The Annotated Wizard of Oz

A portrait poster of L. Frank Baum issued
by the George M. Hill Co. in 1900. *Courtesy
Martin Gardner.*

L. FRANK BAUM.
AUTHOR OF
"FATHER GOOSE" AND "THE WONDERFUL WIZARD OF OZ"

The Annotated
WIZARD OF OZ

The Wonderful Wizard of Oz

By L. ^YMAN FRANK BAUM

Pictures by W. W. DENSLOW

With an Introduction, Notes, and Bibliography by

MICHAEL PATRICK HEARN

 *Clarkson N. Potter, Inc./Publisher* NEW YORK

ENDPAPERS: Maps of The Land of Oz and surrounding
countries designed by L. Frank Baum for *Tik-Tok of
Oz*, 1914. *Courtesy the personal collection of Justin G.
Schiller.*

For Cynthia, Colleen, and Christopher

Acknowledgments

I am grateful to the following persons for contributing in one way or another to the preparation of this work: Doris Frohnsdorff, Martin Gardner, James E. Haff, Margaret Hamilton, Peter E. Hanff, C. Warren Hollister, Bernhard Larsen, Russell P. MacFall, Daniel P. Mannix, Dick Martin, Fred M. Meyer, Brian Nielsen, and Justin G. Schiller. Special thanks is due David L. Greene and Douglas G. Greene for reading the manuscript and offering innumerable valuable suggestions. I am also indebted to the following institutions for their kind help in the research and illustration of this book: the George Arents Research Library, Syracuse University; Columbia University Libraries; the Arents Tobacco Collection, Prints Division, and Theatre Collection of the New York Public Library; Metro-Goldwyn-Mayer, Inc.; the Albert R. Mann Library at Cornell University; the Harvard College Library; the United States Military Academy Library, West Point, New York; the William Allan Nielson Library, Smith College; the History Department, Minneapolis Public Library; the Library of Congress; and the Copyright Office.

Table of Contents.

Introduction.

A caricature of L. Frank Baum drawn by W. W. Denslow for *Father Goose, His Book*, 1899. *Courtesy Dick Martin.*

No children's book of the twentieth century has proven to be as popular or as controversial as *The Wizard of Oz*. When Bobbs-Merrill issued their first edition in 1903, a reviewer remarked: "Mr. L. Frank Baum's last delicious bit of nonsense is amusing to the little people, and even more so to their elders. It is no small gift to write a juvenile which is not inane, and this gift Mr. Baum possesses to a degree which is almost monopoly." Nearly sixty years later when the first paperback editions of the Oz books were being published, another reviewer, noting "the genius of this American author," said, "Frank Baum had a flow of imagination, a depth of humor, a sense of character and a narrative control rare in writers of fantasy."[1] The first book of the long Oz series is one of the fifteen best-selling books of the twentieth century and remains as popular with children today as when it was first published. Yet, librarians and critics of children's books have refused to recognize Baum's Oz books as important juvenile literature. Only in the last decade have a number of appreciations and literary studies appeared in several scholarly journals. A full-length biography of Baum, *To Please a Child*, by Russell P. MacFall and Frank J. Baum, has been published.[2] Also, such writers as Ray Bradbury, Gore Vidal, William Styron, and Shirley Jackson have acknowledged their affection for the Oz

[1] The first-mentioned review appeared in *The Bookseller, Newsdealer and Stationer*, November 15, 1903, the second in the London *Times Literary Supplement*, March 4, 1969.

[2] See Bibliography. This biography is the major study of Baum's life and work. It has been most helpful in compiling the facts of Baum's life (especially those of his days before South Dakota) in this introduction.

3 Baum did not like his first name "Lyman." From childhood he was called "Frank" by his family and friends. Throughout his life he altered his name professionally. As an actor he was "Louis F. Baum." When he first edited the Aberdeen *Saturday Pioneer* (South Dakota), he signed his articles "L. F. Baum" and finally decided on "L. Frank Baum."

stories. Although there remains some resistance on the part of educators and librarians, *The Wizard of Oz* is a major American work of juvenile literature.

Despite the long popularity and the growing critical interest in the Oz books, their author is not widely known. Besides writing fairy tales, Baum had various other interests, ranging from the editing of a midwestern newspaper to the production of musical comedies and early motion pictures. His importance has been judged by his books rather than by his life, but Baum the man was as fascinating as anything he ever wrote.

Lyman Frank Baum[3] was born in Chittenango, a quiet New York State town, on May 15, 1856. His father, Benjamin Ward Baum, who had made his fortune in the early oil industry in Pennsylvania, built for his wife, Cynthia Stanton, a country house named Rose Lawn near Chittenango. Many years later, in *Dot and Tot at Merryland* (1901), Baum was to describe his childhood home:

> The cool but sun-kissed mansion seemed delightful after the formal city house. It was built in a quaint but pretty fashion, and with many wings and gables and broad verandas on every side. Before it were acres and acres of velvety green lawns, sprinkled with shrubbery and dotted with beds of bright flowers. In every direction were winding paths covered with white gravel, which led to all parts of the grounds, looking for all the world like a map.

Although one of several children, Baum had a sheltered childhood. On the great estate he could escape to one of the many rooms of the mansion to read or to the fields to daydream.

Even as a boy Baum was a dreamer who preferred to spend his time alone. He had been born with a defective heart and was forbidden to play any of the rough games of childhood. He was educated by private tutors and soon became enthralled with the fat novels of the popular Victorian authors. Besides reading, he had an early interest in writing poetry and novels.

To cure him of his daydreaming his mother sent him to the Peekskill Military Academy. Unaccustomed to the harsh treatment of a military school he suffered a heart attack and was immediately withdrawn. Years later he described the preference of his instructors to slap or use a cane for discipline purposes. These early experiences at school evidently were responsible for the many caricatures of educators and military men in his stories. Professor Woggle-bug of *The Marvelous Land of Oz* (1904) is the most famous; another notable schoolteacher is Professor Sharpe of *American Fairy Tales* (1901), who is described as "stern and frowning as usual." The Soldier with the Green Whiskers of *The Wizard of Oz* and the Army of Oogaboo of *The Tik-Tok Man of Oz* (1913) may be seen as Baum's reflections on his early experiences at military school. After his disaster at the military academy his parents became more lenient and evidently encouraged his interests.

It was at Rose Lawn that Baum first experienced the joy of printer's ink. While on a business trip with his father he was left to wait in a printer's office; by the time his father returned, he had to have a little printing press of his own. With his brother Harry he published a small newspaper called *The Rose Lawn Home Journal*. He was just fifteen years old. In the pages of this amateur publication, Baum began to develop his writing talents. Several pieces of juvenilia that first appeared in this newspaper so pleased him that many years later he included them in his book of poems, *By the Candelabra's Glare* (1898). With a friend, Thomas G. Alford, he founded *The Empire*, which they described as "a first class amateur monthly newspaper, containing poetry, literature, postage stamp news, amateur items, etc."[4] While working on this paper he prepared a pamphlet called *Baum's Complete Stamp Dealers Directory*, published by Baum, Norris & Co. in 1873. He was also involved in the breeding of chickens, developing new strains and winning prizes for "Baum's Thoroughbred Fowls." This interest encouraged him to write his first book, *The Book of the Hamburgs*, a technical treatise on chickens, published in 1886.

In addition to his oil interests, Baum's father owned a number of theatres. His sister (Aunt Catherine) was already a well-established actress under the name of Katherine Grayson. Young Baum became an actor, and under the name of George Brooks toured throughout New York State with several Shakespearean companies in the late

[4] This is quoted from MacFall's biography, which is the source for most of the information on Baum's youth.

1870s. His father was able to bring him back home to work for a time as a salesman in the family business, but he soon returned to the theatre where as Louis F. Baum he appeared in several productions at the Union Street Theater in New York. While in New York he returned to newspaper reporting and later secured a job with *The New Era* of Bradford, Pennsylvania. He then acted as manager for several of his father's theatres. By 1882, Baum was ready to form a company and produce his own play.

The Maid of Arran was an Irish melodrama (typical of the times), based upon William Black's popular novel *A Princess of Thule* (1874). Book, lyrics, and music were all written by Louis F. Baum, who was also stage manager and took one of the leading roles. Aunt Catherine joined the company to look after young Frank. The play proved to be so successful in Syracuse that the production went on the road, traveling north into Canada and as far west as Kansas, as well as spending a profitable week in New York. Baum wrote several more melodramas (most unproduced), but none repeated the early success of *The Maid of Arran*. The personal triumph of this first theatrical venture remained with him throughout his life; his many miscalculated interests in musical productions and motion pictures may have been in part an attempt to repeat this success of his early twenties. He was to know theatrical prosperity only once more, in the 1902 musical of *The Wizard of Oz*.

On a visit home during the run of *The Maid of Arran* he met Maud Gage of Fayetteville, New York, the daughter of the prominent suffragette Matilda Joslyn Gage. Mrs. Gage was instrumental in drafting the Woman's Bill of Rights, as well as in the first women's rights convention held in New York State. With Elizabeth Cady Stanton and Susan B. Anthony she wrote the four-volume *History of Woman Suffrage*. At first, Mrs. Gage did not approve of the young actor as a son-in-law, but she could not change her daughter's mind. In November 1882, Maud and Frank were married. Later, her son-in-law was influenced by her ideas and satirized the "new woman" in his writings, notably in the character of General Jinjur and her Army of Revolt in *The Marvelous Land of Oz*.

THE

Book of the Hamburgs,

A BRIEF TREATISE

UPON THE

MATING, REARING AND MANAGEMENT

OF THE

DIFFERENT VARIETIES OF HAMBURGS.

By L. FRANK BAUM.

HARTFORD, CONN.:
H. H. STODDARD, Publisher.
1886.

The title page and frontispiece of Baum's first book, *The Book of Hamburgs*, 1886. *Courtesy Albert R. Mann Library, Cornell University.*

Maud Gage Baum's wedding portrait. *Courtesy the personal collection of Justin G. Schiller.*

5 From "The Autobiography of Robert Stanton Baum," *The Baum Bugle,* Christmas 1970 and Spring 1971.

Maud was greatly influenced by her mother. She was strong willed and practical while Frank was careless and dreamy. More than once she had to take over his finances after a great plan of his failed. She also had quite a temper. She thought nothing of using a hairbrush on one of their sons as a punishment, but Frank could not bear to enforce such justice. The second son, Robert Stanton Baum, born in February 1886 (their first son, Frank Joslyn, was born in 1883), recalled one incident in his autobiography:

We had a cat and due to some childish perversity I took it upstairs one day and threw it out the second story window. Fortunately the cat wasn't hurt, but my mother saw me do it and to teach me a lesson, caught me up and held me out the window pretending that she was going to drop me. But it was quite real to me and I screamed so loudly that the neighbors all rushed out and were quite horrified by the spectacle of my mother dangling me out of the window, not sure but she would let me drop. Needless to say, I was quite cured of throwing cats out of windows but I did heave one into a barrel one day and was promptly chucked in myself to see how I liked it.**5**

These punishments must have horrified her husband, but he generally went along with Maud's decisions. Their union may have seemed a mismatch, but Baum spoke of his wife only with affection. He dedicated his most famous work, *The Wizard of Oz*, to "my good friend & comrade, My Wife."

With a wife and two sons to support he had to leave the theatre. He returned to the family business in Syracuse in 1886 where he sold Baum's Castorine, an axle lubricant, for two years. This business did not prove to be as profitable as expected, and with the death of his father and the forced sale of the Castorine company, the Baums had to look elsewhere for a new life. Several years earlier, Maud's brother and sisters had settled in the Dakota Territory, lured by the land boom of the 1880s. The great American frontier had not been officially closed, and news from the West was encouraging. In September 1888, Baum and his family settled in Aberdeen (in what is now South Dakota) where he opened a variety store called Baum's Bazaar.

But the boom had passed and depression had set in. Farmers, trying to make a living off the dry and treeless plains, were hit by recurrent droughts. Aberdeen was not, however, without an energetic social life, and the Baums frequented the card parties, dances, and many local theatricals. Baum also managed a baseball team that reportedly won the South Dakota championship. He had become adept at amateur photography, and on his first visit to Dakota the Aberdeen *Daily News* reported:

Mr. L. Frank Baum of Syracuse, New York, who has been visiting his in-laws here finds recreation from the cares of an extensive business in the fascinating pursuit, amateur photography. Mr. Baum was proficient in the art and during his stay in the city secured a number of fine negatives of Dakota land and cloud scapes. One picture taken by the glorious twilight of Dakota will, when finished up, prove of special interest as an example of advanced photography.[6]

He was to pursue this interest all his life, preparing his own negatives and prints, in later years with the help of his sons. He was fascinated

[6] I quote from Matilda J. Gage's "The Dakota Days of L. Frank Baum," *The Baum Bugle,* Spring to Christmas 1966. Baum's niece's article is an extensive account of Baum's early days in the Dakotas.

with the Dakota landscape, and the opening pages of *The Wizard of Oz* refer to these early days in the Dakota Territory.

He had, as well, a reputation for entertaining the local children with his wonder stories. However, business was bad and did not improve. There was always the hope that the next crop would end the depression, but the store could no longer support the Baum family. On New Year's Day, 1890, Baum's Bazaar closed, only a few weeks before the birth of a third son, Harry Neal.

About this time a friend from Baum's Syracuse days, John H. Drake, who had also emigrated to the Dakotas, was appointed United States Consul to Kiel, Germany, by President Benjamin Harrison. Drake was editor of one of the nine local Aberdeen newspapers, *The Dakota Pioneer*, and asked Baum if he would like to rent the paper and act as its new editor. On January 25, 1890, the first issue of the Aberdeen *Saturday Pioneer* appeared with "L. F. Baum, Editor." Half of each weekly issue was printed from "boiler plates," prepared material (such as a column by Bill Nye with illustrations by Walt McDougall, or national and fashion news), which were syndicated to many local newspapers. The rest of the paper was almost entirely written by Baum. The most popular feature was his column "Our Landlady," which dealt with a fictional Mrs. Bilkins and her opinions on local and world affairs. These columns reflected the tastes and aspirations of the time and also provided an outlet for Baum's fantasy world. Among the topics discussed were the possibilities of lighter-than-air craft, horseless carriages, and the potential of electrical inventions. One of the most interesting columns is Baum's parody of Edward Bellamy's popular *Looking Backward* (1888); in writing a letter meant to be read in the future, Mrs. Bilkins mentions selling an enormous book called *Baum's Hourly Newspaper* which contains all the world events of the last hour, like Glinda's Great Book of Records in the later Oz stories. So popular was "Our Landlady" that several of the other Aberdeen papers tried to compete; "Faithful Zeke" of the Aberdeen *Daily News* wrote editorials against Mrs. Bilkins and her creator.

Baum wrote most of the *Pioneer*'s editorials, frequently reflecting upon contemporary views of spiritualism and women's suffrage. He became interested in Theosophy and other occult sciences and frequently disputed in his paper with the local established churches.

The influence of Matilda Joslyn Gage, his mother-in-law, was evident in his views on women's right to vote. The paper published her "manifesto" and urged its readers to vote for equal suffrage in South Dakota; there were frequent reports on the work of Susan B. Anthony and Mrs. Gage, as well as reviews of the latter's articles for *The Arena* and other publications.

Baum's editorials also reflected the hard times on the Dakota prairies. Drought and a lack of seed wheat for the needy farmers did not improve meager business profits. The year 1890 proved a disastrous one for the crops; seed had to be brought from neighboring states, and work was further complicated by the cyclone that hit Aberdeen on May 23. There was also the threat of the Messiah War, which was to become the last Indian uprising. This religious movement centered on the hope of invoking the spirits of dead warriors to drive out the white settlers. No one was fearful until Chief Sitting Bull, one of the chieftains responsible for Custer's last stand, was asked to join the movement. (Baum's editorials on the Indian situation were the least tolerant of all his work.) The American army killed Sitting Bull on orders to prevent him from leaving for the Black Hills. Soon after, Custer's former regiment, the Seventh Cavalry, slaughtered the entire village of Wounded Knee. Although Congress had already officially closed continental western expansion, this brutality concluded the Indian wars and ended the frontier.

At the time of the South Dakota State Fair of 1890, held in Aberdeen in July, conditions seemed to be better, but the year did not improve. Baum expanded his publishing to include the official program of the State Fair and several issues of *The Western Investor*, a financial publication, but these did not ease his financial pressures. The *Pioneer*'s subscription and advertising revenue had dropped considerably by February 1891. That same month Baum had to undergo minor surgery to remove a tumor beneath his tongue. Times had worsened for everyone; many residents were now leaving. In April 1891, Baum returned the paper to Drake. A fourth son, Kenneth Gage, was born a week or two before Baum's resignation. Baum had failed twice in the Dakotas and now he looked for another place to make his home and fortune.

The enthusiasm surrounding the approaching World's Columbian

Exposition of 1893 inspired Baum to visit Chicago in July 1890. He returned soon after and secured a position on the *Evening Post* as a reporter. His family was soon to follow him there. His salary with the *Post* was not as good as he had hoped so he became a buyer in the crockery department of the Siegel Cooper and Company store. When there was an opening for a traveling salesman with Pitkin and Brooks, Baum took the job and journeyed throughout the Midwest selling china and glassware. As he became more experienced, his salary increased and soon the family could live in relative comfort.

But Baum was a family man and his new job kept him away from Chicago for weeks at a time. Mrs. Gage frequently visited her daughter to help with the raising of the family. Whenever he was home he would spend as much time as possible with his four sons. His favorite activity was the family hour when he read books to them or told them his own stories. His sons were well acquainted with the rhymes of Mother Goose and demanded fictive elaborations of their favorites. One evening his mother-in-law was listening to one of these original fairy tales and advised him to write his stories down. On June 17, 1896, he applied for copyright of the titles to two manuscripts, "Adventures in Phunniland" and "Tales from Mother Goose."**7**

Because of his early newspaper days Baum frequented the Chicago Press Club. Here he met the western novelist Opie Read who, when he heard Baum had a manuscript, introduced him to Chauncey L. Williams of the Way & Williams publishing house. Williams had come to Chicago to produce fine books, in the manner of the reputable Chicago publishers Stone & Kimball. His home, designed by the young Frank Lloyd Wright, was the meeting place of a circle of prominent midwestern writers and artists, including Hamlin Garland, George Barr and John T. McCutcheon, Will Bradley, and William Allen White. Williams agreed to publish the stories of Baum based upon old nursery rhymes as *Mother Goose in Prose* in 1897. Williams employed the young Philadelphia artist Maxfield Parrish (he had previously designed the cover for a collection of Read's stories published by Way & Williams) as illustrator; his magazine and poster work was gaining a reputation, but Baum's first

7 From Peter Hanff's report on Baum's early copyright records in *The Baum Bugle*, Christmas 1968.

children's book was also the first book Parrish illustrated.**8** Way & Williams produced a most attractive volume, but, as Baum admitted in a letter to Frank K. Reilly of December 16, 1916, "the book was not appealing to children, although adults went wild over the beautiful drawings." As quoted by Martin Gardner in *The Wizard of Oz and Who He Was*, Baum, in the copy of *Mother Goose in Prose* presented to his sister Mary Louise Brewster, wrote:

When I was young I longed to write a great novel that should win me fame. Now that I am getting old my first book is written to amuse children. For, aside from my evident inability to do anything "great," I have learned to regard fame as a will-o-the-wisp which, when caught, is not worth the possession; but to please a child is a sweet and lovely thing that warms one's heart and brings its own reward. I hope my book will succeed in that way—that the children will like it. You and I have inherited much the same temperament and literary taste and I know you will not despise these simple tales, but will understand me and accord me your full sympathy.

The book sold well enough to encourage Williams to plan to publish Baum's "Phunniland" story, but the following year (1898) Way & Williams failed and the book was postponed indefinitely.

The income from his first children's book was helpful, for Baum at the advice of a heart specialist had to give up the strenuous life of a traveling salesman for another kind of employment. With Williams as publisher, Baum founded *The Show Window*, a periodical for window trimmers, in 1897. It was quickly accepted by the trade who were soon to form the National Association of Window Trimmers at the suggestion of the magazine. At the first national convention Baum was elected secretary. His magazine grew large enough to allow Baum to publish it himself, and in 1900 he produced *The Art of Decorating Dry Goods Windows and Interiors*, based upon material printed in *The Show Window* during its first three years.

Also at the Chicago Press Club Baum was introduced to the artist

8 Baum and Parrish were approached once more as possible collaborators. Parrish was to design the sets and illustrations, Baum the script and book, for an operetta based upon a British play, *Snow White*, to be produced in 1917; evidently nothing came of this proposal.

William Wallace Denslow through Opie Read, whose *An Arkansas Planter* Denslow had recently illustrated. "Den" was the same age as Baum. He had been educated in Philadelphia, his birthplace, and at the National Academy of Design in New York. His first job as an office boy led to his preparing wood engravings for the *American Agriculturist* magazine. He returned to Pennsylvania where he illustrated a number of county atlases. Back in New York in the late 1880s he became a staff artist of *The Theater* magazine and supposedly designed costumes for several musical revues. Around 1890 he drifted into newspaper work and traveled west to Chicago, Denver (where he also had an interest in the mining industry), and San Francisco. On a visit to Chicago for the 1893 Columbian Exposition he established a studio. His reputation in the United States and Europe was built on his poster work, which was favorably compared to that of the Frenchman Jules Chèret and Denslow's friend Will Bradley. His work won a nod of approval from no less an artist than Alphonse Mucha, whose designs for Sarah Bernhardt were in part responsible for the poster craze. Denslow was chosen by Elbert Hubbard to be the first artist employed by the Roycroft Shops in East Aurora, New York, where Hubbard established his own version of William Morris's Arts and Crafts Movement of Great Britain. Denslow spent part of the year in East Aurora where he designed the Roycroft chapel and decorated the walls of the inn; he prepared initial decorations and cartoons for many of the Roycroft publications, including the magazines *The Philistine* and *The Fra*. In Chicago he designed countless book covers and posters for Rand McNally & Company and became one of the instructors of Frank Holme's School of Illustrating that boasted also the talents of cartoonist John T. McCutcheon and the Leyendecker brothers. Denslow often entertained many of the important artists and writers of the day at his studio. It was here that Denslow and several of his friends agreed to contribute the illustrations to Baum's proposed book of verse, *By the Candelabra's Glare*.

As a break from the editing of *The Show Window* Baum, in 1897, borrowed a foot-powered printing press and several fonts of type to run off a limited edition of his modest collection of poems, "one of my greatest treasures—a book I set in type out of my head without writing it, and which I personally printed and bound."**9** "Unassisted I have set the type and turned the press and accomplished the binding," he writes in the foreword. "Such as it is, the book is 'my very own.' " Friends contributed the paper, endsheets, ink, and binding materials; the author's only cost was his labor. Besides including work from *The Rose Lawn Home Journal* and the *Saturday Pioneer* the collection also contained a selection of children's verse that would appear in his next book.

9 In a previously unpublished letter to Isadore Witmark, April 19, 1903, courtesy Special Collections, Columbia University Libraries.

An altered photograph of W. W. Denslow, which appeared in *The Inland Printer*, March 1901.

Baum approached Denslow on the possibility of collaborating on another project, a picture book of children's poems. The original verses had been written on old envelopes and scraps of paper while Baum was on the road selling crockery and glassware. Denslow was amused by them and agreed to do the illustrations. He became a frequent visitor to the Baums' quiet household. "I recall that 'Den,' as we called him, had a striking red vest of which he was inordinately fond," reports Harry Baum in the December 1962 *American Book Collector*. "And whenever he came to our house, he would always complain of the heat as an excuse to take off his coat and spend the evening displaying his beautiful red vest. The family used to joke about it among ourselves, but it was a touchy subject with Denslow, and we were careful not to say anything about this vanity during his visit." This vest was not the only striking characteristic of the artist. He had a large walrus moustache, and, as the late Elbert Hubbard explained, he "was a pretty gruff old fellow."**10** When he wasn't smoking a corncob pipe, he would be chewing tobacco. As a friend described him in MacFall's *To Please a Child*, Denslow had "the voice of a second mate in a storm—a fog horn voice," a twisted sense of humor, "always grumbling about nothing, always carping, always censorious, and laughing uproariously when he had secured an effect." In contrast to his personality his young bride Ann Waters was a gracious hostess who provided good looks and bright conversation for Denslow's many and varied friends. She was the daughter of "Amber," Martha Holden, a Chicago newspaperwoman whose work was often illustrated by her son-in-law; Ann was also an author whose own press connections had furthered her husband's career. Baum enjoyed the artistic companionship of the Denslows, and soon he and the illustrator were ready to look for a publisher.

Williams suggested that they go to the George M. Hill Company, a young printing and binding firm. When Baum first met him, Hill was still interested primarily in the manufacturing rather than the editorial part of the book trade. Also consulted on the publishing of the book of verses were Sumner C. Britton, Hill's secretary and head salesman, and Frank K. Reilly, the production manager. Hill offered to print, bind, and promote a small edition of several thousand copies if Baum and Denslow would pay the production costs.

10 In a letter to MacFall, quoted in *To Please a Child.*

To save some printing costs Denslow engaged the young artist Ralph Fletcher Seymour to hand-letter the pages; they resembled a series of miniature posters.**11** Both Baum and Denslow paid to have color illustrations, which produced a bright, attractive book. Because it was on the same lines as a Mother Goose picture book, the volume was christened *Father Goose, His Book.*

The first printing was quickly sold out; several subsequent printings were soon exhausted. Much to the pleasant surprise of Baum, Denslow, and Hill, *Father Goose* became the best-selling juvenile of 1899. A dozen imitations flooded the market. The following year Hill released *The Songs of Father Goose,* a book similar in format with a black-and-white selection of the *Father Goose* illustrations and verses set to music by Mrs. Alberta N. Hall (later Burton). Both the public and the critics were pleased with the *Father Goose* phenomenon. A major review by Chauncey Williams with several reproductions from the book appeared in *The Home Magazine,* September 1899. MacFall reports that even William Dean Howells took a copy of Baum's book of jingles to a young niece in the country so that he too could enjoy reading it. Several publishers now approached Baum for a manuscript, any manuscript. He gave his "Adventures in Phunniland" to R. H. Russell of New York; perhaps because of the similarity in title to F. Opper's *Frolics in Phunniland* that Russell was to publish the same year, Baum's book became *A New Wonderland.* (At the turn of the century it was commonplace to link the titles of wonder tales with the famous *Alice* books.) Baum prepared two more books of verse, *The Army Alphabet* and *The Navy Alphabet,* both issued by Hill in 1900. *Father Goose* both encouraged and established him as a major writer of children's books.

The success of *Father Goose* now afforded the Baum family luxuries that were denied earlier. A few summers were spent at Macatawa Park, Michigan, along the shore of Lake Michigan. Here Baum wrote the first of his "old-fashioned" fairy tales, *The Life and Adventures of Santa Claus,* as well as a number of other books, including several of the Oz stories. With the earnings of *Father Goose* Baum bought a summer cottage that he named The Sign of the Goose. Out of wrought iron and painted wood he made a large

11 According to *To Please a Child,* another young artist, Frederic Goudy, was hired to help Seymour. Goudy was to become a noted type designer. He later hand-lettered *Denslow's Mother Goose,* published by McClure, Phillips & Co., in 1901.

A photograph of the Baums in Egypt which first appeared in *In Other Lands than Ours*, 1907. *Courtesy the personal collection of Justin G. Schiller.*

sign to hang on the porch; on it he cut out a great white goose (after Denslow's cover design) and in bold black letters printed the name of the cottage. About 1901, to recover from an attack of facial paralysis, Baum took up light manual labor as a hobby. All the oak furniture in the house was handmade by the author. He built two large rocking chairs whose sides were outlines of white enameled geese; the framework was painted green, and the leather upholstery was fastened with decorative brass goose-head nails, designed by his friend—Williams's brother-in-law—Harrison H. Rountree of the Turner brass foundry in Chicago. Baum also built a grandfather's clock for the hall and a small bookcase, both of which were decorated with characters from his books. For the living room he commissioned a stained glass window of a large goose against a green background; he personally stenciled the walls with a frieze of green geese. This summer house became a popular gathering place with the young residents along Lake Michigan. It was at The Sign of the Goose that Baum described why he preferred to write for children:

> To write fairy stories for children, to amuse them, to divert restless children, sick children, to keep them out of mischief on rainy days, seems of greater importance than to write grown-up novels. Few of the popular novels last the year out, responding as they do to a certain psychological demand, characteristic of the time; whereas, a child's book is, comparatively speaking, the same always, since children are always the same kind of little folks with the same needs to satisfy.[12]

At The Sign of the Goose Baum wrote one other Father Goose book, *Father Goose's Year Book*, but by 1907 the novelty of the original picture book had faded and Baum was to concern himself thereafter with other writing.

The production of his first picture book inspired Baum to complete a more ambitious work. For at least a couple years a fairy tale had been running through his head. It began as a bedtime story for his children and their friends and soon was carried over into several evening sessions. He knew there was something special about this story, and he planned to expand it into a novel-length children's book. Busy with the editing of *The Show Window* he did not begin writing his fairy tale until some time after the initial inspiration. As he explained to his publishers years later, "I was sitting . . . in the hall, telling the kids a story and suddenly this one moved right in and took possession. I shooed the children away and grabbed a piece of paper that was lying there on the rack and began to write. It really seemed to write itself. Then I couldn't find any regular paper, so I took anything at all, even a bunch of old envelopes."[13] He was so enthusiastic that he quickly wrote the story in longhand on letter-size typewriter paper. He attached the stub of the pencil to an extra sheet on which was written: "With this pencil I wrote the Ms. of 'The Emerald City.'" This sheet with the pencil stub was framed and years later hung in the study of his home in Hollywood. Although Baum was left-handed and wrote backhanded, the longhand copy was clear enough to be given to the printer as setting copy. In a letter to Britton, dated January 23, 1912, Baum described his general procedure in preparing his manuscripts:

> I think you misunderstood me in regard to the new Oz book. I said I had it written, and doubtless misled you. A lot of thought is required on one of these fairy tales. The odd characters are a sort of inspiration, liable to strike me any time, but the plot and plan of adventures takes me considerable time to develop. When I get at a thing of that sort I live with it day by day, jotting down on odd slips of paper the various ideas that occur and in this way getting my material together. The new Oz book is in this stage. I've got it all—all the hard work has been done—and it's a dandy I think. But . . . it's a long way from being ready for the printer yet. I must rewrite it, stringing the incidents into consecutive order, elaborating the characters, etc. Then it's type-written. Then it's revised, retypewritten and sent on to Reilly & Britton. By close application there's about six weeks work on it.

12 Baum is quoted in "How the Wizard of Oz Spends His Vacation," Grand Rapids *Herald*, August 18, 1907.

13 Quoted by Roland Baughman in "L. Frank Baum and the 'Oz Books,'" *Columbia Library Columns*, May 1955.

If I took my time I'd devote two months to getting it ready for the press.

"The Emerald City" was submitted to George M. Hill in its original first draft, having had little or no editing. Denslow was immediately shown the manuscript and he agreed to supply the illustrations. Tradition claims that Baum and Denslow had considerable difficulty in finding a publisher. Hill supposedly offered the same deal as for *Father Goose*, but, as Denslow's account book proves, Hill assumed all printing costs and paid the author and illustrator equal royalties.[14] If Hill did not readily agree to publication, he may have been disputing the appropriate time to issue another Baum-Denslow title. By the fall of 1899 the author and illustrator had enough material to present their project to a publisher. The copyright date "1899," appearing on the original drawing and on the printed copyright page of Denslow's design, suggests that there was a desire to publish the book for the Christmas season of 1899. But Hill was just issuing *Father Goose* whose success was still in doubt, and he may have been put off by the idea of Baum's "modernized fairy tale." By September *Father Goose* was a hit, and Hill was willing to publish anything Baum and Denslow could bring him.

But after the manuscript was submitted the Hill company contacted Baum and told him that they would not publish the book under the title "The Emerald City." They told him of a publishers' superstition that claimed that any book with a jewel in its title was doomed to failure. His next suggested title was "From Kansas to Fairyland," and as late as November 17, 1899, the story was known by this title.[15] It was referred to as "The Fairyland of Oz" in *The Bookseller, Newsdealer and Stationer* of February 1900. A report appeared in the April issue that the title had been shortened to "The Land of Oz." Baum and Denslow were confident enough in this decision to file a joint copyright under this title on January 18, 1900.[16] Denslow used it on the title page, and the book was ready to go to press, but Baum was still not satisfied; he wanted something more colorful and eye-catching. In early March Denslow pasted a paper label with Baum's final decision over the title page drawing, and the book went to press as *The Wonderful Wizard of Oz*.

14 See C. Warren Hollister's description of Denslow's account book in *The Baum Bugle*, Spring 1964.

15 In a letter to me, Russell P. MacFall describes a memo from a member of the staff of Reilly & Lee concerning Maud's claim to the copyright of *The Wizard of Oz*. This alludes to the original manuscript (now lost) on which was written "From Kansas to Fairyland" and dated November 17, 1899.

16 Hanff, *op. cit.*

Baum dated his introduction "May 1900," and the official publication was to be on May 15, 1900, Baum's forty-fourth birthday. A letter of April 8, 1900, from Baum to his favorite brother, Harry, in Syracuse records the author's thoughts at this turning point in his life. I quote from MacFall's biography:

The financial success of my books is yet undetermined, and will only be positively settled after the coming fall season. We only had three months sale of *Father Goose*, and though it made a hit and sold plenteously we cannot tell what its future might be. . . . I have been grateful for its success. The money has been a pleasure to me and my work is sought by publishers who once scorned my contributions. Harper Bros. sent a man here last week to try to make a contract for a book next year. Scribner's writes offering a cash advance for a manuscript. Appleton's, Lothrop's and the Century have asked for a book—no matter what it is. This makes me proud, especially as my work in *Father Goose* was not good work, and I know I can do better. But I shall make no contracts with anyone till next January. If my books succeed this year I can dictate terms and choose my publishers. If they fall down I will try to discover the fault and to turn out some better work.

A lady here, Mrs. Alberta N. Hall, has written some charming music to the *Father Goose* verses. *The Songs of Father Goose* was the result and is now in preparation, being announced for publication June 1st. *The Army Alphabet*, wonderfully illustrated by Harry Kennedy, will be issued May 15th. The book surely *ought* to catch on. *The Navy Alphabet*, also illustrated by Kennedy, will appear August 1st. I have received some proofs of the illustrations Frank Verbeck has made for my Phunniland book, which appears July 1st from R. H. Russell's, New York. The work is splendid. This is the man who has illustrated Kipling's new book of animal stories, having been selected over all other American artists to do that work. **17** The title of the book will be *A New Wonderland*. Then there is the other book, the best thing I have ever written, they tell me, *The Wonderful Wizard of Oz*. It is now on the press and will be ready soon

17 Baum is probably referring to Ver Beck's illustrations for the serialization of *Just So Stories* that was then appearing in the *Ladies' Home Journal*. The book itself was illustrated by Kipling and his father.

18 This unusual copy is described in Justin G. Schiller's book catalog "Juvenile Temptations" (*Chapbook Miscellany*, Summer 1970). The inscription reads: "Richard Adlai Watson from his Godfather, R. J. Street, May 23, 1900." Schiller suggests that Street was involved with the production of the book and took a copy as soon as it was completed by the printer, at least a few days before Baum received his own copies.

19 This is quoted from Dick Martin's article on the bibliographical points of the first edition of *The Wizard of Oz*, in the December 1962 *American Book Collector*.

19a The Copyright Office recorded receiving only one copy. Baum had personally sent two copies for copyright purposes in September, 1900, but these evidently were lost in the mail. The Library's copy was a third copy sent by the publishers, with the corrected text. The copyright was not completed until 1903 when Bobbs-Merrill sent two copies of their edition, *The New Wizard of Oz*.

after May 1st. Denslow has made profuse illustrations for it and it will glow with bright colors. Mr. Hill, the publisher, says he expects a sale of at least a quarter of a million copies on it. If he is right, that book alone solves my problem. But the queer, unreliable Public has not yet spoken. I only need one hit this year to make my position secure, and three of these books seem fitted for public approval. But there—who knows anything! I'm working at my trade, earning a salary to keep my family and holding fast to a certainty until the fiat has gone forth.

Hill advertised in the April *Bookseller and Latest Literature* that the new Baum-Denslow book would be ready about June. The first copy (sewn but unbound) to be inscribed by Baum was the one presented to his sister Mary Louise Brewster. On the flyleaf it is dated May 17 with the inscription: "This 'dummy' . . . was made from sheets I gathered from the press as fast as printed and bound up by hand. It is really the very first book ever made of this story." The earliest bound copy has an inscription with the date "May 23, 1900,"**18** but in a book he gave his brother Baum wrote: "This, the first copy of *The Wonderful Wizard of Oz* that left the hands of the publishers, is presented to my dear brother Dr. Harry C. Baum by the Author. May 28th, 1900." **19** *The Bookseller* noted in its June issue: "Although the book has been offered but a fortnight over 5,000 have already been ordered. A second edition of 5,000 is in the press." The copies of the book given his mother and sister were inscribed in June; this delay may have resulted from an illness that also prevented him from continuing as editor of *The Show Window*. Hill again postponed the official publication and distribution of the book until August 1. As reported in *The Bookseller*, the first glimpse the trade had of the new Baum titles was at the Chicago Book Fair, held at the Palmer House July 5 to 20, and the result was enthusiastic. Orders increased and Hill was unable to fill them until September. The official copyright was August, but the Library of Congress did not receive its copies until December 12, 1900.**19a** Hill advertised in October that the first printing of ten thousand copies was exhausted within two weeks of publication, and because the second printing of fifteen thousand was nearly gone, a third of ten thousand was to be run off. Another thirty thousand were produced in November, and the last Hill printing of twenty-five thousand came in January 1901. *The Wonderful Wizard of Oz* became the best-selling children's book of the 1900 Christmas season and continued its success into the next year. Nearly ninety thousand copies were published by the Hill company.

The publishers produced one of the most attractive children's books of the time. On the light green cover the principal characters of the story were stamped in dark green and red. The same illustration was printed in dark green on the light green paper book jacket. The book contained over a hundred text illustrations in two colors and twenty-four plates in three colors. At the back of the book was a colophon that read:

> Here ends the story of "The Wonderful Wizard of Oz," which was written by L. Frank Baum and illustrated by William Wallace Denslow. The engravings were made by the Illinois Engraving Company, the paper was supplied by Dwight Bros. Paper Company, and Messrs. A. R. Barnes & Company printed the book for the publishers, the George M. Hill Company, completing it on the fifteenth day of May, in the year nineteen hundred.

When *Life* magazine planned to reprint a number of the original Denslow drawings in an article on *The Wizard of Oz* in the Christmas 1953 issue, the art director, Charles Tudor, reported (in a brief printed letter that was distributed as an answer to inquiries about the article) that the color printing was done by four plates: a zinc etching or "black plate," which was printed in blue ink, and three wood engravings. *Life* also consulted Arthur Bernhard who had been an apprentice engraver with the Illinois Engraving Company. He claimed that the text illustrations were reproduced by "zinc etchings" or "zinc plates," not woodcuts; the color was put in by the Benday process, a method of adding tone in printing, patented by Benjamin Day of New York in 1879. The Hill printing was so attractive that when Bobbs-Merrill bought the plates in 1903 all copies of the book into the early 1920s were printed from these originals with

20 Quoted from Dick Martin's bibliographical article on *A New Wonderland*, in *The Baum Bugle*, Spring 1967.

21 The letter is now in the L. Frank Baum Manuscripts, Columbia University Libraries.

only a few minor alterations in the text and makeup of the book.

The publisher spared no expense in the printing of the illustrations. Baum's personal response to Denslow's work for *The Wizard of Oz* has never been recorded. Although he praised the illustrations for *Dot and Tot of Merryland* (1901) in its introduction, Baum was evidently not so impressed with those for *The Wizard*. In an inscribed copy of *A New Wonderland* dated October 8, 1900, Baum writes in reference to Ver Beck's pictures: "I like the illustrations more than any of my other books up to the present."**20** References in Baum's letters to Denslow's work are generally cool. Perhaps he resented the disproportionate critical and popular attention given the pictures over the verses of *Father Goose*. He may have also resented Denslow's comic pages, books, and other works derived from Baum characters but with no such acknowledgment. (See the Denslow Appendix.) Then again, Baum may not have cared for the Art-Nouveau-style drawings that illustrated *The Wizard*. In referring to Frederick Richardson and his work for *Queen Zixi of Ix*, Baum wrote W. W. Ellsworth of the Century Company, on September 9, 1904: "If however he could be induced to make the small pictures broadly humorous—even to the verge of burlesque—it would be a good thing all around."**21** Evidently Baum did not see eye to eye with his illustrators. He had a preference for cartoonists, such as Winsor McCay (famous for "Little Nemo") and George McManus (creator of "Bringing Up Father"). In a letter to Reilly & Britton of September 11, 1915, he wrote: "What we need is more *humorous* pictures." His work with the cartoonist Walt McDougall on "The Visitors from Oz" comic page pushed this to an extreme; these stories and pictures are humorous but their jokes are dated, unlike the text and illustrations of most of Baum's many fairy-tale books. Baum finally admitted in a letter to his publishers, October 25, 1915, that "perhaps no author is satisfied with his illustrations, and I see my characters and incidents so differently from the artist that I fail to appreciate his talent." He may not have personally cared for Denslow's work, but if they pleased his readers he was pleased. In the above-mentioned letter of September 11, he commented: "I used to receive many compliments on Denslow's pictures when he was illustrating my books, from children and others."

PLATE II

Romola Remus as Dorothy, Frank Burns as the Scarecrow, Joseph Schrode as the Cowardly Lion, and others in Baum's *Fairylogue and Radio Plays*, 1908–09. *Courtesy the private collection of Justin G. Schiller.*

PLATE I

Poster advertising *The Wonderful Wizard of Oz*, issued by George M. Hill, 1900. *Reproduction courtesy Peter E. Hanff.*

PLATE III

The earliest map of The Land of Oz designed by L. Frank Baum for *The Fairylogue and Radio Plays*, 1908–09. *Courtesy the personal collection of Justin G. Schiller.*

PLATE IV

"Father Goose" comic page drawn by Denslow for the New York *World*, January 21, 1900. *Courtesy the William Allan Nielson Library, Smith College.*

PLATE V

Illustration for *Denslow's Night Before Christmas*, 1902. Note the Tin Woodman in Santa Claus' bag. *Courtesy the personal collection of Justin G. Schiller.*

PLATE VI

Illustration from *Denslow's The House That Jack Built*, 1903. *Courtesy the personal collection of Justin G. Schiller.*

PLATE VII
A poster advertising the first New York run of the musical *The Wizard of Oz*, 1903. *Courtesy Theatre Collection, New York Public Library, Astor, Lenox and Tilden Foundations.*

PLATE VIII
Cover from Denslow's *Pictures from the Wonderful Wizard of Oz*, c. 1903. *Courtesy Theatre Collection, New York Public Library, Astor, Lenox, and Tilden Foundations.*

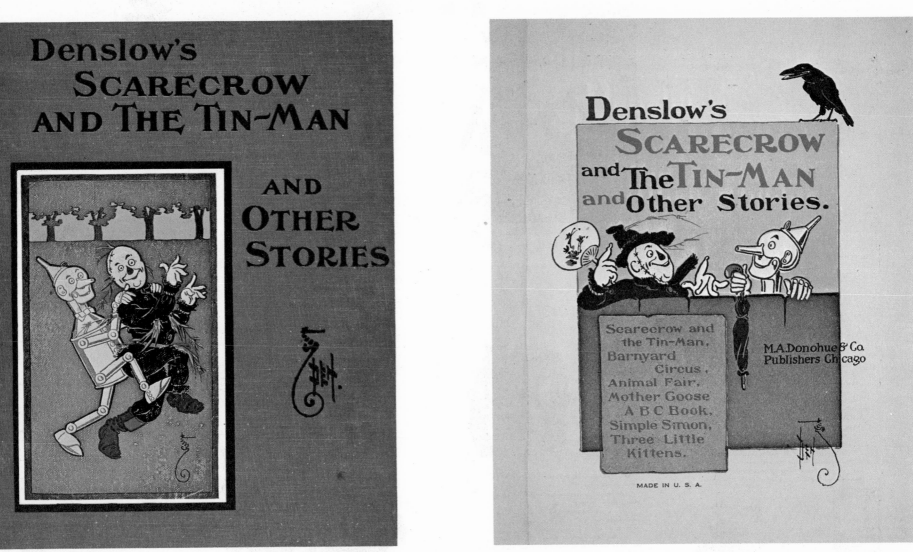

The cover and title page from a later M. A. Donohue
reprint of the collected edition of six of the Denslow
picture books published by G. W. Dillingham in 1904.
Courtesy the personal collection of Justin G. Schiller.

The following plates are of Denslow's *Scarecrow and the Tin-Man* (New York, G. W. Dillingham Co., 1904). *Courtesy the personal collection of Justin G. Schiller.*

PLATE XI

PLATE XII

PLATE XIII

PLATE XIV

Plate XV

advantage of the confusion the two friends dodged down an alley, out on another street and were soon far away.

By and by they found themselves in Madison Square near the fountain, when a man carelessly threw a lighted match directly into the straw that was sticking out of the Scare-crow's chest and set him in a blaze.

The Tin-man seeing this danger, with rare presence of mind caught up his friend and dumped him into the fountain, but in doing so he stumbled and fell in himself.

Now, what was good for the Scare-crow was not good for the Tin-man, and after they had crawled out of the water he began to rust, and as he had left his

Plate XVI

oil-can at the theater, he was soon stiff in all his joints, so that the Scare-crow had to help him along.

Just then they heard a voice behind them say, "There they are; arrest them."

It was the voice of the manager who was hunting them with a squad of policemen.

There was no escape, as the Tin-man was so rusty by this time that he could scarcely move, and the happy pair were soon hustled into a patrol wagon and given a ride to the station.

When they came before the judge, and he had heard the complaint of the manager, he sentenced the Scare-crow and the Tin-man to another year in the theater to make fun for the children.

Plate XVII

"That's all right," said the Scare-crow. "We have had our little fun and it's all right. We go back with pleasure."

The Scare-crow oiled up the Tin-man so that he was as good as ever, and got some new straw to swell out his own chest, and the two friends shone with new luster at the evening performance that night. The children laughed as they had never laughed before at the droll antics of the Scare-crow and the Tin-man.

Press of J. J. Little & Co.,
New York.

Plate XVIII

The critical response to both the text and illustrations of the new Baum-Denslow book was generally favorable. There was a tendency to compare it to *Alice in Wonderland*. The book trade's response to Lewis Carroll's death in 1898 was to put out books of both adulation and imitation. Several memoirs (including the excellent *Life and Letters of Lewis Carroll* by the author's nephew, Stuart Dodgson Collingwood) appeared as did numerous new editions of *Alice in Wonderland* and *Through the Looking-Glass*. *The Dial* (December, 1, 1900), in reviewing *A New Wonderland*, referred to the similarities between Baum's "Phunniland" book and Carroll's more famous predecessor. The reviewer explained that "Mr. Dodgson had a real distinction of style which is wholly lacking here, though to be found in a chapter or two of Mr. Baum's other book, *The Wonderful Wizard of Oz*." *The Bookseller and Latest Literature* (July 1900) claimed that the new Baum-Denslow work "is penned with the wild extravagance of fancy that is noticeable in that children's classic, *Alice in Wonderland*." Baum was perhaps flattered to have his first full-length fairy tale compared to the most famous of modern fairy stories. The similarities are, of course, superficial, and no reviewer attempted a detailed comparison of the two works.

The reviews generally could not decide who deserved more credit, Baum or Denslow. *The Dial* found the book "remarkably illustrated by W. W. Denslow, who possesses all the originality of method which is denied his collaborator." The Chicago *Post* (September 21, 1900) remarked that Denslow could not draw a childlike Dorothy, but admitted that if the book were a success it would be due more to the illustrator than the author. In an unidentified clipping in one of the Baum family scrapbooks is a newspaper review that remarks: "Mr. Baum has given us a clever and original story that deserves a good reception," but "the illustrations are uncommon, suggesting frequently the upset ink-bottle." Most reviews tended to agree with *Kindergarten Magazine* (October 1900):

> Impossible as are the little girl's odd companions, the magic pen of the writer, ably assisted by the artist's brush, has made them seem very real, and no child but will have a warm corner in his heart for the really thoughtful Scarecrow, the truly tender Tin Woodman, the fearless Cowardly Lion. Delightful humor and

rare philosophy are found on every page. The artist, whose fertile invention has so seconded the author's imagination, is W. W. Denslow, who illustrated *Father Goose*.

The critics also predicted that the book would be as entertaining for adults as for children. "Little folks will go wild over it," wrote *The Bookseller and Latest Literature*, "and older people will read it to them with pleasure, since it will form a pleasing interlude with more serious fiction." Reviewers also sensed a depth to the story that made it stand out from the usual fare for children. Even *The Dial* admitted that Baum's book "is really notable among the innumerable publications of the young, making an appeal which is fairly irresistible to a certain standard of taste." *Book News* (October 1900) quoted a Philadelphia newspaper review: "It is not lacking in philosophy and satire which will furnish amusement to the adult and cause the juvenile to think some new and healthy thoughts. At the same time it is not objectionable in being too knowing and cannot be fairly charged with unduly encouraging precocity." However, the most significant and prophetic review was that which appeared in *The New York Times* on September 8, 1900. To preserve this excellent contemporary analysis of *The Wonderful Wizard of Oz* the piece is reprinted here without alteration.

It is impossible to conceive of a greater contrast than exists between the children's books of antiquity that were new publications during the sixteenth century and modern children's books of which "The Wonderful Wizard of Oz" is typical. The crudeness that was characteristic of the old-time publications that were intended for the delectation and amusement of ancestral children would now be enough to cause the modern child to yell with rage and vigor and to instantly reject the offending volume, if not to throw it out of the window. The time when anything was good enough for children has long since passed, and the volumes devoted to our youth are based upon the fact that they are the future citizens: that they are the country's hope, and are thus worthy of the best, not the worst, that art can give. Kate Greenaway has forever driven out the lottery book and the horn book.

In "The Wonderful Wizard of Oz" the fact is clearly recognized that the young as well as their elders love novelty. They are pleased with dashes of color and something new in the place of the old, familiar, and winged fairies of Grimm and Andersen.

Neither the tales of Aesop and other fableists, nor the stories such as the "Three Bears" will ever pass entirely away, but a welcome place remains and will easily be found for such stories as "Father Goose: His Book," "The Songs of Father Goose," and now "The Wonderful Wizard of Oz," that have all come from the hands of Baum and Denslow.

This last story of "The Wizard" is ingeniously woven out of commonplace material. It is of course an extravaganza, but will surely be found to appeal strongly to child readers as well as to the younger children, to whom it will be read by mothers or those having charge of the entertaining of children. There seems to be an inborn love of stories in child minds, and one of the most familiar and pleading requests of children is to be told another story.

The drawing as well as the introduced color work vies with the texts drawn, and the result has been a book that rises far above the average children's book of today, high as is the present standard. Dorothy, the little girl, and her strangely assorted companions, whose adventures are many and whose dangers are often very great, have experiences that seem in some respects like a leaf out of one of the old English fairy tales that Andrew Lang or Joseph Jacobs has rescued for us. A difference there is, however, and Baum has done with mere words what Denslow has done with his delightful draughtsmanship. The story has humor and here and there stray bits of philosophy that will be a moving power on the child mind and will furnish fields of study and investigation for the future students and professors of psychology. Several new features and ideals of fairy life have been introduced into the "Wonderful Wizard," who turns out in the end to be only a wonderful humbug after all. A scarecrow stuffed with straw, a tin woodman, and a cowardly lion do not, at first blush, promise well as moving heroes in a tale when merely mentioned, but in actual practice they take on something of the living and breathing quality that is so gloriously exemplified in the "Story of the Three Bears," that has become a classic.

The book has a bright and joyous atmosphere, and does not dwell upon killing and deeds of violence. Enough stirring adventure enters into it, however, to flavor it with zest, and it will indeed be strange if there be a normal child who will not enjoy the story.

These reviews offer only a slight indication of why *The Wizard of Oz* appealed to the imaginations of the turn-of-the-century young. Certainly Baum and Denslow had learned something from the complaint in *Alice in Wonderland:* "What is the use of a book without pictures or conversations?" Denslow embellished the book with many of his best designs. As *Book News* observed: "Mr. Denslow has managed to maintain the reputation for originality that he earned in his former pictures. Besides originality, the illustrations have live action, and humor." His designs had the clarity of a Japanese print, but the elegance and control of Art Nouveau. His bold outlines and flat solid colors were a relief from the overly sketchy black-and-white illustrations that marred many contemporary children's books. J. M. Bowles in his article "Children's Books for Children," in *Brush and Pencil*, September 1903, tried to describe the appeal of Denslow's work to a child:

> Den's panels, circles, and spots, and his solid pages of gorgeous hues with perhaps one tiny figure or object in a lower corner are simply baits to catch my attention through my eye, which as yet gets only general impressions. In other words, my friend W. W. Denslow is an impressionist for babies. He omits all but fundamentals and essentials. He leaves out of his books everything except things that exist in our own little world of fact.

Besides the novelty of his style the book was unique in Denslow's lavish use of color. There were few children's books that experimented with the possibilities of color; there were, of course, the picture books published by Edmund Evans and lithographed reprints of popular rhymes and fairy tales for the very young. But few children's books had tipped-in color plates, and none had the elaborate color scheme of Baum's story. The text illustrations were printed in accordance with the changing geography of the story to increase the child's interest as he read from page to page. The twenty-four full-page color illustrations were inserted between text pages to break up the regularity of the design so as to keep the child's interest. The bright cover and the jacket design are as attractive as the elaborate bindings of an adult's novel.

The success of this extensive use of color encouraged other publishers to experiment with the possibilities of color in a child's book. Color plates and numerous text illustrations appear in nearly all important juveniles of the next two decades. The first edition of *Queen Zixi of Ix* (perhaps Baum's best fairy tale next to *The Wizard of Oz*) is an imitation of the design of the earlier and more famous Baum book; besides the many color plates the later book contains text illustrations in pastel colors and has a binding of green cloth stamped in dark green and red, the same colors as those of the Hill edition of *The Wizard of Oz*. Another imaginative use of color appears in the first edition of *The Road to Oz;* although there are no color plates, the pages are of different colored paper to give a rainbow effect as the pages are leafed. But the novelty of the first Oz book's design was lost in the many lavishly illustrated children's books thereafter, which did not retain a balance between text and illustration.

Another reason for the success of *The Wizard of Oz* was Baum's awareness of what a child likes. His chapters are full of comic and casual conversations, quite different from the stilted language usual in children's books of the period. He was not interested in being didactic; his work is free of the cloying sentimentality and moralizing of much of the now forgotten but once popular children's literature of the last century. Most of the literature of that time, still read by children now, deals with the lives of people of other times. One reason why Louisa May Alcott's *Little Men* and *Little Women* and Mark Twain's *Tom Sawyer* still fascinate children is because of the "old-fashioned" life-style they portray. Before Baum there were few fairy tales written by Americans. There were, of course, the fairy tales of Howard Pyle and Frank Stockton, but there was nothing in the United States to compare with the flowering of the Victorian fairy tale. The American child had to look to Great Britain for his tales of fantasy, to George Macdonald, Lewis Carroll, John Ruskin, Charles Kingsley, Oscar Wilde. The control of American education by the Sunday schools and the American Tract Society discouraged the publication of children's books that did not have a conscious moral purpose. Rarely were children given books "just for fun." One of Baum's aims was to fill this void with entertaining tales of magic lands.

There were other distractions in children's literature that he felt should be eliminated. He avoided the horrors common to the Grimm and Andersen fairy tales; in his later stories he nearly succeeded in eliminating all killing and other brutal acts. He had no interest in the romantic tales of princes and princesses and preferred not to emphasize romantic love or marriage. He also avoided long descriptive passages that would hinder the action of the story. Of Hans Christian Andersen, Baum wrote in his article "Modern Fairy Tales" in *The Advance*, August 19, 1909: "The great Dane had not only a marvelous imagination but was a poet as well, and surrounded his tales with some of the most beautiful descriptive passages known to our literature. As children you skipped those passages—I can guess that, because as a child I skipped them myself." With the simplest use of detail and emphasis Baum was able to create both the atmospheric and physical sense of a locale, whether imaginary or real. The first few paragraphs of *The Wizard of Oz* demonstrate this power to create a concrete reality through the barest means. Baum was interested in telling a good story so he worked hard on a strong plot in all his stories. He criticized Carroll's work for being "rambling and incoherent," but he admired the ability of Alice to be "doing something every moment, and doing something strange and marvelous, too; so the child follows her with rapturous delight." Baum wrote for children, but never down to them. He was also writing to please himself. He wanted to entertain, but he did not think it below him to insert a lesson if he could. In the copy of *The Wizard of Oz* that he gave to the music publisher Isidore Witmark (now in the Butler Library, Columbia University), Baum confided that this book was "my most truthful tale." In the foreword to *Baum's American Fairy Tales* he explained his intentions in writing "modern tales about modern fairies": "They are not serious in purpose, but aim to amuse and entertain, yet I trust the more thoughtful readers will find a wholesome lesson hidden beneath such extravagant notion and humorous incident." He could have been thinking of *The Wizard of Oz* as well.

Of course, his story is not intended to have an overriding and didactic moral, as in the fables of Aesop and the tales of Perrault. Baum was creating a personal mythology, although intended for children, in which many truths of the world could be expressed. The characters and incidents in his book can be viewed as symbolic, and a symbol can represent many things at the same time. For example, besides possessing the qualities of courage, intelligence, and kindness, Dorothy's three companions also embody the three states of nature —animal, vegetable, and mineral. The grayness of Kansas is in contrast to the multicolored Land of Oz. Is this to be read that reality is less colorful than a world created by one's imagination? "But," as W. H. Auden writes in reference to the stories of George Macdonald, "to hunt for symbols in a fairy tale is absolutely fatal."**22**

One cannot overemphasize Baum's conscious development of the "modernized" or "American" fairy tale. Earlier American writers had explored the possibilities of fantasy in the New World. In the short tales of Washington Irving and Nathaniel Hawthorne can be seen the origins of the search for a mythology of the American people. Baum was, however, neither concerned with the preservation of folk traditions as was Irving nor with great metaphysical morality as was Hawthorne. Baum was concerned with the interests and objects familiar to a child of that time. He did not feel a need to imitate the folktales of Grimm (as Howard Pyle did) to tell a wonder story; he did not have to return to the Greco-Roman tradition (as Hawthorne did) to understand mythology. As Baum mentions in his introduction to *Baum's American Fairy Tales* (1908), his stories "bear the stamp of our own times and depict the progressive fairies of today." As Dr. Edward Wagenknecht observes in *Utopia Americana* (a University of Washington chapbook, 1929), "Baum taught American children to look for wonder in the life around them, to realize even smoke and machinery may be transformed into fairy lore if only we have sufficient energy and vision to penetrate to their significance and transform them to our use."

22 W. H. Auden's "Afterword" for George Macdonald's *The Light Princess* (New York: Farrar, Straus & Giroux, Inc., 1967).

Baum never, however, succeeded in creating a purely "American" fairy tale; he borrowed freely from European fairy-tale forms so that witches and wizards, magic shoes and caps exist in the same world with scarecrows, patchwork girls, and magic dishpans. Many of his finest tales were what he called "old-fashioned" fairy tales, such as *The Life and Adventures of Santa Claus* and *Queen Zixi of Ix*, which took place in centuries gone by and dealt with traditional types and situations of European fairy tales. Only when the children clamored for more about "Oz" did Baum return to his "modernized fairy tales."

Still more reason for the popularity of the book was its appeal to adults. Although juvenile literature is written for children, adults buy it. Both Denslow's pictures and Baum's text were sophisticated enough to amuse the turn-of-the-century mind. His characters were the result of a mature mind, no matter how they entertained children. Baum slipped many bits of wit and wisdom into his narrative; often those who read the book as children discover these subtleties upon rereading it as adults. As MacFall explains in *To Please a Child*, the popularity of children's books may be seen in relationship to that of adult fiction. The best-selling novels were romances like Edwin Caskoden's *When Knighthood Was in Flower* and Anthony Hope's *The Prisoner of Zenda*; George Barr McCutcheon's *Graustark* became the first best-seller of the twentieth century and influenced popular fiction for the next three decades. The naturalist novelists were replaced by the realist journalists. For reality one now looked to nonfiction; the romantic novel provided escape. The age of Dreiser and Sandburg was in the future. The public wanted stories, and Baum was first of all a storyteller. If parents were going off to lands of the Middle Ages and to mythical European duchies, why shouldn't children read about a fairyland?

Baum had more stories to tell, and his new popularity gave him the flexibility to try his hand at several different kinds of writing. The year after *The Wizard*'s great success, Baum produced *The Master Key* ("an electrical fairy tale"), *American Fairy Tales* (a collection of short stories based upon contemporary American themes), and *Dot and Tot of Merryland*. This last was a full-length fairy tale written and designed along the same lines as *The Won-*

derful Wizard of Oz. It was illustrated by Denslow who was now riding the crest of the wave of his new reputation as a major illustrator of children's books. His work was being compared to that of the English illustrators Walter Crane, Kate Greenaway, and Randolph Caldecott. In their tradition he illustrated an elaborate volume called *Denslow's Mother Goose* for McClure, Phillips & Co. of New York. When women's magazines were asked what books should be given the young, the editors often replied *Father Goose* or anything illustrated by Denslow. Denslow spent one more summer with the Roycrofters before opening his own studio in New York. During all this activity Denslow still found time to produce some of his finest work for *Dot and Tot of Merryland.*

This book was the last Baum-Denslow collaboration. The actual cause of their split is not clear. It probably resulted from a number of different factors. The first was probably practical. *Dot and Tot of Merryland* failed to repeat the great success of the previous Baum-Denslow titles. Baum's *The Master Key* (illustrated by Fanny Y. Cory) proved to be both a critical and financial success. The author wrote on the flyleaf of the copy he gave his son Robert, to whom the book was dedicated: "The book has been so well received that I am sorry, now, I did not end it differently and leave an opening for a sequel." In August 1903, *St. Nicholas* listed *The Master Key* as having been chosen one of the most popular books by their readers. *Denslow's Mother Goose* also proved to be widely received; in its first two months of publication forty thousand copies were purported to have been sold. Clearly both Baum and Denslow realized that neither was dependent upon the other to succeed in the children's book trade.

There had been considerable rivalry between Baum and Denslow since the unprecedented success of *Father Goose, His Book* about who was responsible for the great response to their books. Baum admitted that his work on the first book was not good and that Denslow was indeed instrumental in the book's wide reception, but he did not approve of Denslow's attitudes toward this success. Denslow was certainly better known than Baum in the publishing world, and there was no reason why on the original cover design of *Father Goose* (now in the New York Public Library) the artist drew in large letters "Pictures by W. W. Denslow" and included only a minority credit line for Baum. In 1900, Denslow produced a "Father Goose" comic page that appeared in the New York *World* and other papers; this also minimized Baum's claim to the originality of the book on which the comic was based. Baum admitted with some bitterness in a letter of August 10, 1915, to his publishers: "Denslow was allowed to copyright his pictures jointly with my claim to authorship," and "having learned my lesson from my unfortunate experiences with Denslow, I will never permit another artist to have an interest in the drawings he makes of my described characters, if I ever can help it." This rivalry culminated in 1901 in a dispute over the proposed musical version of *The Wizard of Oz*. Baum and Paul Tietjens were to be the librettist and composer, Denslow the costume designer. Denslow, however, as half owner of the copyright of the book, demanded a share of the royalties from the dramatization, although he was in no way responsible for the preparation of the story on the stage. To avoid a threatened lawsuit Baum and Tietjens agreed to Denslow's terms.

Evidently Baum and Denslow had gone their separate ways by the end of 1901, for in none of the publicity for the new Baum book for 1902, *The Life and Adventures of Santa Claus*, is there any indication that Denslow was even considered as the possible illustrator. The failure of the Hill company made it convenient for Baum and Denslow to cease their collaboration.

George M. Hill filed bankruptcy claims in February 1902, just a few weeks after advertising the construction of a new building and the expansion of the firm. Evidently these plans were responsible for the company's financial failure. On April 26, Robert O. Law was named as temporary receiver and trustee, and he ordered the property sold. *Publishers' Weekly* of March 29, 1902, announced the sale of "a modern book bindery . . . several hundred sets of plates . . . juvenile books (including a number of the famous Baum-Denslow copyrighted juveniles) . . . and books in sheets and in 'process.' " Hill tried to regain control of the company, but on May 8 negotiations were completed to form the George W. Ogilvie Company to handle the Hill property. Ogilvie, the brother of the New York publisher

J. S. Ogilvie, advertised that the Baum-Denslow titles would soon be issued under his imprint. No copies of these titles have been found with the Ogilvie name. As late as August 1902, the Ogilvie company was advertising its publication of the Baum-Denslow books. Hill's manufacturing plant was sold to C. O. Owen & Co., and then resold to the newly formed Hill Bindery Company, of which George M. Hill was manager. At the failure of Hill's publishing house, Frank Kennicott Reilly and Sumner Charles Britton quickly founded the Madison Book Company, which secured control of the technical books published by Hill and which acted as the sole western distributors of the Ogilvie (and Jamieson-Higgins) books. Cupples & Leon Co. in New York became the sole distributor of these books in the East.

Baum was personally involved in the financial troubles of his publisher. According to *The Bookseller and Latest Literature*, on April 4, 1902, at a meeting of the Illinois Women's Press Association, Baum gave a lecture on "The Relationship between the Author and Publisher." He was obviously referring to the Hill company when he advised authors to stick to one publisher; he explained the injustice of deserting a publisher after he had invested heavily in advertising to make a reputation for the author. He insisted on small royalties to encourage greater advertising, which would result in greater sales. He also expressed his disfavor of editorial revision of an author's manuscript, as only the author could make changes fully in the spirit of the original work.

With the production of *The Wizard of Oz* musical, obviously Baum pushed to get the book on which the play was based reissued, but the debts and troubles inherited by Ogilvie from the Hill company prevented this.

Besides referring to the legal tangles of the Hill disputes, the August 1902 *Bookseller and Latest Literature* reported: "In the Baum-Denslow matter the court allowed the claim of Mr. Denslow and ruled that the author and artist were not partners; so the payments to one would not apply to the royalties due both. A large sum is tied up pending the decision of the court on the disputed matters." This suggests that there was also a lawsuit between Baum and Denslow that was involved with the Hill problems, but its cause is not clear; perhaps in support of his friend Hill, Baum had agreed to a cut in royalties, and Denslow had disputed the author's right to make such a deal. Denslow may also have wished his collaboration with Baum legally dissolved so that the illustrations could become his sole property. By January 1903, the Hill company had still not settled all its debts. The legal situation was further complicated by the failure of Jamieson-Higgins Co. in January 1903 and by the financial troubles suffered by Ogilvie in May when one of his backers left the firm. Ogilvie was now desperate to make up his losses and may have produced at this time (1903) *Pictures from the Wonderful Wizard of Oz* (see the Denslow Appendix). This was a short pamphlet made from sheets of the Hill color plates with a story by Thomas Russell printed on the versos of the plates; there is no mention of Baum in the booklet, so one may assume that Denslow now was in complete control of his illustrations. The pamphlet emphasized the musical with a cover drawing of the Scarecrow and the Tin Woodman based on a photograph of Fred Stone and David Montgomery, the stars of the show; the pamphlet may have been sold in the lobbies of the theatres where the musical was playing, but it did not help Ogilvie. In a last attempt to save his company Ogilvie negotiated with Bobbs-Merrill to buy the plates of the Baum-Denslow titles. Bobbs-Merrill reissued the Oz story as *The New Wizard of Oz,* the word "new" added to avoid confusion with the script of the musical that bears only the slightest similarity to the book. Denslow designed a new cover, endpapers, and title page, but the text was printed from the Hill plates with only a few minor alterations. The Madison Book Company with much of its revenue gone, because of Jamieson-Higgins' failure and the financial problems of Ogilvie (whose company closed down before 1908), decided to increase its own publishing and negotiated with Baum to become his publisher. In 1904, the Madison Book Company became the Reilly & Britton Co., and published its first title, Baum's *The Marvelous Land of Oz.*

With the financial situation nearing settlement the Denslows moved to New York. The artist made at least two visits to Chicago after establishing a studio in New York, but he was soon involved in personal problems. According to MacFall in *To Please a Child,* Ann Waters filed suit for separation from her husband in

September 1903 and later obtained a divorce. She had fallen in love with the young artist Lawrence Mazzanovich, whom Denslow had met at the Roycroft Shops and had invited to live with the Denslows; she and "Mazzy" were wed in Paris and she bore him a son there. On Christmas Eve 1904, Denslow took a new wife, Mrs. Frances Doolittle, who was reputed to be wealthy. With a new wife and the establishment of an advertising design service, Denslow bought a house in Long Island, and continued writing and illustrating children's books, including several more projects based upon *The Wizard of Oz*, none of which repeated the success of their more illustrious predecessor (see the Denslow Appendix). He purchased an island off the coast of Bermuda and crowned himself King Denslow I of Denslow Island with his native boatman named Archie as the admiral of his fleet and his Japanese cook as prime minister. The minor success of the Broadway musical *The Pearl and the Pumpkin* (based upon a children's book written in collaboration with the songwriter Paul West) kept his name in the public eye, but after 1910 when his commissions lessened, he had to sell the island and return to New York where he spent his last days working in a second-rate advertising agency and drinking heavily. His future began to look brighter after he sold a number of drawings and children's verses to *John Martin's Book*. He also sold a full-color cover design to the old *Life* magazine, which so elated him that he went out to celebrate, got drunk, and caught pneumonia.[23] He died soon after on May 27, 1915 (the same year Elbert Hubbard and his wife died on the *Lusitania*). During these years from 1902 to 1915 Baum heard little of Denslow. Soon after the artist's death Baum was told the false rumor that Denslow had committed suicide.

After 1902, although he had lost both his illustrator and publisher, Baum continued undaunted with several projects, most notably the musical production of *The Wizard of Oz*. Who had the original idea of dramatizing the book is not known. Baum met the composer Paul Tietjens through Ike Morgan (who had illustrated Baum's *American Fairy Tales* and his *The Woggle-Bug Book*), and the two began work on a comic opera called *The Octopus* or *The Title Trust*. They failed to find a producer, but were able to interest Frederick R. Hamlin, the business manager of the Chicago Grand

[23] In a letter to David L. Greene, May 11, 1968, from Maurice Kursh, an acquaintance of Denslow during his last years.

Opera House, in another project. What Baum presented to Hamlin was a five-act children's operetta of *The Wizard of Oz* (somewhat in the tradition of the British Christmas "pantomime" plays). Hamlin approached Julian Mitchell, stage director of the Weber & Fields musical revues, to get his opinion. "But after Julian Mitchell had seen the manuscript he urged my adapting it to a modern extravaganza, on account of the gorgeous scenic effects and absurd situations suggested by the story," Baum was quoted as saying in an interview in an unidentified newspaper.

> This I accomplished after much labor, for I found it necessary to alter materially the story of the book. When I wrote the fairy tale I allowed my imagination full play, so that a great deal of the action is absolutely impossible to adapt to the limitations of the stage. So I selected the most available portions and filled the gaps by introducing several new characters and minor plots which serve to throw the story of Dorothy and her unique companions into stronger relief. The main plot of the book is retained, and its readers will have little difficulty in recognizing the well-known characters as they journey in search of the Emerald City and the wonderful Wizard. . . . I was told that what constituted fun in a book would be missed by the average audience, which is accustomed to a regular gatling-gun discharge of wit—or what stands for wit. So I secured the assistance of two experts in this line of work, selected by the advice of Manager Hamlin, and they peppered my prosy lines with a multitude of "laughs."

The produced play did indeed resemble the book only slightly. But on opening night, June 16, 1902, at the Grand Opera House in Chicago, Mitchell's decision proved to be a good one. The musical became one of the greatest successes of the first decade of twentieth-century American theatre. A New York engagement was quickly secured, and the play opened at the new Majestic Theater in New York in early 1903. During this era only the revue *Florodora* and, many years later, *The Merry Widow* were more successful Broadway shows. And no one was more pleased with this triumph than the author himself. An interview in an unidentified newspaper quoted Baum as saying:

The Cyclone scene from the first act of the musical *The Wizard of Oz*, 1902. *Courtesy Theatre Collection, New York Public Library, Astor, Lenox, and Tilden Foundations.*

Anna Laughlin as "Dorothy."

Fred A. Stone as the "Scarecrow," David C. Montgomery as the "Tin Woodman." *Photographs courtesy Theatre Collection, New York Public Library, Astor, Lenox and Tilden Foundations.*

48

Few people can understand the feelings of an author who for the first time sees his creations depicted by living characters upon the stage. The Scarecrow, the Tin Woodman, and the Cowardly Lion were real children of my brain, having no existence in fact or fiction until I placed them in the pages of my book. But to describe them with pen and ink is very different from seeing them actually live. When the Scarecrow came to life on the first night of *The Wizard of Oz* I expected strange sensations of wonder and awe; the appearance of the Tin Woodman made me catch my breath spasmodically, and when the gorgeous poppy field, with its human flowers, burst on my view—more real than my fondest dreams had ever conceived—a big lump came into my throat and a wave of gratitude swept over me that I had lived to see the sight. I cannot feel ashamed at these emotions.

Much of the success of the musical was due to the actors' performances and Julian Mitchell's direction. The script was adequate, but today seems dated and lifeless. The music was mediocre and none has survived the play. Fred A. Stone and David Montgomery as the Scarecrow and the Tin Woodman were the hit of the show. They had been minor vaudeville stars, but *The Wizard of Oz* established them as an important musical comedy team. From *The Wizard* they would go on to other successes, including *The Red Mill* and *Chin-Chin*. Anna Laughlin played Dorothy, but the most celebrated actresses of the show were Bessie Wynn and Lotta Faust, who popularized several non-Baum interpolated songs. The cow Imogene (impersonated by Edwin Stone) and the Cowardly Lion (portrayed by Arthur Hill, a star of the English "pantomime") were also popular with audiences. Julian Mitchell's production turned Baum's fairy tale into little more than an expanded musical revue, with everything from opening with a cyclone to armies of marching girls and a magic box disappearing act. The most elaborate and effective staging was in the poppy scene where the chorus were dressed as flowers; the Good Witch of the North created a snowstorm to save Dorothy and her companions from eternal sleep. Mitchell added songs and eliminated characters and jokes as the show survived year after year. It

The Wizard of Oz

GRAND OPERA HOUSE

Program cover announcing the forthcoming production of the musical *The Wizard of Oz*, c. June 1902. The illustration is an "Inland Gnome" drawn by Denslow in 1894 for *The Inland Printer*.

played eighteen months on Broadway and continued on the road with various companies as late as 1911 when it played at the Castle Square Theater in Boston. Mitchell and Hamlin quickly put together the musical *Babes in Toyland* (which established Victor Herbert as a major musical comedy composer) in 1903 to capitalize on the great success of *The Wizard;* this was the first of many musical comedies of the next decade that tried to capture the magic and success of Baum's musical.

The financial and personal boost given him by the musical encouraged Baum to write a second Oz book, *The Marvelous Land of Oz*. Since the publication of the first he had been bombarded with letters from children demanding more about Oz; he may have fulfilled their request in the hope that the sequel could also be adapted as a musical. His publishers engaged the young Philadelphia artist John R. Neill (1877–1943) to illustrate the book and it proved to be as popular as its predecessor. *The Marvelous Land of Oz* was adapted for the stage as the musical *The Woggle-Bug* with lyrics by Baum and music by Frederic Chapin. It was a complete failure; it was labeled a "kiddies'" show, which discouraged adult paying audiences. Baum had not learned from his association with Mitchell for he made a faithful adaptation of his book without considering the demands of a sophisticated cosmopolitan audience.

Before the play closed Baum actively publicized both the book and the show. With the cartoonist Walt McDougall (1858–1938), Baum prepared a Sunday comic page entitled "Queer Visitors from the Marvelous Land of Oz," which was syndicated in several newspapers across the country in late 1904 and into 1905, a few months before the opening of the musical. The early installments carried a Woggle-bug contest to familiarize the public with the title character of the forthcoming musical. To advertise this contest Baum and Tietjens wrote the song "What Did the Woggle-Bug Say?" Baum also wrote a picture book *The Woggle-Bug Book*, which may have been sold in the lobby of the theatre where the musical was playing. But nothing could save the show. It lasted less than a month.

After this debacle, Baum returned to his major concern: writing fairy tales. Despite the failure of *The Woggle-Bug*, the royalties from *The Wizard of Oz* musical and his children's books provided security for himself and his family. To increase his income he also began writing potboilers—several adult and teen-age popular novels—including the first of the Aunt Jane's Nieces books, a series that was nearly as popular as the Oz books. With several manuscripts in the publisher's hands the Baums afforded themselves the luxury of an overseas vacation. During the first six months of 1906 Frank and Maud traveled through Egypt, Greece, Italy, North Africa, Switzerland, and France. The following year Baum privately published a selection of Maud's letters describing the trip. *In Other Lands Than Ours* describes Maud's ascent of the Great Pyramid, a volcanic eruption of Mount Vesuvius, and the Baums' visit to the Uffizi in Florence. The book was illustrated with photographs of and by Baum. He continued to write while traveling; evidently several of the books published in the next two years were influenced by this trip. *Publishers' Weekly*, January 6, 1906, noted that the author was preparing a new series of fairy tales based upon characters from "The Fairies of the Nile"; these stories were never published but perhaps some of these ideas were incorporated in his subsequent Oz, and other, books.

During his stay in Paris, Baum became interested in the early film industry. Some film footage had been shot for the 1902 musical, but Baum did not take the possibilities of the motion picture seriously until he looked for a novel way of advertising his books. Initially, he had intended to produce several short films based upon his Oz books for nickelodeons, but he soon expanded this to the conception of the "Radio-Plays."**24** These were a series of hand-colored movies and picture slides to be presented with an explanatory lecture called a "fairylogue" that was described as a travelogue that takes you to Oz rather than to China. Although superficially intended as advertising for his books, the production was paid for by Baum himself. His friend Harrison Rountree lent him the money. The movie portion of the program was filmed at the Chicago studios of Colonel William Nicholas Selig, who patented a motion-picture camera in 1896 and reputedly built the first studio in Hollywood. The films were sent to Paris to be hand-colored by Duval Frères as were the set of picture slides based upon drawings by E. Pollack after the Denslow and Neill illustrations. The films were based upon

Sidney Deane as "The Regent," Blanche Deyo as "Tip" in the musical *The Woggle-Bug*, 1905. *Courtesy the Library of Congress.*

24 This was several years before the word "radio" received its current usage; the "Radio-Plays" were named after Michel Radio, the inventor of Parisian transparent coloring of film.

incidents from *The Wizard of Oz*, *The Marvelous Land of Oz*, *Ozma of Oz*, and *John Dough and the Cherub* (the slides also included publicity about the forthcoming *Dorothy and the Wizard in Oz*) all under the direction of Frank Boggs who was also in charge of production.**25** In an interview that appeared in the New York *Herald*, September 26, 1909, Baum described a number of tricks in the film:

25 I am grateful to Richard Mills and his article on "Radio-Plays" in *The Baum Bugle*, Christmas 1970. This early film project is also considered by Russell P. MacFall in the August 1962 *Baum Bugle*, which is devoted to studies of Baum's musical and motion-picture productions.

> One of the simplest of [tricks] is the introduction to my fairy story entertainment, when my little characters step from the pages of an Oz book preparatory to becoming the moving actors of my little tales. A closed book is first shown, which the fairies open. On the first page is disclosed a black and white picture of little Dorothy.... I beckon, and she straightway steps out of its pages, becomes imbued with the colors of life and moves about. The fairies then close the book, which opens again and again until the Tin Man, Scarecrow and all the others step out of the pages and come, colored, to life....
>
> How is it done? Well, grooves were cut to the exact shape of each character [who stood within the book] and so was photographed in black and white. At the signal each steps forth, and the groove, being backed by white, no grotto can be seen ... Between each character the camera is stopped, [and] the new character is arranged in his grotto, [and] the camera starts again. [It was] necessary to color the figures . . . artificially, as we found a difficulty in changing from black and white to colors on the one film, but even this needed ingenuity. [When] figures are enlarged from three-quarters of an inch to eight feet high . . . smudges of tint would occur upon the screen. So the films had to be colored under a great magnifying glass....
>
> There is another illusion . . . which required a good deal more ingenuity. Little Dorothy in a chicken coop is seen to be dashed about in the middle of a storm at sea—[and the] little girl was never at sea in her life. [First] I took motion pictures of a storm at sea. [Then,] in the studio, I draped with black cloth a space

in which I placed Dorothy in her chicken coop. This was built upon rockers, which were fitted with a series of casters, and invisible wires were attached, all being concealed beneath the black cloth except the coop and the child. [Next] I projected upon a screen at one side the picture of the sea, and as the waves rolled in we made the chicken coop follow its curve and float across the black space, at the same time taking another motion picture of it. . . .

When this strip was developed it showed the girl in the coop plainly, but the dead black surrounding made the film transparent. . . . We next placed the chicken coop film above the film containing the sea scene and printed them together against the strip of positive film which is now used for projection. The result is that the child appears to be floating upon the sea since the sea scene is pictured through the transparent portion of the film, while the child in her coop is shown upon the surface. To make the chicken coop follow the roll of the waves was quite difficult and seven trials were required to obtain a satisfactory result.

In another scene some characters build a flying machine under the roof of a palace and fly away in it. They first drag in two sofas, which are placed with the seats together and bound with a clothesline. They place a stuffed . . . deer head at one end and a broom at the other to serve as a tail. Then they run off the stage and fetch some big palm leaves [for] wings. When the characters have all climbed into this queer flying machine and begin to wave the palm leaf wings, the machine rises into the air and flies away with them.

The effect is startling—but easily explained. When the characters leave the stage, the camera is stopped and then workmen come and attach invisible wires to the sofa. These wires extend into the flies where they are joined to a runway. When everything is [ready] the workmen leave the stage and the camera again begins taking the succession of minute pictures, and the characters appear with their palm leaf wings and climb aboard the sofas. Next moment the invisible wires pull them into the sky and the effect is complete.

[Another] class of illusion in fairy photography is bewitchment. Thus a boy is changed into a little girl. He melts before your eyes, [and] out of the mist appears a girl, and vague and shadowy at first, until she at length stands before you, solid as she can be. Moving picture film is prepared for a tremendously quick exposure. Should the exposure be made longer—that is, the camera to be made to go more slowly—the film becomes overexposed and the picture becomes more shadowy. So . . . to efface the boy we gradually slow down the camera till it finally stops. Then we take the boy away and put the little girl in exactly the same place. . . . [Then] we slowly start the camera again, gradually increasing its speed [to normal, taking care, however, to make the two "slows" overlap]. Thus the little girl will gradually strengthen on the film until . . . she appears as her little solid self. . . . A camera can be made a fine liar!

These are all elementary tricks; but considering that these films were made in 1907–1908, only a few years after the Frenchman George Melies explored the possibilities of the trick film, they were remarkable. Baum toured with the films as lecturer, accompanied by an orchestra that played a musical score composed by Nathaniel D. Mann (who had been responsible for several of the songs in *The Wizard of Oz* musical). The show premiered on September 24, 1908, in Grand Rapids, Michigan.

The audiences were fascinated with Baum. He appeared in a white frock coat with silk-faced lapels and trousers of white woolen broadcloth. Several papers could not avoid the temptation of comparing him to the then most famous American lecturer and humorist Mark Twain; the St. Paul *News* noted that, despite his fierce moustache, Baum, like James M. Barrie and Eugene Field, was the "Eternal Boy." The poet Eunice Tietjens, wife of the composer, described Baum at this time in her autobiography *The World at My Shoulder* (1938): "L. Frank Baum was a character. He was tall and rangy, with an imagination and vitality which constantly ran away with him. . . . Constantly exercising his imagination as he did, he had come to the place where he could honestly not tell the difference between what he had done and what he had imagined. Everything he said had to be taken with at least a half-pound of salt. But he was a fascinating companion." His imagination and innocent charm evidently added to the entertainment of the show. "Mr. Baum reveals himself as a trained public speaker of abilities unusual in a writer," wrote a reviewer in the Chicago *Tribune* in October. "His enunciation is clear and incisive, and his ability to hold a large audience's attention during two hours of tenuous entertainment was amply demonstrated." Most critics found the "Radio-Plays" unique entertainment, equally enjoyable for parent and child.

But Baum proved himself to be the "Eternal Boy" not only theatrically but in financial matters as well. The "Radio-Plays," although popular, were not profitable. The expense of moving a projector, its projectionist (his son Frank), an orchestra, and a heavy screen as well as the lecturer himself cut deeply into the profits. He was forced to close the show just before Christmas at the Hudson Theater in New York. He obviously owed Selig for the filming; perhaps to pay off part of his debt Baum allowed Selig to release in 1910 several films based upon the film portion of the "Radio-Plays" as four one-reelers: *The Wizard of Oz, Dorothy and the Scarecrow in Oz, The Land of Oz,* and *John Dough and the Cherub.* Baum was now drastically in need of funds and tried during this period to negotiate several theatrical productions. He and Mrs. Carter Harrison (wife of the mayor of Chicago) made plans for a children's theater to be built near Carnegie Hall in New York. Its first production was to be the operetta *Prince Silverwings,* which Baum and Mrs. Harrison had adapted from her book of the same name as early as 1903; as late as 1915 they were still trying to encourage a production, this time with the Metropolitan Opera Company. If Baum did invest in this children's theatre, it could not have improved his financial state since the project did not materialize. He also wrote a dramatization of the third Oz book, incorporating incidents from other books, for a musical under the name *Ozma of Oz,* but he was unable to find a producer.

On June 3, 1911, Baum filed bankruptcy in the Los Angeles Federal District Court. According to the article, "L. Frank Baum Is

L. Frank Baum at Coronado Beach, California, c. 1909. *Courtesy Fred M. Meyer.*

Ozcot, Hollywood, California, March 1911. *Courtesy Fred M. Meyer.*

'Broke,' He Says" (New York *Morning Telegraph*, June 5, 1911), he claimed his only assets were clothing, a worn typewriter, and a reference book. Harrison Rountree was declared trustee of the estate and was responsible to Baum's many creditors. To pay these debts Baum turned over the rights to all his Bobbs-Merrill titles to Rountree who was to pay off the debts with the royalties. L. Frank Baum had no further financial interest in *The Wizard of Oz* in his lifetime. Not until the 1930s was the copyright returned to the Baum estate.

In 1910, the Baums moved to Hollywood, California, where they found the climate more congenial to Baum's health. For several summers they had spent their vacations near Coronado Beach. With the remainder of Maud's inheritance from her mother a house was built in Hollywood in 1910. Baum lived at Ozcot (as he named his home) until his death; the house remained with Maud until she died in 1953 when it was demolished and replaced by an apartment house.

Building a house did not improve Baum's financial troubles, which were not completely solved by the relinquishing of his royalties from the Bobbs-Merrill books. Because he had other fairy tales to write, he decided that with the sixth Oz book, *The Emerald City of Oz* (1910), he would end the series. The book concludes with a letter from Dorothy stating that Oz was henceforth cut off from the rest of the world by a Barrier of Invisibility that would protect the kingdom from further invasion. Baum then produced the two "Trot" books, *The Sea Fairies* (1911) and *Sky Island* (1912)—this last he considered his finest work—but these did not repeat the great success of the Oz books. Because of disappointing sales of *The Sea Fairies* Baum included characters from the Oz books in *Sky Island* to interest more readers, but its sales were equally discouraging. In 1913, with *The Patchwork Girl of Oz* and the six *Little Wizard* stories Baum returned to writing Oz books. In the introduction to *The Patchwork Girl* he explained that communication with the Land of Oz had been made through the use of the "wireless." He had actually returned to Oz for financial aid; but even the new Oz books didn't sell as well as he had hoped. His publishers suggested that the decrease in sales was due largely to the Donohue reprints issued the same year. Without Baum's consent or knowledge, Bobbs-Merrill (perhaps encouraged by Rountree in the hope of quickening the payment of Baum's debts) rented the plates of their Baum books to M. A. Donohue & Company of Chicago, a reprint house, which sold cheap editions of these books for as low as a sixth of the Reilly & Britton retail price. Baum was now in effect competing with himself.

At this time Baum approached Oliver Morosco with the possibility of introducing his musical *Ozma of Oz* (which was then in its third writing). Morosco was a prominent showman responsible for the successful *Peg O' My Heart;* in later years he would have an even greater success with *Abie's Irish Rose.* He produced Baum's play as *The Tik-Tok Man of Oz,* starring Frank Moore and James Morton as the Shaggy Man and Tik-Tok, with music by Louis F. Gottschalk. The musical was well received on the West Coast, but it did not fare as well on the road. To its disadvantage, it was compared in the press to the earlier and more successful *Wizard of Oz.* As Mac-Fall records in *To Please a Child,* Morosco was smart enough to take the show off the road while it was still in the black. With the musical's minor success Baum's financial troubles were eased. He capitalized on this production by deriving the story of his 1914 book *Tik-Tok of Oz* from the musical.

A few months after the closing of *The Tik-Tok Man of Oz* Baum consulted with a group of men who met socially at the Los Angeles Athletic Club on the possibilities of independent production of motion pictures. Baum and the others were members of the "Lofty and Exalted Order of Uplifters" as well as being actors and businessmen involved in the young Hollywood film industry. Baum proposed the establishment of the Oz Film Manufacturing Company (to be owned by certain members of the club) to produce the famous Oz stories for the screen. When the company was formed, Baum was elected president, the composer Gottschalk vice-president, Clarence R. Rundel secretary, and Harry F. Haldeman treasurer. A studio was built across the street from the Universal Film Company, and in July 1914, production of the first film, *The Patchwork Girl of Oz,* was begun. *The Patchwork Girl* had originally been dramatized as a play to follow *Tik-Tok Man of Oz;* but when Morosco lost interest in its production Baum rewrote the musical as a scenario for the film

L. Frank Baum's library at Ozcot where he wrote many of the "Oz" books. *Courtesy Fred M. Meyer.*

An advertisement for *The Tik-Tok Man of Oz* that appeared in the Los Angeles *Times*, April 10, 1913. *Courtesy the Library of Congress.*

L. Frank Baum and Louis F. Gottschalk during the production of *The Tik-Tok Man of Oz*, from the Los Angeles *Times*, April 3, 1913. *Courtesy the Library of Congress.*

From a program for a screening of the 1914 Oz Film Manufacturing Company's production of *His Majesty, the Scarecrow of Oz* (released as *The New Wizard of Oz*). *Courtesy the personal collection of Justin G. Schiller.*

studio. Within a month the five-reeler was completed, but the new company soon learned that it was easier to produce a film than to distribute it.**26** Most motion-picture studios were controlled by big producers who also controlled the theatres. Eventually, Paramount Pictures agreed to distribute the Oz company's films, but then the Motion Pictures Patent Company, claiming to own Thomas Edison's patent rights, filed suit against all independents. After several months of legal entanglements filming resumed at the Oz Film Manufacturing Company. In all, the company produced *The Patchwork Girl of Oz; The Magic Cloak of Oz; His Majesty, the Scarecrow of Oz* (released as *The New Wizard of Oz*); *The Last Egyptian; The Gray Nun of Belgium;* and four one-reelers released under the title *Violet's Dreams*. Only the first three are known to be extant. All were evidently well photographed and a cut above the stilted film production of the period. The company continued to have distribution problems; theatres refused to book anything with the "Oz" label when their adult audiences refused to pay for "kiddie shows." The company was forced to close. The studio was sold to Universal; the distribution rights were bought by several companies, and as late as 1920 footage shot by the Oz company was infrequently released.

The next filmed version of his work was the 1925 Chadwick *Wizard of Oz*, the script for which was credited to his son Frank. The film starred Larry Semon as the Scarecrow and his wife Dorothy Dwan as Dorothy; Semon was also the director. Oliver Hardy (who had not yet teamed with Stan Laurel) played the Tin Woodman. This film was only slightly based upon the book and was not successful. On occasion it has been revived at film festivals of silent comedies.

Baum had had great faith in the possibilities of adapting his stories for the screen, but the only successful adaptation of his work is the 1939 MGM movie of *The Wizard of Oz*, certainly one of the most popular motion pictures ever made. This time the scriptwriters returned to Baum's original text instead of trying to update the 1902 musical. Judy Garland will always be identified with her portrayal of Dorothy. Ray Bolger, Jack Haley, and Bert Lahr gave memorable performances as the Scarecrow, the Tin Woodman, and the Cowardly Lion. They were supported by Frank Morgan as the Wizard,

26 See Frank J. Baum's "The Oz Film Co.," *Films in Review*, August–September 1956.

Oliver Hardy, Dorothy Dwan, Larry Semon in the 1925 Chadwick Pictures film of *The Wizard of Oz.*

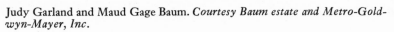

Judy Garland and Maud Gage Baum. *Courtesy Baum estate and Metro-Gold-wyn-Mayer, Inc.*

Judy Garland, Bert Lahr, Jack Haley, Ray Bolger in the 1939 MGM film of *The Wizard of Oz. Courtesy Metro-Goldwyn-Mayer, Inc.*

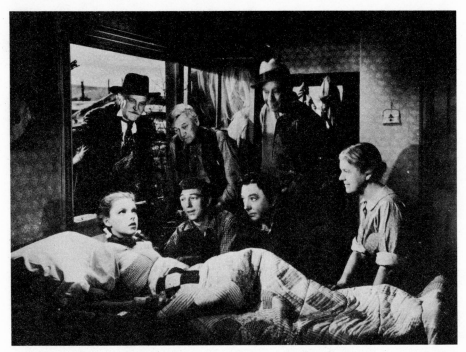

Top, left to right: Frank Morgan, Charley Grapewin, Bert Lahr. Bottom: Judy Garland, Ray Bolger, Jack Haley, Clara Blandick. From the 1939 MGM film of *The Wizard of Oz*. *Courtesy Metro-Goldwyn-Mayer, Inc.*

Billie Burke as Glinda the Good, and Margaret Hamilton as the Wicked Witch. The score by Harold Arlen and E. Y. Harburg included "Over the Rainbow," which won the Academy Award for Best Song of 1939. Despite the many changes (Glinda becomes the Good Witch of the North, the Silver Shoes become the Ruby Slippers), the film is faithful to the spirit and plot of Baum's book. The movie received new life on television where it has become an annual institution. For over thirty years this motion picture has remained a principal introduction for thousands of children to Baum's Land of Oz.

After the failure of the film company Baum settled down at Ozcot to concern himself once again with writing fairy tales. Although the Donohue reprints continued to threaten his profits and the financial situation during the First World War threatened his sales, Baum lived comfortably, though modestly. He spent much of his time in his garden, caring for the flowers that were to win him numerous awards at local garden shows, and writing his books. "My father wrote all his books in longhand on a clip board containing plain single sheets of white typewriter paper," writes his son Harry in the December 1962 *American Book Collector*, "and a great deal of his writing was done in his garden which he loved and cherished. He would make himself comfortable in a garden chair, cross his legs, place the clip board on his knee, and with a cigar in his mouth, begin writing whenever the spirit moved him. This is the picture of him in my mind which I most frequently recall. When he finished an episode or adventure, he would get up and work in his garden. He might putter around for two or three hours before returning to his writing; or it might be two or three days or a week before the idea he was seeking came to him. 'My characters just won't do what I want them to,' he would explain." He revised his original manuscripts in a reconverted bedroom upstairs in the house, which acted as a study. "After a book was completed, Father typed it himself, using the first two fingers of each hand and developing quite a speed. It was during this typing that he made any changes or revisions that seemed necessary." In the garden was an enormous circular birdcage that Baum had constructed with a constantly running fountain and which he supplied with a large variety of songbirds.

Dr. E. P. Ryland, a retired Presbyterian minister and friend of Baum, recalled many years later**27** the resident of Ozcot: "He was a very handsome man, but very modest and reserved. He liked to meet people, mingle with them, talk with them. He was a good listener as well as an easy mixer, and had a keen sense of humor. If he'd not taken to writing children's books he might have been one of the country's best known technical writers for he had a strong leaning toward technical matters." In his garden Baum also answered the hundreds of letters from children that were a constant delight to him. Frequently he had the opportunity to entertain one or two of his child admirers and would think up tales to tell them on their visits to his garden.

Although there is little in his stories to indicate this, Baum in his last year was confined to bed because of a series of painful angina attacks and a gall bladder infection. Since early boyhood he had suffered from a poor heart, and surgery to remove his defective gall bladder and the further complication of an inflamed appendix weakened him. Despite his illness he continued his work. "I want to tell you, for your complete protection, that I have finished the writing of the *second* Oz book—beyond *The Tin Woodman of Oz*—which will give you a manuscript for 1919 and 1920," Baum wrote his publishers on February 14, 1918. "Also there is material for another book, so in case anything happens to me the Baum books can be issued until and including 1921. And the two stories which I have here in the safety deposit I consider as good as anything I have ever done, with the possible exception of *Sky Island*, which will probably always be considered my best work." Despite his failing health, Baum remained in good spirits. In a letter dated September 2, 1918, quoted by MacFall in *To Please a Child*, Baum wrote his son Frank who was then fighting in Europe: "But do not be too downhearted, my boy, for I have lived long enough to learn that in life nothing adverse lasts very long. And it is true that as years pass, and we look back on something which, at the time, seemed unbelievably discouraging and unfair, we come to realize, after all, God was at all times on our side. The eventual outcome was, we discover, by far the best solution for us, and what then we thought should have been to our best advantage, would in reality have been quite detri-

27 Jeanne O. Potter, "The Man Who Invented Oz," Los Angeles *Times Sunday Magazine*, August 13, 1939, p. 12.

Judy Garland, Margaret Hamilton in the 1939 film of *The Wizard of Oz. Courtesy Metro-Goldwyn-Mayer, Inc.*

mental." On May 6, 1919, at his home in Hollywood, Baum died.

So popular were the Oz books that the children refused to let the series end with their creator's death. William F. Lee of Reilly & Lee secured permission from Maud Baum to have the stories continued by Ruth Plumly Thompson, a young Philadelphia writer of children's verse and stories. Starting with *The Royal Book of Oz* in 1921, Miss Thompson was to add a new title to the series each year for nineteen years until she retired from her role as "Royal Historian of Oz" in 1939. She still writes verse and stories and receives dozens of letters a year from children still captivated by her Oz stories. Her view of Oz was distinct from Baum's, but her own magic has ensured many devoted readers. Edward Eager, writing in the *Horn Book* in 1948, believes that Miss Thompson brought back the vigor lacking in Baum's last work. "In her earlier books, she shows a fine ear for pun, a real feeling for nonsense, and in lieu of style, a contagious zest and pace that sweep the reader beyond criticism."**28** The books written by John R. Neill (who illustrated all the Oz stories except the first, until his death in 1943) are not as successful. Neill was a fine illustrator, but he was not as gifted with words. He had a wild imagination demonstrated in both text and picture, but he was careless with plot. The late Jack Snow (who had loved Baum's books since a child) contributed two Oz books, *Magical Mimics in Oz* (1946) and *The Shaggy Man of Oz* (1949), plus the encyclopedic *Who's Who in Oz*. Snow assembled one of the earliest collections of Baum's work and also hoped to write a biography of his favorite author. Although well plotted, his books borrow too freely from Baum's work and lack the humor essential to the Oz series. The two other books in the series, *The Hidden Valley of Oz* (1951) by Rachel R. Cosgrove and *Merry Go Round in Oz* (1963) by Eloise Jarvis McGraw and Lauren McGraw Wagner, are good adventure stories but are not distinctive in their views of the Land of Oz. In addition to the long series published by Reilly & Lee, *The Laughing Dragon of Oz* was issued by Whitman Publishing Company in 1934 as a "Big Little Book." This was an abbreviated version of the story "Rosine in Oz" written by the author's son Frank J. Baum on his return from the service in Europe. Frank had hoped to continue the series, but his mother had already given per-

28 See also Russel B. Nye's appreciation of Miss Thompson's work in *The Baum Bugle*, Autumn 1965.

mission to Reilly & Lee to employ Miss Thompson as "Royal Historian of Oz." Frank's book was sold in dime stores until it was recalled by Whitman when Reilly & Lee threatened a lawsuit. His second story, "The Enchanted Princess of Oz," had been bought and illustrations prepared for it by Milt Youngren before Whitman decided not to publish it.

Although the Oz books were the leading juveniles of their day, almost no mention of these stories and their creator appeared in the major contemporary magazines. As Martin Gardner observes in *The Wizard of Oz and Who He Was*, in an era when the major publications noted the best children's books of the year in their Christmas issues, Baum's name is conspicuously absent from these lists. Many of these periodicals were controlled by the major book-publishing houses. These magazines aimed to promote the authors of the various companies by printing short stories and literary comment on those writers under contract. The titles of many of these publications reflect this control: *Harper's, Scribner's, The Century*. Among the book trade journals, Scribner's owned *The Book Buyer*, Macmillan *Book Reviews*, and Bobbs-Merrill *The Reader*. Baum did serialize a book in the leading juvenile magazine *St. Nicholas*, but he was to write on February 9, 1912, to Reilly & Britton that the Century Co. (who owned *St. Nicholas*) had paid him "for the serial rights of *Queen Zixi of Ix*, and Mr. Ellsworth lately gave me to understand that they would materially advance the price for another book. But they will not serialize anything in *St. Nicholas* which they do not own the book rights for." These magazines controlled their lists of "suggested reading"; generally the only books reviewed were their own and those of other publishers who advertised in their pages. With the exception of the Bobbs-Merrill books, Baum's stories were not widely reviewed. George M. Hill was concerned primarily with the printing and distributing of books, not the editing; it was never a major publishing house and did not invest heavily in advertising. *Father Goose, His Book* was a freak success, for it was well received by the critics without extensive advertising; but the other Baum-Hill books (including *The Wonderful Wizard of Oz*) did not need to be advertised and were not reviewed in the major magazines. "When the Hill company published *Father Goose* and *The Wizard of Oz,*" Frank Reilly wrote Baum on New Year's Eve, 1914, "Mr. Britton and the writer were able to put over a lot of stunts—the best sort of advertising, free publicity in the newspapers—because we had something absolutely new. Now, however, there is nothing new in presenting—either to the trade or to the public—a new Oz book. The professional buyers do not read such books and merely regard the annual Baum book as one of a thousand other items of merchandise." Evidently the press also viewed each new Oz book as no different from the last and so failed to acknowledge it.

Baum chose his own publishers, so the lack of critical opinion may have been in part his fault. As Martin Gardner explains in "Why Librarians Dislike Oz" (*The American Book Collector,* December 1962), most of his books were published by the Reilly & Britton Company (later Reilly & Lee) a small Chicago publishing house that specialized in Baum, teen-age fiction, and the verse of Edgar Guest. His own reputation might have improved if his name had been included with the more prestigious authors on the lists of a major eastern firm. (In surviving letters of the Baum family are references to his being approached by several leading publishers for manuscripts.) He paid little attention to the critics. He knew the children enjoyed his stories, and if they sold well he was pleased. Also, he had a special agreement with Reilly & Britton who paid him a monthly salary on his royalties, a rare contract between publisher and author at the time. Moreover, the Baums were personal friends of the Reillys and the Brittons, even before the failure of the Hill company. Baum received certain special courtesies from his publishers that he would not have received from any other. He knew they would devote most of their attention to the promotion of the Baum books (although after 1910 this interest waned). Previously when associated with Bobbs-Merrill (whose reputation and sales were based on their extensive advertising interests), Baum was disappointed with the sales of his books and considered this due to the company's poor promotion of his interests. Although they failed to appear on recommended reading lists, the Reilly & Britton books by Baum never failed to make the best-seller lists.

In recent years a number of critical studies of Baum and his work have appeared. Only a few, however, deal exclusively or extensively with *The Wizard of Oz*. One of the most interesting of these is Henry M. Littlefield's "The Wizard of Oz: Parable on Populism" (*American Quarterly*, Spring 1964). The basis of Mr. Littlefield's article is that Baum was interpreting his own times allegorically when he wrote the first of the Oz series. Mr. Littlefield raises several valid points (mentioned in my notes to Baum's text) on how Baum's writing did, in fact, reflect its own time in terms of the Populist movement. But too often he strains metaphors to support his ideas. For instance, for Littlefield, the Silver Shoes reflect the silver issue and the Yellow Brick Road alludes to William Jennings Bryan's famous "Cross of Gold" speech (but *are* the streets of Oz really paved with gold?); because the Wizard is from Omaha, Baum must be consciously suggesting Bryan who was nominated by his party in Nebraska for the Presidency. Of course, it isn't difficult to find evidence for various ideologies in a child's book, but Mr. Littlefield's article cannot be ignored.

I cannot say the same for Osmond Beckwith's "The Oddness of Oz" (*Kulchur*, Fall 1961). Considerable space is devoted to a psycho-analytical interpretation of *The Wizard of Oz*. Beckwith suggests (among other things) that the Wicked Witch of the West is Dorothy's evil mother figure and must therefore be killed; the lack of a brain, a heart, and courage suggests that Baum had a castration complex. These rather obvious Freudian interpretations are amusing rather than enlightening.

Another curious piece on *The Wizard of Oz* is "The Art of Being," one of the *Lecture-Lessons* of Marc Edmund Jones, published in 1964 by the Sabian Assembly, a society interested in occult sciences. Each chapter of *The Wizard* is seen in terms of a particular virtue, which each child must follow toward maturity. Each act is seen as a moral choice in accordance with the tenets of this society. The argument is not convincing but it is of some interest. The author of *The Wizard of Oz* was indeed well read in the occult sciences. When he lived in Aberdeen, Baum became interested in Theosophy and was rumored to be a Buddhist. His wife and her mother, Matilda Gage, were also interested in spiritualism; they were known to have

29 Robert Baum in his autobiography (published in part in *The Baum Bugle*, Christmas 1970) records one peculiar psychic occurrence at their first home in Chicago:

> My brother Kenneth was just a baby and Father had rigged up a "jumper" between the door way, a little chair suspended by strings in which he sat and could be jumped up and down to quiet him. A cord was attached to it so Mother could sit in a chair and jump him up and down by pulling the cord while she was doing her sewing or reading. One night when the baby was especially fretful and Mother was tired of pulling the cord, she cried out, "If there is any such thing as spirits I wish they would rock this baby for me." And, according to the story as told by my mother, the jumper immediately began to go up and down for a considerable length of time without anyone touching it.

Another recollection of Robert Baum in his autobiography (which was not published in *The Baum Bugle*) concerns his grandmother Gage's wide interest in the occult:

> She was more or less interested in Spiritualism and had also made a study of the science of Palmistry. She used to delight in reading our hands and I can remember how she would have us place our palm on an ink pad and then make an impression on a piece of paper so she could study the lines of our hands at her leisure. She was also interested in Astronomy and used to take us children out doors at night and point out to us the various stars and constellations.

entertained clairvoyants and held seances in their home.**29** This was not especially unusual; the spiritualist movement had begun in America in 1848 and was still widely followed in the latter part of the nineteenth century. In an article on the power of the clairvoyant in the April 5, 1890, Aberdeen *Saturday Pioneer*, Baum described the following cosmology:

> Scientists have educated the world to the knowledge that no portion of the universe, however infinitesimal, is uninhabited. Every bit of wood, every drop of liquid, every grain of sand or portion of rock has its myriads of inhabitants—creatures deriving their origin from and rendering involuntary allegiance to a common Creator. The creatures of the atmosphere, while admittedly existent, are less widely known in that they are microscopically and otherwise invisible to ordinary humanity. No student of Nature can conceive that the Creator, in peopling every other portion of the universe, neglected to give the atmosphere its quota of living creatures. These invisible and vapory beings are known as Elementals, and play an important part in the lives of humanity. They are soulless, but immortal; frequently possessed of extraordinary intelligence, and again remarkably stupid. Some are exceedingly well disposed toward mankind, but the majority are maliciously inclined and desirous of influencing us to evil. The legendary "guardian spirit" which each human being has, is nothing more or less than an Elemental, and happy is he who is influenced thereby for good and not incited to evil.

The theory of "elementals" was popularized by such works as Edward Bulwer-Lytton's *Zanoni* (1848) and Mme. Blavatsky's *Isis Unveiled* (1877). These, however, have their source in an ancient occult tradition. The belief that everything is composed of "elementals," or the four building blocks from which all matter is made, is of the Aristotelian tradition. In the fifth century A.D., Proclus divided all spirits into five groups, the first four associated with the elements—earth, air, fire, water—the fifth being underground. Paracelsus, the sixteenth-century Swiss alchemist and physician, divided all spirits into four categories: Air, sylphs; Water, nymphs or undines; Earth, gnomes; Fire, salamanders. These could be expanded to the ancient idea of the four states of matter—gas, liquid, solid, and energy. From Paracelsus the occult group known as the Rosicrucians adopted this categorizing of spirits. This influence is also seen in Alexander Pope's *The Rape of the Lock* (1712) as well as Le Motte-Fouqué's *Undine* (1811) and Sir Walter Scott's *The Monastery* (1820). A quick glance at Baum's fairy tales reveals that he wrote about each Paracelsian classification of spirits. His sylphs are the "winged fairies" (Lulea of *Queen Zixi of Ix*, Lurline of *The Tin Woodman of Oz*); the undines are the mermaids (Aquareine of *The Sea Fairies*, the water fairies of the first chapter of *The Scarecrow of Oz*); the gnomes are the Nomes (the Nome King of *The Life and Adventures of Santa Claus* and *Ozma of Oz*); and the salamanders are the fairies of energy (the Demon of Electricity of *The Master Key*, the Lovely Lady of Light of *Tik-Tok of Oz*). Baum seems to have created a highly sophisticated cosmology by interpreting this theory of spirits or "elementals" in terms of traditional fairies.

This is basically a religion of Nature. Modern science itself has its origins in the occult sciences, in the search for the secrets of Nature. Baum claimed that the basic belief of Theosophy was that "God is Nature, and Nature God." As editor of the *Pioneer* (February 22, 1890) he writes: "Of all that is inexplicable in our daily lives, we can only say that they are Nature's secrets, and a sealed book to ignorant mortals; but none the less do we marvel at their source and desire to unravel their mystery." It is not by mistake that the Shaggy Man in *The Patchwork Girl of Oz* refers to Oz as being a fairyland "where magic is a science." Both science and magic have the same ends.

In his article on Theosophy (January 25, 1890) Baum described his own era as an "Age of Unfaith," but "this is not atheism of the last century. It is rather an eager longing to penetrate the secrets of Nature—an aspiration for knowledge we have thought is forbidden." The Theosophists are "searchers for Truth" and "admit the existence of God—not necessarily a personal God." The growth of the theo-

30 In a letter to Martin Gardner, November 21, 1955.

31 In a letter to Jack Snow, June 7, 1943 (quoted by Martin Gardner in *The Wizard of Oz and Who He Was*), Baum's nephew Henry B. Brewster writes:

> Mr. Baum always liked to tell wild stories, with a perfectly straight face, and earnestly, as though he really believed them himself. . . . His mother was very religious . . . and felt she knew her Bible well. Frank Baum seemed to take particular delight in teasing her and I recall, not once but many times, how he would pretend to quote from the Bible, with which he definitely was not familiar. For example, once she said, "Frank, you are telling a story," and he said, "Well, Mother, as you know, in St. Paul's epistle to the Ephesians he said, 'All men are liars.'" Whereupon his mother said, "Why, Frank, you are wrong, I do not recall that," and irrespective of the fact that she had been fooled so many times she would look up in her Bible to see if she were wrong, and he right. Frank Baum was one of the most imaginative men. There was nothing wrong, but he did love to "Fairytale," or as you might say, tell "white lies."

A similar joke occurs in the Aberdeen *Saturday Pioneer*. In response to the claim of the rector of Saint Mark's Church that there are no such things as psychic phenomena Baum suggests that the clergyman refer to Acts V: 38, 39, of course, this passage has nothing to do with the minister's point.

sophical movement and spiritualism in general was a reaction to the increasing strength of science. Twice in the nineteenth century the occult sciences became a popular form of religious expression. The first was after the church and state became one under the French Republic. In response to the apparent failure of the church, the Romantic Age developed a new "paganism," a return to a religion of Nature where emotion rather than reason reigned. This is evident in the Swedenborgian philosophy of William Blake; in the works of the German Romantic E. T. A. Hoffman the occult influence is obvious in his complicated references to then archaic or "secret" practices. The second was the compromise between the Protestant churches and Darwinism. Science had divorced religion from Nature. The theory of "elementals" is in agreement with scientific theory, but with the addition of spiritual possibilities. The rebirth of secret societies like the Rosicrucians was in pursuit of communion with God and Nature. Writers such as Arthur Rimbaud and William Butler Yeats searched for (in different ways) a new mysticism in a world that preferred to agree with Huxley's "agnosticism."

Whether Baum actually believed all this is debatable. His son Frank admitted the author's interest in Theosophy, but also reported that the elder Baum could not accept all its teachings.[30] He firmly believed in reincarnation; he had faith in the immortality of the soul and believed that he and his wife had been together in many past states and would be together in future reincarnations, but he did not accept the possibility of the transmigration of souls from human beings to animals or vice versa, as in Hinduism. He was in agreement with the Theosophist belief that man on Earth was only one step on a great ladder that passed through many states of consciousness, through many universes, to a final state of Enlightenment. He did believe in Karma, that whatever good or evil one does in his lifetime returns to him as reward or punishment in future reincarnations. Baum could not accept the idea of a wrathful godhead. Perhaps he had been taught too early by his grandfather Baum, a Methodist preacher, about hellfire and damnation. His mother was also strong willed about her religion, which often amused her son.[31] But Baum could not accept the idea of the Devil, a denial that prevented him from joining any Christian church. In the October 18, 1890, *Saturday Pioneer* he blasted the organized church: "When the priests acknowledge their fallibility; when they abolish superstition, intolerance and bigotry; when they abhor the thought of a vindictive and revengeful God; when they are able to reconcile reason and religion and fear not to let the people think for themselves, then, and then only will the Church regain its old power and be able to draw to its pulpits the whole people." He believed that all the great religious teachers of history had found their inspiration from the same source, a common Creator. He could not accept the rivalries between different sects; the few references to the church and ministers in his books (notably *American Fairy Tales*) are not generally favorable. "He wasn't what you'd call a strictly religious man," the Reverend Mr. Ryland was quoted as saying in the previously mentioned article in the Los Angeles *Times*, "that is, he wasn't a denominationalist. When he went to church at all in Hollywood he attended mine, but he wasn't a member of it. He had a gospel of his own and he preached it through his books, although you certainly couldn't call them religious either. I once asked him how he came to write the first Oz book. 'It was pure inspiration,' he said. 'It came to me right out of the blue. I think that sometimes the Great Author has a message to get across and He has to use the instrument at hand. I happened to be that medium, and I believe the magic key was given me to open the doors to sympathy and understanding, joy, peace and happiness. That is why I've always felt there should never be anything except sweetness and happiness in the Oz books, never a hint of tragedy or horror. They were intended to reflect the world as it appears to the eyes and imagination of a child.' That was as close as we ever came to a discussion of religion. But he certainly had one, and he lived and wrote by it."

The world of Oz as described in *The Wizard of Oz* significantly differs from that developed in the later sequels. S. J. Sackett's "The Utopia of Oz" (*The Georgia Review*, Fall 1961) is a convincing study of the Land of Oz in economic, social, and cultural terms. After the coronation of Princess Ozma,**32** the rightful ruler of Oz, in *The Marvelous Land of Oz*, both social structure and certain

32 The second syllable of the name "Ozma" may be an abbreviation of Maud, the name of Baum's wife. When the musical *The Tik-Tok Man of Oz* was adapted as the book *Tik-Tok of Oz*, the Rose Princess "Ozma" became "Ozga"; the second syllable of this name may be an abbreviation of Gage, Maud's maiden name.

aspects of the geography of Oz are radically different from what they were during the Wizard's reign.

The flora and fauna of each of the four kingdoms become the same color as the favorite color of that region. The great desert that surrounds Oz has some mysterious magic power that threatens to destroy anyone who dares step foot on it. In the third chapter of *The Emerald City of Oz*, Baum explains most fully the utopian nature of his fairyland:

No disease of any sort was ever known among the Ozites, and so no one ever died unless he met with an accident that prevented him from living. This happened very seldom, indeed. There were no poor people in the Land of Oz, because there was no such thing as money, and all property of every sort belonged to the Ruler. The people were her children, and she cared for them. Each person was given freely by his neighbors whatever he required for his use, which is as much as any one may reasonably desire. Some tilled the lands and raised great crops of grain, which was divided equally among the entire population, so that all had enough. There were many tailors and dress makers and shoe-makers and the like, who made things that any one who desired them might wear. Likewise there were jewelers who made ornaments for the person, which pleased and beautified the people, and these ornaments also were free to those who asked for them. Each man and woman, no matter what he or she produced for the good of the community, was supplied by the neighbors with food and clothing and a house and furniture and ornaments and games. If by chance the supply ever ran short, more was taken from the great storehouses of the Ruler, which were afterwards filled up again when there was more of any article the people needed.

Every one worked half the time and played half the time, and the people enjoyed the work as much as they did the play, because it is good to be occupied and to have something to do. There were no cruel overseers set to watch them, and no one to rebuke them or to find fault with them. So each one was proud to do all he could for his friends and neighbors, and was glad when they would accept the things he produced.

Ozma preserves a few minor laws (such as that which forbids picking a six-leaf clover in *The Patchwork Girl of Oz*), but the most important law is: "Do whatever you will as long as it does not hurt anyone else." There are, of course, uncivilized tribes throughout the unexplored territory of Oz and many discontented magicians and witches who infrequently try to take over the fairyland, but generally Oz is a gentle kingdom where the good are rewarded and the evil forgiven. Under Ozma of Oz the country becomes "The Land of Love." This is in marked contrast to the struggle between Good and Evil in *The Wizard of Oz*. If the country under the Wizard where there is still death and taxes may be seen as a dark age, the reign of Ozma may be its return to a golden age. The new period of the history of Oz reflects (as MacFall explains in *To Please a Child*) the contemporary utopian novels, notably Edward Bellamy's *Looking Backward* (1888) and William Morris's rural *News from Nowhere* (1891). The seemingly "socialist" character of the Oz culture is only superficial; Oz is closer to a benevolent despotism than to either a Marxist or welfare state.

The alleged "socialist" structure of Oz may in part be responsible for the continual controversy over the Oz books. In "The Red Wizard of Oz" (*New Masses*, October 4, 1938), Stewart Robb in jest suggested that the reason for banning the Oz books from the shelves of the children's room in the New York Public Library may have been political; he noted the anarchistic culture of Oz was an approximation of the Marxist dream. In the age of Senator Joe McCarthy (when even Robin Hood's legend was to be viewed as a Marxist tract), it is not surprising that Baum's quiet utopia could be misconstrued as something it was not. Ray Ulveling, the Detroit library system's director, caused a wave of protest when he candidly mentioned in early April 1957 that he was proud to say that his libraries never had and never intended to stock any of Baum's Oz books. The press quickly accepted this as meaning a "ban" of the Oz stories. Ulveling claimed that these books were "of no value"; they sup-

33 Quoted from Neil Hunter's "Librarian Raps 'Oz' Books," *The State Journal* (Lansing, Michigan), April 4, 1957.

34 C. Warren Hollister in "Baum's Other Villains" (*The Baum Bugle*, Spring 1970) refers to a passage from *The Magic of Oz* (1919), which may be a reflection on the Bolshevik Revolution of Russia in 1917. Hollister views the speech of the Nome King before the animals of the Forest of Gugu as Baum's attempt to show how innocent creatures are motivated into war and revolt through the effective use of Marxist dialectic.

posedly encouraged "negativism" and misled minds to accept a cowardly approach to life. "There is nothing uplifting or elevating about the Baum series," he continued. "They do not compare in quality to fairy tales by Grimm and Andersen."**33** He noted that the public preferred do-it-yourself books to mysteries, fairy tales, and other popular fiction. His opinions were supported by his colleagues who explained that after 1920 there was a new approach to children's literature and *The Wizard of Oz* was not in keeping with this approach. The press came to the defense of the Oz books in protest to the growing censorship, but as late as April 1961 the Westwood-Brentwood, California, *Villager* published an article accusing Baum of Communist leanings.**34** The Detroit libraries still do not have the Baum books on their shelves.

Another frequent complaint of librarians and critics is that *The Wizard of Oz* is poorly written. This would seem to be a matter of taste rather than of criticism. Baum was not a stylist as were many writers of juvenile literature, including Andersen, Robert Louis Stevenson, Kenneth Grahame, and others. Baum's main concern was in telling a good story, but his style is generally good and without the archaisms and long descriptive passages that, though of interest to an adult, sometimes confuse a child. It is also free of the sentimentality and class consciousness that mar many juvenile books of the nineteenth century. As with all great works of fantasy its style and mood are timeless; it reads as well today as when it was first written.

The Wizard of Oz is also well structured. Dichotomy is important. The first and last chapter take place in Kansas; the loss of home is comfortably restored. Dorothy is befriended by two good witches; in the second chapter the Good Witch of the North presents her with a pair of Silver Shoes, in the next to the last chapter the Good Witch of the South discloses their power. The center of the book is the Discovery of Oz, the Terrible. Dorothy is disappointed twice by the Wizard; first, after she kills the Wicked Witch of the East and he appears as a great head; second, after she kills the Wicked Witch of the West and he escapes in his balloon. The second half of the story reflects the first. The first concerns the discovery of intelligence, kindness, and courage; after the brain, heart, and courage are received, their qualities, embodied now with outer symbols, must be put into practice in the second half. There are conscious rephrasings of conversations of the first part in the second. In Chapter 18 the discussion about Glinda the Good reflects one in the second chapter between Dorothy and the Good Witch of the North about the Wizard. Within this framework Baum has created several of the most memorable characters in children's literature. The Scarecrow, Tin Woodman, and Cowardly Lion in their search for a brain, heart, and courage are today as much a part of the child's world as any traditional nursery characters.

Today, the Oz books often remain ignored by librarians and critics of juvenile literature. There has been the complaint that it is impractical for a public library to stock any books of a series; if the child likes one, the library is supposedly obligated to buy the complete set. Perhaps this is true, but nearly every children's library has at least several of C. S. Lewis's *Narnia* chronicles or Beatrix Potter's *Peter Rabbit* tales. Also, it is true that fantasy is not for everyone, for, as E. M. Forster has written, "fantasy asks us to pay something extra."[35] Libraries when they do buy nontraditional fairy tales generally choose only those by British authors. The long history of English literature proves that Americans prefer British literature to their own. The American Library Association has named its awards for the most distinguished picture book and general contribution to juvenile literature after the English illustrator Randolph Caldecott and the English publisher John Newbery. The editors of the *Horn Book*, which is responsible for nearly all critical reviews of children's books, still fail to recognize L. Frank Baum as a major American author of juvenile literature. While it will ignore Baum's books, the *Horn Book* will devote bibliographies and articles to such secondary American writers as Laura E. Richards and Susan Coolidge. Notwithstanding the failure of these librarians and critics to consider Baum's work, the Oz stories have remained among the most popular American juveniles ever published.

A number of prominent scholars and writers have, however, voiced their appreciation of the Oz books. Dr. Edward Wagenknecht

35 E. M. Forster, *Aspects of the Novel* (New York: Harcourt, Brace & World, Inc., 1927), p. 109.

of Boston University wrote the first monograph on Baum and his work, *Utopia Americana,* in 1929. C. Beecher Hogan, retired lecturer of English at Yale University, and C. Warren Hollister, professor of history at the University of California, Santa Barbara, are major collectors of Baum's books. The late Roland Baughman, the curator of Special Collections at Columbia University and a collector of Baum, was responsible for the Columbia library's centennial exhibition of L. Frank Baum. Important studies of the Oz books have appeared in such scholarly journals as *The Georgia Review, The New York Review of Books, American Quarterly,* and *Chicago Review.* Baum is also becoming recognized in critical histories of juvenile literature. Selma G. Lanes in her study *Down the Rabbit Hole* devotes much of her discussion of American fairy tales to Baum's work. Two essays in Oxford University's *Only Connect,* a collection of studies of juvenile literature, concern the Oz stories. Collectors, artists, writers, and Baum enthusiasts in general have formed The International Wizard of Oz Club, Inc. (Box 95, Kinderhook, Illinois) which is instrumental in every project dealing with Oz and Baum. The organization's periodical, *The Baum Bugle,* published three times a year, contains articles on various topics such as little known stories by Baum and bibliographical material on early editions of his books. Since the club's founding in 1957 by a twelve-year-old Brooklyn boy, Justin G. Schiller, the club has grown to more than a thousand members from every state in the country and from several foreign nations.

Certainly the influence of *The Wizard of Oz* has not been confined to the United States. This American fairy tale has been translated into countless foreign languages and is often included in collections of translations of the more critically favored English classics such as *Alice in Wonderland, Peter Pan,* and *The Wind in the Willows.* The earliest known translation was in French and appeared in 1932. Bobbs-Merrill sold the British distribution rights to several of their Baum titles when they first came out, and Reilly & Britton sold copies of Baum's books in Canada through the Copp Clark Company; but Baum evidently was unconcerned with foreign editions of his work.[36] The many translations that have appeared in

36 In an article on Baum, that appeared in the St. Paul *Pioneer Press,* October 11, 1908, are mentioned foreign editions in Germany, France, Italy, and Japan, but no copies of these possible early translations have been seen. Foreign editions of *The Wizard of Oz* have been frequently discussed in *The Baum Bugle.* Through the help of David and Douglas Greene a checklist of the most notable editions is included in the bibliography at the back of the book.

the last three decades were encouraged by the international popularity of the 1939 MGM film. As the Spring 1962 *Baum Bugle* reports, *The Wizard of Oz* has been so popular in Italy that several of the earliest sequels have also been translated. The first Oz book has proven to be especially popular in the Soviet Union. A. Volkov, the translator, has written two original sequels, *Urfin Dzhus and His Wooden Soldiers* and *The Seven Underground Kings*. Also, the texts of *The Wizard* and *The Magic of Oz* are used to teach Russian children the English language. The illustrations for *The Wizard* vary as often as the languages. They range from the Denslowlike drawings of the 1963 Tamil (one of the national languages of India) edition to the surreal illustrations (not unlike the work of Paul Klee) of the 1962 Czech edition by Arnost Karasek. These many translations are complemented by over a dozen different editions in the United States.

This edition is intended as an introduction to Baum's great body of work. I have tried to keep in mind the note to "Margery Daw" in *Mother Goose's Melody:* "It is mean and scandalous practice in authors to put notes to things that deserve no notice." (I hesitate to recommend to the sensitive reader Robert Benchley's humorous essay "Shakespeare Explained.") A checklist of Baum's published and projected work is included at the back indicating to the novice Baum's profuse output and the great wealth of material the annotator has had to consider. This edition also includes all the Denslow illustrations (in their original colors) from the George M. Hill edition, as well as a number of later drawings, some of which have never appeared in any edition. It is an accurate facsimile of the first edition, including all the two-color text illustrations plus the twenty-four color plates. To capture a correct reproduction of the original printing has been most difficult. The old process of color reproduction used for the first edition is no longer used. The color plates were printed in three colors: blue, red, and yellow. This common trichromatic process avoided the use of a black plate. The addition of a black plate seems to have become more popular a few years later than the first printing of *The Wonderful Wizard of Oz*. A comparison of the trichromatic and the four-color processes can be made by viewing the plates for both *The Wizard of Oz* and *Denslow's Scarecrow and the Tin-Man*, which is published in facsimile in the Denslow Appendix. Denslow's original drawings for *The Wizard of Oz* are in black and white; the colors were chosen by the printers, perhaps with the artist's assistance. The drawings were probably reproduced photographically on zinc plates. The changes in subtle tones were done by fine parallel lines or cross-hatching; contemporary color reproduction is generally determined by the quality of dots. The original plates no longer exist having been worn by exhaustive later printings by the Bobbs-Merrill Co. and M. A. Donohue & Co. By the early 1920s Bobbs-Merrill had to produce a new edition, reset and use illustrations redrawn by another artist after Denslow's work; by the 1940s Denslow's drawings were replaced by contemporary drawings by Evelyn Copelman. Although Bobbs-Merrill produced the greatest number of copies of *The Wizard of Oz*, the original Hill edition is the most attractive. Besides eliminating a number of the text illustrations in their earliest edition, Bobbs-Merrill used muted inks for the color plates and an illogical color scheme for the text illustrations; the press work is careless, and these printings of *The New Wizard of Oz* from the original Hill plates are generally muddy and clumsy. But the Hill edition is especially bright in its use of color, and nearly three quarters of a century has failed to date the edition. This edition of *The Annotated Wizard of Oz* is faithful to the beautifully printed original plates of *The Wonderful Wizard of Oz*. A Denslow Appendix is included in the back to indicate his many separate projects derived from his collaboration with Baum. The current interest in Art Nouveau encourages the reprint of the most important work of this once influential children's illustrator. Denslow's pictures may once again entertain children as they first did nearly three quarters of a century ago.

This edition is intended for adults. I hope it will be of interest to the already avid and often purist Oz enthusiast. I also hope that for one who has been long exiled from Baum's domain it will serve as an interesting reintroduction. Children have never needed one.

The Wonderful Wizard of Oz.

The WONDERFUL WIZARD OF OZ

By L. Frank Baum

With Pictures by

W.W. Denslow.

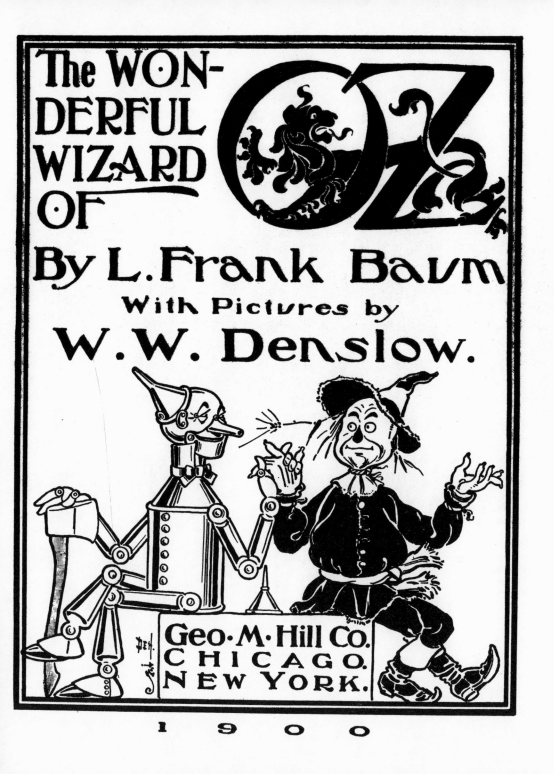

Geo. M. Hill Co.
CHICAGO.
NEW YORK.

1900

This fine drawing of the Tin Woodman is from the copyright page of the first edition. On the original drawing is the line "Copyright 1899/by L. Frank Baum and W. W. Denslow." There is no evidence in the Copyright Office in Washington, D.C., that there was any attempt by either Baum or Denslow to file a copyright on any part of the story prior to 1900. Both Baum and Denslow may have hoped that their book would appear in the last months of 1899, but the book's production dragged on into the next year. Denslow perhaps simply forgot to change the copyright line when the drawings were sent to the printer. In the final production the copyright page was carelessly prepared. In the first edition it appears on page 6, instead of on the verso of the title page, as is required by copyright law. In some copies of the first edition a rubber stamp copyright notice appears in the correct place, and in later issues the notice was printed in its proper place so that most copies have two copyright notices.

INTRODUCTION

Folk lore, legends, myths and fairy tales have followed childhood through the ages, for every healthy youngster has a wholesome and instinctive love for stories fantastic, marvelous and manifestly unreal. The winged fairies of Grimm and Andersen have brought more happiness to childish hearts than all other human creations.

Yet the old-time fairy tale, having served for generations, may now be classed as "historical" in the children's library; for the time has come for a series of newer "wonder tales" in which the stereotyped genie, dwarf and fairy are eliminated, together with all the horrible and blood-curdling incident devised by their authors to point a fearsome moral to each tale. Modern education includes morality; therefore the modern child seeks only entertainment in its wonder-tales and gladly dispenses with all disagreeable incident.

Having this thought in mind, the story of "The Wonderful Wizard of Oz" was written solely to pleasure children of today. It aspires to being a modernized fairy tale, in which the wonderment and joy are retained and the heart-aches and nightmares are left out.

L. FRANK BAUM.

CHICAGO, APRIL, 1900.

1 The ideas presented by Baum in this introduction reflect the trend of the Chicago literary circles at the turn of the century. Their major spokesman was Hamlin Garland, who in his essay "The Literary Emancipation of the West" (*Forum*, October 1893) and the collection of essays entitled *Crumbling Idols* (Chicago: Stone & Kimball, 1894) called for the rejection of Europe and New England's literary traditions. He demanded the acceptance and development of new literary forms, American literary forms, which he felt could come from only the writers of the West. These thoughts were discussed and followed by the Chicago writers of this period. Baum was clearly under the influence of these authors when he wrote *The Wonderful Wizard of Oz*.

2 *fairies of Grimm and Andersen.* Baum is, of course, referring to the fairy tales of the brothers Jacob (1785–1863) and Wilhelm (1786–1859) Grimm and those of Hans Christian Andersen (1805–1875). The Grimm brothers, German philologists, were interested in the preservation of traditional German folktales. Andersen was a Danish Romantic writer whose nontraditional fairy tales came from his own fertile imagination. The stories of Grimm and Andersen are still the world's most popular fairy tales.

Generally, the tales of Grimm and Andersen do not deal with "winged fairies." Most are about what J. R. R. Tolkien in "On Fairy Stories" of *Tree and Leaf* (Boston: Houghton Mifflin, 1965), calls *Faërie*, concerning "many things besides elves and fays, and besides dwarfs, witches, trolls, giants, or dragons; it holds the seas, the sun, the moon, the sky; and the earth, and all things that are in it: tree and bird, water and stone, wine and bread, and ourselves, mortal men, when we are enchanted." Dr. Tolkien continues: "Stories that are actually concerned primarily with 'fairies' . . . are relatively rare, and as a rule not very interesting." As Baum did, Tolkien avoids "that long line of flower-fairies and fluttering sprites with antennae that I so disliked as a child, and which my children in their turn detested." For supplementary material on Baum's opinions on fairy literature see his article "Modern Fairy Tales" in *The Advance*, August 19, 1909.

3 *library;* It is somewhat ironic that many librarians and critics of children's literature now classify Baum's stories as of only "historic" interest in the field of juvenile books. This opinion is now changing due to such articles as Martin Gardner's "The Librarians in Oz" (*Saturday Review*, April 11, 1959) and "Why Librarians Dislike Oz" (*The American Book Collector*, December 1962).

4 *eliminated.* Fortunately, Baum did not eliminate all the traditional fairy-tale forms. "The Oz books conform to the accepted pattern far more than they deviate," observes Russel B. Nye in *The Wizard of Oz and Who He Was* (p. 2). Baum's "strength as a storyteller for children lay in his unique ability to implement and adapt the familiar apparatus of the older tale by reworking old materials into new forms." An obvious example of such an adaptation is the Nome King of *Ozma of Oz,* a traditional character reworked to fit Baum's needs. (His son Frank Joslyn Baum once suggested that his father eliminated the "g" in "Gnome" because the original spelling was too difficult for a child to learn.) As his storytelling powers developed, Baum was able to write successfully both "modernized" fairy tales, like *The Wizard of Oz,* and (what he termed stories based upon European folk traditions) "old-fashioned" stories, like *Queen Zixi of Ix.*

5 *fearsome moral to each tale.* The moral ending is more characteristic of the French tales of Charles Perrault (1628–1703) and others than of the stories of Grimm and Andersen. Denslow may have been influenced by Baum's principles given in this introduction. When he illustrated a series of picture books for G. W. Dillingham of New York in 1903 and 1904, he rewrote the old tales to make them less terrifying. In the September 1903 *Brush and Pencil,* Denslow's description of one of these "horrible and bloodcurdling" tales is quoted as follows:

See what a perfectly outrageous thing is Jack and the Bean-Stalk. A lad gains admittance to a man's house under false pretense, through lying and deceit, imposing on the sympathy of the man's wife, then he commits theft upon theft. He is a confidence man, a sneak-thief, and a burglar. After which, when the man attempts to defend his property, he is slain by the hero (?), who not only commits murder, but mutilates the corpse, much to the delight of his mother.

Later for Arthur Nicholas Hosking's *The Artist's Year Book* (Chicago: Fine Arts Building, 1905) Denslow declared that his

"aim is to make books for children that are replete with good, clean, wholesome fun and from which all coarseness and vulgarity are excluded." (The letter is now in the Alexander McCook Craighead Collection, United States Military Academy Library, West Point, New York.)

6 *pleasure.* Most modern editions corrupt the word "pleasure" to "please." This change first occurred in the Bobbs-Merrill edition of 1944.

7 *heart-aches and nightmares are left out.* "I am glad, in spite of this high determination, Mr. Baum failed to keep them out," writes James Thurber in his article "The Wizard of Chittenango" (*The New Republic,* December 12, 1934). "Children love a lot of nightmare and at least a little heartache in their books. And they get them in the Oz books. I know that I went through excruciatingly lovely nightmares and heartaches when the Scarecrow lost his straw, when the Tin Woodman was taken apart, when the Saw-Horse broke his wooden leg (it hurt for me, even if it didn't for Mr. Baum)."

LIST OF CHAPTERS.

This book is dedicated to my
good friend & comrade.
My Wife
L·F·B·

Chapter I.
The Cyclone.

Dorothy LIVED IN **1** the midst of the great Kansas prairies, with Uncle Henry, **2** who was a farmer, and Aunt Em, who was the farmer's wife. Their house was small, for the lumber to build it had to be carried by wagon many miles. There were four walls, a floor and a roof, which made one room; and this room contained a rusty looking cooking stove, a cupboard for the dishes, a table, three or four chairs, and the beds. Uncle

1 *Dorothy.* Dorothy of Kansas is not the only Dorothy to appear in Baum's stories. "Little Bun Rabbit," the last story in Baum's first children's book, *Mother Goose in Prose*, has as its heroine a Dorothy who is, as Roland Baughman has observed in his article "L. Frank Baum and the 'Oz Books' " (*Columbia Library Columns*, May 1955), "a farm girl with all of the qualities of simplicity, common sense, and gentleness that later became identified with the Dorothy of the Oz books." When the story was reprinted several years later in *L. Frank Baum's Juvenile Speaker*, her name was changed to Doris. Baum gives to the title heroine of *Dot and Tot of Merryland* a common nickname for Dorothy (although her real name is Evangeline Josephine); the doll Queen of Merryland is given another —Dolly.

Who Baum had in mind when he created the young heroine of *The Wizard of Oz* is not known. Frank Joslyn Baum, the author's older son, offered perhaps the best explanation of this question in a letter in *The Best of The Baum Bugle: 1957–1961*:

Many times during the fifty-seven years since *The Wonderful Wizard of Oz* was first published, many rumors have circulated and some have been printed, to the effect that my father, L. Frank Baum, had named "Dorothy" of the book after some particular child he knew. One such claim, made by a certain lady in the Midwest, recently came to my attention. There is no truth in any of these stories. At the time that he wrote *The Wizard of Oz* he did not know any girl or woman by the name of Dorothy. It was a name he selected because he liked the sound of it. You see he loved babies, especially little girl babies. And he wanted very much to have a daughter of his own. But Fate decided otherwise—he had only four sons. But several times, just before

the arrival of a child, he had selected a possible name, trusting it would be a girl. The name of "Dorothy" was one such name he hoped to give a daughter. This he was never able to do. So he used the name for the little Kansas girl who was carried away to the Land of Oz by a cyclone.

The reason that he selected a child heroine for his story may be found in the following passage from Baum's article "Modern Fairy Tales":

Singularly enough, we have no recognized author of fairy literature between Andersen's day and that of Lewis Carroll, the quaint and clever clergyman who recorded Alice's Adventures in Wonderland. Carroll's method of handling fairies was as whimsical as Andersen's was reverential, yet it is but fair to state that the children loved Alice better than any prince or princess that Andersen ever created. The secret of Alice's success lay in the fact that she was a real child, and any normal child could sympathize with her all through her adventures. The story may often bewilder the little one—for it is bound to bewilder us, having neither plot nor motive in its relation—but Alice is doing something every moment, and doing something strange and marvelous, too; so the child follows her with rapturous delight. It is said that Dr. Dodgson, the author, was so ashamed that he had written a child's book that he could only allow it to be published under the pen name of Lewis Carroll; but it made him famous, even then, and "Alice in Wonderland," rambling and incoherent as it is, is one of the best and perhaps the most famous of modern fairy tales.

There is no detailed description of Dorothy in any of Baum's Oz stories, and her appearance is left to the imagination of the illustrator and the reader. But the following from *The Emerald City of Oz* (p. 22) is the best description Baum gave of her personality:

This little girl, Dorothy, was like dozens of little girls you know. She was loving and usually sweet-tempered, and had a round rosy face and earnest eyes. Life was a serious thing to Dorothy, and a wonderful thing, too, for she had encountered more strange adventures in her short life than many other girls her age.

(All page references in this edition correspond to the pages of the first editions, first issues, of Baum's books.)

Certainly, the most popular conception of Dorothy is Judy Garland's portrayal in the 1939 MGM film of *The Wizard of Oz.*

2 *prairies.* In *The Ozmapolitan,* a four-page newspaper (perhaps written by Baum) issued by Reilly & Britton in 1904 to advertise *The Marvelous Land of Oz* (reprinted in the Spring 1963 *Baum Bugle*), a letter appears from Dorothy whose address is "Uncle Henry's Farm near Topeka, Kansas." This is a reference to the 1902 musical in which Dorothy lives near Topeka, the capital of Kansas.

3 *gray.* Martin Gardner writes in *The Wizard of Oz and Who He Was:* "The word 'gray' appears nine times in the space of four paragraphs. Baum is clearly contrasting the grayness of life on the Kansas farm, and the solemnity of Uncle Henry and Aunt Em, with the color and gaiety of Oz." In describing the landscape in harsh, naturalistic terms, Baum begins his story in the manner common to many novels dealing with the Midwest during the last decade of the nineteenth century.

This illustration of Dorothy and Toto originally appeared on a poster drawn by Denslow to advertise *The Songs of Father Goose* (reprinted on the back cover of the December 1968 *Baum Bugle*). The complete drawing also appeared as the inside title page of the Father Goose song folios. Both the poster and folios were issued by the George M. Hill Company in 1900.

Henry and Aunt Em had a big bed in one corner, and Dorothy a little bed in another corner. There was no garret at all, and no cellar—except a small hole, dug in the ground, called a cyclone cellar, where the family could go in case one of those great whirlwinds arose, mighty enough to crush any building in its path. It was reached by a trap-door in the middle of the floor, from which a ladder led down into the small, dark hole.

When Dorothy stood in the doorway and looked around, she could see nothing but the great gray prairie on every side. Not a tree nor a house broke the broad sweep of flat country that reached the edge of the sky in all directions. The sun had baked the plowed land into a gray mass, with little cracks running through it. Even the grass was not green, for the sun had burned the tops of the long blades until they were the same gray color to be seen everywhere. Once the house had been painted, but the sun blistered the paint and the rains washed it away, **3** and now the house was as dull and gray as everything else.

When Aunt Em came there to live she was a young, pretty wife. The sun and wind had changed her, too. They had taken the sparkle from her eyes and left them a sober gray; they had taken the red from her cheeks and lips, and they were gray also. She was thin and gaunt, and never smiled, now. When Dorothy, who was an orphan, first came to her, Aunt Em had been so startled by the child's laughter that she would scream and press her hand upon her heart whenever Dorothy's merry voice reached her ears; and she still looked at the little girl with wonder that she could find anything to laugh at.

Uncle Henry never laughed. He worked hard from morning till night and did not know what joy was. He was gray also, from his long beard to his rough boots, and he looked stern and solemn, and rarely spoke. **4**

It was Toto that made Dorothy laugh, and saved her from growing as gray as her other surroundings. Toto was not gray; he was a little black dog, **5** with long, silky hair and small black eyes that twinkled merrily on either side of his funny, wee nose. Toto played all day long, and Dorothy played with him, and loved him dearly.

To-day, however, they were not playing. Uncle Henry sat upon the door-step and looked anxiously at the sky, which was even grayer than usual. Dor- **6** othy stood in the door with Toto in her arms, and looked at the sky too. Aunt Em was washing the dishes.

From the far north they heard a

4 *stern and solemn.* The lives of Dorothy's aunt and uncle reflect the late nineteenth century belief that environment was crucial in developing one's physical and psychological character. (In *The Emerald City of Oz* where Aunt Em and Uncle Henry change their environment by settling in the Land of Oz, they are no longer the grim foster parents as portrayed in the first Oz book.) This idea is central to the naturalist school of fiction in America, founded by Hamlin Garland, a major literary force in Chicago at the turn of the century. Possibly Baum knew Garland through Chauncey Williams, the publisher of Baum's *Show Window* magazine and *Mother Goose in Prose*. Another friend of Williams who may have influenced Baum was William Allen White, whose sketches of Kansas life, *The Real Issue and Other Stories*, were published by Way & Williams in 1896. These sketches (particularly "The Story of Aqua Pura" and "A Story of the Highlands") are similar in tone to the first chapter of Baum's story. (For a discussion of the influence of the Oz environment on its people, see S. J. Sackett's "The Utopia of Oz," *The Georgia Review*, Fall 1960.)

5 *Toto.* "Toto" as a name for a dog was popular in the Victorian Age; in France it is a common nickname, often for little boys. For the 1902 musical of *The Wizard of Oz* the dog Toto was replaced by a spotted calf named Imogene. "I regret that one favorite character of the children—the dog Toto—will be missing," Baum was quoted in an interview in an unidentified newspaper just prior to the opening of the production:

We found Toto an impossibility from the dramatic viewpoint, and reluctantly abandoned him. But we put the cow in his place. It may seem a long jump from a dog to a cow, but in the latter animal we have a character that really ought to amuse the youngsters exceedingly, and the eccentric creature accompanies Dorothy on her journey from Kansas just as Toto did in the book.

The reason for the change was probably practical; it is easier for an actor to impersonate a cow than a dog (although Nana the Dog was a popular attraction of the 1908 James M. Barrie play, *Peter Pan*). Imogene was played by Fred Stone's brother Edwin until his death; the role was then taken by Joseph Schrode. Although Baum probably intended Toto to be a mongrel, different illustrators have seen him as different breeds. Daniel P. Mannix writes me that Baum's description resembles that of a Cairn terrier. In *The Road to Oz* and *The Emerald City of Oz* John R. Neill pictures him as a Boston bull terrier; in the Neill illustrations to the subsequent Oz books he returns to being a mongrel. Also, in *The Road to Oz* (p. 163) Neill plays with Denslow's conceptions of Dorothy and Toto. The two travelers come upon statues of themselves in the gardens of the Tin Woodman's tin palace, just as "they first appeared in the Land of Oz." Neill pictures this by showing his graceful and realistic Dorothy and Toto amused by the cruder replicas of themselves in Denslow's style, complete with the date "1900" and Denslow's device, a seahorse, on each pedestal. Toto was also the name of a cocker spaniel owned by the Baums in Hollywood, but he was, of course, named after Dorothy's pet.

6 *even grayer than usual.* The scenes in this chapter are largely Baum's recollections of the great gray prairie of the Dakota Territory (now South Dakota) where he lived before settling in Chicago. One wonders how often he stared off into the lonely gray sky in hope of escaping to a fairyland like Oz. (Eva Catherine Gibson's *Zauberlinda, the Wise Witch*, published by the Robert Smith Printing Co., Chicago, in 1901 and the most blatant imitation in both text and appearance of *The Wizard of Oz*, occurs in the Black Hills of Dakota instead of the Kansas prairie.)

low wail of the wind, and Uncle Henry and Dorothy could see where the long grass bowed in waves before the coming storm. There now came a sharp whistling in the air from the south, and as they turned their eyes that way they saw ripples in the grass coming from that direction also.

Suddenly Uncle Henry stood up.

"There's a cyclone coming, Em," he called to his wife; "I'll go look after the stock." Then he ran toward the sheds where the cows and horses were kept.

Aunt Em dropped her work and came to the door. One glance told her of the danger close at hand.

"Quick, Dorothy!" she screamed; "run for the cellar!"

Toto jumped out of Dorothy's arms and hid under the bed, and the girl started to get him. Aunt Em, badly frightened, threw open the trap-door in the floor and climbed down the ladder into the small, dark hole. Dorothy caught Toto at last, and started to follow her aunt. When she was half way across the room there came a great shriek from the wind, and the house shook so hard that she lost her footing and sat down suddenly upon the floor.

A strange thing then happened.

The house whirled around two or three times and rose slowly through the air. Dorothy felt as if she were going up in a balloon.

The north and south winds met where the house stood, and made it the exact center of the cyclone. In the middle of a cyclone the air is generally still, but the great **7** pressure of the wind on every side of the house raised it up higher and higher, until it was at the very top of the cyclone; and there it remained and was carried miles and miles away as easily as you could carry a feather.

It was very dark, and the wind howled horribly around her, but Dorothy found she was riding quite easily. After the first few whirls around, and one other time when the house tipped badly, she felt as if she were being rocked gently, like a baby in a cradle.

Toto did not like it. He ran about the room, now here, now there, barking loudly; but Dorothy sat quite still on the floor and waited to see what would happen.

Once Toto got too near the open trap-door, and fell in; and at first the little girl thought she had lost him. But soon she saw one of his ears sticking up through the hole, for the strong pressure of the air was keeping him up so that he could not fall. She crept to the hole, caught **8** Toto by the ear, and dragged him into the room again; afterward closing the trap-door so that no more accidents could happen.

Hour after hour passed away, and slowly Dorothy got over her fright; but she felt quite lonely, and the wind shrieked so loudly all about her that she nearly became deaf. At first she had wondered if she would be dashed to pieces when the house fell again; but as the hours passed and nothing terrible happened, she stopped worrying and

7 *cyclone*. Baum family tradition claims that when *The Wonderful Wizard of Oz* was first published, a Chicago newspaper published an open letter to the George M. Hill Company with the complaint that Baum in his story described a tornado, not a "cyclone." Hill conceded to the mistake and promised that in the next edition of the book all references to the "cyclone" would be changed to read "tornado"; the Hill company failed, and no subsequent edition made this change. Technically Baum does describe a tornado rather than a cyclone; a cyclone has a center of low atmospheric pressure, between 30 and 40 mph, a tornado has a high atmospheric pressure above 200 mph. In common speech, however, the word "cyclone" is used to mean tornado, hurricane, or any destructive windstorm.

8 *he could not fall.* "The author of the chronicle of Dorothy's adventures explains that the same force which held up the house held up Toto," writes Norman E. Gilbert in J. Malcolm Bird's *Einstein's Theories of Relativity and Gravitation* (New York: Scientific American Publishing Co., 1922, pp. 338–39), "but this explanation is not necessary. Dorothy was now floating through space, and house and dog were subject to the same forces of gravitation which gave them identical motions. Dorothy must have pushed the dog onto the floor and in doing so must herself have floated to the ceiling whence she might have pushed herself to the floor. In fact gravitation was apparently suspended and Dorothy was in a position to have tried certain experiments which Einstein has never tried because he was never in Dorothy's unique position." Although Baum does not state whether this actually happens to Dorothy, it may well occur when she is transported by the cyclone. Such "weightlessness" has been experienced by cosmonauts and astronauts in outer space.

9 *asleep.* One of the unforgivable changes made in the 1939 MGM film was the revelation at the end of the movie that Dorothy's adventure in Oz was merely a dream. One reason for the success of Baum's story is that Oz exists without the trickery of a dream. In *The Bookman* (December 1900) a reviewer classified fairy tales in two categories—those that are concerned with traditional winged fairies and those that occur in dreamland. The popularity of the first was due to the success of the works of Grimm and Andersen, the second to that of Lewis Carroll's *Alice* books. The books of the 1900 Christmas season reflect these traditions: Andrew Lang and others had collections of old tales, and such books as *The Dream Fox Story Book, The Road to Nowhere, The Little Dreamer's Adventures* (all now forgotten) take place in dreamland. The only fairy-tale book published in 1900 that did not depend upon these two traditions was *The Wonderful Wizard of Oz*. Oz is "a real, truly live place" to the children, even if not to MGM Studios. While Oz is unquestionably real, Baum realized the ambiguity of fairyland when as "Laura Bancroft" he wrote in the preface to *Policeman Bluejay:*

The question is often asked me whether Twinkle and Chubbins were asleep or awake when they encountered these wonderful adventures; and it grieves me to reflect that the modern child has been deprived of fairy tales to such an extent that it does not know . . . that in a fairy story it does not matter whether one is awake or not. You must accept it as you would a fragrant breeze that cools your brow, a draught of sweet water, or the delicious flavor of a strawberry, and be grateful for the pleasure it brings you, without stopping to question its source.

Located on the 1914 map of the Land of Oz and its surrounding countries is a strange little country labeled "The Kingdom of Dreams." It is bordered by the Deadly Desert of Oz, Boboland, the Rippleland, and the Country of the Growleywogs. This is the only location on the map that does not appear in any of Baum's known writings. A possible reference to it is in *Ozma of Oz* (p. 190) where Dorothy falls asleep in the Caverns of the Nome King and enters "the land of dreams."

resolved to wait calmly and see what the future would bring. At last she crawled over the swaying floor to her bed, and lay down upon it; and Toto followed and lay down beside her.

In spite of the swaying of the house and the wailing of the wind, Dorothy soon closed her eyes and fell fast **9** asleep.

Chapter II.
The Council with
The Munchkins.

She WAS AWAKENED by a shock, so sudden **1** and severe that if Dorothy had not been lying on the soft bed she might have been hurt. As it was, the jar made her catch her breath and wonder what had happened; and Toto put his cold little nose into her face and whined dismally. Dorothy sat up and noticed that the house was not moving; nor was it dark, for the bright sunshine came in at the window, flooding the little room. She sprang from her bed and with Toto at her heels ran and opened the door. **2**

The little girl gave a cry of amazement and looked

1 *shock*. Several science-fiction enthusiasts believe that the continent where the Land of Oz exists is in a parallel universe in another dimension from our own, another world that may be the same size and occupy the same space as our own. Entry into a parallel world is often accompanied by a jolt, a violent upheaval, or a sudden feeling of uneasiness at the momentary meeting between the two worlds. An editorial note to Barbara Hughes's article on the Deadly Desert in the Autumn 1968 *Baum Bugle* suggests that Dorothy's awakening by a shock may be evidence of such an entry. All recorded journeys from our world to the Land of Oz by means other than magic are associated with violent physical upheavals. (Dorothy journeys by air, water, and earth: the cyclone in *The Wizard of Oz*, the storm at sea in *Ozma of Oz*, the earthquake in *Dorothy and the Wizard in Oz*.) That Oz is on another planet is hinted in some of the publicity for *The Marvelous Land of Oz* (e.g., in the 1904 *Ozmapolitan* and introductory material of the "Queer Visitors from the Marvelous Land of Oz" comic page), but whether or not Baum wrote any or all these pieces is not known.

The most popular theory as to where the Land of Oz is situated, however, is that the continent of Oz and its surrounding countries is somewhere in the South Pacific. Evidence to support this opinion appears in Baum's unpublished and unproduced play, *The Girl from Oz*, in which a character remarks that Oz is "some island far away in the Pacific." In his short story, "Nelebel's Fairyland" (*The Russ*, June 1905) Oz is placed in the Pacific, for the heroine travels east from the Forest of Burzee (which is on the same continent as Oz) to the bay of Coronado in California. In *Ozma of Oz*, Dorothy is shipwrecked on the shores of the continent where Oz is located while on a journey to Australia. Wherever it may be, the Land of Oz, be-

cause it is a fairyland, is not known to mortal men except through the travels of a fortunate few. Baum has written that Dorothy at her birth was blessed by the fairies (*The Emerald City of Oz*, p. 22); perhaps this in part explains why she was allowed to visit Oz while it remained invisible to most mortals. Evidently Baum himself was confronted with the question of the location of the Land of Oz. "Baum spent hours revealing to me the beauties of 'The Wizard of Oz' and explaining how he came to think of the book," writes Walt McDougall in his humorous article on Baum (St. Paul *Dispatch*, July 30, 1904, reproduced in *The Baum Bugle*, Spring 1970). "I tried to discourage him by introducing him to people who would ask him whether the accent was on the 'o' or the 'z,' and where Oz is situated; but upon obtaining a grave answer that 'Oz was the domain of children, young and old, wherever they may be found,' they would regard him with suspicion and flee from him, avoiding Baum and myself thereafter."

A number of modern science-fiction writers have expressed their appreciation of Baum's work. One of the most interesting references to the Oz stories appears in Keith Laumer's *The Otherside of Time* (1968). Among the discoveries made by the hero Brion Bayard in an alternate universe (in 1814 our two worlds separated and have been developing independently ever since) is a red leather-bound book entitled *The Sorceress of Oz* and written by one Lyman F. Baum. Besides a date of 1896 with a publisher's imprint of Wiley & Cotton (Reilly & Britton in another universe?) of New York, New Orleans, and Paris, it contains a Denslowlike frontispiece of "Sorana the Sorceress" surrounded by a band of Nomes; the capital of this story's fairyland is the Sapphire City. In this other world "Lyman F. Baum" died in 1897. Ray Bradbury, perhaps America's most distinguished writer of science fantasy, has frequently acknowledged Baum as one of his favorite authors. His short story "The Exiles" in *The Illustrated Man* (1951) ends with the fall of the Emerald City of Oz.

2 *opened the door.* One of the imaginative touches of the 1939 MGM film occurred when Dorothy's house landed after the cyclone. The Kansas episodes were filmed in sepia tones, but when Judy Garland opened the door, the movie changed to technicolor.

3 *for her age.* Baum had no particular child in mind when he wrote *The Wizard of Oz*, so Dorothy's exact age is difficult to determine. In *The Tin Woodman of Oz* (p. 156), Princess Ozma is said to appear to be fourteen or fifteen years old, Dorothy to be much younger. "She had been a little girl when first she came to the Land of Oz," Baum continues, "and she was a little girl still, and would never seem to be a day older while she lived in this wonderful fairyland." From this we might conclude Dorothy's age to have been not more than ten years in *The Emerald City of Oz* when she came to live in the Land of Oz. If each preceding Oz book (with the possible exception of *The Marvelous Land of Oz* in which she does not appear) is a year of her short life, she could have been five or six years old at the time of her first trip to Oz. Denslow pictures a child no older than this and dresses her in frocks suitable for this age group at the turn of the century.

about her, her eyes growing bigger and bigger at the wonderful sights she saw.

The cyclone had set the house down, very gently—for a cyclone—in the midst of a country of marvelous beauty. There were lovely patches of green sward all about, with stately trees bearing rich and luscious fruits. Banks of gorgeous flowers were on every hand, and birds with rare and brilliant plumage sang and fluttered in the trees and bushes. A little way off was a small brook, rushing and sparkling along between green banks, and murmuring in a voice very grateful to a little girl who had lived so long on the dry, gray prairies.

While she stood looking eagerly at the strange and beautiful sights, she noticed coming toward her a group of the queerest people she had ever seen. They were not as big as the grown folk she had always been used to; but neither were they very small. In fact, they seemed about as tall **3** as Dorothy, who was a well-grown child for her age, although they were, so far as looks go, many years older.

Three were men and one a woman, and all were oddly dressed. They wore round hats that rose to a small point a foot above their heads, with little bells around the brims that tinkled sweetly as they moved. The hats of the men were blue; the little woman's hat was white, and she wore a white gown that hung in plaits from her shoulders; over it were sprinkled little stars that glistened in the sun like diamonds. The men were dressed in blue, of the same shade as their hats, and wore well polished boots with a deep roll of blue at the tops. The men, Dorothy thought, **4** were about as old as Uncle Henry, for two of them had beards. But the little woman was doubtless much older: her face was covered with wrinkles, her hair was nearly white, and she walked rather stiffly.

When these people drew near the house where Dorothy was standing in the doorway, they paused and whispered among themselves, as if afraid to come farther. But the little old woman walked up to Dorothy, made a low bow and said, in a sweet voice,

"You are welcome, most noble Sorceress, to the land of the Munchkins. We are so grateful to you for having **5** killed the wicked Witch of the East, and for setting our people free from bondage."

Dorothy listened to this speech with wonder. What could the little woman possibly mean by calling her a sorceress, and saying she had killed the wicked Witch of the East? Dorothy was an innocent, harmless little girl, who had been carried by a cyclone many miles from home; and she had never killed anything in all her life.

But the little woman

4 *blue at the tops.* The following from *The Patchwork Girl of Oz* (pp. 23–24) is a more detailed description of the native costume of the Munchkins:

> [The boy] wore silk stockings, blue knee-pants with gold buckles, a blue ruffled waist and a jacket of bright blue braided with gold. His shoes were of blue leather and turned up at the toes, which were pointed. His hat had a peaked crown and a flat brim, and around the brim was a row of tiny golden bells that tinkled when he moved. This was the native costume of those who inhabited the Munchkin Country. . . . Instead of shoes, the old man wore boots with turn-over tops and his blue coat had wide cuffs of gold braid.

5 *the Munchkins.* No known notes by Baum exist that might explain the sources of his names of people and places. An explanation is pure speculation; as with the word "Oz" (see Note 12) most were chosen by chance or for their sound. In a 1961 Russian edition of *The Wizard of Oz* (entitled *The Magic of Oz*) designed to teach Soviet children English, the name Munchkin is said to derive from the verb "to munch." I suspect Münchhausen, the eighteenth-century German baron whose name is now synonymous with the fabulous, may have been on Baum's mind. Perhaps the Munchkins are related to Thumbkin, Bumpkin, Linkin, etc., pet names given the fingers of the hand in nursery rhymes of the British Isles and parts of the United States. The second syllable of "Munchkin" in accordance with the names of the other countries of Oz is an affectionate diminutive suffix, of course referring to the size of the natives of the East. "Munchkin" has found its way into common usage in the United States, notably in the paintings of Pop artist Idelle Weber whose modern mute urbanites are called "Munchkins."

6 *East.* A common error in later Oz books and elsewhere is the reversal of the Munchkin Country to the West and the Winkie Country to the East. The earliest known map of Oz was made for the 1908 *Fairylogue and Radio-Plays*; this simple version, one of the glass slides shown between reels of the film, has the correct directions. (See color plate xxviii.) Perhaps this slide was the source for the "official" map of the Land of Oz, believed to have been sketched by Baum and then redrawn. He may have looked on the back side of the slide, thus reversing the two countries. The official map appeared in 1914 as the front endpaper of *Tik-Tok of Oz.* The recent and most accurate of Oz maps designed by James E. Haff and executed by Dick Martin for the International Wizard of Oz Club has corrected the error by placing the Munchkins in the East and the Winkies in the West as stated in the first Oz book.

7 *North.* Not until the second Oz story does Baum disclose the favorite color and name of the land of the North—the purple Country of the Gillikins. Gillikin is similar to "Gilligren," the hero of the first story of Baum's 1897 *Mother Goose in Prose.* Martin Gardner has called my attention to the possibility that the purple land of the North may take its name from the purple gillyflower of New England.

8 *"came at once."* Fred Meyer, secretary of the Oz Club, notes in a letter to me that this messenger must have been swift indeed if he was able to summon the Good Witch of the North just a few minutes after Dorothy's house landed on the Wicked Witch of the East. This messenger may not necessarily have been human; swift birds are often used as carriers of important news.

9 *I am the Witch of the North*. Notice that the color plate of this meeting is the first opportunity in this book that Denslow has, as MacFall observes in *To Please a Child*, "to parade rows of figures across the pages like comic friezes, but with each tiny figure amusingly individualized by some feature or item of clothing." Other examples of this are found in the book in the drawings of the Winkies, Hammer-Heads, and Glinda's Guards.

10 *good witch*. In European fairy tales there is no "good" witch. To receive her powers a wicked witch must make a pact with the Devil. There is no indication in Baum's story that either the Good or the Wicked Witches have any dealings with Satan. Baum claimed (in an editorial in the October 18, 1890, *Saturday Pioneer*) "the absurd and legendary devil is the enigma of the Church." He did admit that the pact between the Devil and all witches was a common misconception, for in "The Witchcraft of Mary-Marie" in *Baum's American Fairy Tales* (1908) the young heroine cries that all witches "sell their souls to Satan, in return for a knowledge of witchcraft" (p. 45).

The closest analogy to a "good" witch in European tradition is the pagan sorceress. Technically, a witch serves Satan, a sorceress serves herself. Baum may have known this distinction; in all the later Oz stories Glinda the Good Witch is referred to as Glinda the Sorceress.

The change from a wicked to a good witch here is one of Baum's many conscious contradictions of traditional fairy-tale stereotypes. Certainly, the most famous example of such a paradox in the Oz stories is the Cowardly Lion. The Foolish Owl and the Wise Donkey of *The Patchwork Girl of Oz* are also notable examples.

In the 1902 musical the Good Witch of the North is given the name "Locasta," but this name may have been the invention of the producer Julian Mitchell rather than of Baum. "Tattypoo" is her name in Ruth Plumly Thompson's *The Giant Horse of Oz* (1928), in which the Good Witch of the North has quite a remarkable adventure of her own.

11 *Oh, no; that is a great mistake*. Because the Devil is not instrumental in Baum's stories, a witch or wizard must be judged according to his own nature rather than by the source of his powers. An incident similar to this occurs in *The Master Key* when the boy Rob who has summoned up the Demon of Electricity exclaims that he had "always understood that demons were bad things." His visitor replies:

Not necessarily. . . . If you take the trouble to consult your dictionary, you will find that demons may be either good or bad, like any other class of beings. Originally all demons were good, yet of later years people have come to consider all demons evil. I do not know why. Should you read Hesiod, you will find he says:

Soon was a world of holy demons made,
Aerial spirits, by great Juno designed,
To be on Earth the guardians of mankind. (pp. 16–17)

Likewise in "The Witchcraft of Mary-Marie" in *Baum's American Fairy Tales* (1908), when an old traveler suggests that Mary-Marie become a witch, the little girl cries in astonishment, "I'm not old enough. Witches, you know, are withered dried-up old hags. . . . And they sell their souls to Satan. . . ." The old traveler replies:

One might think you knew all about witches, to hear you chatter. But your words prove you to be very ignorant of the subject. You may find good people and bad people in the world; and so, I

evidently expected her to answer; so Dorothy said, with hesitation,

"You are very kind; but there must be some mistake. I have not killed anything."

"Your house did, anyway," replied the little old woman, with a laugh; "and that is the same thing. See!" she continued, pointing to the corner of the house; "there are her two toes, still sticking out from under a block of wood."

Dorothy looked, and gave a little cry of fright. There indeed, just under the corner of the great beam the house rested on, two feet were sticking out, shod in silver shoes with pointed toes.

"Oh, dear! oh, dear!" cried Dorothy, clasping her hands together in dismay; "the house must have fallen on her. What ever shall we do?"

"There is nothing to be done," said the little woman calmly.

"But who was she?" asked Dorothy.

"She was the wicked Witch of the East, as I said," answered the little woman. "She has held all the Munchkins in bondage fo many years, making them slave for her night and day. Now they are all set free, and are grateful to you for the favour."

"Who are the Munchkins?" enquired Dorothy.

"They are the people who live in this land of the East, where the wicked Witch ruled." **6**

"Are you a Munchkin?" asked Dorothy.

"No; but I am their friend, although I live in the land of the North. When they saw the Witch of the East was **7** dead the Munchkins sent a swift messenger to me, and I came at once. I am the Witch of the North." **8,9**

"Oh, gracious!" cried Dorothy; "are you a real witch?"

"Yes, indeed;" answered the little woman. "But I am a good witch, and the people love me. I am not as **10** powerful as the wicked Witch was who ruled here, or I should have set the people free myself."

"But I thought all witches were wicked," said the girl, who was half frightened at facing a real witch.

"Oh, no; that is a great mistake. There were only **11** four witches in all the Land of Oz, and two of them, those **12** who live in the North and the South, are good witches. I know this is true, for I am one of them myself, and cannot be mistaken. Those who dwelt in the East and the West were, indeed, wicked witches; but now that you have killed one of them, there is but one wicked Witch in all the Land of Oz—the one who lives in the West." **13**

"But," said Dorothy, after a moment's thought, "Aunt

suppose, you may find good witches and bad witches. But I must confess most of the witches I have known were very respectable, indeed, and famous for their kind actions. (pp. 45–46).

12 *Oz.* A number of theories concerning the origin of the word "Oz" have been suggested since the initial publication of *The Wizard of Oz.* The generally accepted story as described in MacFall's *To Please a Child* concerns a small filing cabinet in the Baum home. One evening while telling his children and their friends a story about a little girl named Dorothy who was carried off by a cyclone to a fairyland, Baum was asked what was the name of the strange country. Looking about the room, his eye fell upon the drawers of the filing cabinet, which were labeled "A–N" and "O–Z"; he told the children it was the Land of Oz. The earliest known appearance of the filing-cabinet story is in an interview in the St. Louis *Republic* (May 10, 1903). Here the story was published in a slightly different version:

I have a little cabinet letter file on my desk in front of me. I was thinking and wondering about a title for my story, and I had settled on 'Wizard' as part of it. My gaze was caught by the gilt letters on the three drawers of the cabinet. The first was A–G; the next drawer was labeled H–N; and on the last were the letters O–Z. And Oz it at once became.

Variants of this filing cabinet story appeared as publicity for the New York run of the musical in 1903, but with no significant changes. The accuracy of this version is doubtful. Baum must have had a name for the fairyland even before considering the title. "Oz" was part of at least two early titles for the book before "wizard" was even considered (see my introduction).

Several less prosaic theories have been

suggested. In *The Wizard of Oz and Who He Was* Gardner notes the similarity between the Land of Oz and the Land of Uz, where Job lived. Because he was an admirer of the works of Dickens whose pseudonym was "Boz," Baum may have merely dropped the "B" for "Baum" and was left with "Oz". The late Jack Snow, in the introduction to *Who's Who in Oz*, preferred to think that Baum liked stories that caused the reader to exclaim with "Ohs" and "Ahs" of wonder. The word "Oz" can be pronounced either way. Baum's preferred pronunciation of Oz is indicated in the following verse from the unpublished first dramatization of his story:

Hear me, fear me! Never dare to jeer me!
I'm the greatest necromancer ever was!
All my deeds with magic reek,
I'm the whole thing, so to speak!
I'm the Wonderful Wizard of Oz!

In *Dorothy and the Wizard in Oz* (p. 196) the meaning of the word "Oz" is given as "Great and Good."

Martin Gardner in the "Mathematical Games" column of *Scientific American* (February 1972) discloses an unintended correlation between Baum's home state and the name of his fairyland. Mary Scott, a member of the International Wizard of Oz Club, writes that a one-step word shift of the abbreviation of New York produces OZ:

N→O
Y→Z

Gardner writes me that since his column has appeared he has learned that another one-step word shift discloses the abbreviation of the home state of Ruth Plumly Thompson, the second Royal Historian of Oz:

O→P
Z→A

Also in this article Gardner diagrams the alphabetical symmetry of the word "WIZARD."

13 *the one who lives in the West.* Perhaps at this point in the history of Oz there were only four witches. A quick survey of Baum's other Oz stories show a number of other witches in the four countries of Oz (e. g., Mrs. Yoop of *The Tin Woodman of Oz*, Reera the Red and Coo-ee-oh of *Glinda of Oz*). In *Dorothy and the Wizard in Oz* it is explained that there were once four Wicked Witches who each ruled a country of Oz. The Wicked Witch of the North was Mombi who makes her first appearance in the second Oz story. She was conquered by the Good Witch of the North and forced to be only a minor witch. Glinda the Good overthrew the Wicked Witch of the South who may have been Blinkie, the witch of *The Scarecrow of Oz*. Now powerless she lives in Jinxland with a band of witches who perhaps fled with her when Glinda came into power.

14 *"years ago."* This statement repeats the attitude of the following verse "Who's Afraid?":

Ev'ry giant now is dead—
Jack has cut off ev'ry head.
Ev'ry goblin, known of old,
Perished years ago, I'm told.

Ev'ry witch on broomstick riding
Has been burned or is in hiding.
Ev'ry dragon seeking gore,
Died an age ago or more.

Lions now you only see
Caged in the menagerie;
And the grizzly bear can't hug
When he's made into a rug.
　Who's afraid?

This poem first appeared in the section of children's verse in Baum's privately printed *By the Candelabra's Glare* and was later included in *Father Goose, His Book*.

15 *civilized.* Baum presents an interesting paradox. Although Kansas is civilized, it is a wasteland; Oz is not, and it is a paradise. This paradox suggests that civilization may not be beneficial to its people. Progress, an important force of the nineteenth century, is of little value in a paradise. David Greene has written to me that in Lord Dunsany's *The King of Elfland's Daughter* perfection exists in a fairyland where stasis, or the absence of motion-force, is the ideal. The Land of Oz must be between this perfection and modern civilization. Marius Bewley in "Oz Country" (*The New York Review of Books*, December 3, 1964) observes that numerous examples in the Oz stories suggest a preference for Jeffersonian agrarianism, a system in which each citizen tends his own garden and is unconcerned with national and foreign affairs. This is, of course, related to the American dream of rugged individualism. The witch's remark is one of several similar comments about notions of civilization. The Demon of Electricity in *The Master Key* reminds the young hero: "One of your writers has said, in truth, that among civilized people things are seldom what they seem" (p. 93). One of the citizens of *Prairie-Dog Town* (one of the *Twinkle Tales*, 1906) explains that civilization is "a very big word which means some folks have found a better way to live than other folks" (p. 5). In *The Road to Oz* the King of Foxville gives his own definition: "To become civilized means to dress as elaborately and prettily as possible, and to make a show of your clothes so your neighbors will envy you, and for that reason both civilized foxes and civilized humans spend most of their time dressing

Em has told me that the witches were all dead—years and **14** years ago."

"Who is Aunt Em?" inquired the little old woman.

"She is my aunt who lives in Kansas, where I came from."

The Witch of the North seemed to think for a time, with her head bowed and her eyes upon the ground. Then she looked up and said,

"I do not know where Kansas is, for I have never heard that country mentioned before. But tell me, is it a civilized country?"

"Oh, yes;" replied Dorothy.

"Then that accounts for it. In the civilized countries I believe there are no witches left; nor wizards, nor sorceresses, nor magicians. But, you see, the Land of Oz has **15** never been civilized, for we are cut off from all the rest of the world. Therefore we still have witches and wizards amongst us."

"Who are the Wizards?" asked Dorothy.

16 "Oz himself is the Great Wizard," answered the Witch, sinking her voice to a whisper. "He is more powerful than all the rest of us together. He lives in the City **17** of Emeralds."

Dorothy was going to ask another question, but just then the Munchkins, who had been standing silently by, gave a loud shout and pointed to the corner of the house where the Wicked Witch had been lying.

"What is it?" asked the little old woman; and looked, and began to laugh. The feet of the dead Witch had disappeared entirely and nothing was left but the silver shoes.

"She was so old," explained the Witch of the North, "that she dried up quickly in the sun. That is the end of her. But the silver shoes are yours, and you shall have them to wear." She reached down and picked up the shoes, and after shaking the dust out of them handed them to Dorothy.

18

"The Witch of the East was proud of those silver shoes," said one of the Munchkins; "and there is some charm connected with them; but what it is we never knew."

Dorothy carried the shoes into the house and placed them on the table. Then she came out again to the Munchkins and said,

"I am anxious to get back to my Aunt and Uncle, for I am sure they will worry about me. Can you help me find my way?"

The Munchkins and the Witch first looked at one

themselves" (p. 56). Civilization is one of the themes of *The Enchanted Island of Yew*. When Man was young, he lived in the Golden Age: "Men and women lived simply and quietly. They were Nature's children, and breathed fresh air into their lungs instead of smoke and coal gas; and tramped through green meadows and deep forests instead of riding in street cars; and went to bed when it was dark and rose with the sun—which is vastly different from the present custom" (p. 2). Man was also helpless, but had the fairies to protect him; now they are shy and seldom are seen by modern man. "Great cities had been built and great Kingdoms established. Civilization had won the people, and they no longer robbed or fought or indulged in magic arts, but were busily employed and leading respectable lives" (p. 242). Baum's opinion of the modern world is somewhat ambiguous; people are now occupied with other things than exciting adventures. Luckily, the Land of Oz was never civilized.

The Good Witch's comment on civilization has a deeper historical significance. The High Renaissance, one of the great periods of Western civilization, was also the time of greatest persecution of witches and wizards. Edicts condemning the practice of witchcraft were issued by the Roman Church, several kings of France, Queen Elizabeth I of Britain, and most notably by James VI of Scotland (later King James I of Great Britain). The frenzy seems to have reached its zenith in 1524 when more than one thousand men and women were executed near Lake Como in Switzerland. The Salem witch trials in New England were as late as the end of the seventeenth century. The last execution for witchcraft in Scotland was not until 1722. History has proven how barbaric an age of high civilization can be, for only in a highly organized culture can the brutal execution of thousands be effectively carried out.

16 *Oz.* It is disclosed in *Dorothy and the Wizard in Oz* (p. 196) that "Oz" was always the name of the ruler of Oz when the country was under one head. If the ruler happened to be a woman, her name was "Ozma." Prior to the Wizard's arrival in the Land of Oz, the country was ruled by the grandfather of Princess Ozma, the present ruler. Both he and his son were enchanted by Mombi the Witch who with the other Wicked Witches took power over the four countries of Oz. (In *The Marvelous Land of Oz* Pastoria, Ozma's father, is said to have been ruler of the Emerald City. This is an obvious reference to the 1902 musical, but it does not agree with the history of Oz as given in the other Oz stories. The Wizard of Oz built the Emerald City after Pastoria's enchantment.) Mombi was also the guardian of Ozma before her enchantment was broken by Glinda the Good who proclaimed the girl to be the rightful ruler of Oz. A thorough study of the pre-Dorothean history of Oz is included in *Unexplored Territory in Oz*, a booklet of four essays written by the late Robert R. Pattrick, published by the International Wizard of Oz Club in 1963.

17 *Emeralds.* Russell MacFall suggests in *To Please a Child* that the reason that Baum made the emerald the predominant jewel of the capital of Oz may have been to honor his mother's ancestral homeland, the "Emerald Isle." It is also possible that Baum chose the emerald because it is his own birthstone.

18 *dust.* David Greene, an editor of *The Baum Bugle*, has written to me about the possible spiritual and physical irony of the Wicked Witch turning to dust. He suggests that Baum had in mind the biblical phrase "for dust thou art and unto dust shalt thou return." (Genesis, 3:19).

19 *desert.* The actual nature of this desert is obscure in the Oz stories. The first indication that its danger is magical is in *The Road to Oz* (p. 126). A sign warns travelers not to attempt to cross the desert for its deadly sands will turn any living flesh to dust. Baum's reference in the first Oz story suggests that it is so expansive a wasteland that no one has been able to survive long enough to cross it. All other recorded attempts to cross the desert (including the flight of Mombi the Witch as a Griffin in Chapter 22 of *The Marvelous Land of Oz*) are by magic means. Only when Ozma is on the throne of Oz is the desert enchanted as described in *The Road to Oz*. See also Barbara Hughes's interesting article on the Deadly Desert in the Autumn 1968 *Baum Bugle.*

On the 1914 map of the Land of Oz the desert is divided like the countries of Oz into four geographical areas, each with its own name. Although this name is frequently given to the entire desert that surrounds Oz, the "Deadly Desert" is the name only of the part that cuts the Winkie Country off from the rest of the world. To the north is the "Impassable Desert" and to the south the "Great Sandy Waste." The desert beyond the Munchkin Country is the "Shifting Sands." Family tradition holds that Baum's last words were: "Now we can cross the Shifting Sands. . . ."

20 *Quadlings.* The name "Quadling" ends in a diminutive like the other names of the countries of Oz. If one accepts the syllable "Quad" to mean fourth, a free translation of the name of a native of the Southland might be "a small inhabitant of the fourth country."

21 *Winkies.* Although wink usually means to blink (the Winkies "wink" in the Russian Oz books), the name of the yellow country of Oz may refer instead to the colloquial expression meaning "a little bit of light." That "light" is the important word is evidenced in Chapter 12 where the Country of the West is described as "where the sun sets." In parts of the British Isles and the United States "winkie" is a children's pet name for the index finger. The name of the land of the West also suggests William Miller's nursery rhyme, "Wee Willie Winkie," the nickname of William of Orange.

22 *one, two, three.* The number three is traditionally a mystic number. It is an important element in much of the magic performed throughout this story.

23 *white chalk marks.* Slates and white chalk were basic writing tools of schoolchildren at the turn of the century. Like Hans Christian Andersen, Baum had the ability to relate his fairyland to the immediacy of a child's world. (In "The Tinder Box" Andersen describes the soldier's wealth in terms of all the rocking horses, tin soldiers, and sugar pigs one could buy.) Besides slate and white chalk, other examples of "homely, American things that you'd hardly expect in Fairyland" (as Clifton Fadiman calls them in his afterword to the Macmillan edition of *The Wizard of Oz*) are the scarecrow, a funnel for a hat, an oilcan, and the big clothes basket used for the Wizard's balloon.

another, and then at Dorothy, and then shook their heads.

"At the East, not far from here," said one, "there is a **19** great desert, and none could live to cross it."

"It is the same at the South," said another, "for I have been there and seen it. The South is the country of the **20** Quadlings."

"I am told," said the third man, "that it is the same at **21** the West. And that country, where the Winkies live, is ruled by the wicked Witch of the West, who would make you her slave if you passed her way."

"The North is my home," said the old lady, "and at its edge is the same great desert that surrounds this land of Oz. I'm afraid, my dear, you will have to live with us."

Dorothy began to sob, at this, for she felt lonely among all these strange people. Her tears seemed to grieve the kind-hearted Munchkins, for they immediately took out their handkerchiefs and began to weep also. As for the little old woman, she took off her cap and balanced the point on the end of her nose, while she counted **22** "one, two, three" in a solemn voice. At once the cap changed to a slate, on which was written in **23** big, white chalk marks:

"LET DOROTHY GO TO THE CITY OF EMERALDS."

The little old woman took the slate from her nose, and, having read the words on it, asked, **24** "Is your name Dorothy, my dear?"

"Yes," answered the child, looking up and drying her tears.

"Then you must go to the City of Emeralds. Perhaps Oz will help you."

"Where is this City?" asked Dorothy.

"It is exactly in the center of the country, and is ruled by Oz, the Great Wizard I told you of."

"Is he a good man?" enquired the girl, anxiously.

"He is a good Wizard. Whether he is a man or not I cannot tell, for I have never seen him."

"How can I get there?" asked Dorothy.

"You must walk. It is a long journey, through a country that is sometimes pleasant and sometimes dark and terrible. However, I will use all the magic arts I know of to keep you from harm."

"Won't you go with me?" pleaded the girl, who had begun to look upon the little old woman as her only friend.

"No, I cannot do that," she replied; "but I will give you my kiss, and no one will dare injure a person who has been kissed by the Witch of the North." **25**

She came close to Dorothy and kissed her gently on the forehead Where her lips touched the girl they left a round, shining mark, as Dorothy found out soon after.

"The road to the City of Emeralds is paved with yel- **26** low brick," said the Witch; "so you cannot miss it. When you get to Oz do not be afraid of him, but tell your story and ask him to help you. Good-bye, my dear."

24 *Is your name Dorothy*. Dorothy *Gale*, to be exact. Her last name first appears in the script for the 1902 musical of *The Wizard of Oz*. The addition of her surname may have been made to prepare the audience for the following uninspired exchange:

> DOROTHY: My name is Dorothy, and I am one of the Kansas Gales.
>
> SCARECROW: That accounts for your breezy manner.

"Dorothy Gale" appears at the closing of a letter from her printed in *The Ozmapolitan* (see Chapter 1, Note 2.) The first appearance of her last name in the Oz books is in *Ozma of Oz*.

25 *kissed by the Witch of the North*. Although the Good Witch is not powerful enough to defeat the Wicked Witch, her kiss symbolizes abstract Good, which is more powerful than Evil. The Witch's kiss plays an important part in Ruth Plumly Thompson's *The Wishing Horse of Oz* (1935).

26 *yellow brick*. What would be more logical than a yellow brick road to travel on through a blue countryside en route to a green city? Yellow brick was a common building material in late nineteenth-century architecture; New York's first Metropolitan Opera House was nicknamed "the yellow brick brewery." Although this is the most famous road in Oz, it is not the only yellow brick road there. The road through the Gillikin Country followed by Tip and Jack Pumpkinhead in *The Marvelous Land of Oz* is made of yellow brick. A second road of yellow brick in the Munchkin Country is that traveled by Scraps and Ojo in *The Patchwork Girl of Oz*. No one has yet determined how many yellow brick roads there must be in the Winkie Country.

27 *not surprised in the least.* A similar reaction to a magical disappearance occurs in "The Queen of Quok," one of Baum's *American Fairy Tales.* When the Slave of the Royal Bedstead (a genie who presents the boy king with a purse that is never empty) disappears, the King of Quok admits, "I expected that, yet I am sorry he did not wait to say goodby."

The three Munchkins bowed low to her and wished her a pleasant journey, after which they walked away through the trees. The Witch gave Dorothy a friendly little nod, whirled around on her left heel three times, and straightway disappeared, much to the surprise of little Toto, who barked after her loudly enough when she had gone, because he had been afraid even to growl while she stood by.

But Dorothy, knowing her to be a witch, had ex-**27** pected her to disappear in just that way, and was **not** surprised in the least.

Chapter III
How Dorothy saved the Scarecrow.

This chapter title page was originally drawn for Chapter 2. A paper label with the title of the third chapter is pasted over the first title on the pen and ink drawing (now in the Henry Goldsmith collection in the New York Public Library).

This picture of the Scarecrow originally appeared in a copy of the first edition, inscribed by Denslow to his friend Charles Warren Stoddard, whose *A Cruise Under the Crescent* Denslow illustrated in 1898. The inscription includes the "sincerest regards" of Baum. *Courtesy Harvard College Library.*

WHEN DOROTHY WAS left alone she began to feel hungry. So she went to the cupboard and cut herself some bread, which she spread with butter. She gave some to Toto, and taking a pail from the shelf she carried it down to the little brook and filled it with clear, sparkling water. Toto ran over to the trees and began to bark at the birds sitting there. Dorothy went to get him, and saw such delicious fruit hanging from the branches that she gathered some of it, finding it just what she wanted to help out her breakfast.

Then she went back to the house, and having helped

1 *only one other dress*. But Denslow pictures three—the one she is wearing, the blue-and-white checked, and the dotted one shown in the opening pages of the book. (See also Chapter 23, Note 1.)

2 *made for her*. The dresses of the Emerald City and the Golden Cap of the Wicked Witch of the East also fit her exactly. Baum is reemphasizing the fact that Dorothy is the same size as the natives of the Land of Oz.

herself and Toto to a good drink of the cool, clear water, she set about making ready for the journey to the City of Emeralds.

1   Dorothy had only one other dress, but that happened to be clean and was hanging on a peg beside her bed. It was gingham, with checks of white and blue; and although the blue was somewhat faded with many washings, it was still a pretty frock. The girl washed herself carefully, dressed herself in the clean gingham, and tied her pink sunbonnet on her head. She took a little basket and filled it with bread from the cupboard, laying a white cloth over the top. Then she looked down at her feet and noticed how old and worn her shoes were.

"They surely will never do for a long journey, Toto," she said. And Toto looked up into her face with his little black eyes and wagged his tail to show he knew what she meant.

At that moment Dorothy saw lying on the table the silver shoes that had belonged to the Witch of the East.

"I wonder if they will fit me," she said to Toto. "They would be just the thing to take a long walk in, for they could not wear out."

She took off her old leather shoes and tried on the silver ones, which fitted her as well as if they had been **2** made for her.

Finally she picked up her basket.

"Come along, Toto," she said, "we will go to the Emerald City and ask the great Oz how to get back to Kansas again."

She closed the door, locked it, and put the key carefully in the pocket of her dress. And so, with Toto trotting along soberly behind her, she started on her journey. **3**

There were several roads near by, but it did not take her long to find the one paved with yellow brick. Within a short time she was walking briskly toward the Emerald City, her silver shoes tinkling merrily on the hard, yellow roadbed. The sun shone bright and the birds sang sweet and Dorothy did not feel nearly as bad as you might think a little girl would who had been suddenly whisked away from her own country and set down in the midst of a strange land.

She was surprised, as she walked along, to see how pretty the country was about her. There were neat fences at the sides of the road, painted a dainty blue color, and beyond them were fields of grain and vegetables in abundance. Evidently the Munchkins were good farmers and able to raise large crops. Once in a while she would pass a house, and the people came out to look at her and bow low as she went by; for everyone knew she had been the means of destroying the wicked witch and setting them free from bondage. The houses

3 *key.* "Dorothy may still have this key," writes Gardner in Note 5 of *The Wizard of Oz and Who He Was.* "It would be interesting to know if the old farm house is still standing at the spot where the cyclone left it."

4 *dwellings.* Notice the human characteristics given by Denslow to the Munchkin house and other Oz architecture, a Baumian touch not indicated by the text but continued in Neill's illustrations to the other Oz books. This fantastic architecture, perfectly suited to Baum's fairyland, is a playful borrowing from Italian Mannerism (primarily the Orsini Gardens at Bomarzo and those of the Palazzo Zuccari in Rome), and is also evident in examples of Art Nouveau. Such a style carried to excess is exemplified by a comic but horrifying episode in Neill's *The Wonder City of Oz* (1940) where a battle results from an argument among these personified buildings.

5 *color.* Each country of Oz has its own distinctive color, possibly because on geographical maps countries are generally distinguished by different colors. Baum refers to the coloring of maps in the opening chapter of *The Magical Monarch of Mo* when he states that if cartographers would put the Land of Mo "on the maps of our geographies and paint it pink or green, and put a round dot where the King's castle stands, it would be easy enough to point out to you its exact location." Martin Gardner has called my attention to a passage in the third chapter of Mark Twain's *Tom Sawyer Abroad* (1894), which discusses the colors of geographies. During a balloon trip the scenery below is green, and Huck Finn says to Tom Sawyer:

"I know by the color. We're right over Illinois. And you can see for yourself that Indiana ain't in sight."

"I wonder what's the matter with you,

Huck. You know by the color?"

"Yes, of course I do."

"What's the color got to do with it?"

"It's got everything to do with it. Illinois is green. Indiana is pink. . . . I've seen it on the map and it's pink. You show me any pink down there, if you can. No, sir, it's green. . . . there ain't no two states the same color."

The colors of Baum's fairyland are not arbitrary. The change of color from one region to another is in accordance with the principles of color theory. Each of the three major countries visited in *The Wizard of Oz* is a primary color, one of the three colors from which all others are made. The travelers do not journey directly from one primary color to another but instead travel through a secondary color. Before she visits the Land of the West, Dorothy travels through the green countryside of the Emerald City, which is merely a link between the blue land of the Munchkins and the yellow Winkie Country. Before arriving at the castle of Glinda the Good, the girl travels from the Winkie Country to the red land of the Quadlings by way of the Emerald City; as indicated by the text and the illustrations she visits a brown region. Brown is a combination of the three primary colors; it can also be made from red and green, green being a combination of the other two primary colors. The standard color wheel often presents the blue to the right, the yellow to the left, and the red at the bottom; this may explain why the blue Munchkins are in the East, the yellow Winkies in the West, and the red

4 of the Munchkins were odd looking dwellings, for each was round, with a big dome for a roof. All were painted blue, for in this country of the East blue was the favorite **5** color.

Towards evening, when Dorothy was tired with her long walk and began to wonder where she should pass the night, she came to a house rather larger than the rest. On the green lawn before it many men and women were dancing. Five little fiddlers played as loudly as possible and the people were laughing and singing, while a big table near by was loaded with delicious fruits and nuts, pies and cakes, and many other good things to eat.

The people greeted Dorothy kindly, and invited her to supper and to pass the night with them; for this was the home of one of the richest Munchkins in the land, and his friends were gathered with him to celebrate their freedom from the bondage of the wicked witch.

Dorothy ate a hearty supper and was waited upon by the rich Munchkin himself, whose name was Boq. Then she sat down upon a settee and watched the people dance.

When Boq saw her silver shoes he said,

"You must be a great sorceress."

"Why?" asked the girl.

"Because you wear silver shoes and have killed the wicked witch. Besides, you have white in your frock, and only witches and sorceresses wear white."

"My dress is blue and white checked," said Dorothy, smoothing out the wrinkles in it.

"It is kind of you to wear that," said Boq. "Blue is the color of the Munchkins, and white is the witch color; **6** so we know you are a friendly witch."

Dorothy did not know what to say to this, for all the people seemed to think her a witch, and she knew very well she was only an ordinary little girl who had come by the chance of a cyclone into a strange land.

When she had tired watching the dancing, Boq led her into the house, where he gave her a room with a pretty bed in it. The sheets were made of blue cloth, and Dorothy slept soundly in them till morning, with Toto curled up on the blue rug beside her.

She ate a hearty breakfast, and watched a wee Munchkin baby, who played with Toto and pulled his tail and crowed and laughed in a way that greatly amused Dorothy. Toto was a fine curiosity to all the people, for they had never seen a dog before.

"How far is it to the Emerald City?" the girl asked.

"I do not know," answered Boq, gravely, "for I have never been there. It is better for people to keep away from Oz, unless they

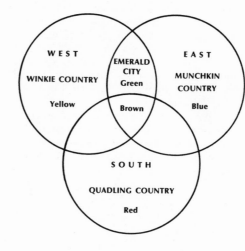

Quadlings in the South. A diagram of the geography of Oz according to color is as follows:

```
         WEST              EAST
              EMERALD
              CITY
      WINKIE COUNTRY   MUNCHKIN
              Green    COUNTRY
        Yellow              Blue
               Brown

              SOUTH

         QUADLING COUNTRY
                Red
```

Baum was aware of color theory when he wrote the first Oz story. A principal article in the September and October 1899 issues of Baum's trade magazine *The Show Window* is "The Scientific Arrangement of Colors" by William M. Couran. Baum wrote his own explanation of color theory in the fifth chapter of *The Art of Decorating Dry Goods Windows and Interiors*, published by the Show Window Publishing Co. in 1900.

The color scheme of the story is also related to the colors of the changing seasons. The story begins in the grays of winter and continues to the blues, reds, and greens of spring, then to the yellows and greens of summer, and finally to the browns and reds of autumn until the return to the grays of winter with Dorothy's homecoming.

6 *white is the witch color.* Although some witch cults in Europe in the Middle Ages wore white, black is generally considered the witch color. Black is traditionally the color of evil, white the color of good. Baum's use of white as the witch color is another reversal of the generally accepted ways of the world. That white is the witch color in Oz is evidenced by the garments worn by the Good Witches of both North and South. Maetta the Sorceress of *A New Wonderland* and the good witch of "The Witchcraft of Mary-Marie" in *Baum's American Fairy Tales* (1908) also wear white. Note that Denslow's Wicked Witch of the West does not wear white, but Baum makes no such distinction.

7 *never seen a dog before.* A similar reaction occurs in *A New Wonderland* when a dog visits the lovely Valley of Mo. There are no dogs in Mo, but (despite this passage in *The Wizard of Oz*) at one time there must have been dogs in Oz. According to the map of the Land of Oz and its surrounding countries (prepared by James E. Haff for the International Wizard of Oz Club), the only country beyond the mountains of Mo and the great desert is the Land of Oz. (To cross the desert at the point dividing Oz and Mo is obviously easier than at any other place. The Foolish Donkey of *A New Wonderland*, which was later revised and published under the title *The Magical Monarch of Mo*, journeys across the desert from Mo before Glinda cuts Oz off from the rest of the world, as disclosed in *The Patchwork Girl of Oz*, p. 93.) Evidently, the dog who visited Mo was native to the Land of Oz.

8 *Scarecrow.* As a boy Baum must have had his first glimpse of a scarecrow in the cornfields of his father's farm in New York State. In *To Please a Child* MacFall reports a story Baum told to his children: When a boy he had recurring dreams of being chased by a scarecrow who would collapse into a pile of straw just before catching him. MacFall suggests that Baum looked back to this dream scarecrow when he wrote *The Wizard of Oz.*

"The American scarecrow had its heyday in the latter part of the nineteenth century," writes Avon Neal in *Ephemeral Folk Figures* (New York: Clarkson N. Potter, Inc., 1969).

It cut such a figure of sartorial elegance among the corn rows that tramps exchanging their worn-out wardrobes for the scarecrow's finer garb became legendary. Since then the art of scarecrow making has declined appreciably, depending more on working clothes and such pop art accouterments as aluminum pie tins held dangling in the wind. There was a time in America when no rustic scene would have seemed complete without some representation of this spectral image standing guard among the farmer's crops, but they are rare today. Science now has more effective ways of discouraging marauding crows.

The original role of the Scarecrow was played by Fred Stone in the 1902 musical. Because it made his reputation, Stone devoted an entire chapter of his autobiography, *A Rolling Stone* (1943), to the musical. Larry Semon, a silent film comedian, who had once worked as an illustrator with Neill, took the role in the 1925 Chadwick movie. Ray Bolger danced as the Scarecrow in the 1939 MGM film. He has recently narrated an album based on Baum's 1914 book *The Scarecrow of Oz* for Walt Disney Productions.

have business with him. But it is a long way to the Emerald City, and it will take you many days. The country here is rich and pleasant, but you must pass through rough and dangerous places before you reach the end of your journey."

This worried Dorothy a little, but she knew that only the great Oz could help her get to Kansas again, so she bravely resolved not to turn back.

She bade her friends good-bye, and again started along the road of yellow brick. When she had gone several miles she thought she would stop to rest, and so climbed to the top of the fence beside the road and sat down. There was a great cornfield beyond the fence, and

8 and not far away she saw a Scarecrow, placed high on a pole to keep the birds from the ripe corn.

Dorothy leaned her chin upon her hand and gazed thoughtfully at the Scarecrow. Its head was a small sack stuffed with straw, with eyes, nose and mouth painted on it to represent a face. An old, pointed blue hat, that had belonged to some Munchkin, was perched on this head, and the rest of the figure was a blue suit of clothes, worn and faded, which had also been stuffed with straw. On the feet were some old boots with blue tops, such as every man wore in this country, and the figure was raised above the stalks of corn by means of the pole stuck up its back.

While Dorothy was looking earnestly into the queer, painted face of the Scarecrow, she was surprised to see one of the eyes slowly wink at her. She thought she must have been mistaken, at first, for none of the scarecrows in Kansas ever wink; but presently the figure nodded its head to her in a friendly way. Then she climbed down from the fence and walked up to it, while Toto ran around the pole and barked.

"Good day," said the Scarecrow, in a rather husky **9** voice.

"Did you speak?" asked the girl, in wonder.

"Certainly," answered the Scarecrow; "how do you do?"

"I'm pretty well, thank you," replied Dorothy, politely; "how do you do?"

"I'm not feeling well," said the Scarecrow, with a smile, "for it is very tedious being perched up here night and day to scare away crows."

"Can't you get down?" asked Dorothy.

"No, for this pole is stuck up my back. If you will please take away the pole I shall be greatly obliged to you."

Dorothy reached up both arms and lifted the figure off the pole; for, being stuffed with straw, it was quite light.

"Thank you very much," said the Scarecrow, when he had been set down on the ground. "I feel like a new man."

Dorothy was puzzled at this, for it sounded queer to

9 *husky*. This is the first of numerous puns scattered throughout the book. Mac-Fall, in *To Please a Child*, records Baum's statement that he liked a good pun almost as well as a good cigar, his other major weakness. Although children tend to enjoy puns, modern critics of juvenile books generally agree that puns lower the literary value of a work. The pun depends only on verbal relations, while wit depends on intellectual connections. In the Elizabethan Age the pun was highly respected, but by the eighteenth century it had lost favor; Thomas Addison called it false wit, and Dr. Samuel Johnson considered it the lowest form of humor. Lewis Carroll, one of the most gifted creators of nonsense, enjoyed the pun but also realized its controversial aspect in the Victorian Age. When the King of Hearts makes a pun, there is dead silence, and one of the traits of the Snark is that "he looks gravely at a pun." Contemporary critics tend to agree with Dr. Johnson in spite of the frequency of puns in the works of such major modern writers as James Joyce and Vladimir Nabokov. In *The Marvelous Land of Oz* Baum admits the habit of many to turn in disgust at hearing a pun, but he (with his tongue firmly in his cheek) also gives a defense of the pun in the following speech of the Woggle-bug (p. 160):

A joke derived from a play upon words is considered among educated people to be eminently proper. . . . Our language contains many words having a double meaning; and that to pronounce a joke that allows both meanings of a certain word, proves the joker a person of culture and refinement, who has, moreover, a thorough command of language.

This fine drawing of the Scarecrow first appeared on the front cover of the Bobbs-Merrill edition of 1903, *The New Wizard of Oz*. The entire cover drawing (see Chapter IV, page 130) was adapted as a poster to advertise the book.

hear a stuffed man speak, and to see him bow and walk along beside her.

"Who are you?" asked the Scarecrow, when he had stretched himself and yawned, "and where are you going?"

"My name is Dorothy," said the girl, "and I am going to the Emerald City, to ask the great Oz to send me back to Kansas."

"Where is the Emerald City?" he enquired; "and who is Oz?"

"Why, don't you know?" she returned, in surprise.

"No, indeed; I don't know anything. You see, I am stuffed, so I have no brains at all," he answered, sadly.

"Oh," said Dorothy; "I'm awfully sorry for you."

"Do you think," he asked, "If I go to the Emerald City with you, that the great Oz would give me some brains?"

"I cannot tell," she returned; "but you may come with me, if you like. If Oz will not give you

any brains you will be no worse off than you are now."

"That is true," said the Scarecrow. "You see," he continued, confidentially, "I don't mind my legs and arms and body being stuffed, because I cannot get hurt. If anyone treads on my toes or sticks a pin into me, it doesn't matter, for I can't feel it. But I do not want people to call me a fool, and if my head stays stuffed with straw instead of with brains, as yours is, how am I ever to know anything?"

"I understand how you feel," said the little girl, who was truly sorry for him. "If you will come with me I'll ask Oz to do all he can for you."

"Thank you," he answered, gratefully.

They walked back to the road, Dorothy helped him over the fence, and they started along the path of yellow brick for the Emerald City.

Toto did not like this addition to the party, at first. He smelled around the stuffed man as if he suspected there might be a nest of rats in the straw, and he often growled in an unfriendly way at the Scarecrow.

"Don't mind Toto," said Dorothy, to her new friend; "he never bites."

"Oh, I'm not afraid," replied the Scarecrow, "he can't hurt the straw. Do let me carry that basket for you. I shall not mind it, for I can't get tired. I'll tell you a secret," he continued, as he walked along; "there is only one thing in the world I am afraid of."

"What is that?" asked Dorothy; "the Munchkin farmer who made you?"

"No," answered the Scarecrow; "it's a lighted match."

The illustration on this page originally appeared in *Denslow's A B C Book*, published by G. W. Dillingham in 1903. The verse illustrated is:

    S is the Scarecrow
      who lives in the corn,
    That the crows think so foolish
      they laugh him to scorn.

Although there is no reference to Baum or *The Wizard of Oz*, the Scarecrow pictured here is clearly the same as the one Dorothy found in the Munchkin cornfield. See Chapter VII, page 161.

Chapter IV.
~The Road through the Forest~

After A FEW HOURS the road began to be rough, and the walking grew so difficult that the Scarecrow often stumbled over the yellow brick, which were here very uneven. Sometimes, indeed, they were broken or missing altogether, leaving holes that Toto jumped across and Dorothy walked around. As for the Scarecrow, having no brains he walked straight ahead, and so stepped into the holes and fell at full length on the hard bricks. It never hurt him, however, and Dorothy would pick him up and set him upon his feet again, while he joined her in laughing merrily at his own mishap.

This previously unpublished drawing was presented to Townsend Walsh, the publicity manager of the 1902 musical. *Courtesy Theatre Collection, New York Public Library, Astor, Lenox, and Tilden Foundations.*

The farms were not nearly so well cared for here as they were farther back. There were fewer houses and fewer fruit trees, and the farther they went the more dismal and lonesome the country became.

At noon they sat down by the roadside, near a little brook, and Dorothy opened her basket and got out some bread. She offered a piece to the Scarecrow, but he refused.

"I am never hungry," he said; "and it is a lucky thing I am not. For my mouth is only painted, and if I should cut a hole in it so I could eat, the straw I am stuffed with would come out, and that would spoil the shape of my head."

Dorothy saw at once that this was true, so she only nodded and went on eating her bread.

"Tell me something about yourself, and the country you came from," said the Scarecrow, when she had finished her dinner. So she told him all about Kansas, and how gray everything was there, and how the cyclone had carried her to this queer land of Oz. The Scarecrow listened carefully, and said,

"I cannot understand why you should wish to leave this beautiful country and go back to the dry, gray place you call Kansas."

"That is because you have no brains," answered the girl. "No matter how dreary and gray our homes are, we people of flesh and blood would rather live there than in any other country, be it ever so beautiful.   There is no place **1** like home."

The Scarecrow sighed.

"Of course I cannot understand it," he said.   "If your heads were stuffed with straw, like mine, you would probably all live in the beautiful places, and then Kansas would have no people at all.   It is fortunate for Kansas that you have brains."

"Won't you tell me a story, while we are resting?" asked the child.

The Scarecrow looked at her reproachfully, and answered,

"My life has been so short that I really know nothing whatever.   I was only made day before yesterday.   What happened in the world before that time is all unknown to me.   Luckily, when the farmer made my head, one of the first things he did was to paint my ears, so that I heard what was going on.   There was another Munchkin with him, and the first thing I heard was the farmer saying,

"'How do you like those ears?'

"'They aren't straight,' answered the other.

"'Never mind,' said the farmer; 'they are ears just the same,' which was true enough.

"'Now I'll make the eyes,' said the farmer. So he painted my right eye, and as soon as it was finished I found myself looking at him and at everything around me with a great deal of curiosity, for this was my first glimpse of the **2** world.

1   *There is no place like home*. Although this particular area of the Munchkin Country has just been described as "dismal and lonesome," the Land of Oz is more beautiful than Kansas. Baum is being ironic when Dorothy states her preference to live in gray Kansas rather than in the colorful land of Oz. His point is also metaphysical; Dorothy's home means something more than the most beautiful foreign land. This passage reinforces the importance of environment, mentioned in Chapter 1, Note 4. Of course, Dorothy's feeling is not logical so the intellectually oriented Scarecrow is confused.

2   *my first glimpse of the world*. "The problem of language aside," writes Sackett in his article "The Utopia of Oz," "it would be difficult to imagine a better description of the awakening of a new mind, the first initial marks made upon the *tabula rasa*, than the following account told by the Scarecrow to Dorothy, of his early moments." Sackett interprets this as Baum's answer to "the unchangeability of human nature."

The key to the problem is epistemology. You must assume with Locke that the mind at birth is a *tabula rasa*, an empty page; that there are no innate ideas, no Jungian archetypes or other inherited memories. According to this theory the individual's environment will completely mold his personality, for he has no inherited psychological characteristics. Each experience he has will form his personality, little by little.

Sackett also notes a passage in *The Marvelous Land of Oz* (pp. 47–51), the bringing to life of the Sawhorse, as "well worth reading as an account of the way one sensation after another marks the empty page of the mind at birth."

3 *the other a little bigger.* In *The Wizard of Oz and Who He Was*, Gardner observes in Note 6: "Both Denslow and Neill drew the Scarecrow with a larger left eye, showing a respect for the text of the Royal History that has not been shared by other Oz illustrators." An exception is Dick Martin whose pictures of the Scarecrow are in agreement with this point of the text. Baum's emphasis of the left eye is one of several examples throughout his writing suggesting an interest in sinistrality, or the preference for the left over the right of the body's double organs. There is no mystical or Freudian significance to this; Baum himself was left-handed. When the boy Ojo declares that one reason he is called unlucky is that he is left-handed, Baum in the guise of the Tin Woodman slyly replies, "Many of our greatest men are that way" (*The Patchwork Girl of Oz*, p. 329).

4 *brains.* That a scarecrow with his soft straw-stuffed head should wish a brain is, of course, ironic. Folktales are often concerned with a quest for the one object that will make the individual whole. It is generally something unusual or, as in the Scarecrow's case, highly improbable. This search is, as M.-L. Franz describes in her chapter on psychic growth included in Carl G. Jung's *Man and His Symbols* (New York: Doubleday & Company, 1964), the process of individuation. According to her, the problem of an individual's imperfection can only be solved within himself.

"'That's a rather pretty eye,' remarked the Munchkin who was watching the farmer; 'blue paint is just the color for eyes.'

3 "'I think I'll make the other a little bigger,' said the farmer; and when the second eye was done I could see much better than before. Then he made my nose and my mouth; but I did not speak, because at that time I didn't know what a mouth was for. I had the fun of watching them make my body and my arms and legs; and when they fastened on my head, at last, I felt very proud, for I thought I was just as good a man as anyone.

"'This fellow will scare the crows fast enough,' said the farmer; 'he looks just like a man.'

"'Why, he is a man,' said the other, and I quite agreed with him. The farmer carried me under his arm to the cornfield, and set me up on a tall stick, where you found me. He and his friend soon after walked away and left me alone.

"I did not like to be deserted this way; so I tried to walk after them, but my feet would not touch the ground, and I was forced to stay on that pole. It was a lonely life to lead, for I had nothing to think of, having been made such a little while before. Many crows and other birds flew into the cornfield, but as soon as they saw me they flew away again, thinking I was a Munchkin; and this pleased me and made me feel that I was quite an important person. By and by an old crow flew near me, and after looking at me carefully he perched upon my shoulder and said,

"'I wonder if that farmer thought to fool me in this clumsy manner. Any crow of sense could see that you are only stuffed with straw.' Then he hopped down at my feet and ate all the corn he wanted. The other birds, seeing he was not harmed by me, came to eat the corn too, so in a short time there was a great flock of them about me.

"I felt sad at this, for it showed I was not such a good Scarecrow after all; but the old crow comforted me, saying: 'If you only had brains in your head you would be as good a man as any of them, and a better man than some of them. Brains are the only things worth having in this world, no matter whether one is a crow or a man.'

"After the crows had gone I thought this over, and decided I would try hard to get some brains. **4** By good luck, you came along and pulled me off the stake, and from what you say I am sure the great Oz will give me brains as soon as we get to the Emerald City." **5**

"I hope so," said Dorothy, earnestly, "since you seem anxious to have them."

"Oh yes; I am anxious," returned the Scarecrow. "It is such an uncomfortable feeling to know one is a fool." **6**

The resolution is clearly defined in the folktale described in Tolkien's "On Fairy Tales": "The Monkey's Heart" is about the search for the creature's heart, supposedly left behind in a bag. The irony of the tale is that the monkey's heart has been in his own breast all along. A similar metaphysical conclusion occurs in Oscar Wilde's fine fairy tale "The Fisherman and His Soul" in *The House of Pomegranates* (1891). When it has been separated from the fisherman, the soul goes in search of God and is led to a room in the temple of an enchanted country where it discovers a mirror. What the monkey and the soul of these two tales discover can be compared to what the Scarecrow learns about himself when he discovers Oz, the Terrible.

5 *as soon as we get to the Emerald City.* A different version of the Scarecrow's story is given in "The Scarecrow Tells A Fairy Tale to Children and Hears an Equally Marvelous True Story," one of the "Queer Visitors from the Marvelous Land of Oz" comic-page stories that were syndicated in 1904–1905, written by Baum and illustrated by McDougall. (This particular story was revised and published in 1960 in *The Visitors from Oz* with pictures by Dick Martin.) The Scarecrow is the narrator of the following tale:

You must know, my dears, that in the Land of Oz everything has life that can become of any use by living. Now, I do not know of what use a live Scarecrow can be unless he serves to amuse children; but it is a fact that, as soon as the farmer had stuffed me into the shape of a man,

and made me a head by using this excellent cotton sack, I began to realize that I was a part of the big world and had come to life.

Of course, I could not see, nor hear, nor talk at first, but the farmer brought a paint pot and a brush, and upon the surface of my head, where a face properly belongs, he began to paint. First he made this left eye, which you observe is a beautiful circle, with a dot in the centre of it. The first object I saw with this eye was the farmer himself, and, you may be sure, I watched him carefully as he painted my other eye. I have always considered that man an artist; otherwise he could not have made me so handsome. My right eye is even finer than the left; and, after making it, the farmer gave me this exquisite nose, with which I gathered the scent of the wild flowers and the new-mown hay and the furrows of sweet and fertile earth. Next my mouth was manufactured, so excellently shaped that I have never ceased to be proud of it; but I could not then speak, for I knew no words by which to express my feelings. Then followed these lovely ears, which completed my features. And now I heard the loud breathing of the farmer, who was fat and inclined to asthma, and the twittering songs of the birds and the whisper of the winds as they glided through the meadows, and the chatter of the field mice—and many other pleasant and delightful sounds.

Indeed, I now believed myself fully the equal of the man who had made me; but the idea was soon dispelled when the farmer sat me upon a stout pole in the cornfield and then walked away with his paint pot and left me. I tried at once to follow, but my feet would not touch the earth, and so I could not escape from the pole.

Near me was a stile, and people crossing the fields would often stop at the stile and converse; so that by listening to them I soon learned how to speak properly. I had a fine view of the country from my elevation, and plenty of time to examine it curiously. Moreover, the crows often came and perched upon my head and shoulders and talked of the big world they had seen; so my education was unusually broad and diverse. But I longed to see the big world of Oz for myself, and my real mission in life—to scare the crows—seemed to be a failure. The crows even grew fond of me and spoke to me pleasantly while they dug up the grains of the corn the farmer had planted.

This story appeared in several newspapers on November 27, 1904, and was reproduced in the Spring 1969 *Baum Bugle*.

6 *to know one is a fool.* In a revision of this episode, which appeared as "The Scarecrow's Story" in *L. Frank Baum's Juvenile Speaker*, Baum adds the following:

I realize at present that I'm only an imitation of a man, and I assure you it's a very uncomfortable feeling to know one is a fool. It seems to me that a body is only a machine for brains to direct, and those who have no brains themselves are liable to be directed by the brains of others.

But I may be wrong. I'm only a Scarecrow, you know.

"Well," said the girl, "let us go." And she handed the basket to the Scarecrow.

There were no fences at all by the road side now, and the land was rough and untilled. Towards evening they came to a great forest, where the trees grew so big and close together that their branches met over the road of yellow brick. It was almost dark under the trees, for the branches shut out the daylight; but the travellers did not stop, and went on into the forest.

"If this road goes in, it must come out," said the Scarecrow, "and as the Emerald City is at the other end of the road, we must go wherever it leads us."

"Anyone would know that," said Dorothy.

"Certainly; that is why I know it," returned the Scarecrow. "If it required brains to figure it out, I never should have said it."

After an hour or so the light faded away, and they found themselves stumbling along in the darkness. Dorothy could not see at all, but Toto could, for some dogs see very well in the dark; and the Scarecrow declared he could see as well as by day. So she took hold of his arm, and managed to get along fairly well.

"If you see any house, or any place where we can pass the night," she said, "you must tell me; for it is very uncomfortable walking in the dark."

Soon after the Scarecrow stopped.

"I see a little cottage at the right of us," he said, "built of logs and branches. Shall we go there?"

"Yes, indeed;" answered the child. "I am all tired out."

So the Scarecrow led her through the trees until they reached the cottage, and Dorothy entered and found a bed of dried leaves in one corner. She lay down at once, and with Toto beside her soon fell into a sound sleep. The Scarecrow, who was never tired, stood up in another corner and waited patiently until morning came.

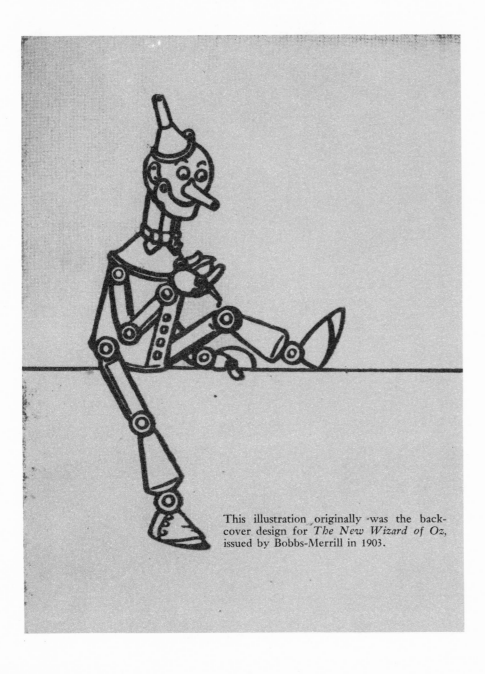

This illustration originally was the back-
cover design for *The New Wizard of Oz*,
issued by Bobbs-Merrill in 1903.

Chapter V.
The Rescue of
the Tin Woodman

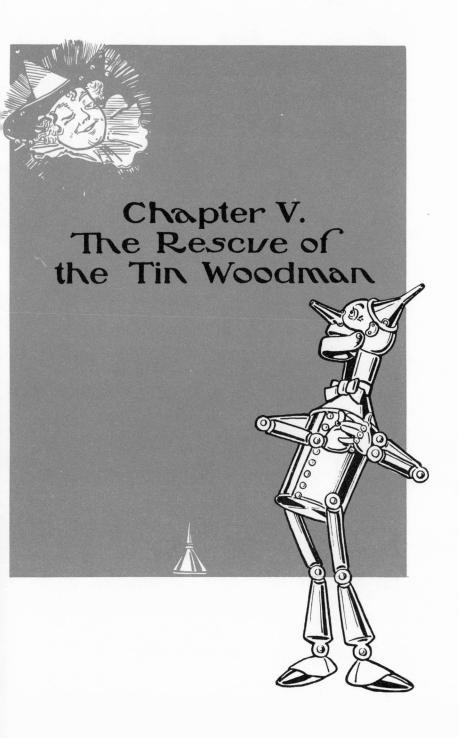

When DOROTHY awoke the sun was shining through the trees and Toto had long been out chasing birds and squirrels. She sat up and looked around her. There was the Scarecrow, still standing patiently in his corner, waiting for her.

"We must go and search for water," she said to him.

"Why do you want water?" he asked.

"To wash my face clean after the dust of the road, and to drink, so the dry bread will not stick in my throat."

"It must be inconvenient to be made of flesh," said the **1** Scarecrow, thoughtfully; "for you must sleep, and eat and

1 *made of flesh.* In the combined version of portions from the present and previous chapters, under the title "An Adventure in Oz" in *L. Frank Baum's Juvenile Speaker,* is the following revision of this exchange between Dorothy and the Scarecrow:

Presently she brought a cup of water from the brook and drank it.

"You people of flesh and blood," remarked the Scarecrow, who had been watching her, "take a good deal of trouble to keep alive. You must eat and drink and sleep, and those are three things that a straw man need not worry about. However, you have brains, and it is worth a lot of bother to be able to think properly."

"Yes," said Dorothy; "take it altogether, I'm glad I'm not straw."

2 *a man made entirely of tin.* One of the many jobs Baum held before settling in Chicago as a writer of children's books was that of dressing a hardware-store window. His son Harry explained, in Joseph Haas's "A Little Bit of 'Oz' in Northern Indiana" (Indianapolis *Times*, May 3, 1965), that "he wanted to create something eye-catching so he made a torso out of a washboiler, bolted stovepipe legs and arms to it and used the underside of a saucepan for a face. He topped it with a funnel hat and what would become the inspiration for the Tin Woodman was born."

The Tin Woodman is one of several mechanical men to clank through Baum's fairy tales. "One of Baum's major contributions to the tradition of the fantasy tale," writes Nye in *The Wizard of Oz and Who He Was*, "is his recognition of the inherent wonder of the machine, his perception of the magic of *things* in themselves. . . . By transforming the talking beasts of ancient folktales into talking machines, Baum grafted twentieth century technology to the fairy tale tradition." Other notable examples are the Cast-Iron Man of *A New Wonderland*, Mr. Split who divides himself in half in *Dot and Tot of Merryland*, and his not-too-distant relatives, Tik-Tok (whose prototype is the clockwork man of a poem in *Father Goose, His Book*) and the Giant-With-The-Hammer, both built by the firm of Smith & Tinker in *Ozma of Oz*.

drink. However, you have brains, and it is worth a lot of bother to be able to think properly."

They left the cottage and walked through the trees until they found a little spring of clear water, where Dorothy drank and bathed and ate her breakfast. She saw there was not much bread left in the basket, and the girl was thankful the Scarecrow did not have to eat anything, for there was scarcely enough for herself and Toto for the day.

When she had finished her meal, and was about to go back to the road of yellow brick, she was startled to hear a deep groan near by.

"What was that?" she asked, timidly.

"I cannot imagine," replied the Scarecrow; "but we can go and see."

Just then another groan reached their ears, and the sound seemed to come from behind them. They turned and walked through the forest a few steps, when Dorothy discovered something shining in a ray of sunshine that fell between the trees. She ran to the place, and then stopped short, with a cry of surprise.

One of the big trees had been partly chopped through, and standing beside it, with an uplifted axe in his hands, **2** was a man made entirely of tin. His head and arms and legs were jointed upon his body, but he stood perfectly motionless, as if he could not stir at all.

Dorothy looked at him in amazement, and so did the

Scarecrow, while Toto barked sharply and made a snap at the tin legs, which hurt his teeth.

"Did you groan?" asked Dorothy.

"Yes," answered the tin man; "I did. I've been groaning for more than a year, and no one has ever heard me before or come to help me."

"What can I do for you?" she enquired, softly, for she was moved by the sad voice in which the man spoke.

"Get an oil-can and oil my joints," he answered. "They are rusted so badly that **3** I cannot move them at all; if I am well oiled I shall soon be all right again. You will find an oil-can on a shelf in my cottage."

Dorothy at once ran back to the cottage and found the oil-can, and then she returned and asked, anxiously,

"Where are your joints?"

"Oil my neck, first," replied the Tin Woodman. So she oiled it, and as it was quite badly rusted the Scarecrow took hold of the tin head and moved it gently from side to side until it worked freely, and then the man could turn it himself.

3 *rusted*. Technically, only iron rusts, but other metals during corrosion are commonly said to "rust." (David Greene writes me that in the Russian Oz books the Woodman is made of iron.) Perhaps Baum intended the Woodman's joints to be made of iron rather than tin; this chapter refers only to the joints, and in Denslow's color plate these are a different color from the rest of the tin man.

In the Metropolitan Life Insurance Company's advertisement in the November 1954 *National Geographic*, the rusting of the Tin Woodman's joints is likened to arthritis, or the stiffening of the joints of the human body. The ad stresses proper medical care to help the joints remain "flexible and workable despite arthritis."

"Now oil the joints in my arms," he said. And Dorothy oiled them and the Scarecrow bent them carefully until they were quite free from rust and as good as new.

The Tin Woodman gave a sigh of satisfaction and lowered his axe, which he leaned against the tree.

"This is a great comfort," he said. "I have been holding that axe in the air ever since I rusted; and I'm glad to be able to put it down at last. Now, if you will oil the joints of my legs, I shall be all right once more."

So they oiled his legs until he could move them freely; and he thanked them again and again for his release, for he seemed a very polite creature, and very grateful.

"I might have stood there always if you had not come along," he said; "so you have certainly saved my life. How did you happen to be here ?"

"We are on our way to the Emerald City, to see the great Oz," she answered, "and we stopped at your cottage to pass the night."

"Why do you wish to see Oz?" he asked.

"I want him to send me back to Kansas; and the Scarecrow wants him to put a few brains into his head," she replied.

The Tin Woodman appeared to think deeply for a moment. Then he said:

"Do you suppose Oz could give me a heart?"

"Why, I guess so," Dorothy answered; "it would be as easy as to give the Scarecrow brains."

"True," the Tin Woodman returned. "So, if you will allow me to join your party, I will also go to the Emerald City and ask Oz to help me."

"Come along," said the Scarecrow, heartily; and Dorothy added that she would be pleased to have his company. So the Tin Woodman shouldered his axe and they all passed through the forest until they came to the road that was paved with yellow brick.

The Tin Woodman had asked Dorothy to put the oil-can in her basket. "For," he said, "if I should get caught in the rain, and rust again, I would need the oil-can badly."

It was a bit of good luck to have their new comrade join the party, for soon after they had begun their journey again they came to a place where the trees and branches grew so thick over the road that the travellers could not pass. But the Tin Woodman set to work with his axe and chopped so well that soon he cleared a passage for the entire party.

Dorothy was thinking so earnestly as they walked along that she did not notice when the Scarecrow stumbled into a hole and rolled over to the side of the road. Indeed, he was obliged to call to her to help him up again.

"Why didn't you walk around the hole?" asked the Tin Woodman.

"I don't know enough," replied the Scarecrow, cheer- **4** fully. "My head is stuffed with straw, you know, and that is why I am going to Oz to ask him for some brains."

4 *I don't know enough.* Here is, in fact, the first opportunity the Scarecrow has had to use his intelligence; he fails dismally. This mistake will act as a lesson to him, for from now on he will trust to and use this experience to avoid a recurrence. It will encourage him to use his judgment in other situations.

5 *When I grew up.* This does not agree with our subsequent knowledge of the nature of aging in Oz. The following account appears in *The Tin Woodman of Oz* (pp. 156-57):

Oz was not always a fairyland, I am told. Once it was much like other lands, except it was shut in by a dreadful desert of sandy wastes that lay all around it, thus preventing its people from all contact with the rest of the world. Seeing this isolation, the fairy band of Queen Lurline left one of her fairies to rule this enchanted Land of Oz, and then passed on and forgot all about it.

From that moment on no one in Oz ever died. Those who were old remained old; those who were young and strong did not change as years passed them by; the children remained children always, and played and romped to their hearts' content, while all the babies lived in their cradles and were tenderly cared for and never grew up. So people in Oz stopped counting how old they were in years, for years made no difference in their appearance and could not alter their station. They did not get sick, so there were no doctors among them. Accidents might happen to some, on rare occasions, it is true, and while no one could die naturally, as other people do, it was possible that one might be totally destroyed. Such incidents, however, were very unusual, and so seldom was there anything to worry over that the Oz people were as happy and contented as can be.

Under the rule of the Wizard this enchantment was significantly different from that described above. Perhaps when the Wizard (and not the fairy that Lurline left as rightful ruler and protector of Oz) was on the throne of Oz, the fairyland may have regressed to its pre-enchantment state. This may explain why deaths occur during the reign of the Wizard and not under that of Princess Ozma. (See Note 7 below.)

6 *I too became a wood-chopper.* Nick Chopper is the name of the woodman, before and after he became a man of tin (*The Marvelous Land of Oz*, p. 117). The first appearance of this name (also as "Niccolo" Chopper) is in the final script for the 1902 musical. David C. Montgomery took the role of the Tin Woodman in this production. Prior to his teaming with Stan Laurel, Oliver Hardy played the role in the 1925 Chadwick silent film. Jack Haley portrayed him in the 1939 MGM movie.

7 *father died.* Gardner observes in Note 7 of *The Wizard of Oz and Who He Was*: "The many references in this book to the deaths of men and beasts are hard to reconcile with our later knowledge concerning the extreme difficulty of 'destroying' living beings in Oz." However, it is only after Ozma officially becomes ruler of all Oz that it becomes impossible to kill a living creature in the Land of Oz, though it remains possible to "destroy" one. Jack Snow wrote a clever short story entitled "Murder in Oz," which concerns the "death" of Ozma and its aftermath. It is reprinted in *The Best of The Baum Bugle: 1957–1961*:

8 *to love her.* Another theme in children's literature that Baum decided should not appear in his "modernized fairy tales" was that of romance. "Love, as depicted in literature," Baum is quoted as saying in the St. Louis *Republic* (May 30, 1903), "is a threadbare and unsatisfactory topic which children can comprehend neither in its esoteric nor exoteric meaning. Therefore it

"Oh, I see;" said the Tin Woodman. "But, after all, brains are not the best things in the world."

"Have you any?" enquired the Scarecrow.

"No, my head is quite empty," answered the Woodman; "but once I had brains, and a heart also; so, having tried them both, I should much rather have a heart."

"And why is that?" asked the Scarecrow.

"I will tell you my story, and then you will know."

So, while they were walking through the forest, the Tin Woodman told the following story:

"I was born the son of a woodman who chopped down trees in the forest and sold the wood for a living. When I grew up I too became a wood-chopper, and after my father died I took care of my old mother as long as she lived. Then I made up my mind that instead of living alone I would marry, so that I might not become lonely.

"There was one of the Munchkin girls who was so beautiful that I soon grew to love her with all my heart. She, on her part, promised to marry me as soon as I could earn enough money to build a better house for her; so I set to work harder than ever. But the girl lived with an old woman who did not want her to marry anyone, for she was so lazy she wished the girl to remain with her and do the cooking and the housework. So the old woman went to the wicked Witch of the East, and promised her two sheep and a cow if she would prevent the marriage. Thereupon the wicked Witch enchanted my axe, and when I was chopping away at my best one day, for I was anxious to get the new house and my wife as soon as possible, the axe slipped all at once and cut off my left leg.

"This at first seemed a great misfortune, for I knew a one-legged man could not do very well as a wood-chopper. So I went to a tin-smith and had him make me a new leg **10** out of tin. The leg worked very well, once I was used to it; but my action angered the wicked Witch of the East, for she had promised the old woman I should not marry the pretty Munchkin girl. When I began chopping again my axe slipped and cut off my right leg. Again I went to the tinner, and again he made me a leg out of tin. After this the enchanted axe cut off my arms, one after the other; but, nothing daunted, I had them replaced with tin ones. The wicked Witch then made the axe slip and cut off my head, and at first I thought that was the end of me. But the tinner happened to come along, and he made me a new head out of tin.

"I thought I had beaten the wicked Witch then, and I worked harder than ever; but I little knew how cruel my enemy could be. She thought of a new way to kill my love for the beautiful Munchkin maiden, and made my axe

has no place in their storybooks." (A similar view was expressed by John Ruskin in his introduction to an 1868 edition of *German Popular Tales* in which he writes the word love, "in the modern child-story, is too often restrained and darkened into the hieroglyph of an evil mystery, troubling the sweet peace of youth with premature gleams of uncomprehended passion, and flitting shadows of unrecognized sin.") When *The Wizard of Oz* was written Baum had not yet decided to eliminate such references from his children's books as is evident in the Tin Woodman's narrative and the story of Gayelette and Quelala in Chapter 14. Love stories, however, do occur in *Tik-Tok of Oz* and *The Scarecrow of Oz*, both of which were based upon theatricals (the first a musical, the second a movie), which may in part explain the inclusion of romance. Baum was well aware that these romances might have been out of place in his children's stories. "In the 'Scarecrow' I introduced a slightly novel theme, for me, in the love and tribulations of Pon the gardner's son and the Princess Gloria," writes Baum in a letter to his publishers dated January 17, 1916. "It smacked a bit of the Andersen fairy tales and I watched its effect upon my readers. They accepted it gleefully, with all the rest, it being well within their comprehension."

9 *the girl.* In *The Tin Woodman of Oz* (p. 22) her name is Nimmee Amee. In this book the Tin Woodman tells a somewhat different story of his early life, including a number of puns and satiric touches avoided in the first. In this later version the girl is said to have worked for the Wicked Witch of the East; "an old woman" is not mentioned. The Tin Woodman had evidently learned (by this time) that the old woman was the Wicked Witch herself.

10 *a tin-smith.* His name is Ku-Klip (*The Tin Woodman of Oz*, p. 22). One of the episodes in this book is a visit to the tin-smith's workshop where the Tin Woodman has a discussion with his former head, one of the most unusual and fascinating chapters in all of Baum's writing. (It may

This illustration of the Wicked Witch of the East is from one of a set of six lithographed broadsides drawn by Denslow to advertise the 1902 musical. (*See also* pages 348-49). *Courtesy Dick Martin.*

have been suggested by "The Strange Adventures of the King's Head" in *A New Wonderland,* a story that James Thurber called " a fine, fantastic fairy tale.") Besides building the Tin Woodman, Ku-Klip was responsible for the construction of Captain Fyter, the Tin Soldier who at the wrath of the Wicked Witch of the East suffered a fate similar to the Tin Woodman, a situation Gardner has noted as the cause of "profound metaphysical questions concerning personal identity." (These are increased when one learns that an early title of the book was "The Twin Tin Woodman of Oz.") Ku-Klip also tries to manufacture a flesh-and-blood human being. His result is the unsocial Chopfyte, made of spare pieces of the former bodies of Nick Chopper and Captain Fyter, a man who "is always someone else." As Nye observes: "Baum comments on technological overdevelopment, which may undo the unwary in America as it does in Oz."

11 *I had now no heart.* Henry M. Littlefield in his article "The Wizard of Oz: A Parable on Populism" (cited in my introduction) sees the Tin Woodman's story as "a Populist view of evil Eastern influences on honest labor." By replacing the Woodman's flesh with tin, "Eastern witchcraft dehumanized a simple laborer so that the faster and better he worked the more he became a machine." Mr. Littlefield's article attempts to explain *The Wizard of Oz* in terms of the times in which it was written. As I have mentioned in my introduction, his view suggests a number of interesting and valid points, but he tends to restrict Baum's broad use of metaphor to an allegory based upon the Populist movement. An allegory is a tale in which every object and incident is directly representative of something else, whereas to my mind *The*

Wizard of Oz is a symbolic narrative · in which certain objects and actions give the tale (in an overall way) a universal meaning. A symbol may represent many things at the same time.

11 slip again, so that it cut right through my body, splitting me into two halves. Once more the tinner came to my help and made me a body of tin, fastening my tin arms and legs and head to it, by means of joints, so that I could move around as well as ever. But, alas! I had now no heart, so that I lost all my love for the Munchkin girl, and did not care whether I married her or not. I suppose she is still living with the old woman, waiting for me to come after her.

"My body shone so brightly in the sun that I felt very proud of it and it did not matter now if my axe slipped, for it could not cut me. There was only one danger—that my joints would rust; but I kept an oil-can in my cottage and took care to oil myself whenever I needed it. However, there came a day when I forgot to do this, and, being caught in a rainstorm, before I thought of the danger my joints had rusted, and I was left to stand in the woods until you came to help me. It was a terrible thing to undergo, but during the year I stood there I had time to think that the greatest loss I had known was the loss of my heart. While I was in love I was the happiest man on earth; but no one can love who has not a heart, and so I am resolved to ask Oz to give me one. If he does, I will go back to the Munchkin maiden and marry her." **12**

13

Both Dorothy and the Scarecrow had been greatly interested in the story of the Tin Woodman, and now they knew why he was so anxious to get a new heart.

"All the same," said the Scarecrow, "I shall ask for brains instead of a heart; for a fool would not know what to do with a heart if he had one."

"I shall take the heart," returned the Tin Woodman; "for brains do not make one happy, and happiness is the best thing in the world." **14**

Dorothy did not say anything, for she was puzzled to know which of her two friends was right, and she decided **15** if she could only get back to Kansas and Aunt Em it did not matter so much whether the Woodman had no brains and the Scarecrow no heart, or each got what he wanted.

What worried her most was that the bread was nearly gone, and another meal for herself and Toto would empty the basket. To be sure neither the Woodman nor the Scarecrow ever ate anything, but she was not made of tin nor straw, and could not live unless she was fed. **16**

12 *heart.* Just as with the Scarecrow and his brains, it is ironic that a cold, hollow, metallic individual should wish a soft and loving heart. The Tin Woodman is a machine in search of a human characteristic. One of the tragedies of the Industrial Age of the nineteenth century was the rapid growth away from basic human values. The close of the century encouraged many diverse hopes and prophecies of twentieth-century technological progress. A frequent prediction was the inevitable superiority of the machine; it would eventually perform all the labors of man. Baum realized that with this advancement man must not lose his humanity. The creation of Tik-Tok in *Ozma of Oz* clearly expresses this belief. This clockwork man is so skillfully made that he can do everything a man can do, everything but live.

13 *marry her.* In a revised version of this chapter, under the title "The Heart of a Man of Tin," which appeared in *L. Frank Baum's Juvenile Speaker,* Baum added the following exchange:

"Perhaps," said Dorothy, "she won't care very much for a tin husband."

"Perhaps not," sighed the tin man; "yet I am brighter than most husbands, and am considered a polished gentleman."

Not until the twelfth Oz book, *The Tin Woodman of Oz,* does he attempt to fulfill his promise to marry the girl.

14 *best thing in the world.* This dispute brings to mind a similar discussion in the dialogue of Plato, "Charmides." Socrates speaks of a dream he has had of universal knowledge, but then reverts to the opinion that knowledge does not ensure happiness.

15 *which of her two friends was right.* Dorothy is puzzled because she is confronted with the traditional philosophical choice between the dictates of the mind and those of the heart. Her two companions could easily represent the opposing views of the Age of Reason and the Romantic Movement. Similar discussions appear throughout the Oz series (notably the last paragraphs of *The Marvelous Land of Oz*). Baum suggests that both reason and emotion are necessary; the Scarecrow and the Tin Woodman remain inseparable friends throughout the series.

16 *she was fed.* Dorothy's solution to the above discussion is purely practical; as long as she is fed she will let others talk about philosophy. Baum hints at another reason why Dorothy does not care whether the Tin Woodman lacks a brain or the Scarecrow a heart; Dorothy has both a mind and a heart—in the persons of the Tin Woodman and the Scarecrow—to guide her so she need not determine which is greater.

In respect to the discussion between the Scarecrow and Tin Woodman, I quote Gardner's question in his introduction to the 1960 Dover edition of *The Wizard of Oz*: "Was T. S. Eliot thinking vaguely (among other things) of the Tin Woodman and the Scarecrow when he wrote, 'We are the hollow men / We are the stuffed men'?"

This illustration was the front endpaper design of the Hill edition.

Chapter VI.
The Cowardly Lion.

All THIS TIME DOROTHY and her companions had been walking through the thick woods. The road was still paved with yellow brick, but these were much covered by dried branches and dead leaves from the trees, and the walking was not at all good.

There were few birds in this part of the forest, for birds love the open country where there is plenty of sunshine; but now and then there came a deep growl from some wild animal hidden among the trees. These sounds made the little girl's heart beat fast, for she did not know what made them; but Toto knew, and he walked close to Dorothy's side, and did not even bark in return.

"How long will it be," the child asked of the Tin Woodman, "before we are out of the forest?"

"I cannot tell," was the answer, "for I have never been to the Emerald City. But my father went there once, when I was a boy, and he said it was a long journey through a dangerous country, although nearer to the city where Oz dwells the country is beautiful. But I am not afraid so long as I have my oil-can, and nothing can hurt the Scarecrow, while you bear upon your forehead the mark of the good Witch's kiss, and that will protect you from harm."

"But Toto!" said the girl, anxiously; "what will protect him?"

"We must protect him ourselves, if he is in danger," replied the Tin Woodman.

Just as he spoke there came from the forest a terrible roar, and the next moment a great Lion bounded into the road. With one blow of his paw he sent the Scarecrow spining over and over to the edge of the road, and then he struck at the Tin Woodman with his sharp claws. But, to the Lion's surprise, he could make no impression on the tin, although the Woodman fell over in the road and lay still.

Little Toto, now that he had an enemy to face, ran barking toward the Lion, and the great beast had opened his mouth to bite the dog, when Dorothy, fearing Toto would be killed, and heedless of danger, rushed forward and slapped the Lion upon his nose as hard as she could, while she cried out:

"Don't you dare to bite Toto! You ought to be ashamed of yourself, a big beast like you, to bite a poor little dog!"

"I didn't bite him," said the Lion, as he rubbed his nose with his paw where Dorothy had hit it.

"No, but you tried to," she retorted. "You are nothing but a big coward." **1**

"I know it," said the Lion, hanging his head in shame; "I've always known it. But how can I help it?"

"I don't know, I'm sure. To think of your striking a stuffed man, like the poor Scarecrow!"

"Is he stuffed?" asked the Lion, in surprise, as he watched her pick up the Scarecrow and set him upon his feet, while she patted him into shape again.

"Of course he's stuffed," replied Dorothy, who was still angry.

"That's why he went over so easily," remarked the Lion. "It astonished me to see him whirl around so. Is the other one stuffed, also?"

"No," said Dorothy, "he's made of tin." And she helped the Woodman up again.

"That's why he nearly blunted my claws," said the Lion. "When they scratched against the tin it made a

1 *big coward.* Baum was not the first author to conceive of a gentle lion. The Cowardly Lion is a creation not too distantly related to other lions in legend and literature. In heraldry, a lion portrayed with his tail hanging between his legs is considered a coward. The legends of Androcles and Saint Jerome both concern lions who are tamed after thorns are removed from their paws. Una's lion in Booke I, Canto iii, of Spenser's *Faerie Queene* also reminds one of the Cowardly Lion.

One of the highlights of the MGM film was Bert Lahr's performance as the Cowardly Lion. "Not all characters from children's literature, of course, are ruined by conversion to stage or screen," writes William K. Zinsser in "John Dolittle, M.D., Puddleby-on-the-Marsh" (*The New York Times Children's Book Review*, November 6, 1966). "On the contrary, the Cowardly Lion of Oz, thanks to one of those genetical surprises that occasionally tweak the nose of science, looked more authentic when the part was played by Bert Lahr than if it had been taken by a lion." John Lahr's biography of his father, *Notes on a Cowardly Lion* (1969), devotes considerable space to a discussion of the MGM film.

2 *a meat dog.* This discussion discloses that Dorothy's companions, besides personifying the qualities of courage, intelligence, and kindness, also represent the three states of nature—animal, vegetable, and mineral. This is also the first use of the term "meat" creature that Baum uses throughout his books to distinguish flesh-and-blood beings from his non-natural fantastic characters such as the Scarecrow and the Tin Woodman.

3 *King of Beasts.* Although this belief originated in ancient times and was accepted in the Middle Ages, not until the Renaissance did a belief in the Lion as the King of Beasts appear in a highly sophisticated world view. In such works as Raymond de Symonde's *Natural Theology* (1550) and Peacham's *The Compleat Gentleman* (1622), the lion as King of Beasts fitted neatly into their theory of primates: in every class of every level of existence there is a primate. The eagle is chief of the birds, the dolphin or whale head of the fish, the lion King of Beasts. There seems to have been a controversy however, as to the primate of beasts. Gelli's *Circe* (1548) and other works of this period gave the title King of Beasts to the elephant. The lion, however, received wider recognition and is referred to even today as King of Beasts. (See also Chapter 11, Note 16.)

2 cold shiver run down my back. What is that little animal you are so tender of?"

"He is my dog, Toto," answered Dorothy.

"Is he made of tin, or stuffed?" asked the Lion.

"Neither. He's a—a—a meat dog," said the girl.

"Oh. He's a curious animal, and seems remarkably small, now that I look at him. No one would think of biting such a little thing except a coward like me," continued the Lion, sadly.

"What makes you a coward?" asked Dorothy, looking at the great beast in wonder, for he was as big as a small horse.

"It's a mystery," replied the Lion. "I suppose I was born that way. All the other animals in the forest naturally expect me to be brave, for the Lion is every- **3** where thought to be the King of Beasts. I learned that if I roared very loudly every living thing was frightened and got out of my way. Whenever I've met a man I've been awfully scared; but I just roared at him, and he has always run away as fast as he could go. If the elephants and the tigers and the bears had ever tried to fight me, I should have run myself—I'm such a coward; but just as soon as they hear me roar they all try to get away from me, and of course I let them go."

"But that isn't right. The King of Beasts shouldn't be a coward," said the Scarecrow.

"I know it," returned the Lion, wiping a tear from his eye with the tip of his tail; "it is my great sorrow, and makes my life very unhappy. But whenever there is danger my heart begins to beat fast."

"Perhaps you have heart disease," said the Tin Wood-man. **4**

"It may be," said the Lion. **5**

"If you have," continued the Tin Woodman, "you ought to be glad, for it proves you have a heart. For my part, I have no heart; so I cannot have heart disease."

"Perhaps," said the Lion, thoughtfully, "if I had no heart I should not be a coward."

"Have you brains?" asked the Scarecrow.

"I suppose so. I've never looked to see," replied the Lion.

"I am going to the great Oz to ask him to give me some," remarked the Scarecrow, "for my head is stuffed with straw."

"And I am going to ask him to give me a heart," said the Woodman.

"And I am going to ask him to send Toto and me back to Kansas," added Dorothy.

4 *heart disease.* This is one of several jokes about heart ailments. Baum had been born with a defective heart and had suffered infrequent attacks throughout his life. Perhaps his own trouble was on his mind when he penned this story.

5 *the Lion.* In a revised version of this chapter, which appeared in *L. Frank Baum's Juvenile Speaker*, the following is added:

"No," declared Dorothy, "that doesn't 'splain it. I guess it's lion nature, because it's human nature. Out West in Kansas, where I live, they always say that the cowboy that roars the loudest and claims he's the baddest man, is sure to be the biggest coward of all."

"Do you think Oz could give me courage?" asked the cowardly Lion.

"Just as easily as he could give me brains," said the Scarecrow.

"Or give me a heart," said the Tin Woodman.

"Or send me back to Kansas," said Dorothy.

"Then, if you don't mind, I'll go with you," said the Lion, "for my life is simply unbearable without a bit of courage."

"You will be very welcome," answered Dorothy, "for you will help to keep away the other wild beasts. It seems to me they must be more cowardly than you are if they allow you to scare them so easily."

"They really are," said the Lion; "but that doesn't make me any braver, and as long as I know myself to be a coward I shall be unhappy."

So once more the little company set off upon the journey, the Lion walking with stately strides at Dorothy's side. Toto did not approve this new comrade at first, for he could not forget how nearly he had been crushed between the Lion's great jaws; but after a time he became more at ease, and presently Toto and the Cowardly Lion had grown to be good friends.

During the rest of that day there was no other adventure to mar the peace of their journey. Once, indeed, the Tin Woodman stepped upon a beetle that was crawling along the road, and killed the poor little thing. This made the Tin Woodman very unhappy, for he was always careful not to hurt any living creature; and as he walked along he wept several tears of sorrow and regret. These tears ran slowly down his face and over the hinges of his jaw, and there they rusted. When Dorothy presently asked him a question the Tin Woodman could not open his mouth, for his jaws were tightly rusted together. He became greatly frightened at this and made many motions to Dorothy to relieve him, but she could not understand. The Lion was also puzzled to know what was wrong. But the Scarecrow seized the oil-can from Dorothy's basket and oiled the Woodman's jaws, so that after a few moments he could talk as well as before.

"This will serve me a les- **6** son," said he, "to look where I step. For if I should kill another bug or beetle I should surely cry again, and crying rusts my jaw so that I cannot speak."

Thereafter he walked

6 *lesson.* This is the first instance in which the Woodman realizes the consequences of a heartless act. From this moment on he will be as kind and loving as if he did in fact have heart.

7 *unkind to anything*. The Tin Woodman's sensibility could easily rival that of an eighteenth-century man. He would agree with the following sentiments of the poet William Cowper (1731–1800):

I would not enter on my list of friends,
Though graced with polished manners
 and fine sense,
Yet wanting sensibility, the man
Who needlessly sets foot upon a worm.

Baum is clearly expressing his own belief that even the lowliest insect has its place in the universe. He does not, however, claim that insects are of equal value or on a level with man. The minister in "The Wonderful Pump" in *American Fairy Tales* explains to a farmer and his wife who have received a great deal of money from the ruler of the insects: "Even bugs which can speak have no consciences and can't tell the difference between right and wrong." But the beetle befriended by the farmer's wife admits: "Bugs value their lives as much as human beings," and, therefore, should be treated with kindness. In "The Mandarin and the Chinaman," also in *American Fairy Tales*, the Chinaman tells the captive butterfly who fears death that that "is the end of everything," that "Butterflies do not have souls and, therefore, cannot live again"; but a butterfly deserves kindness just as any creature. In *The Patchwork Girl of Oz* the Tin Woodman refuses to let a little boy take the wing from a yellow butterfly to use in a magic potion that will free the boy's uncle from an enchantment; the Tin Woodman cannot bear to let even one butterfly suffer.

Another fine example of the cultivation of "sensibility" is the Tin Woodman's crying at the loss of the Wizard's balloon in Chapter 18.

8 *I must be very careful*. Baum is being ironic in suggesting that those with hearts are not as kind as this man of tin.

very carefully, with his eyes on the road, and when he saw a tiny ant toiling by he would step over it, so as not to harm it. The Tin Woodman knew very well he had no heart, and therefore he took great care never to be cruel or unkind to anything.

"You people with hearts," he said, "have something to guide you, and need never do wrong; but I have no
8 heart, and so I must be very careful, When Oz gives me a heart of course I needn't mind so much."

This illustration of the Scarecrow and the Tin Woodman originally appeared on the title page of *The New Wizard of Oz*, issued by Bobbs-Merrill in 1903.

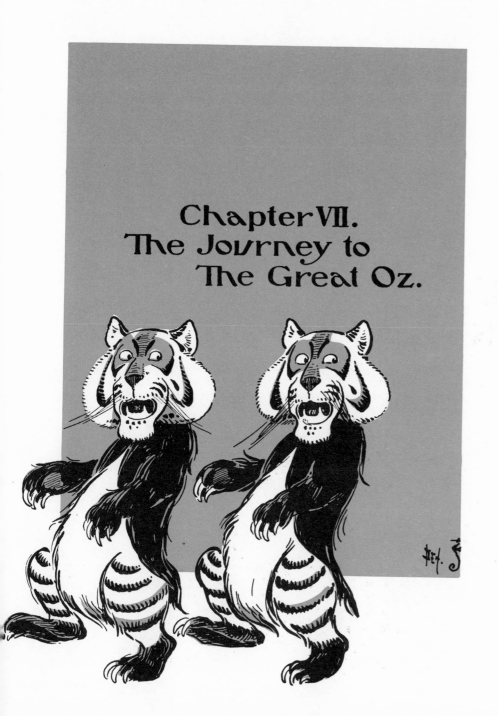

Chapter VII.
The Journey to
The Great Oz.

They WERE obliged to camp out that night under a large tree in the forest, for there were no houses near. The tree made a good, thick covering to protect them from the dew, and the Tin Woodman chopped a great pile of wood with his axe and Dorothy built a splendid fire that warmed her and made her feel less lonely. She and Toto ate the last of their bread, and now she did not know what they would do for breakfast.

"If you wish," said the Lion, "I will go into the forest

1 *I should certainly weep*. Despite his lack of a heart, the Tin Woodman is able to express concern for all living creatures; evidently he had learned from the experience that closed the last chapter. One suspects that the Tin Woodman is here expressing the sentiments of the author. Baum's love of wildlife is reflected in many passages of his stories. In the introduction to *Policeman Bluejay* he writes that "if a little tenderness for the helpless animals and birds is acquired with the amusements, the value of the tales will be doubled."

2 *nuts*. "Oz was free from many of the fads which have attracted much attention in the outside world," writes S. J. Sackett in "The Utopia of Oz." "At one time, however, Dorothy was taken by an idea which was rather close to vegetarianism." He cites a passage in Chapter 2 of *Ozma of Oz* that reflects upon this, but there are also indications of it in the first Oz book. A close look at Dorothy's diet while in Oz reveals no meat of any kind. The views expressed by the Tin Woodman above may also indicate Baum's possible second thoughts on eating animals. Baum himself, however, was not a vegetarian.

3 *burn him up*. In contrast with this, the scarecrow of Nathaniel Hawthorne's short story "Feathertop; A Moralized Legend" remains living only as long as a spark remains burning in the pipe given him by an old witch, his creator. The description of the making of Hawthorne's Feathertop is similar in some details to that of the Scarecrow in Chapter 4. Marius Bewley suggests in "Oz Country" that in reading Baum's books "one becomes aware of allegorical themes and attitudes that put one in mind of Hawthorne's short stories." He suggests a comparison between the creation of Feathertop and Tip's "manufacture" of Jack Pumpkinhead in *The Marvelous Land of Oz*. Mombi the Witch, who brings Jack Pumpkinhead to life, may have derived her name (as my sister Cynthia Hearn has pointed out to me) from the name of the witch responsible for Feathertop, "Mother Rigby."

and kill a deer for you. You can roast it by the fire, since your tastes are so peculiar that you prefer cooked food, and then you will have a very good breakfast."

"Don't! please don't," begged the Tin Woodman.

1 "I should certainly weep if you killed a poor deer, and then my jaws would rust again."

But the Lion went away into the forest and found his own supper, and no one ever knew what it was, for he didn't mention it. And the Scarecrow found a tree full

2 of nuts and filled Dorothy's basket with them, so that she would not be hungry for a long time. She thought this was very kind and thoughtful of the Scarecrow, but she laughed heartily at the awkward way in which the poor creature picked up the nuts. His padded hands were so clumsy and the nuts were so small that he dropped almost as many as he put in the basket. But the Scarecrow did not mind how long it took him to fill the basket, for it enabled him to keep away from the fire, as he feared a spark might get into his straw and

3 burn him up. So he kept a good distance away from the flames, and only came near to cover Dorothy with dry leaves when she lay down to sleep. These kept her very snug and warm and she slept soundly until morning.

When it was daylight the girl bathed her face in a little rippling brook and soon after they all started toward the Emerald City.

This was to be an eventful day for the travellers. They had hardly been walking an hour when they saw before them a great ditch that crossed the road and divided the forest as far as they could see on either side. It was a very wide ditch, and when they crept up to the edge and looked into it they could see it was also very deep, and there were many big, jagged rocks at the bottom. The sides were so steep that none of them could climb down, and for a moment it seemed that their journey must end.

"What shall we do?" asked Dorothy, despairingly.

"I haven't the faintest idea," said the Tin Woodman; and the Lion shook his shaggy mane and looked thoughtful. But the Scarecrow said:

"We cannot fly, that is certain; neither can we climb down into this great ditch. Therefore, if we cannot jump over it, we must stop where we are." **4**

"I think I could jump over it," said the Cowardly Lion, after measuring the distance carefully in his mind.

"Then we are all right," answered the Scarecrow, "for you can carry us all over on your back, one at a time."

"Well, I'll try it," said the Lion. "Who will go first?"

"I will," declared the Scarecrow; "for, if you found that you could not jump over the gulf, Dorothy would be

4 *we must stop where we are.* Note that this is the first instance where the Scarecrow uses his head; his fall into the hole in the road taught him to think before acting.

5 *across the ditch again.* This is the first time the Lion has proven his bravery. Certainly he always had the ability to be courageous.

killed, or the Tin Woodman badly dented on the rocks below. But if I am on your back it will not matter so much, for the fall would not hurt me at all."

"I am terribly afraid of falling, myself," said the Cowardly Lion, "but I suppose there is nothing to do but try it. So get on my back and we will make the attempt."

The Scarecrow sat upon the Lion's back, and the big beast walked to the edge of the gulf and crouched down.

"Why don't you run and jump?" asked the Scarecrow.

"Because that isn't the way we Lions do these things," he replied. Then giving a great spring, he shot through the air and landed safely on the other side. They were all greatly pleased to see how easily he did it, and after the Scarecrow had got down from his back the Lion sprang **5** across the ditch again.

Dorothy thought she would go next; so she took Toto in her arms and climbed on the Lion's back, holding tightly to his mane with one hand. The next moment it seemed as if she was flying through the air; and then, before she had time to think about it, she was safe on the other side. The Lion went back a third time and got the Tin Woodman, and then they all sat down for a few moments to give the beast a chance to rest, for his great leaps had made his breath short, and he panted like a big dog that has been running too long.

They found the forest very thick on this side, and it looked dark and gloomy. After the Lion had rested they started along the road of yellow brick, silently wondering, each in his own mind, if ever they would come to the end of the woods and reach the bright sunshine again. To add to their discomfort, they soon heard strange noises in the depths of the forest, and the Lion whispered to them that it was in this part of the country that the Kalidahs lived.

"What are the Kalidahs?" asked the girl.

"They are monstrous beasts with bodies like bears and heads like tigers," replied the Lion; "and with claws **6** so long and sharp that they could tear me in two as easily as I could kill Toto. I'm terribly afraid of the Kalidahs."

6 *heads like tigers.* The Kalidahs make one more appearance in the Oz books, in Chapter 9 of *The Magic of Oz*. Baum, perhaps in answer to Reilly & Britton's concern that the Kalidahs might have appeared in other books besides *The Wizard of Oz* (which they did not publish), assured them in a letter dated November 2, 1918: "The 'Kalidahs' do not appear in any of my books except the 'Wizard'—and not much about them there." Jack Snow speculates in *Who's Who in Oz* that the name "Kalidah" originates from kaleidoscope, the children's toy that forms fanciful symmetrical patterns from transparent colored shapes and mirrors. Or Baum may have intended the name of these beasts to be an ironic use of the Greek term *kaloseidos* (from which "kaleidoscope" derives) which means "beautiful form." These monsters also suggest the "heads-and-bodies" toy books popular at the turn of the century; the pages of "turn-ups" are cut in sections, so that as one flips through them, fantastical creatures are formed by the exchange of different animal heads and bodies. A recent example of these toy books is Denis Wirth-Millar and Richard Chopping's *Heads, Bodies and Legs*, published by Puffin Books. The Kalidahs are the first example of conglomerate beasts encountered in Baum's stories. Other such creatures of various mythologies are cataloged and described in Jorge Luis Borges's excellent *The Book of Imaginary Beasts* (New York: E. P. Dutton & Co., 1969), which defines an imaginary beast as being "a combination of parts of real beings, and the possibilities of permutation border on the infinite." (See Chapter 11, Note 13.)

"I'm not surprised that you are," returned Dorothy "They must be dreadful beasts."

The Lion was about to reply when suddenly they came to another gulf across the road; but this one was so broad and deep that the Lion knew at once he could not leap across it.

So they sat down to consider what they should do, and after serious thought the Scarecrow said,

"Here is a great tree, standing close to the ditch. If the Tin Woodman can chop it down, so that it will fall to the other side, we can walk across it easily."

"That is a first rate idea," said the Lion. "One would almost suspect you had brains in your head, instead of straw."

The Woodman set to work at once, and so sharp was his axe that the tree was soon chopped nearly through. Then the Lion put his strong front legs against the tree and pushed with all his might, and slowly the big tree tipped and fell with a crash across the ditch, with its top branches on the other side.

They had just started to cross this queer bridge when a sharp growl made them all look up, and to their horror they saw running toward them two great beasts with bodies like bears and heads like tigers.

"They are the Kalidahs!" said the Cowardly Lion, beginning to tremble.

"Quick!" cried the Scarecrow, "let us cross over."

So Dorothy went first, holding Toto in her arms; the Tin Woodman followed, and the Scarecrow came next. The Lion, although he was certainly afraid, turned to face the Kalidahs, and then he gave so loud and terrible a roar that Dorothy screamed and the Scarecrow fell over backwards, while even the fierce beasts stopped short and looked at him in surprise.

But, seeing they were bigger than the Lion, and remembering that there were two of them and only one of him, the Kalidahs again rushed forward, and the Lion crossed over the tree and turned to see what they would do next. Without stopping an instant the fierce beasts also began to cross the tree, and the Lion said to Dorothy,

"We are lost, for they will surely tear us to pieces with their sharp claws. But stand close behind me, and I will fight them as long as I am alive."

"Wait a minute!" called the Scarecrow. He had been thinking what was best to be done, and now he asked the Woodman to chop away the end of the tree that rested on their side of the ditch. The Tin Woodman began to use his axe at once, and, just as the two Kalidahs were nearly across, the tree fell with a crash into the gulf, carrying the ugly, snarling brutes with it, and both were dashed to **pieces** on the sharp rocks at the bottom.

"Well," said the Cowardly Lion, drawing a long breath of relief, "I see we are going to live a little while longer, and I am glad of it, for it must be a very uncomfortable

This illustration of the Tin Woodman first appeared in *Denslow's A B C Book* (1903). It illustrated the following verse:

T is the Tin
that they make into toys,
That walk by themselves
and puzzle small boys.

Peering over Santa Claus's bag in *Denslow's Night Before Christmas* (G. W. Dillingham, 1902) is another of these toy tin woodmen. (See color plate V).

161

thing not to be alive. Those creatures frightened me so badly that my heart is beating yet.

"Ah," said the Tin Woodman, sadly, "I wish I had a heart to beat."

This adventure made the travellers more anxious than ever to get out of the forest, and they walked so fast that Dorothy became tired, and had to ride on the Lion's back. To their great joy the trees became thinner the further they advanced, and in the afternoon they suddenly came upon a broad river, flowing swiftly just before them. On the other side of the water they could see the road of yellow brick running through a beautiful country, with green meadows dotted with bright flowers and all the road bordered with trees hanging full of delicious fruits. They were greatly pleased to see this delightful country before them.

"How shall we cross the river?" asked Dorothy.

"That is easily done," replied the Scarecrow. "The Tin Woodman must build us a raft, so we can float to the other side."

So the Woodman took his axe and began to chop down small trees to make a raft, and while he was busy at this the Scarecrow found on the river bank a tree full of fine fruit. This pleased Dorothy, who had eaten nothing but nuts all day, and she made a hearty meal of the ripe fruit.

But it takes time to make a raft, even when one is as industrious and untiring as the Tin Woodman, and when night came the work was not done. So they found a cozy place under the trees where they slept well until the morning; and Dorothy dreamed of the Emerald City, and of the good Wizard Oz, who would soon send her back to her own home again.

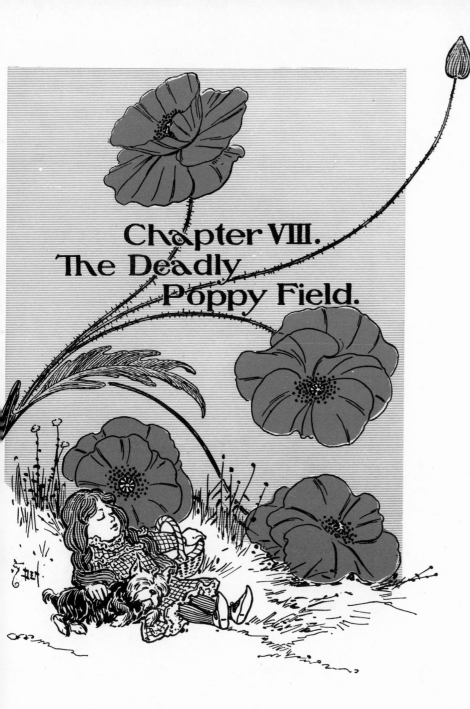

Chapter VIII.
The Deadly Poppy Field.

Our LITTLE PARTY of travellers awakened next morning refreshed and full of hope, and Dorothy breakfasted like a princess off peaches and plums from the trees beside the river. Behind them was the dark forest they had passed safely through, although they had suffered many discouragements; but before them was a lovely, sunny country that seemed to beckon them on to the Emerald City.

To be sure, the broad river now

cut them off from this beautiful land; but the raft was nearly done, and after the Tin Woodman had cut a few more logs and fastened them together with wooden pins, they were ready to start. Dorothy sat down in the middle of the raft and held Toto in her arms. When the Cowardly Lion stepped upon the raft it tipped badly, for he was big and heavy; but the Scarecrow and the Tin Woodman stood upon the other end to steady it, and they had long poles in their hands to push the raft through the water.

They got along quite well at first, but when they reached the middle of the river the swift current swept the raft down stream, farther and farther away from the road of yellow brick; and the water grew so deep that the long poles would not touch the bottom.

"This is bad," said the Tin Woodman, "for if we cannot get to the land we shall be carried into the country of the wicked Witch of the West, and she will enchant us and make us her slaves."

"And then I should get no brains," said the Scarecrow.

"And I should get no courage," said the Cowardly Lion.

"And I should get no heart," said the Tin Woodman.

"And I should never get back to Kansas," said Dorothy.

"We must certainly get to the Emerald City if we can," the Scarecrow continued, and he pushed so hard on his long pole that it stuck fast in the mud at the bottom of the river, and before he could pull it out again, or let go, the raft was swept away and the poor Scarecrow left clinging to the pole in the middle of the river.

"Good bye!" he called after them, and they were very sorry to leave him; indeed, the Tin Woodman began to cry, but fortunately remembered that he might rust, and so dried his tears on Dorothy's apron.

Of course this was a bad thing for the Scarecrow.

"I am now worse off than when I first met Dorothy," he thought. "Then, I was stuck on a pole in a cornfield, where I could make believe scare the crows, at any rate; but surely there is no use for a Scarecrow stuck on a pole in the middle of a river. I am afraid I shall never have any brains, after all!"

Down the stream the raft floated, and the poor Scarecrow was left far behind. Then the Lion said:

"Something must be done to save us. I think I can swim to the shore and pull the raft after

1 *They were all tired*. All except the Tin Woodman who, not being made of flesh and blood, never tires.

me, if you will only hold fast to the tip of my tail."

So he sprang into the water and the Tin Woodman caught fast hold of his tail, when the Lion began to swim with all his might toward the shore. It was hard work, although he was so big; but by and by they were drawn out of the current, and then Dorothy took the Tin Woodman's long pole and helped push the raft to the land.

1 They were all tired out when they reached the shore at last and stepped off upon the pretty green grass, and they also knew that the stream had carried them a long way past the road of yellow brick that led to the Emerald City.

"What shall we do now?" asked the Tin Woodman, as the Lion lay down on the grass to let the sun dry him.

"We must get back to the road, in some way," said Dorothy.

"The best plan will be to walk along the river bank until we come to the road again," remarked the Lion.

So, when they were rested, Dorothy picked up her basket and they started along the grassy bank, back to the road from which the river had carried them. It was a lovely country, with plenty of flowers and fruit trees and sunshine to cheer them, and had they not felt so sorry for the poor Scarecrow they could have been very happy.

They walked along as fast as they could, Dorothy only stopping once to pick a beautiful flower; and after a time the Tin Woodman cried out,

"Look!"

Then they all looked at the river and saw the Scarecrow perched upon his pole in the middle of the water, looking very lonely and sad.

"What can we do to save him?" asked Dorothy.

The Lion and the Woodman both shook their heads, for they did not know. So they sat down upon the bank and gazed wistfully at the Scarecrow until a Stork flew by, **2** which, seeing them, stopped to rest at the water's edge.

"Who are you, and where are you going?" asked the Stork.

"I am Dorothy," answered the girl; "and these are my friends, the Tin Woodman and the Cowardly Lion; and we are going to the Emerald City."

"This is n't the road," said the Stork, as she twisted her long neck and looked sharply at the queer party.

"I know it," returned Dorothy, "but we have lost the Scarecrow, and are wondering how we shall get him again."

"Where is he?" asked the Stork.

"Over there in the river," answered the girl.

"If he wasn't so big and heavy I would get him for you," remarked the Stork.

2 *Stork.* The traditional stork theme appears in examples of Baum's most beautiful and personal writing. One of the seven valleys of Merryland in *Dot and Tot of Merryland* is the Valley of Babies where baby blossoms fall from the sky and unfold their petals, disclosing a sleeping child in each flower; the infants are cared for by the storks until ready to be winged into the world. In the copy of *The Road to Oz* presented to his grandson Joslyn Stanton ("Tik-Tok") Baum to whom the book was dedicated, Baum wrote the following inscription:

Once on a time the Storks brought a baby to Frank Joslyn and Helen Snow Baum, and the baby was so smiling and sweet and merry that he won his way to all hearts—those of strangers as well as those of his doting relatives. For, as the Stork was flying Earthward, it met the Love Fairy, who stopped to kiss the babe; and next the Laughing Fairy tossed it in his arms; and then Glinda the Good blessed it and decreed it happiness. So on the Stork flew with its burden until it passed the Emerald City, where the Shaggy Man took the Love Magnet from the Great Gates and pressed it against the infant's brow.

And so, what do you think will be the fate of this youngster—so favored by the fairies? I know. He will find in life joy and prosperity, and since he has touched the Love Magnet he will win all hearts. It is so decreed.

This inscription first appeared in print in the Christmas 1964 *Baum Bugle*.

3 *"Tol-de-ri-de-oh."* I am grateful to Miss Judith Brownlow, a friend in Crompond, New York, for bringing my attention to the similarity between the Scarecrow's phrase and the last line of the refrain to a seventeenth-century ballad, "A carrion crow sat on an oak" (first published as early as 1796 and frequently included in collections of Mother Goose rhymes):

With a heigh ho! the carrion crow!
Sing tol de rol, de riddle row!

It seems appropriate that the Scarecrow would sing this song.

This illustration first appeared as the end-paper of the 1903 edition issued as *The New Wizard of Oz* by Bobbs-Merrill.

"He isn't heavy a bit," said Dorothy, eagerly, "for he is stuffed with straw; and if you will bring him back to us we shall thank you ever and ever so much."

"Well, I'll try," said the Stork; "but if I find he is too heavy to carry I shall have to drop him in the river again."

So the big bird flew into the air and over the water till she came to where the Scarecrow was perched upon his pole. Then the Stork with her great claws grabbed the Scarecrow by the arm and carried him up into the air and back to the bank, where Dorothy and the Lion and the Tin Woodman and Toto were sitting.

When the Scarecrow found himself among his friends again he was so happy that he hugged them all, even the **3** Lion and Toto; and as they walked along he sang "Tol-de-ri-de-oh!" at every step, he felt so gay.

"I was afraid I should have to stay in the river forever," he said, "but the kind Stork saved me, and if I ever get any brains I shall find the Stork again and do it some kindness in return."

"That's all right," said the Stork, who was flying along beside them. "I always like to help anyone in trouble. But I must go now, for my babies are waiting in the nest for me. I hope you will find the Emerald City and that Oz will help you."

"Thank you," replied Dorothy, and then the kind Stork flew into the air and was soon out of sight.

They walked along listening to the singing of the

bright-colored birds and looking at the lovely flowers which now became so thick that the ground was carpeted with them. There were big yellow and white and blue and purple blossoms, besides great clusters of scarlet poppies, which were so brilliant in color they almost dazzled Dorothy's eyes.

"Aren't they beautiful?" the girl asked, as she breathed in the spicy scent of the flowers.

"I suppose so," answered the Scarecrow. "When I have brains I shall probably like them better."

"If I only had a heart I should love them," added the Tin Woodman.

"I always did like flowers," said the Lion; "they seem so helpless and frail. But there are none in the forest so bright as these."

They now came upon more and more of the big scarlet poppies, and fewer and fewer of the other flowers; and soon they found themselves in the midst of a great meadow of poppies. Now it is well known that when there are many of these flowers together their odor is so powerful that anyone who breathes it falls asleep, and if the sleeper is not carried away from the scent of the flowers he sleeps on and on forever. But Dorothy did not know this, nor could she get away from the bright red flowers that were everywhere about; so presently her eyes grew heavy and she felt she must sit down to rest and to sleep.

4

4 *sleep*. This would seem to be an obvious allusion to opium, but the scarlet poppy has since ancient times been associated with both sleep and death. Because they are the color of blood, poppies are believed to be related to the dead. In Greco-Roman myth they were an offering to the dead as a symbol of sleep. Sleep and the poppy have been associated primarily because of the narcotic produced from the seeds of the "sleep poppy," the scarlet flower grown largely in the Orient. Opium and its derivatives are extracted from the seeds. When taken medicinally in small quantities, the narcotic produces a dreamlike sleep from which the patient awakens refreshed, but there is danger of dependence on the drug. Opium was a major ingredient in the many pain-killers of the nineteenth century and was widely smoked for pleasure in Bohemian circles at the end of the century; not until the close of the first decade of the twentieth century were there laws against international traffic of the drug.

The poppy was also a popular motif in Art Nouveau, which was still flourishing at the time of publication of *The Wizard of Oz*. Neill often portrayed Ozma of Oz with scarlet poppies in her hair, but this was in accordance with the Art Nouveau style rather than a reference to the Deadly Poppy Field.

Deadly flowers frequently appear both in literature and popular myth. The legendary upas tree of Java supposedly drips and breathes poison, killing living creatures for miles due to its poisonous fragrance; another mythical plant is the kerzra flower of Persia, which poisons anyone who dares smell its deadly perfume. Nathaniel Hawthorne may have had one of these legends in mind when he wrote "Rapaccini's Daughter." In this short story the poisonous odor of the flowers in Beatrice's garden causes anyone (except the immune Beatrice) to die. A variant of the death flower reportedly discovered by Captain Arkwright in 1581 on the island of El Banoor in the South Pacific is the species of "Man-Eating Plants" encountered in *The Patchwork Girl of Oz* (p. 118). These great Venus flytraps attack unsuspecting travelers in the Munchkin Country.

But the Tin Woodman would not let her do this.

"We must hurry and get back to the road of yellow brick before dark," he said; and the Scarecrow agreed with him. So they kept walking until Dorothy could stand no longer. Her eyes closed in spite of herself and she forgot where she was and fell among the poppies, fast asleep.

"What shall we do?" asked the Tin Woodman.

"If we leave her here she will die," said the Lion. "The smell of the flowers is killing us all. I myself can scarcely keep my eyes open and the dog is asleep already."

It was true; Toto had fallen down beside his little mistress. But the Scarecrow and the Tin Woodman, not being made of flesh, were not troubled by the scent of the flowers.

"Run fast," said the Scarecrow to the Lion, "and get out of this deadly flower-bed as soon as you can. We will bring the little girl with us, but if you should fall asleep you are too big to be carried."

So the Lion aroused himself and bounded forward as fast as he could go. In a moment he was out of sight.

"Let us make a chair with our hands, and carry her," said the Scarecrow. So they picked up Toto and put the dog in Dorothy's lap, and then they made a chair with their hands for the seat and their arms for the arms and carried the sleeping girl between them through the flowers.

On and on they walked, and it seemed that the great carpet of deadly flowers that surrounded them would never end. They followed the bend of the river, and at last came upon their friend the Lion, lying fast asleep among the poppies. The flowers had been too strong for the huge beast and he had given up, at last, and fallen only a short distance from the end of the poppy-bed, where the sweet grass spread in beautiful green fields before them.

"We can do nothing for him," said the Tin Woodman, sadly; "for he is much too heavy to lift. We must leave him here to sleep on forever, and perhaps he will dream that he has found courage at last."

"I'm sorry," said the Scarecrow; "the Lion was a very good comrade for one so cowardly. But let us go on."

They carried the sleeping girl to a pretty spot beside the river, far enough from the poppy field to prevent her breathing any more of the poison of the flowers, and here they laid her gently on the soft grass and waited for the fresh breeze to waken her.

Chapter IX.
The Queen of the Field Mice.

"WE CANNOT BE FAR from the road of yellow brick, now," remarked the Scarecrow, as he stood beside the girl, "for we have come nearly as far as the river carried us away."

The Tin Woodman was about to reply when he heard a low growl, and turning his head (which worked beautifully on hinges) he saw a strange beast come bounding over the grass towards them. It was, indeed, a great, yellow wildcat, and the Woodman thought it must be chasing something, for its ears were lying close to its head and its mouth was wide open, showing two rows of ugly teeth, while its red eyes glowed like balls of fire. As it came nearer the Tin

1 *pieces.* Although the Oz books are generally free of the many horrors found in the tales of Grimm and Andersen, the occasional references to decapitation have upset several modern critics of juvenile literature who feel a child's book should be free of all violence. Violence, however, has always existed in children's stories. "Bluebeard" and "Little Red Riding Hood" with their emphasis on murder with Freudian undertones appear in the first classic of juvenile literature, Perrault's *Contes de Ma Mère l'Oye (Mother Goose Tales);* these still delight the young to the surprise of educators. Baum must have realized the sentiments of some parents about violence, for in his other tales the mayhem, if not eliminated, is minimized. His publishers' policy was: "No Baum story ever sent a child to bed to troubled dreams." In his article on fairy tales (cited in Chapter 1, Note 1) Baum advocated children's books that were not "marred by murder or cruelties, by terrifying characters, or by maudlin sentimentality, love or marriage." Whatever the effect of the Oz books, children do enjoy some violence and sentimentality in their books.

2 *Queen of all the field-mice.* See "The Wonderful Pump" in *American Fairy Tales,* in which a beetle whose life has been saved by a kindhearted farm woman reveals that he is king of all the insects and will use his powers to return her kindness. David Greene suggests a comparison to the Androcles and the Lion legend whose theme is gratitude.

Woodman saw that running before the beast was a little gray field-mouse, and although he had no heart he knew it was wrong for the wildcat to try to kill such a pretty, harmless creature.

So the Woodman raised his axe, and as the wildcat ran by he gave it a quick blow that cut the beast's head clean off from its body, and it rolled over at his feet in two **1** pieces.

The field-mouse, now that it was freed from its enemy, stopped short; and coming slowly up to the Woodman it said, in a squeaky little voice,

"Oh, thank you! Thank you ever so much for saving my life."

"Don't speak of it, I beg of you," replied the Woodman. "I have no heart, you know, so I am careful to help all those who may need a friend, even if it happens to be only a mouse."

"Only a mouse!" cried the little animal, indignantly; **2** "why, I am a Queen—the Queen of all the field-mice!"

"Oh, indeed," said the Woodman, making a bow.

"Therefore you have done a great deed, as well as a brave one, in saving my life," added the Queen.

At that moment several mice were seen running up as fast as their little legs could carry them, and when they saw their Queen they exclaimed,

"Oh, your Majesty, we thought you would be killed! How did you manage to escape the great Wildcat?" and they all bowed so low to the little Queen that they almost stood upon their heads.

"This funny tin man," she answered, "killed the Wild-cat and saved my life. So hereafter you must all serve him, and obey his slightest wish."

"We will!" cried all the mice, in a shrill chorus. And then they scampered in all directions, for Toto had awakened from his sleep, and seeing all these mice around him he gave one bark of delight and jumped right into the middle of the group. Toto had always loved to chase mice when he lived in Kansas, and he saw no harm in it.

But the Tin Woodman caught the dog in his arms and held him tight, while he called to the mice: "Come back! come back! Toto shall not hurt you."

At this the Queen of the Mice stuck her head out from a clump of grass and asked, in a timid voice,

"Are you sure he will not bite us?"

"I will not let him," said the Woodman; "so do not be afraid."

One by one the mice came creeping back, and Toto did not bark again, although he tried to get out of the Woodman's arms, and would have bitten him had he not known very well he was made of tin. Finally one of the biggest mice spoke.

"Is there anything we can do," it asked, "to repay you for saving the life of our Queen?"

"Nothing that I know of," answered the Woodman; but the Scarecrow, who had been trying to think, but could not because his head was stuffed with straw, said, quickly,

"Oh, yes; you can save our friend, the Cowardly Lion, who is asleep in the poppy bed."

"A Lion!" cried the little Queen; "why, he would eat us all up."

"Oh, no;" declared the Scarecrow; "this Lion is a coward."

"Really?" asked the Mouse.

"He says so himself," answered the Scarecrow, "and he would never hurt anyone who is our friend. If you will help us to save him I promise that he shall treat you all with kindness."

"Very well," said the Queen, "we will trust you. But what shall we do?"

"Are there many of these mice which call you Queen and are willing to obey you?"

"Oh, yes; there are thousands," she replied.

"Then send for them all to come here as soon as possible, and let each one bring a long piece of string."

The Queen turned to the mice that attended her and told them to go at once and get all her people. As soon as they heard her orders they ran away in every direction as fast as possible.

"Now," said the Scarecrow to the Tin Woodman, "you must go to those trees by the river-side and make a truck that will carry the Lion."

So the Woodman went at once to the trees and began to work; and he soon made a truck out of the limbs of trees, from which he chopped away all the leaves and branches. He fastened it together with wooden pegs and made the four wheels out of short pieces of a big tree-trunk. So fast and so well did he work that by the time the mice began to arrive the truck was all ready for them.

They came from all directions, and there were thousands of them: big mice and little mice and middle-sized mice; and each one brought a piece of string in his mouth. It was about this time that Dorothy woke from her long sleep and opened her eyes. She was greatly astonished to find herself lying upon the grass, with thousands of mice standing around and looking at her timidly. But the Scarecrow told her about everything, and turning to the dignified little Mouse, he said,

"Permit me to introduce to you her Majesty, the Queen."

Dorothy nodded gravely and the Queen made a courtesy, after which she became quite friendly with the little girl.

The Scarecrow and the Woodman now began to fasten the mice to the truck, using the strings they had brought. One end of a string was tied around the neck of each mouse and the other end to the truck. Of course the truck was a thousand times bigger than any of the mice who were to draw it; but when all the mice had been harnessed they were able to pull it quite easily. Even the Scarecrow and the Tin Woodman could sit on it, and were drawn swiftly by their queer little horses to the place where the Lion lay asleep.

After a great deal of hard work, for the Lion was heavy, they managed to get him up on the truck. Then

the Queen hurriedly gave her people the order to start, for she feared if the mice stayed among the poppies too long they also would fall asleep.

At first the little creatures, many though they were, could hardly stir the heavily loaded truck; but the Woodman and the Scarecrow both pushed from behind, and they got along better. Soon they rolled the Lion out of the poppy bed to the green fields, where he could breathe the sweet, fresh air again, instead of the poisonous scent of the flowers.

3 *flowers.* The only original device of the 1902 musical that was incorporated into the MGM film is the snowstorm, created by the Good Witch, to break the spell of the Deadly Poppy Field; the snowstorm became a part of the stage play through the suggestion of Baum himself. In the first dramatization Baum retained the Field Mice for the same purposes as in the book.

4 *homes.* In *The Marvelous Land of Oz* the Queen and her subjects make a second appearance in the History of Oz; this time they are not encountered in the Munchkin Country but rather in their village in the Winkie Country.

Dorothy came to meet them and thanked the little mice warmly for saving her companion from death. She had grown so fond of the big Lion she was glad he had been rescued.

Then the mice were unharnessed from the truck and **4** scampered away through the grass to their homes. The Queen of the Mice was the last to leave.

"If ever you need us again," she said, "come out into the field and call, and we shall hear you and come to your assistance. Good bye!"

"Good bye!" they all answered, and away the Queen ran, while Dorothy held Toto tightly lest he should run after her and frighten her.

After this they sat down beside the Lion until he should awaken; and the Scarecrow brought Dorothy some fruit from a tree near by, which she ate for her dinner.

Chapter X.
The Guardian of the Gate.

It WAS SOME TIME BEFORE THE Cowardly Lion awakened, for he had lain among the poppies a long while, breathing in their deadly fragrance; but when he did open his eyes and roll off the truck he was very glad to find himself still alive.

"I ran as fast as I could," he said, sitting down and yawning; "but the flowers were too strong for me. How did you get me out?"

Then they told him of the field-mice, and how they had generously saved him from death; and the Cowardly Lion laughed, and said,

"I have always thought myself very big and terrible; yet such small things as flowers came near to killing me,

1 *mice have saved my life.* This suggests Aesop's fable "The Lion and the Mouse" whose moral is: "The least may help the greatest." Baum has added a corollary: "The weak may destroy the strong."

1 and such small animals as mice have saved my life. How strange it all is! But, comrades, what shall we do now?"

"We must journey on until we find the road of yellow brick again," said Dorothy; "and then we can keep on to the Emerald City."

So, the Lion being fully refreshed, and feeling quite himself again, they all started upon the journey, greatly enjoying the walk through the soft, fresh grass; and it was not long before they reached the road of yellow brick and turned again toward the Emerald City where the great Oz dwelt.

The road was smooth and well paved, now, and the country about was beautiful; so that the travelers rejoiced in leaving the forest far behind, and with it the many dangers they had met in its gloomy shades.

Once more they could see fences built beside the road, but these were painted green, and when they came to a small house, in which a farmer evidently lived, that also was painted green. They passed by several of these houses during the afternoon, and sometimes people came to the doors and looked at them as if they would like to ask questions; but no one came near them nor spoke to them because of the great Lion, of which they were much afraid. The people were all dressed in clothing of a lovely emerald green color and wore peaked hats like those of the Munchkins.

"This must be the Land of Oz," said Dorothy, "and we are surely getting near the Emerald City."

"Yes," answered the Scarecrow; "everything is green here, while in the country of the Munchkins blue was the favorite color. But the people do not seem to be as friendly as the Munchkins and I'm afraid we shall be unable to find a place to pass the night."

"I should like something to eat besides fruit," said the girl, "and I'm sure Toto is nearly starved. Let us stop at the next house and talk to the people."

So, when they came to a good sized farm house, Dorothy walked

2 *Land of Oz.* Dorothy is referring to the green countryside surrounding the Emerald City, the land controlled by Oz the Wizard; she has been in the country known as the Land of Oz ever since her house landed in the Munchkin Country. Baum's ambiguous use of the name "Oz" in *The Wizard of Oz* is studied in depth in Jay Delkin's article "The Meaning of 'Oz' " (*The Baum Bugle*, Autumn 1971).

2

boldly up to the door and knocked. A woman opened it just far enough to look out, and said,

"What do you want, child, and why is that great Lion with you?"

"We wish to pass the night with you, if you will allow us," answered Dorothy; "and the Lion is my friend and comrade, and would not hurt you for the world."

"Is he tame?" asked the woman, opening the door a little wider.

"Oh, yes;" said the girl, "and he is a great coward, too; so that he will be more afraid of you than you are of him."

"Well," said the woman, after thinking it over and taking another peep at the Lion, "if that is the case you may come in, and I will give you some supper and a place to sleep."

So they all entered the house, where there were, besides the woman, two children and a man. The man had hurt his leg, and was lying on the couch in a corner. They seemed greatly surprised to see so strange a company, and while the woman was busy laying the table the man asked,

"Where are you all going?"

"To the Emerald City," said Dorothy, "to see the Great Oz."

"Oh, indeed!" exclaimed the man. "Are you sure that Oz will see you?"

"Why not?" she replied.

"Why, it is said that he never lets any one come into his presence. I have been to the Emerald City many times, and it is a beautiful and wonderful place; but I have never been permitted to see the Great Oz, nor do I know of any living person who has seen him."

"Does he never go out?" asked the Scarecrow.

"Never. He sits day after day in the great throne room of his palace, and even those who wait upon him do not see him face to face."

"What is he like?" asked the girl.

"That is hard to tell," said the man, thoughtfully. "You see, Oz is a great Wizard, and can take on any form he wishes. So that some say he looks like a bird; and some say he looks like an elephant; and some say he looks like a cat. To others he appears as a beautiful fairy, or a brownie, or in any other form that pleases him. But who the real Oz is, when he is in his own form, no living person can tell."

"That is very strange," said Dorothy; "but we must try, in some way, to see him, or we shall have made our journey for nothing."

"Why do you wish to see the terrible Oz?" asked the man.

3 *any other form.* This passage and the appearance of the Wizard as a winged fairy in the subsequent chapter is evidence that Baum does not completely succeed in eliminating the "stereotyped" fairy as he claims in his introduction. In a passage in "The Ryl of the Lilies" (first appearing in several papers on Easter Sunday 1903, later reprinted as "The Ryl" in *Baum's American Fairy Tales*, 1908), Baum admits that both the winged fairy and the brownie have a place in children's books, though not necessarily in his. The fairy creatures in this story are the ryls who are the "servants of nature." When he is mistaken for a fairy, the Ryl indignantly replies: "Do you see any wings growing out of my body? Do you see any golden hair flowing over my shoulders, or any gauzy cobweb skirts floating about my form in graceful folds?" When mistaken for a brownie he replies: "Really now, do I look like one of those impossible, crawly, mischievous elves? Is my body ten times bigger than it should be? Do my legs look like toothpicks and my eyes like saucers?" Baum is describing the contemporary popular conception of the Brownie, created by the American cartoonist Palmer Cox (1840–1924) in his many popular "Brownie" books published in the last quarter of the nineteenth century and into the twentieth. (So popular were Cox's designs that Denslow imitated them with his "Inland Gnomes" created in 1894 for *The Inland Printer* as calling cards and other decorations. See illustration on page 50.) That Baum had Cox in mind is obvious as the Ryl continues his discussion:

"Old nurses prefer to talk about those stupid fairies and hobgoblins, and never mention ryls to the children. And the people who write fairy tales and goose books and brownie stories and such rubbish sit down at writing-tables and invent all sorts of impossible and unbelieveable things" (pp. 176–77). The author of "fairy tales and goose books" is, of course, Baum himself.

A few years later in his article on fairy tales (see Chapter 1, Note 1) Baum broadened his view of the creature known as the fairy:

I once asked a little fellow, a friend of mine, to tell me what a "fairy" is. He replied, quite promptly: "A fairy has wings, and is much like an angel, only smaller." Now that, I believe is the general conception of fairies; and it is a pretty conception, is it not? Yet we know the family of immortals generally termed "fairies" has many branches and includes fays, sprites, elves, nymphs, ryls, knooks, gnomes, brownies and many other subdivisions. There is no blue book or history of the imaginative little creatures to guide us in classifying them, but they all have their uses and peculiar characteristics; as, for example, the little ryls, who carry around paint-pots, with which they color, most brilliantly and artistically, the blossoms of the flowers.

4 *no living person can tell.* This description could be compared to the process by which the unsophisticated understand the unknown. Gods have been described throughout history as having the appearance of various beasts, including the bird, elephant, and cat. The word "Oz" in this passage could be replaced by "God" without making the statements false. The fairy and brownie were also imaginative creations resulting from the attempt to understand what could not be explained by common sense. "Every normal human being is interested in two kinds of worlds: the Primary, everyday world which he knows through his senses and a Secondary world or worlds which he not only can create in his imagination, but also cannot stop himself creating," writes W. H. Auden in the "Afterword" to George Macdonald's *The Light Princess* cited in my introduction. "A person incapable of imagining another than that given him by his senses is subhuman, and a person who identifies his imaginary world with the world of sensory fact has become insane." The fairy tale was created to fulfill the need to express this secondary world, whether spiritual or purely imaginative.

5 *to keep it from running over.* In Chapter 16, however, the Wizard stores his "courage" in green bottles.

6 *could not speak.* Gardner writes in Note 11 of *The Wizard of Oz and Who He Was:* "In *Tik-Tok of Oz* (p. 268) we discover that Toto was capable of speaking the moment he entered Oz. He just didn't feel like it."

"I want him to give me some brains," said the Scarecrow, eagerly.

"Oh, Oz could do that easily enough," declared the man. "He has more brains than he needs."

"And I want him to give me a heart," said the Tin Woodman.

"That will not trouble him," continued the man, "for Oz has a large collection of hearts, of all sizes and shapes."

"And I want him to give me courage," said the Cowardly Lion.

"Oz keeps a great pot of courage in his throne room," said the man, "which he has covered with a golden plate **5** to keep it from running over. He will be glad to give you some."

"And I want him to send me back to Kansas," said Dorothy.

"Where is Kansas?" asked the man, in surprise.

"I don't know," replied Dorothy, sorrowfully; "but it is my home, and I'm sure it's somewhere."

"Very likely. Well, Oz can do anything; so I suppose he will find Kansas for you. But first you must get to see him, and that will be a hard task; for the great Wizard does not like to see anyone, and he usually has his own way. But what do you want?" he continued, speaking to Toto. Toto only wagged his tail; for, strange to say, he **6** could not speak.

The woman now called to them that supper was ready

o they gathered around the table and Dorothy ate some delicious porridge and a dish of scrambled eggs and a plate of nice white bread, and enjoyed her meal. The Lion ate some of the porridge, but did not care for it, saying it was made from oats and oats were food for horses, not for **7** lions. The Scarecrow and the Tin Woodman ate nothing at all. Toto ate a little of everything, and was glad to get a good supper again.

The woman now gave Dorothy a bed to sleep in, and Toto lay down beside her, while the Lion guarded the door of her room so she might not be disturbed. The Scarecrow and the Tin Woodman stood up in a corner and kept quiet all night, although of course they could not sleep.

The next morning, as soon as the sun was up, they started on their way, and soon saw a beautiful green glow in the sky just before them.

"That must be the Emerald City," said Dorothy.

As they walked on, the green glow became brighter and brighter, and it seemed that at last they were nearing the end of their travels. Yet it was afternoon before they came to the great wall that surrounded the City. It was high, and thick, and of a bright green color.

In front of them, and at the end of the road of yellow brick, was a big gate, all studded with emeralds that glittered so in the sun that even the painted eyes of the Scarecrow were dazzled by their brilliancy. **8**

There was a bell beside the gate, and Dorothy pushed

7 *food for horses.* I succumb to the temptation to quote Dr. Johnson's entry under "Oats" in his *Dictionary of the English Language:* "A grain, which in England is generally given to horses, but in Scotland supports the people."

8 *dazzled by their brilliancy.* With economy of language Baum has created the mystery and magnificence of a fairy city. Of the many descriptions of such mythic capitals in literature, that of Camelot in Tennyson's "Gareth and Lynette" in *The Idylls of the King* could as easily refer to the Emerald City of Oz as to the fairy city of King Arthur:

The damp hill-slopes were quicken'd into
    green,
And the live green had kindl'd into
    flowers,
For it was past the time of Easterday.
So, when their feet were planted on the
    plain,
That broaden'd toward the base of Came-
    lot,
Far off they saw the silver-misty morn
Rolling her smoke about the Royal mount,
That rose between the forest and the
    field.
At times the summit of the high city
    flash'd;
At times the spires and turrets half-way
    down
Prick'd thro' the mist; at times the great
    gate shone
Only, that open'd on the field below. . . .

the button and heard a silvery tinkle sound within. Then the big gate swung slowly open, and they all passed through and found themselves in a high arched room, the walls of which glistened with countless emeralds.

Before them stood a little man about the same size as the Munchkins. He was clothed all in green, from his head to his feet, and even his skin was of a greenish tint. At his side was a large green box.

When he saw Dorothy and her companions the man asked,

"What do you wish in the Emerald City?"

"We came here to see the Great Oz," said Dorothy.

The man was so surprised at this answer that he sat down to think it over.

"It has been many years since anyone asked me to see Oz," he said, shaking his head in perplexity. "He is powerful and terrible, and if you come on an idle or foolish errand to bother the wise reflections of the Great Wizard, he might be angry and destroy you all in an instant."

"But it is not a foolish errand, nor an idle one," replied the Scarecrow; "it is important. And we have been told that Oz is a good Wizard."

"So he is," said the green man; "and he rules the Emerald City wisely and well. But to those who are not honest, or who approach him from curiosity, he is most terrible, and few have ever dared ask to see his face. I am the Guardian of the Gates, and since you demand to see the Great Oz I must take you to his palace. But first you must put on the spectacles."

"Why?" asked Dorothy.

"Because if you did not wear spectacles the brightness and glory of the Emerald City would blind you. Even those who live in the City must wear spectacles night and day. They are all locked on, for Oz so ordered it when the City was first built, and I have the only key that will unlock them."

He opened the big box, and Dorothy saw that it was filled with spectacles of every size and shape. All of them had green glasses in them. The Guardian of the gates found a pair that would just fit Dorothy and put them over her eyes. There were

two golden bands fastened to them that passed around the back of her head, where they were locked together by a little key that was at the end of a chain the Guardian of the Gates wore around his neck. When they were on, Dorothy could not take them off had she wished, but of course she did not want to be blinded by the glare of the Emerald City, so she said nothing.

Then the green man fitted spectacles for the Scarecrow and the Tin Woodman and the Lion, and even on little Toto; and all were locked fast with the key.

Then the Guardian of the Gates put on his own glasses and told them he was ready to show them to the palace. Taking a big golden key from a peg on the wall he opened another gate, and they all followed him through the portal into the streets of the Emerald City.

Chapter XI.
The Wonderful
Emerald City of OZ.

Even

WITH EYES protected by the green spectacles Dorothy and her friends were at first dazzled by the brilliancy of the wonderful City. The streets were lined with beautiful houses all built of green marble and studded everywhere with sparkling emeralds. They walked over a pavement of the **1** same green marble, and where the blocks were joined together were rows of emeralds, set closely, and glittering in the brightness of the sun. The window panes were of green glass; even the sky above the City had a green tint, and the rays of the sun were green.

There were many people, men, women and children, **2**

1 *sparkling emeralds.* An indication of the size of the capital city of Oz appears in *The Emerald City of Oz* (p. 29). The number of buildings is 9,654; the population of the city is 57,318 citizens.

2 *many people.* According to *The Magic of Oz* (p. 54), the name of a citizen of the Emerald City is "Ozmie," perhaps a misprint of "Ozmite," the generally accepted name. "Ozite" is the name of a native of the Land of Oz (e.g., in *Dorothy and the Wizard in Oz*, p. 224, and in *The Emerald City of Oz*, p. 30).

3 *green pennies.* These are probably copper pennies, which often turn green. Currency, as a part of the economy of Oz, is known only in the earliest of Baum's Oz stories. As the series progresses, money is abolished by decree of Princess Ozma. In *The Road to Oz* (1909) (pp. 164–165), the Tin Woodman explains why:

Money in Oz! . . . Did you suppose we are so vulgar as to use money here? If we used money to buy things with, instead of love and kindness, the desires to please one another, then we should be no better off than the rest of the world. . . . Fortunately money is not known in the Land of Oz at all. We have no rich, and no poor; for what one wishes the others all try to give him in order to make him happy, and no one in all Oz cares to have more than he can use.

Baum may have decided to abolish money in Oz in the later books in response to the increasing financial pressures that resulted in his bankruptcy, a year after he wrote the above passage.

Prior to the success of *The Wizard of Oz* Baum had seen lean years. In his autobiography (first published in *The Baum Bugle*, Christmas 1970 and Spring 1971) the author's son Robert gives the following account of the early days in Chicago just before the success of Baum's children's books:

Money wasn't very plentiful and a penny went a long way. When I would ask father or mother for money, which was not very often, I would get a penny and go over to the candy store or grocery store to see what I could buy. Standing in front of the case I would ask "How many of these for a penny?" And it was surprising what a penny would buy. Not very good candy probably, but sweet and satisfying to the taste. . . . Red letter days were when father would come home from a sales trip and we would ask for a penny and he would magnanimously hand out a nickel. And all the things a nickel would buy, quite enough to upset our stomachs for the next few days.

4 *animals of any kind.* But, as revealed in the last paragraph of this chapter, the Emerald City is not totally without livestock: the final paragraph refers to a green hen and thus contradicts *Ozma of Oz*, in which Billina the chicken is said to be the first hen in Oz.

5 *a soldier.* In *The Marvelous Land of Oz* (p. 94), the official title of the Soldier with the Green Whiskers is disclosed as "the Royal Army of Oz," but not until the third Oz book, *Ozma of Oz* (p. 261), is his name, Omby Amby, given. In Ruth Plumly Thompson's *Ozoplaning with the Wizard of Oz* (1939) he is renamed "Wantowin Battles."

walking about, and these were all dressed in green clothes and had greenish skins. They looked at Dorothy and her strangely assorted company with wondering eyes, and the children all ran away and hid behind their mothers when they saw the Lion; but no one spoke to them. Many shops stood in the street, and Dorothy saw that everything in them was green. Green candy and green pop-corn were offered for sale, as well as green shoes, green hats and green clothes of all sorts. At one place a man was selling green lemonade, and when the children bought it Dorothy

3 could see that they paid for it with green pennies.

4 There seemed to be no horses nor animals of any kind; the men carried things around in little green carts, which they pushed before them. Everyone seemed happy and contented and prosperous.

The Guardian of the Gates led them through the streets until they came to a big building, exactly in the middle of the City, which was the Palace of Oz, the Great

5 Wizard. There was a soldier before the door, dressed in a green uniform and wearing a long green beard.

"Here are strangers," said the Guardian of the Gates to him, "and they demand to see the Great Oz."

"Step inside," answered the soldier, "and I will carry your message to him."

So they passed through the Palace gates and were led into a big room with a green carpet and lovely green furniture set with emeralds. The soldier made them all wipe their feet upon a green mat before entering this room, and when they were seated he said, politely,

"Please make yourselves comfortable while I go to the door of the Throne Room and tell Oz you are here."

They had to wait a long time before the soldier returned. When, at last, he came back, Dorothy asked,

"Have you seen Oz?"

"Oh, no;" returned the soldier; "I have never seen him. But I spoke to him as he sat behind his screen, and **6** gave him your message. He says he will grant you an audience, if you so desire; but each one of you must enter his presence alone, and he will admit but one each day. Therefore, as you must remain in the Palace for several days, I will have you shown to rooms where you may rest in comfort after your journey."

"Thank you," replied the girl; "that is very kind of Oz."

The soldier now blew upon a green whistle, and at once a young girl, dressed **7** in a pretty green silk gown, entered the

6 *screen*. This screen becomes an important factor in the events of Chapter 15. This is one of several details in this and the next chapter that foreshadow the unmasking of Oz, the Terrible.

7 *a young girl*. Her name is Jellia Jamb ("Jelly or jam?") in *The Marvelous Land of Oz*, p. 77.

8 *queer green pictures*. Could these green books be copies of *The Wonderful Wizard of Oz*? The first edition was bound in green cloth with the text illustrations of the Emerald City episodes printed in green. One is reminded of a device employed in at least two examples of the "nouveau roman." At the close of Michel Butor's *La Modification* the narrator decides to write the book the reader has just finished; in this way Butor's novel is related to Proust's *A la Recherche du Temps Perdu*. Bruce Morissette suggests in his introductory essay to the English translation of Alain Robbe-Grillet's *Dans le Labyrinthe* that the scattered papers left on the narrator's table at the close of the book represent *Dans le Labyrinthe* itself.

room. She had lovely green hair and green eyes, and she bowed low before Dorothy as she said,

"Follow me and I will show you your room."

So Dorothy said good-bye to all her friends except Toto, and taking the dog in her arms followed the green girl through seven passages and up three flights of stairs until they came to a room at the front of the Palace. It was the sweetest little room in the world, with a soft, comfortable bed that had sheets of green silk and a green velvet counterpane. There was a tiny fountain in the middle of the room, that shot a spray of green perfume into the air, to fall back into a beautifully carved green marble basin. Beautiful green flowers stood in the windows, and there was a shelf with a row of little green books. When Dorothy had time to open these books she found them full **8** of queer green pictures that made her laugh, they were so funny.

In a wardrobe were many green dresses, made of silk and satin and velvet; and all of them fitted Dorothy exactly.

"Make yourself perfectly at home," said the green girl, "and if you wish for anything ring the bell. Oz will send for you to-morrow morning."

She left Dorothy alone and went back to the others. These she also led to rooms, and each one of them found himself lodged in a very pleasant part of the Palace. Of course this politeness was wasted on the Scarecrow; for

when he found himself alone in his room he stood stupidly
in one spot, just within the doorway, to wait till morning.
It would not rest him to lie down, and he could not close
his eyes; so he remained all night staring at a little spider
which was weaving its web in a corner of the room, just as
if it were not one of the most wonderful rooms in the
world. The Tin Woodman lay down on his bed from
force of habit, for he remembered when he was made of
flesh; but not being able to sleep he passed the night
moving his joints up and down to make sure they kept in
good working order. The Lion would have preferred a
bed of dried leaves in the forest, and did not like being
shut up in a room; but he had too much sense to let this
worry him, so he sprang upon the bed and rolled himself
up like a cat and purred himself asleep in a minute.

The next morning, after breakfast, the green maiden
came to fetch Dorothy, and she dressed her in one of the
prettiest gowns—made of green brocaded satin. Dorothy
put on a green silk apron and tied a green ribbon around Toto's neck, and they started for the
Throne Room of the Great Oz.

First they came to a great hall in which
were many ladies and gentlemen of the court,
all dressed in rich costumes.
These people had nothing
to do but talk to each other,
but they always came to

9 *never permitted to see Oz.* Bewley writes in the revised version of "Oz Country" in his *Masks and Mirrors:* "Baum's deep affection for monarchy and the trappings of royalty that run through all the books reflect a facet of sensibility shared by many nineteenth century Americans." This passage also expresses certain prejudices Americans had against European royalty.

10 *ask to see him.* David Greene has suggested in a letter to me that there are biblical overtones in this chapter. He mentions a comparison to the meeting between Moses and God at the burning bush in the book of Exodus; Moses is forced to refrain from looking upon the face of God. The Wizard has clearly encouraged his people to think of him as a god. If the Wizard acts as God, the irony of the discovery of Oz, the Terrible, would seem to be especially bitter, almost existential; but it is unlikely that Baum was thinking in these terms. The Wizard is only following the superstitions and rituals expected of a god.

This particular passage is also ironic. The courtiers are curious to know if Dorothy will actually learn the true nature of Oz. She, of course, naïvely concludes that Oz will reveal himself to her at the first meeting. The soldier takes her phrase literally and infers that whether or not she gazes upon "the face of Oz, the Terrible" the Wizard will be able to look upon her. The reason that Oz refuses to let his people have an audience with him becomes evident upon the discovery of Oz, the Terrible, in Chapter 15.

11 *light.* A similar light appears in the dwelling of another wizard in *A New Wonderland* (p. 134), but here it is clearly stated that it is an electric light. The great light that illuminates the Throne Room may also be considered electric. Many of the wonders of fairyland in Baum's stories are electrical. In *The Sea Fairies* (p. 92) the palaces of the mermaids are lit by electrical jellyfish; one of the mermaids explains to the mortal visitors that "we use electric lights in our palaces, and have done so for thousands of years—long before the earth people knew of electric lights." In Chapter 12 of *Tik-Tok of Oz,* of all the lovely maidens in the palace of the Queen of Light, Electra is "the most beautiful"; it seems that "both Sunlight and Daylight regarded Electra with envy and were a little jealous of her."

Baum's one attempt at scientific fantasy, *The Master Key,* in which the Demon of Electricity is accidentally summoned, was published the year following the success of *The Wonderful Wizard of Oz.* The hero of the "electrical fairy tale" is a boy named Rob inspired by Baum's son Robert Stanton. In his autobiography Rob Baum describes his interest in electricity:

> I was interested in anything of a mechanical nature and up in the large attic . . . I had a workshop in which I made many things . . . but my special pet projects I worked out in the back of the house on the second floor. My parents really must have been quite lenient with me, because I bored holes all through the house and installed wires to operate my

9 wait outside the Throne Room every morning, although they were never permitted to see Oz. As Dorothy entered they looked at her curiously, and one of them whispered,

"Are you really going to look upon the face of Oz the Terrible?"

"Of course," answered the girl, "if he will see me."

"Oh, he will see you," said the soldier who had taken her message to the Wizard, "although he does not like to **10** have people ask to see him. Indeed, at first he was angry, and said I should send you back where you came from. Then he asked me what you looked like, and when I mentioned your silver shoes he was very much interested. At last I told him about the mark upon your forehead, and he decided he would admit you to his presence."

Just then a bell rang, and the green girl said to Dorothy,

"That is the signal. You must go into the Throne Room alone."

She opened a little door and Dorothy walked boldly through and found herself in a wonderful place. It was a big, round room with a high arched roof, and the walls and ceiling and floor were covered with large emeralds set closely together. In the center of the roof was a great **11** light, as bright as the sun, which made the emeralds sparkle in a wonderful manner.

But what interested Dorothy most was the big throne of green marble that stood in the middle of the room. It was shaped like a chair and sparkled with gems, as did everything else. In the center of the chair was an enormous Head, without body to support it or any arms or legs whatever. There was no hair upon this head, but it had eyes and nose and mouth, and was bigger than the head of the biggest giant.

As Dorothy gazed upon this in wonder and fear the eyes turned slowly and looked at her sharply and steadily. Then the mouth moved, and Dorothy heard a voice say:

"I am Oz, the Great and Terrible. Who are you, and **12** why do you seek me?"

It was not such an awful voice as she had expected to come from the big Head; so she took courage and answered,

"I am Dorothy, the Small and Meek. I have come to you for help."

The eyes looked at her thoughtfully for a full minute. Then said the voice:

"Where did you get the silver shoes?"

"I got them from the wicked Witch of the East, when my house fell on her and killed her," she replied.

"Where did you get the mark upon your forehead?" continued the voice.

"That is where the good Witch of the North kissed me when she bade me good-bye and sent me to you," said the girl.

Again the eyes looked at her sharply, and they saw she was telling the truth. Then Oz asked,

various gadgets. For instance, when I wanted privacy in my room, I got it by the very simple expedient of installing a wire from a spark coil and battery to the inside handle of the door. When anyone from the outside took hold of the handle and turned it, contact was made and caused him to change his mind about entering.

I also rigged up an apparatus which I attached to our gas lights so that by pushing a button the gas was turned on, and an electric spark ignited it. As I was still going to Lewis [Institute], and we now lived much further away, I had to leave home early in the morning, so I rigged up an annunciator drop in the kitchen to simplify matters for me. As soon as I got out of bed, I pushed a button in my room and the annunciator came down with a sign saying, "start breakfast." This was the signal to our cook and, by the time I got down, my breakfast was ready.

In a letter to his brother, dated April 8, 1900, Baum wrote: "Rob fills the house with electrical batteries and such truck and we are prepared to hear a bell ring whenever we open a door or step on a stair." Baum's interest in mechanical inventions matched his son's, and he had faith in the future of electricity, which was just coming of age at the end of the nineteenth century. One may conclude that it is Baum himself who speaks through Mr. Joslyn of *The Master Key:* "Electricity is destined to become the motive power of the world. The future advance of civilization will be by electrical lines" (pp. 2–3).

12 *Oz, the Great and Terrible.* Compare this to the definition of the word "Oz" given in Chapter 2, Note 12. This title also suggests "the most evil character in all the Oz books" (as Bewley notes, in agreement with Nye, in "Oz Country"), "The First and Foremost" ruler of the Phanfasms in *The Emerald City of Oz.* Bewley continues: "That magnificently sinister title sums up the ultimate meaning of Oz history. The aggrandizement of the individual and private self at the expense of others is the root of all evil." These words are equally true of Oz, the Great and Terrible, now before Dorothy, the Small and Meek.

"What do you wish me to do?"

"Send me back to Kansas, where my Aunt Em and Uncle Henry are," she answered, earnestly. "I don't like your country, although it is so beautiful. And I am sure Aunt Em will be dreadfully worried over my being away so long."

The eyes winked three times, and then they turned up to the ceiling and down to the floor and rolled around so queerly that they seemed to see every part of the room. And at last they looked at Dorothy again.

"Why should I do this for you?" asked Oz.

"Because you are strong and I am weak; because you are a Great Wizard and I am only a helpless little girl," she answered.

"But you were strong enough to kill the wicked Witch of the East," said Oz.

"That just happened," returned Dorothy, simply; "I could not help it."

"Well," said the Head, "I will give you my answer. You have no right to expect me to send you back to Kansas unless you do something for me in return. In this country everyone must pay for everything he gets. If you wish me to use my magic power to send you home again you must do something for me first. Help me and I will help you."

"What must I do?" asked the girl.

"Kill the wicked Witch of the West," answered Oz.

"But I cannot!" exclaimed Dorothy, greatly surprised.

"You killed the Witch of the East and you wear the silver shoes, which bear a powerful charm. There is now but one Wicked Witch left in all this land, and when you can tell me she is dead I will send you back to Kansas—but not before."

The little girl began to weep, she was so much disappointed; and the eyes winked again and looked upon her anxiously, as if the Great Oz felt that she could help him if she would.

"I never killed anything, willingly," she sobbed; "and even if I wanted to, how could I kill the Wicked Witch? If you, who are Great and Terrible, cannot kill her yourself, how do you expect me to do it?"

"I do not know," said the Head; "but that is my answer, and until the Wicked Witch dies you will not see your Uncle and Aunt again. Remember that the Witch is Wicked—tremendously Wicked —and ought to be killed. Now go, and do not ask to see me again until you have done your task."

Sorrowfully Dorothy left the Throne Room and went back

13 *wings.* This is the only appearance of a winged fairy in Baum's Royal History of Oz. Note that Denslow's lovely lady does not wear wings.

where the Lion and the Scarecrow and the Tin Woodman were waiting to hear what Oz had said to her.

"There is no hope for me," she said, sadly, "for Oz will not send me home until I have killed the Wicked Witch of the West; and that I can never do."

Her friends were sorry, but could do nothing to help her; so she went to her own room and lay down on the bed and cried herself to sleep.

The next morning the soldier with the green whiskers came to the Scarecrow and said,

"Come with me, for Oz has sent for you."

So the Scarecrow followed him and was admitted into the great Throne Room, where he saw, sitting in the emerald throne, a most lovely lady. She was dressed in green silk gauze and wore upon her flowing green locks a crown of jewels. Growing from her shoulders were

13 wings, gorgeous in color and so light that they fluttered if the slightest breath of air reached them.

When the Scarecrow had bowed, as prettily as his straw stuffing would let him, before this beautiful creature, she looked upon him sweetly, and said,

"I am Oz, the Great and Terrible. Who are you, and why do you seek me?"

Now the Scarecrow, who had expected to see the great Head Dorothy had told him of, was much astonished; but he answered her bravely.

"I am only a Scarecrow, stuffed with straw. Therefore I have no brains, and I come to you praying that you will put brains in my head instead of straw, so that I may become as much a man as any other in your dominions."

"Why should I do this for you?" asked the lady.

"Because you are wise and powerful, and no one else can help me," answered the Scarecrow.

"I never grant favors without some return," said Oz; "but this much I will promise. If you will kill for me the Wicked Witch of the West I will bestow upon you a great many brains, and such good brains that you will be the wisest man in all the Land of Oz."

"I thought you asked Dorothy to kill the Witch," said the Scarecrow, in surprise.

"So I did. I don't care who kills her. But until she is dead I will not grant your wish. Now go, and do not seek me again until you have earned the brains you so greatly desire."

The Scarecrow went sorrowfully back to his friends and told them what Oz had said; and Dorothy was surprised to find that the great Wizard was not a Head, as she had seen him, but a lovely lady.

"All the same," said the Scarecrow, "she needs a heart as much as the Tin Woodman."

On the next morning the soldier with the green whiskers came to the Tin Woodman and said,

14 *a most terrible Beast.* This conglomerate beast is another of several to appear in Baum's Oz stories. They may either be the fantastic transformation of magicians, as the Li-Mon-Eags of *The Magic of Oz*, or exist naturally, as the Hippo-Gy-Raf of *The Tin Woodman of Oz*.

In Baum's first dramatic version of *The Wizard of Oz* the Wizard appears not as the horrible beast here described but as "a huge crab-like beast." His original conception of the monster may have been thought to be too terrifying or impractical for the stage. This script was never produced and a second play was prepared on request of the stage manager, Julian Mitchell. Neither the crablike nor the original beast appeared in the produced play.

Denslow did prepare a pencil sketch of the Wizard as the "terrible Beast." Baum may well have found it too terrifying for his children's book, for the drawing was abandoned. Over this pencil sketch Denslow drew the black-and-white original of color plate XXXII. The pencil sketch can still be faintly seen on the original in the Henry Goldsmith collection of the New York Public Library.

"Oz has sent for you.   Follow me."

So the Tin Woodman followed him and came to the great Throne Room. He did not know whether he would find Oz a lovely lady or a Head, but he hoped it would be the lovely lady. "For," he said to himself, "if it is the Head, I am sure I shall not be given a heart, since a head has no heart of its own and therefore cannot feel for me. But if it is the lovely lady I shall beg hard for a heart, for all ladies are themselves said to be kindly hearted."

But when the Woodman entered the great Throne Room he saw neither the Head nor the Lady, for Oz had **14** taken the shape of a most terrible Beast. It was nearly as big as an elephant, and the green throne seemed hardly strong enough to hold its weight. The Beast had a head like that of a rhinoceros, only there were five eyes in its face. There were five long arms growing out of its body and it also had five long, slim legs. Thick, woolly hair covered every part of it, and a more dreadful looking monster could not be imagined. It was fortunate the Tin Woodman had no heart at that moment, for it would have beat loud and fast from terror. But being only tin, the Woodman was not at all afraid, although he was much disappointed.

"I am Oz, the Great and Terrible," spake the Beast, in a voice that was one great roar. "Who are you, and why do you seek me?"

"I am a Woodman, and made of tin. Therefore I have no heart, and cannot love. I pray you to give me a heart that I may be as other men are."

"Why should I do this?" demanded the Beast.

"Because I ask it, and you alone can grant my request," answered the Woodman.

Oz gave a low growl at this, but said, gruffly,

"If you indeed desire a heart, you must earn it."

"How?" asked the Woodman.

"Help Dorothy to kill the Wicked Witch of the West," replied the Beast. "When the Witch is dead, come to me, and I will then give you the biggest and kindest and most loving heart in all the Land of Oz."   **15**

So the Tin Woodman was forced to return sorrowfully to his friends and tell them of the terrible Beast he had seen. They all wondered greatly at the many forms the great Wizard could take upon himself, and the Lion said,

"If he is a beast when I go to see him, I shall roar my loudest, and so frighten him that he will grant all I ask. And if he is the lovely lady, I shall pretend to spring upon her, and so compel her to do my bidding. And if he is the great Head, he will be at my mercy; for I will roll this head all about the room until he promises to give us what we desire. So be of good cheer my friends, for all will yet be well."

16

15 *loving heart in all the Land of Oz.* "The Wizard failed to keep this promise," explains Gardner in Note 14 of *The Wizard of Oz and Who He Was.* "We learn in *The Tin Woodman of Oz* (p. 31) that it was a 'kind' but not a 'loving' heart." This is indicated in Chapter 16 when the Tin Woodman receives his heart and asks, "But is it a kind heart?" and the Wizard replies, "Oh, very!"

16 *give us what we desire.* The Lion is expressing the irony of the sequences each of Dorothy's friends follows in their audiences with the great Oz. If each had gone before the other, he might have had a better chance to convince the Wizard of his individual wish. The Scarecrow might have appealed to the intellect of the huge Head for a brain (surely this form's only quality is that of intellect), the Tin Woodman to the kind heart of the lovely lady, and the Lion to the strength of the Beast. Each might have proven to that particular form of the Wizard that he was capable of using the gift so desired, but inevitably each was faced with a form he was unable to comprehend.

17 *a Ball of Fire*. Baum's choice of four particular transformations of Oz, the Great and Terrible, may not have been completely arbitrary. These forms may be explained in terms of the primate factor of "the Great Chain of Being" world view, which has its origins in ancient times and developed in the occult sciences of the Middle Ages to become part of the English world picture from the Elizabethan to the Romantic Age. The world is a great chain, stretching from God to the least of inanimate things. The chain is divided into classes, and each class has a primate. The Wizard Oz, with his magic and political supremacy, is at the apex of the Ozian society and has the ability to take the forms of primates in other classes. Among the elements, fire holds the highest place; among the members of the body, the head is greatest.

In Robert Kirk's *Secret Commonwealth* (1691) the fairy is placed in the "Middle Nature between Man and Angel." The fairy is thus the most perfect of humanlike beings of the earthly existence. The winged fairy is obviously the "sylph" of Paracelsian cosmology (see my introduction). This, the elemental of Air, is occasionally referred to as the highest form of earthly spirit, the primate of elementals.

Baum's Beast may refer to the "Great Beast" of *The Book of Revelation*. This monster of seven heads and seven horns was associated in the early Church with the Roman Empire, in the early nineteenth century with Napoleon Bonaparte. Thomas Macaulay said that the House of Commons in the Victorian Age must surely be the

Beast. Obviously, the term was associated with any contemporary terrifying power.

The Beast may also be seen as the animal manifestation of the primate. Baum was well aware of the occult world picture. He was associated with several spiritualist groups such as the Theosophists and the clairvoyants. Alchemy, astronomy, and other occult sciences saw the world as a chain of progression from inanimate things to God. The remains of this once widely accepted picture of the universe still exist in poetic metaphor. (For additional information on these theories one may consult E. M. W. Tillyard's *The Elizabethan World Picture*, London: Chatto & Williams, 1956, and Arthur O. Lovejoy's *The Great Chain of Being*, Cambridge, Massachusetts: Harvard University Press, 1936.)

18 *low, quiet voice*. The description of this voice betrays the true nature of Oz the Wizard when it is discovered in Chapter 15.

The next morning the soldier with the green whiskers led the Lion to the great Throne Room and bade him enter the presence of Oz.

The Lion at once passed through the door, and glancing around saw, to his surprise, that before the throne was **17** a Ball of Fire, so fierce and glowing he could scarcely bear to gaze upon it. His first thought was that Oz had by accident caught on fire and was burning up; but, when he tried to go nearer, the heat was so intense that it singed his whiskers, and he crept back tremblingly to a spot nearer the door.

18 Then a low, quiet voice came from the Ball of Fire, and these were the words it spoke:

"I am Oz, the Great and Terrible. Who are you, and why do you seek me?" And the Lion answered,

"I am a Cowardly Lion, afraid of everything. I come to you to beg that you give me courage, so that in reality I may become the King of Beasts, as men call me."

"Why should I give you courage?" demanded Oz.

"Because of all Wizards you are the greatest, and alone have power to grant my request," answered the Lion.

The Ball of Fire burned fiercely for a time, and the voice said,

"Bring me proof that the Wicked Witch is dead, and that moment I will give you courage. But so long as the Witch lives you must remain a coward."

The Lion was angry at this speech, but could say nothing in reply, and while he stood silently gazing at the Ball of Fire it became so furiously hot that he turned tail and rushed from the room. He was glad to find his friends waiting for him, and told them of his terrible interview with the Wizard.

"What shall we do now?" asked Dorothy, sadly.

"There is only one thing we can do," returned the Lion, "and that is to go to the land of the Winkies, seek out the Wicked Witch, and destroy her."

"But suppose we cannot?" said the girl.

"Then I shall never have courage," declared the Lion.

"And I shall never have brains," added the Scarecrow.

"And I shall never have a heart," spoke the Tin Woodman.

"And I shall never see Aunt Em and Uncle Henry," said Dorothy, beginning to cry.

"Be careful!" cried the green girl, "the tears will fall on your green silk gown, and spot it."

So Dorothy dried her eyes and said, **19**

"I suppose we must try it; but I am sure I do not want to kill anybody, even to see Aunt Em again."

19. *dried her eyes.* Note how cleverly Baum undercuts Dorothy's tears. A similar incident occurs in Chapter 18 when the Tin Woodman must have his tears wiped away when he feels it his duty to cry at the departure of the Wizard of Oz in his balloon.

"I will go with you; but I'm too much of a coward to kill the Witch," said the Lion.

"I will go too," declared the Scarecrow; "but I shall not be of much help to you, I am such a fool."

"I haven't the heart to harm even a Witch," remarked the Tin Woodman; "but if you go I certainly shall go with you."

Therefore it was decided to start upon their journey the next morning, and the Woodman sharpened his axe on a green grindstone and had all his joints properly oiled. The Scarecrow stuffed himself with fresh straw and Dorothy put new paint on his eyes that he might see better. The green girl, who was very kind to them, filled Dorothy's basket with good things to eat, and fastened a little bell around Toto's neck with a green ribbon.

They went to bed quite early and slept soundly until daylight, when they were awakened by the crowing of a green cock that lived in the back yard of the palace, and the cackling of a hen that had laid a green egg.

Chapter XII.
The Search for the Wicked Witch.

The SOLDIER WITH THE green whiskers led them through the streets of the Emerald City until they reached the room where the Guardian of the Gates lived. This officer unlocked their spectacles to put them back in his great box, and then he politely opened the gate for our friends.

"Which road leads to the Wicked Witch of the West?" asked Dorothy.

"There is no road," answered the Guardian of the Gates; "no one ever wishes to go that way."

"How, then, are we to find her?" enquired the girl.

1 *no longer green.* This is not surprising when one learns in Chapter 15 the true nature of the magic of the Emerald City. Denslow's illustrations follow the text on this point.

"That will be easy," replied the man; "for when she knows you are in the Country of the Winkies she will find you, and make you all her slaves."

"Perhaps not," said the Scarecrow, "for we mean to destroy her."

"Oh, that is different," said the Guardian of the Gates. "No one has ever destroyed her before, so I naturally thought she would make slaves of you, as she has of all the rest. But take care; for she is wicked and fierce, and may not allow you to destroy her. Keep to the West, where the sun sets, and you cannot fail to find her."

They thanked him and bade him good-bye, and turned toward the West, walking over fields of soft grass dotted here and there with daisies and buttercups. Dorothy still wore the pretty silk dress she had put on in the palace, but now, to her surprise, she found it was no longer green, but pure white. The ribbon around Toto's neck had also lost its green color and was as white as Dorothy's dress.

The Emerald City was soon left far behind. As they advanced the ground became rougher and hillier, for there were no farms nor houses in this country of the West, and the ground was untilled.

In the afternoon the sun shone hot in their faces, for here were no trees to offer them shade; so that before night Dorothy and Toto and the Lion were tired, and lay down upon the grass and fell asleep, with the Woodman and the Scarecrow keeping watch.

Now the Wicked Witch of the West had but one eye, yet that was as powerful as a telescope, and could see everywhere. So, as she sat in the door of her castle, she happened to look around and saw Dorothy lying asleep, with her friends all about her. They were a long distance off, but the Wicked Witch was angry to find them in her country; so she blew upon a silver whistle that hung around her neck.

At once there came running to her from all directions a pack of great wolves. They had long legs and fierce eyes and sharp teeth.

"Go to those people," said the Witch, "and tear them to pieces."

"Are you not going to make them your slaves?" asked the leader of the wolves.

"No," she answered, "one is of tin, and one of straw; one is a girl and another a Lion. None of them is fit to work, so you may tear them into small pieces."

"Very well," said the wolf, and he dashed away at full speed, followed by the others.

It was lucky the Scarecrow and the Woodman were wide awake and heard the wolves coming.

2 *forty wolves, and forty times.* Baum's references to "forty wolves," "forty crows," and "forty bees" is a biblical, or rather an archaic, use of the number to indicate "many," an approximative sense of a large group or great length of time. The storm during the Flood lasted forty days and forty nights; Christ fasted in the wilderness for forty days and forty nights. In the Near East "forty" just denotes "many": the centipede ("one hundred-footed") has a Persian and now Turkish name that means "forty-footed."

"This is my fight," said the Woodman; "so get behind me and I will meet them as they come."

He seized his axe, which he had made very sharp, and as the leader of the wolves came on the Tin Woodman swung his arm and chopped the wolf's head from its body, so that it immediately died. As soon as he could raise his axe another wolf came up, and he also fell under the sharp edge of the Tin Woodman's weapon. There **2** were forty wolves, and forty times a wolf was killed; so that at last they all lay dead in a heap before the Woodman.

Then he put down his axe and sat beside the Scarecrow, who said,

"It was a good fight, friend."

They waited until Dorothy awoke the next morning. The little girl was quite frightened when she saw the great pile of shaggy wolves, but the Tin Woodman told her all. She thanked him for saving them and sat down to breakfast, after which they started again upon their journey.

Now this same morning the Wicked Witch came to the door of her castle and looked out with her

one eye that could see afar off. She saw all her wolves lying dead, and the strangers still travelling through her country. This made her angrier than before, and she blew her silver whistle twice.

Straightway a great flock of wild crows came flying toward her, enough to darken the sky. And the Wicked Witch said to the King Crow,

"Fly at once to the strangers; peck out their eyes and tear them to pieces."

The wild crows flew in one great flock toward Dorothy and her companions. When the little girl saw them coming she was afraid. But the Scarecrow said,

"This is my battle; so lie down beside me and you will not be harmed."

So they all lay upon the ground except the Scarecrow, and he stood up and stretched out his arms. And when the crows saw him they were frightened, as these birds always are by scarecrows, and did not dare to come any nearer. But the King Crow said,

"It is only a stuffed man. I will peck his eyes out."

The King Crow flew at the Scarecrow, who caught it by the head and twisted its neck until it died. And then another crow flew at him, and the Scarecrow twisted its neck also. There were forty crows, and forty times the Scarecrow twisted a neck, until at last all were lying dead beside him. Then he called to his companions to rise, and again they went upon their journey.

When the Wicked Witch looked out again and saw all her crows lying in a heap, she got into a terrible rage, and blew three times upon her silver whistle.

Forthwith there was heard a great buzzing in the air, and a swarm of black bees came flying towards her.

"Go to the strangers and sting them to death!" commanded the Witch, and the bees turned and flew rapidly until they came to where Dorothy and her friends were walking. But the Woodman had seen them coming and the Scarecrow had decided what to do.

"Take out my straw and scatter it over the little girl and the dog and the lion," he said to the Woodman, "and the bees cannot sting them." This the Woodman did, and as Dorothy lay close beside the Lion and held Toto in her arms, the straw covered them entirely.

The bees came and found no one but the Woodman to sting, so they flew at him and broke off all their stings against the tin, without hurting the Woodman at all. And as bees cannot live when their stings are broken that was the end of the black bees, and they lay scattered thick about the Woodman, like little heaps of fine coal.

Then Dorothy and the Lion got up, and the girl helped the Tin Woodman put the straw back into the Scarecrow again, until he was as good as ever. So they started upon their journey once more.

The Wicked Witch was so angry when she saw her black bees in little heaps like fine coal that she stamped her foot and tore her hair and gnashed her teeth. And then she called a dozen of her slaves, who were the Winkies, and gave them sharp spears, telling them to go to the strangers and destroy them.

The Winkies were not a brave people, but they had to do as they were told; so they marched away until they came near to Dorothy. Then the Lion gave a great roar and sprang toward them, and the poor Winkies were so frightened that they ran back as fast as they could.

When they returned to the castle the Wicked Witch beat them well with a strap, and sent them back to their work, after which she sat down to think what she should do next. She could not understand how all her plans to destroy these strangers had failed; but she was a powerful Witch, as well as a wicked one, and she soon made up her mind how to act.

There was, in her cupboard, a Golden Cap, with a circle of diamonds and rubies running round it. This Golden Cap had a charm. Whoever owned it could call **3** three times upon the Winged Monkeys, who would obey any order they were given. But no person could command these strange creatures more than three times.

3 *a charm*. The enchanted hat is often referred to in folk legends. It may be associated with magic transportation; *The History of Fortunatus*, a popular English chapbook of the seventeenth century derived from a Dutch legend, concerns a magic hat that will fly its wearer anywhere he might wish. Robert Burton in *The Anatomy of Melancholy* (1628) describes another miraculous cap, somewhat comparable to the Golden Cap: "Erricus, King of Sweden, had an enchanted Cap, by virtue of which, and some magical murmur or whispering terms, he could command spirits, trouble the air, and make the wind stand which way he would; insomuch that when there was any great wind or storm, the common people were wont to say, the King now had on his conjuring Cap."

4 *Ep-pe, pep-pe, kak-ke.* "My wife has called my attention," writes Gardner in Note 15 of *The Wizard of Oz and Who He Was,* "to the close similarity of this incantation to 'ipecac,' the name of a once popular household emetic still sold in drugstores."

5 *Hil-lo, hol-lo, hel-lo.* Evidently part of the magic of the charm is the change in vowels. Another example occurs in *Prince Mud-Turtle* (p. 32): "Uller; aller; iller; oller!" Other incantations may be formed by a change in consonants, as in the charm of the Powder of Life in *The Marvelous Land of Oz:* "Weaugh! Teaugh! Peaugh!"

6 *Ziz-zy, zuz-zy, zik.* Compare this line to the incantation of *A New Wonderland* (revised as *The Magical Monarch of Mo,* p. 46): "Gizzle, guzzle, goo!" The last line of the charm of the Magic Cap is similar to the counting-out rhymes of the nursery. These are used to determine who is "It" in any proposed game. Among the many variants are "One-ery, two-ery, Ziccary zan!"; "Eeny, meeny, miney, mo!"; and "Onesy, twosy, three!" Although other nonsense lines from Mother Goose (e.g., "Higgledy, piggledy, pop!") may also suggest the incantation of the Golden Cap, the witch-queen of *Queen Zixi of Ix* gives the best explanation. When asked what a particular charm means, Zixi as Miss Trust replies: "No one knows; and therefore it is a fine incantation" (p. 153). Baum intends this in fun, but the witch's answer is not so far from the truth. As Richard Cavendish

states in *The Black Arts* (New York: G. P. Putnam's Sons, 1967, p. 130), incantations generally have no meaning (even though they may be derived from meaningful rituals, as the term "hocus-pocus" is from a line in the Latin mass, *Hoc est corpus meum*); their importance is in the fact that they sound impressive.

Twice already the Wicked Witch had used the charm of the Cap. Once was when she had made the Winkies her slaves, and set herself to rule over their country. The Winged Monkeys had helped her do this. The second time was when she had fought against the Great Oz himself, and driven him out of the land of the West. The Winged Monkeys had also helped her in doing this. Only once more could she use this Golden Cap, for which reason she did not like to do so until all her other powers were exhausted. But now that her fierce wolves and her wild crows and her stinging bees were gone, and her slaves had been scared away by the Cowardly Lion, she saw there was only one way left to destroy Dorothy and her friends.

So the Wicked Witch took the Golden Cap from her cupboard and placed it upon her head. Then she stood upon her left foot and said, slowly,

4 "Ep-pe, pep-pe, kak-ke!"

Next she stood upon her right foot and said,

5 "Hil-lo, hol-lo, hel-lo!"

After this she stood upon both feet and cried in a loud voice,

6 "Ziz-zy, zuz-zy, zik!"

Now the charm began

to work. The sky was darkened, and a low rumbling sound was heard in the air. There was a rushing of many wings; a great chattering and laughing; and the sun came out of the dark sky to show the Wicked Witch surrounded by a crowd of monkeys, each with a pair of immense and **7** powerful wings on his shoulders.

One, much bigger than the others, seemed to be their leader. He flew close to the Witch and said,

"You have called us for the third and last time. What do you command?"

"Go to the strangers who are within my land and destroy them all except the Lion," said the Wicked Witch. "Bring that beast to me, for I have a mind to harness him like a horse, and make him work."

"Your commands shall be obeyed," said the leader; and then, with a great deal of chattering and noise, the Winged Monkeys flew away to the place where Dorothy and her friends were walking.

7 *monkeys.* Baum concluded that if men had fairy guardians animals must also; although the Winged Monkeys do not act as animal protectors while under the power of the Golden Cap, they are not too distantly related to what Baum called "animal fairies." The Fairy Beavers of *John Dough and the Cherub* are similar creations. Certainly Baum's best short stories were the "Animal Fairy Tales," which first appeared in *The Delineator* in 1905 and were published as a collection by the International Wizard of Oz Club in 1969.

The function of the Winged Monkeys may be analogous to that of the familiars of the European witches. After performing certain acts and words, a band of "divining familiars" could be conjured by a witch to foretell the future. If the Winged Monkeys act as familiars, it is in respect to controlling, rather than predicting, the future.

Some of the Monkeys seized the Tin Woodman and carried him through the air until they were over a country thickly covered with sharp rocks. Here they dropped the poor Woodman, who fell a great distance to the rocks, where he lay so battered and dented that he could neither move nor groan.

Others of the Monkeys caught the Scarecrow, and with their long fingers pulled all of the straw out of his clothes and head. They made his hat and boots and clothes into a small bundle and threw it into the top branches of a tall tree.

The remaining Monkeys threw pieces of stout rope around the Lion and wound many coils about his body and head and legs, until he was unable to bite or scratch or struggle in any way. Then they lifted him up and flew away with him to the Witch's castle, where he was placed in a small yard with a high iron fence around it, so that he could not escape.

But Dorothy they did not harm at all. She stood, with Toto in her arms, watching the sad fate of her comrades and thinking it would soon be her turn. The leader of the Winged Monkeys flew up to her, his long, hairy arms stretched out and his ugly face grinning terriby; but he saw the mark of the Good Witch's kiss upon her forehead and stopped short, motioning the others not to touch her.

"We dare not harm this little girl," he said to them, "for she is protected by the Power of Good, and that is greater than the Power of Evil. All we can do is to carry her to the castle of the Wicked Witch and leave her there."

So, carefully and gently, they lifted Dorothy in their arms and carried her swiftly through the air until they came to the castle, where they set her down upon the front door step. Then the leader said to the Witch,

"We have obeyed you as far as we were able. The Tin Woodman and the Scarecrow are destroyed, and the Lion is tied up in your yard. The little girl we dare not harm, nor the dog she carries in her arms. Your power over our band is now ended, and you will never see us again."

Then all the Winged Monkeys, with much laughing and chattering and noise, flew into the air and were soon out of sight.

The Wicked Witch was both surprised and worried when she saw the mark on Dorothy's forehead, for she

8

8 *greater than the Power of Evil.* This is, as Roger Samber writes in the dedication to his English translation of Perrault's *Histories, or Tales of the Past* (1729), "the true End and Design of Fable." Perrault, the first important writer of children's fairy tales, realized this purpose of the fairy tale, as witnessed in the following passage from the 1659 preface to his verse tales (quoted from Jacques Branchelon and Henry Pettit's introduction to *The Authentic Mother Goose Fairy Tales and Nursery Rhymes*, Chicago: Alan Swallow, 1960):

We see them [the children] sad and depressed as long as the hero and heroine are unlucky and shouting with joy when the time for their happiness arrives; in the same way, having endured impatiently the property of the wicked man and woman, they are overjoyed when they see them finally punished as they deserved.

This is a necessary element in Baum's stories according to his article on fairy tales (referred to in Note 2 of Baum's Introduction), in which he writes that "never has a fairy tale lived, if one has been told or written, wherein the good did not conquer evil and virtue finally reign supreme." Also, as Baum explains in *The Life and Adventures of Santa Claus*, it "is the Law that while Evil, unopposed, may accomplish terrible deeds, the powers of Good can never be overthrown when opposed to Evil" (p. 117).

9 *keep the fire fed with wood.* Notice how unlike the witches of European fairy tales is Baum's Wicked Witch. The Witch of the West does not threaten to eat Dorothy as does the witch who is encountered by Hansel and Gretel. She does not scratch out the eyes of her prisoner as does the witch in Grimm's "Rapunzel." As Daniel Mannix points out in his article on Baum in the December 1964 *American Heritage*, Dorothy is not tortured by having to wear hot iron shoes and being forced to dance to death as must Snow White. Dorothy is protected by the kiss of the Good Witch; Baum avoids the gruesome tortures associated with the European witches. Dorothy's only tribulation is to do the household chores that any little girl would rightly loathe, but which would not result in nightmares.

The Wicked Witch as played by Margaret Hamilton is one of the highlights of the 1939 MGM film.

10 *not to kill her.* "Many Western farmers have held these same grim thoughts in less mystical terms," writes Henry M. Littlefield in his article cited in my introduction. "The Witch of the West uses natural forces to achieve her ends; she is Baum's version of satient and malign nature." These natural forces are given animal form in her wolves, crows, and bees. "If the Witch of the West is a diabolical force of Darwinian or Spencerian nature, then another contravening force may be counted upon to dispose of her. Dorothy destroys the evil Witch by angrily dousing her with a bucket of water. Water, that precious commodity which the drought ridden farmers in the great plains needed so badly, and which if correctly used could create an agricultural paradise, or at least dissolve a wicked witch. Plain water brings an end to malign nature in the West."

knew well that neither the Winged Monkeys nor she, herself, dare hurt the girl in any way. She looked down at Dorothy's feet, and seeing the Silver Shoes, began to tremble with fear, for she knew what a powerful charm belonged to them. At first the Witch was tempted to run away from Dorothy; but she happened to look into the child's eyes and saw how simple the soul behind them was, and that the little girl did not know of the wonderful power the Silver Shoes gave her. So the Wicked Witch laughed to herself, and thought, "I can still make her my slave, for she does not know how to use her power." Then she said to Dorothy, harshly and severely,

"Come with me; and see that you mind everything I tell you, for if you do not I will make an end of you, as I did of the Tin Woodman and the Scarecrow."

Dorothy followed her through many of the beautiful rooms in her castle until they came to the kitchen, where the Witch bade her clean the pots and kettles and sweep

9 the floor and keep the fire fed with wood.

Dorothy went to work meekly, with her mind made up to work as hard as she could; for she was glad the

10 Wicked Witch had decided not to kill her.

With Dorothy hard at work the Witch thought she would go into the court-yard and harness the Cowardly Lion like a horse; it would amuse her, she was sure, to make him draw her chariot whenever she wished to go to drive. But as she opened the gate the Lion gave a loud roar and bounded at her so fiercely that the Witch was afraid, and ran out and shut the gate again.

"If I cannot harness you," said the Witch to the Lion, speaking through the bars of the gate, "I can starve you. You shall have nothing to eat until you do as I wish."

So after that she took no food to the imprisoned Lion; but every day she came to the gate at noon and asked,

"Are you ready to be harnessed like a horse?"

And the Lion would answer,

"No. If you come in this yard I will bite you."

The reason the Lion did not have to do as the Witch wished was that every night, while the woman was asleep Dorothy carried him food from the cupboard. After he had eaten he would lie down on his bed of straw, and Dorothy would lie beside him and put her head on his soft, shaggy mane, while they talked of their troubles and tried to plan some way to escape. But they could find no way to get out of the castle, for it was constantly guarded by the yellow Winkies, who were the slaves of the Wicked Witch and too afraid of her not to do as she told them.

The girl had to work hard during the day, and often the Witch threatened to beat her with the same old umbrella she always carried in her hand. But, in truth, she did not dare to strike Dorothy, because of the mark upon her forehead. The child did not know this, and was full of fear for herself and Toto. Once the Witch struck Toto a blow with her umbrella and the brave little dog flew at her

11

11 *umbrella.* Although the common implement associated with witches is the broom, the eminently suitable one carried by a witch so afraid of water is the umbrella.

12 *afraid of the dark*. Here is another example of the fear of the unknown. Like a child the Witch is afraid because she does not know what may be in the darkness; she is frightened of what may be there rather than what is. Likewise the Winkies still fear the Witch despite the fact that much of her power is now gone. In Chapter 15, Dorothy and her companions are faced with what they view as the most dreadful form of Oz, the Great and Terrible—the empty Throne Room. One fears what he does not know.

and bit her leg, in return. The Witch did not bleed where she was bitten, for she was so wicked that the blood in her had dried up many years before.

Dorothy's life became very sad as she grew to understand that it would be harder than ever to get back to Kansas and Aunt Em again. Sometimes she would cry bitterly for hours, with Toto sitting at her feet and looking into her face, whining dismally to show how sorry he was for his little mistress. Toto did not really care whether he was in Kansas or the Land of Oz so long as Dorothy was with him; but he knew the little girl was unhappy, and that made him unhappy too.

Now the Wicked Witch had a great longing to have for her own the Silver Shoes which the girl always wore. Her Bees and her Crows and her Wolves were lying in heaps and drying up, and she had used up all the power of the Golden Cap; but if she could only get hold of the Silver Shoes they would give her more power than all the other things she had lost. She watched Dorothy carefully, to see if she ever took off her shoes, thinking she might steal them. But the child was so proud of her pretty shoes that she never took them off except at night and when she **12** took her bath. The Witch was too much afraid of the dark to dare go in Dorothy's room at night to take the shoes, and her dread of water was greater than her fear of the dark, so she never came near when Dorothy was bathing. Indeed, the old Witch never touched water, nor ever let water touch her in any way.

But the wicked creature was very cunning, and she finally thought of a trick that would give her what she wanted. She placed a bar of iron in the middle of the kitchen floor, and then by her magic arts made the iron invisible to human eyes. So that when Dorothy walked across the floor she stumbled over the bar, not being able to see it, and fell at full length. She was not much hurt, but in her fall one of the Silver Shoes came off, and before she could reach it the Witch had snatched it away and put it on her own skinny foot.

The wicked woman was greatly pleased with the success of her trick, for as long as she had one of the shoes she owned half the power of their charm, and Dorothy could not use it against her, even had she known how to do so.

The little girl, seeing she had lost one of her pretty shoes, grew angry, and said to the Witch,

"Give me back my shoe!"

"I will not," retorted the Witch, "for it is now my shoe, and not yours."

"You are a wicked creature!" cried Dorothy. "You have no right to take my shoe from me."

"I shall keep it, just the same," said the Witch, laughing at her,

13 *Didn't you know water would be the end of me.* Dorothy should have known this. A frequent test of an accused witch is ordeal by water. This was considered the most decisive proof of the power of a witch, because man cannot deceive the element of water. The suspect was bound and thrown into a river; if she sank, she was innocent, if she floated, she was guilty and could be unquestionably executed by fire. This method of human justice appears as early as 1950 B.C. in the code of Hammurabi; it was accepted by the Paris parliament into the seventeenth century and was performed with conclusive results as late as June 1696.

Many students of Oz believe that Oz magic may be rationally explained, that it is based on certain scientific principles, and may be seen as an extension of natural law. This is the position taken by Dr. Douglas A. Rossman in his article "On the Liquidation of Witches" (*The Baum Bugle*, Spring 1969). Dr. Rossman views the melting of wicked witches (besides the Wicked Witch of the West, Mombi the Witch is "liquidated" in Ruth Plumly Thompson's *The Lost King of Oz*) as occurring by the process of hydrolysis. Adhesion, the sticking together of molecules in contact with each other, may be broken down either by water or by another powerful force, such as a strong blow. The Witch cannot bleed because her bodily liquids dried up years before; with the loss of natural liquids the ability of adhesion to combat other forces is lessened. Only her black arts have kept her from literally falling apart. When water is poured on this dry substance, the adhesion is disrupted and the molecular structure falls apart. When Dorothy's house falls upon the Wicked Witch of the East, the impact of the blow is so great that this also breaks down the molecular structure, and she falls apart into dust. A slightly revised version of this episode appeared as "Melting A Wicked Witch" in *L. Frank Baum's Juvenile Speaker*.

"and some day I shall get the other one from you, too."

This made Dorothy so very angry that she picked up the bucket of water that stood near and dashed it over the Witch, wetting her from head to foot.

Instantly the wicked woman gave a loud cry of fear; and then, as Dorothy looked at her in wonder, the Witch began to shrink and fall away.

"See what you have done!" she screamed. "In a minute I shall melt away."

"I'm very sorry, indeed," said Dorothy, who was truly frightened to see the Witch actually melting away like brown sugar before her very eyes.

13 "Didn't you know water would be the end of me?" asked the Witch, in a wailing, despairing voice.

"Of course not," answered Dorothy; "how should I?"

"Well, in a few minutes I shall be all melted, and you will have the castle to yourself. I have been wicked in my day, but I never thought a little girl like you would ever be able to melt me and end my wicked deeds. Look out—here I go!"

With these words the Witch fell down in a brown, melted, shapeless mass and began to spread over the clean boards of the kitchen floor. Seeing that she had really melted away to nothing, Dorothy drew another bucket of water and threw it over the mess. She then swept it all out the door. After picking out the silver shoe, which was all that was left of the old woman, she cleaned and dried it with a cloth, and put it on her foot again. Then, being at last free to do as she chose, she ran out to the court-yard to tell the Lion that the Wicked Witch of the West had come to an end, and that they were no longer prisoners in a strange land.

Chapter XIII.
The Rescue ~ 1

1 *The Rescue.* In the early editions of *The Wonderful Wizard of Oz* and *The New Wizard of Oz* this chapter has two titles. The chapter-title page has "The Rescue," while the contents page lists "How the Four Were Reunited." When the chapter-title pages were eliminated and the contents page was reset in a late Bobbs-Merrill edition (about 1920), "The Rescue" was the title retained. Most subsequent editions have had only this title.

The COWARDLY LION WAS much pleased to hear that the Wicked Witch had been melted by a bucket of water, and Dorothy at once unlocked the gate of his prison and set him free. They went in together to the castle, where Dorothy's first act was to call all the Winkies together and tell them that they were no longer slaves.

There was great rejoicing among the yellow Winkies, for they had been made to work hard during many years for the Wicked Witch, who had always treated them with great cruelty. They kept this day as a holiday, then and ever after, and spent the time in feasting and dancing.

"If our friends, the Scarecrow and the Tin Woodman,

were only with us," said the Lion, "I should be quite happy."

"Don't you suppose we could rescue them?" asked the girl, anxiously.

"We can try," answered the Lion.

So they called the yellow Winkies and asked them if they would help to rescue their friends, and the Winkies said that they would be delighted to do all in their power for Dorothy, who had set them free from bondage. So she chose a number of the Winkies who looked as if they knew the most, and they all started away. They travelled that day and part of the next until they came to the rocky plain where the Tin Woodman lay, all battered and bent. His axe was near him, but the blade was rusted and the handle broken off short.

The Winkies lifted him tenderly in their arms, and carried him back to the yellow castle again, Dorothy shedding a few tears by the way at the sad plight of her old friend, and the Lion looking sober and sorry. When they reached the castle Dorothy said to the Winkies,

"Are any of your people tinsmiths?"

"Oh, yes; some of us are very good tinsmiths," they told her.

"Then bring them to me," she said. And when the tinsmiths came, bringing with them all their tools in baskets, she enquired,

"Can you straighten out those dents in the Tin Woodman, and bend him back into shape again, and solder him together where he is broken?"

The tinsmiths looked the Woodman over carefully and then answered that they thought they could mend him so he would be as good as ever. So they set to work in one of the big yellow rooms of the castle and worked for three days and four nights, hammering and twisting and bending and soldering and polishing and pounding at the legs and body and head of the Tin Woodman, until at last he was straightened out into his old form, and his joints worked as well as ever. To be sure, there were several patches on him, but the tinsmiths did a good job, and as the Woodman was not a vain man he did not mind the patches at all.

When, at last, he walked into Dorothy's room and thanked her for rescuing him, he was so pleased that he wept tears of joy, and Dorothy had to wipe every tear carefully from his face with her apron, so his joints would not be rusted. At the same time her own tears fell thick and fast at the joy of meeting her old friend again, and these tears did not need to be wiped away. As for the Lion, he wiped his eyes so often with the tip of his tail that it became quite wet, and he was obliged to go out into the court-yard and hold it in the sun till it dried.

"If we only had the Scarecrow with us again," said the Tin Woodman, when Dorothy had finished telling him everything that had happened, "I should be quite happy."

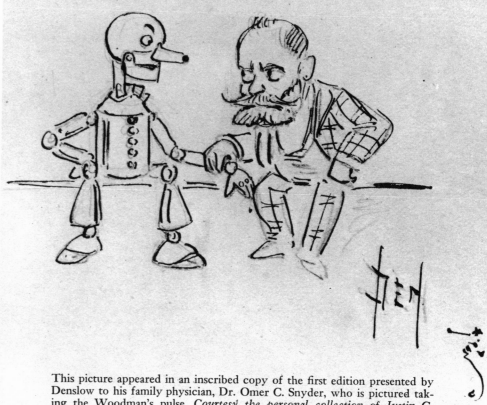

This picture appeared in an inscribed copy of the first edition presented by Denslow to his family physician, Dr. Omer C. Snyder, who is pictured taking the Woodman's pulse. *Courtesy the personal collection of Justin G. Schiller.*

"We must try to find him," said the girl.

So she called the Winkies to help her, and they walked all that day and part of the next until they came to the tall tree in the branches of which the Winged Monkeys had tossed the Scarecrow's clothes.

It was a very tall tree, and the trunk was so smooth that no one could climb it; but the Woodman said at once,

"I'll chop it down, and then we can get the Scarecrow's clothes."

Now while the tinsmiths had been at work mending the Woodman himself, another of the Winkies, who was a goldsmith, had made an axe-handle of solid gold and fitted it to the Woodman's axe, instead of the old broken handle. Others polished the blade until all the rust was removed and it glistened like burnished silver.

As soon as he had spoken, the Tin Woodman began to chop, and in a short time the tree fell over with a crash, when the Scarecrow's clothes fell out of the branches and rolled off on the ground.

Dorothy picked them up and had the Winkies carry them back to the castle, where they were stuffed with nice, clean straw; and, behold! here was the Scarecrow, as good as ever, thanking them over and over again for saving him.

Now they were reunited, Dorothy and her friends spent a few happy days at the Yellow Castle, where they found everything they needed to make them comfortable. But one day the girl thought of Aunt Em, and said,

"We must go back to Oz, and claim his promise."

"Yes," said the Woodman, "at last I shall get my heart."

"And I shall get my brains," added the Scarecrow, joyfully.

"And I shall get my courage," said the Lion, thoughtfully.

"And I shall get back to Kansas," cried Dorothy, clapping her hands. "Oh, let us start for the Emerald City to-morrow!"

This they decided to do. The next day they called the Winkies together and bade them good-bye. The Winkies were sorry to have them go, and they had grown so fond of the Tin Woodman that they begged him to stay and rule over them and the Yellow Land of the West. Finding they were determined to go, the Winkies gave Toto and the Lion each a golden collar; and to Dorothy they presented a beautiful bracelet, studded with diamonds;

2 *diamonds.* Evidently these presents were left behind in Oz, for "Dorothy never brought any jewels home with her" (*The Emerald City of Oz*, p. 23).

2

243

3 *precious jewels.* This may be the same oilcan described in *The Marvelous Land of Oz*, p. 124: "Upon a handsome center-table [in an antechamber of the Tin Woodman's Tin Palace in the Winkie Country] stood a large silver oil-can, richly engraved with scenes from the past adventures of the Tin Woodman, Dorothy, the Cowardly Lion and the Scarecrow: the lines of the engraving being traced upon the silver in yellow gold."

and to the Scarecrow they gave a gold-headed walking stick, to keep him from stumbling; and to the Tin Woodman they offered a silver oil-can, inlaid with gold and set **3** with precious jewels.

Every one of the travellers made the Winkies a pretty speech in return, and all shook hands with them until their arms ached.

Dorothy went to the Witch's cupboard to fill her basket with food for the journey, and there she saw the Golden Cap. She tried it on her own head and found that it fitted her exactly. She did not know anything about the charm of the Golden Cap, but she saw that it was pretty, so she made up her mind to wear it and carry her sunbonnet in the basket.

Then, being prepared for the journey, they all started for the Emerald City; and the Winkies gave them three cheers and many good wishes to carry with them.

This illustration of the Scarecrow pulling the Cowardly Lion's tail was drawn during the last week in August 1902, when Denslow was in Chicago on vacation from New York. He had been asked by a newspaper to give his impression of the stage play of *The Wizard of Oz*, then playing at the Grand Opera House in Chicago, and he produced this sketch, which was printed in an unidentified newspaper.

Chapter XIV.
The Winged
Monkeys

YOU WILL REMEMBER there was no road—not even a pathway—between the castle of the Wicked Witch and the Emerald City. When the four travellers went in search of the Witch she had seen them coming, and so sent the Winged Monkeys to bring them to her. It was much harder to find their way back through the big fields of buttercups and yellow daisies **1** than it was being carried. They knew, of course, they must go straight east, toward the rising sun; and they started off in the right way. But at noon, when the sun was over their heads, they did not know which was east and which was west, and that was the reason they were lost in the great fields. They kept on walking, however,

1 *yellow.* In most editions of *The Wizard of Oz* the word "yellow" is here replaced by "bright." Dick Martin, the illustrator, has noted that the corrupted text contains references in this chapter to scarlet fields and scarlet flowers, although the locale is the Winkie Country where yellow is the favorite color. For some unknown reason this change was made in the earliest printing of the 1903 Bobbs-Merrill edition where the word "scarlet" has replaced the word "yellow." Baum's original text speaks only of buttercups and daisies, yellow fields and yellow flowers.

2 *sometime come to some place.* Compare this logic to the following lines from the meeting of Alice and the Cheshire Cat in Chapter 6 of *Alice in Wonderland:*

"Would you tell me, please, which way I ought to go from here?"

"That depends a good deal on where you want to get to," said the Cat.

"I don't care much where—" said Alice.

"Then it doesn't matter which way you go," said the Cat.

"—so long as I get *somewhere,*" Alice added as an explanation.

"Oh, you're sure to do that," said the Cat, "if you only walk long enough."

The reviewer of *The Dial* may have had this passage in mind when he compared *The Wizard of Oz* to Carroll's classics. As Baum himself suggests in his article on fairy tales (referred to in Chapter 1, Note 1), his debt to Carroll is slight. There are more obvious similarities between *A New Wonderland* and the Alice books. Martin Gardner devotes considerable space in his introduction to the 1968 Dover edition of *The Magical Monarch of Mo* (the slightly revised version of *A New Wonderland*) to a comparison between this and the Carroll books. Some discussion of the Oz books and the possible influence of Carroll on Baum appears in Gardner's "A Child's Garden of Bewilderment," *Saturday Review,* July 17, 1965.

and at night the moon came out and shone brightly. So they lay down among the sweet smelling yellow flowers and slept soundly until morning—all but the Scarecrow and the Tin Woodman.

The next morning the sun was behind a cloud, but they started on, as if they were quite sure which way they were going.

"If we walk far enough," said Dorothy, "we shall **2** sometime come to some place, I am sure."

But day by day passed away, and they still saw nothing before them but the yellow fields. The Scarecrow began to grumble a bit.

"We have surely lost our way," he said, "and unless we find it again in time to reach the Emerald City I shall never get my brains."

"Nor I my heart," declared the Tin Woodman. "It seems to me I can scarcely wait till I get to Oz, and you must admit this is a very long journey."

"You see," said the Cowardly Lion, with a whimper, "I haven't the courage to keep tramping forever, without getting anywhere at all."

Then Dorothy lost heart. She sat down on the grass and looked at her companions, and they sat down and looked at her, and Toto found that for the first time in his life he was too tired to chase a butterfly that flew past his head; so he put out his tongue and panted and looked at Dorothy as if to ask what they should do next.

"Suppose we call the Field Mice," she suggested. "They could probably tell us the way to the Emerald City."

"To be sure they could," cried the Scarecrow; "why didn't we think of that before?"

Dorothy blew the little whistle she had always carried about her neck since the Queen of the Mice had given it to her. In a few minutes they heard the pattering of tiny feet, and many of the small grey mice came running up to her. Among them was the Queen herself, who asked, in her squeaky little voice,

"What can I do for my friends?"

"We have lost our way," said Dorothy. "Can you tell us where the Emerald City is?"

"Certainly," answered the Queen; "but it is a great way off, for you have had it at your backs all this time." Then she noticed Dorothy's Golden Cap, and said, "Why don't you use the charm of the Cap, and call the Winged Monkeys to you? They will carry you to the City of Oz in less than an hour."

"I didn't know there was a charm," answered Dorothy, in surprise. "What is it?"

"It is written inside the Golden Cap," replied the Queen of the Mice; "but if you are going to call the Winged Monkeys we must run away, for they are full of mischief and think it great fun to plague us."

"Won't they hurt me?" asked the girl, anxiously.

"Oh, no; they must obey the wearer of the Cap. Good-bye!" And she scampered out of sight, with all the mice hurrying after her.

Dorothy looked inside the Golden Cap and saw some words written upon the lining. These, she thought, must be the charm, so she read the directions carefully and put the Cap upon her head.

"Ep-pe, pep-pe, kak-ke!" she said, standing on her left foot.

"What did you say?" asked the Scarecrow, who did not know what she was doing.

"Hil-lo, hol-lo, hel-lo!" Dorothy went on, standing this time on her right foot.

"Hello!" replied the Tin Woodman, calmly.

"Ziz-zy, zuz-zy, zik!" said Dorothy, who was now standing on both feet. This ended the saying of the charm, and they heard a great chattering and flapping of wings, as the band of Winged Monkeys flew up to them. The King bowed low before Dorothy, and asked,

"What is your command?"

"We wish to go to the Emerald City," said the child, "and we have lost our way."

"We will carry you," replied the King, and no sooner had he spoken than two of the Monkeys caught Dorothy in their arms and flew away with her. Others took the Scarecrow and the Woodman and the Lion, and one little Monkey seized Toto and flew after them, although the dog tried hard to bite him.

The Scarecrow and the Tin Woodman were rather frightened at first, for they remembered how badly the Winged Monkeys had treated them before; but they saw that no harm was intended, so they rode through the air quite cheerfully, and had a fine time looking at the pretty gardens and woods far below them.

Dorothy found herself riding easily between two of the biggest Monkeys, one of them the King himself. They had made a chair of their hands and were careful not to hurt her.

"Why do you have to obey the charm of the Golden Cap?" she asked.

"That is a long story," answered the King, with a laugh; "but as we have a long journey before us I will pass the time by telling you about it, if you wish."

"I shall be glad to hear it," she replied.

3 *ruby*. This is the first of two references in this chapter indicating that Baum at this time considered the favorite color of the North to be red, as it is in the South. In *The Marvelous Land of Oz* we learn that the color of the North is purple.

"Once," began the leader, "we were a free people, living happily in the great forest, flying from tree to tree, eating nuts and fruit, and doing just as we pleased without calling anybody master. Perhaps some of us were rather too full of mischief at times, flying down to pull the tails of the animals that had no wings, chasing birds, and throwing nuts at the people who walked in the forest. But we were careless and happy and full of fun, and enjoyed every minute of the day. This was many years ago, long before Oz came out of the clouds to rule over this land.

"There lived here then, away at the North, a beautiful princess, who was also a powerful sorceress. All her magic was used to help the people, and she was never known to hurt anyone who was good. Her name was Gayelette, and she lived in a handsome palace built from **3** great blocks of ruby. Everyone loved her, but her greatest sorrow was that she could find no one to love in return, since all the men were much too stupid and ugly to mate with one so beautiful and wise. At last, however, she found a boy who was handsome and manly and wise beyond his years. Gayelette made up her mind that when he grew to be a man she would make him her husband, so she took him to her ruby palace and used all her magic powers to make him as strong and good and lovely as any woman could wish. When he grew to manhood, Quelala, as he was called, was said to be the best and wisest man in all the land, while his manly beauty was so great that

Gayelette loved him dearly, and hastened to make everything ready for the wedding.

"My grandfather was at that time the King of the Winged Monkeys which lived in the forest near Gayalette's palace, and the old fellow loved a joke better than a good dinner. One day, just before the wedding, my grandfather was flying out with his band when he saw Quelala walking beside the river. He was dressed in a rich costume of pink silk and purple velvet, and my grandfather thought he would see what he could do. At his word the band flew down and seized Quelala, carried him in their arms until they were over the middle of the river, and then dropped him into the water.

"'Swim out, my fine fellow,' cried my grandfather, 'and see if the water has spotted your clothes.' Quelala was much too wise not to swim, and he was not in the least spoiled by all his good fortune. He laughed, when he came to the top of the water, and swam in to shore. But when Gayelette came running out to him she found his silks and velvet all ruined by the river.

"The princess was very angry, and she knew, of course, who did it. She had all the Winged Monkeys brought before her, and she said at first that their wings should be tied and they should be treated as they had treated Quelala, and dropped in the river. But my grandfather pleaded hard, for he knew the Monkeys would drown in the river with their wings tied, and Quelala said a kind word for them also; so that Gayelette finally spared them, on condition that the Winged Monkeys should ever after do three times the bidding of the owner of the Golden Cap. This Cap had been made for a wedding present to Quelala, and it is said to have cost the princess half her kingdom. Of course my grandfather and all the other Monkeys at once agreed to the condition, and that is how it happens that we are three times the slaves of the owner of the Golden Cap, whomsoever he may be."

"And what became of them?" asked Dorothy, who had been greatly interested in the story.

"Quelala being the first owner of the Golden Cap," replied the Monkey, "he was the first to lay his wishes upon us. As his bride could not bear the sight of us, he called us all to him in the forest after he had married her and ordered us to always keep where she could never again set eyes on a Winged Monkey, which we were glad to do, for we were all afraid of her.

"This was all we ever had to do until the Golden Cap fell into the hands of the Wicked Witch of the West, who made us enslave the Winkies, and afterward drive Oz himself out of the Land of the West. Now the Golden Cap is yours, and three times you have the right to lay your wishes upon us."

As the Monkey King finished his story Dorothy looked down and saw the green, shining walls of the Emerald City before them. She wondered at the rapid flight of the Monkeys, but was glad the journey was over. The strange creatures set the travellers down carefully before the gate of the City, the King bowed low to Dorothy, and then flew swiftly away, followed by all his band.

"That was a good ride," said the little girl.

"Yes, and a quick way out of our troubles," replied the Lion. "How lucky it was you brought away that wonderful Cap!"

Chapter XV.
The Discovery of OZ, The Terrible.

The Four travellers walked up to the great gate of the Emerald City and rang the bell. After ringing several times it was opened by the same Guardian of the Gate they had met before.

"What! are you back again?" he asked, in surprise.

"Do you not see us?" answered the Scarecrow.

"But I thought you had gone to visit the Wicked Witch of the West."

"We did visit her," said the Scarecrow.

"And she let you go again?" asked the man, in wonder.

"She could not help it, for she is melted," explained the Scarecrow.

"Melted! Well, that is good news, indeed," said the man. "Who melted her?"

"It was Dorothy," said the Lion, gravely.

"Good gracious!" exclaimed the man, and he bowed very low indeed before her.

Then he led them into his little room and locked the spectacles from the great box on all their eyes, just as he had done before. Afterward they passed on through the gate into the Emerald City, and when the people heard from the Guardian of the Gate that they had melted the Wicked Witch of the West they all gathered around the travellers and followed them in a great crowd to the Palace of Oz.

The soldier with the green whiskers was still on guard before the door, but he let them in at once and they were again met by the beautiful green girl, who showed each of them to their old rooms at once, so they might rest until the Great Oz was ready to receive them.

The soldier had the news carried straight to Oz that Dorothy and the other travellers had come back again, after destroying the Wicked Witch; but Oz made no reply. They thought the Great Wizard would send for them at once, but he did not. They had no word from him the next day, nor the next, nor the next. The waiting was tiresome and wearing, and at last they grew vexed that

Oz should treat them in so poor a fashion, after sending them to undergo hardships and slavery. So the Scarecrow at last asked the green girl to take another message to Oz, saying if he did not let them in to see him at once they would call the Winged Monkeys to help them, and find out whether he kept his promises or not. When the Wizard was given this message he was so frightened that he sent word for them to come to the Throne Room at four minutes after nine o'clock the next morning. He had **1** once met the Winged Monkeys in the Land of the West, and he did not wish to meet them again.

The four travellers passed a sleepless night, each thinking of the gift Oz had promised to bestow upon him. Dorothy fell asleep only once, and then she dreamed she was in Kansas, where Aunt Em was telling her how glad she was to have her little girl at home again.

Promptly at nine o'clock the next morning the green whiskered soldier came to them, and four minutes later they all went into the Throne Room of the Great Oz.

Of course each one of them expected to see the Wizard in the shape he had taken before, and all were greatly surprised when they looked about and saw no one at all in the room. They kept close to the door and closer to one another, for the stillness of the empty room was more dreadful than any of the forms they had seen Oz take.

Presently they heard a Voice, seeming to come

1 *four minutes after nine o'clock.* The time of the Wizard's appointment recalls the ridiculous hours kept by another little wizard, in *A New Wonderland* (p. 134). Over the entrance to his cave is the following:

> A. WIZARD, Esq.,
> Office hours:
> From 10:45 until
> a quarter to 11.

261

from somewhere near the top of the great dome, and it said, solemnly.

"I am Oz, the Great and Terrible. Why do you seek me?"

They looked again in every part of the room, and then, seeing no one, Dorothy asked,

"Where are you?"

"I am everywhere," answered the Voice, "but to the eyes of common mortals I am invisible. I will now seat myself upon my throne, that you may converse with me." Indeed, the Voice seemed just then to come straight from the throne itself; so they walked toward it and stood in a row while Dorothy said:

"We have come to claim our promise, O Oz."

"What promise?" asked Oz.

"You promised to send me back to Kansas when the Wicked Witch was destroyed," said the girl.

"And you promised to give me brains," said the Scarecrow.

"And you promised to give me a heart," said the Tin Woodman.

"And you promised to give me courage," said the Cowardly Lion.

"Is the Wicked Witch really destroyed?" asked the Voice, and Dorothy thought it trembled a little.

"Yes," she answered, "I melted her with a bucket of water."

"Dear me," said the Voice; "how sudden! Well, come to me to-morrow, for I must have time to think it over."

"You've had plenty of time already," said the Tin Woodman, angrily.

"We shan't wait a day longer," said the Scarecrow.

"You must keep your promises to us!" exclaimed Dorothy.

The Lion thought it might be as well to frighten the Wizard, so he gave a large, loud roar, which was so fierce and dreadful that Toto jumped away from him in alarm and tipped over the screen that stood in a corner. As it fell with a crash they looked that way, and the next moment all of them were filled with wonder. For they saw, standing in just the spot the screen had hidden, a little, old man, with a bald head and a wrinkled face, who **2** seemed to be as much surprised as they were. The Tin Woodman, raising his axe, rushed toward the little man and cried out,

"Who are you?"

"I am Oz, the Great and Terrible," said the little man, in a trembling voice, "but don't strike me—please don't!—and I'll do anything you want me to."

2 *a bald head*. An ancient tradition claims that the power of a wizard depends upon the abundance of hair upon his head. If this is true, a bald wizard can only be "a very good man, but a very bad wizard." On the other hand, James Hastings's *A Dictionary of the Bible*, published by Charles Scribner's Sons in 1909, notes that Egyptian priests, to retain their supernatural power, shaved their heads. Notice in the illustration on page 267 that the Wizard was not completely bald until after he came to live in the Land of Oz. Evidently he did age in Oz. See Note 9 below.

3 *I am a humbug.* In "The Forest Oracle" (*The Delineator*, April 1905), "the Terrible Unknown, the Mighty Oracle—the Fraud of the Forest" is discovered by a clever monkey. This is one of Baum's "Animal Fairy Tales," first published as a collection by the International Wizard of Oz Club in 1969.

Our friends looked at him in surprise and dismay.

"I thought Oz was a great Head," said Dorothy.

"And I thought Oz was a lovely Lady," said the Scarecrow,

"And I thought Oz was a terrible Beast," said the Tin Woodman.

"And I thought Oz was a Ball of Fire," exclaimed the Lion.

"No; you are all wrong," said the little man, meekly. "I have been making believe."

"Making believe!" cried Dorothy. "Are you not a great Wizard?"

"Hush, my dear," he said; "don't speak so loud, or you will be overheard—and I should be ruined. I'm supposed to be a Great Wizard."

"And aren't you?" she asked.

"Not a bit of it, my dear; I'm just a common man."

"You're more than that," said the Scarecrow, in a grieved tone; "you're a humbug."

3 "Exactly so!" declared the little man, rubbing his hands together as if it pleased him; "I am a humbug."

"But this is terrible," said the Tin Woodman; "how shall I ever get my heart?"

"Or I my courage?" asked the Lion.

"Or I my brains?" wailed the Scarecrow, wiping the the tears from his eyes with his coat-sleeve.

"My dear friends," said Oz, "I pray you not to speak

of these little things.   Think of me, and the terrible trouble I'm in at being found out."

"Doesn't anyone else know you're a humbug?" asked Dorothy.

"No one knows it but you four—and myself," replied Oz. "I have fooled everyone so long that I thought I should never be found out. It was a great mistake my ever letting you into the Throne Room. Usually I will not see even my subjects, and so they believe I am something terrible."

"But, I don't understand," said Dorothy, in bewilderment. "How was it that you appeared to me as a great Head?"

"That was one of my tricks," answered Oz. "Step this way, please, and I will tell you all about it."

He led the way to a small chamber in the rear of the Throne Room, and they all followed him. He pointed to one corner, in which lay the Great Head, made out of many thicknesses of paper, and with a carefully painted face.

"This I hung from the ceiling by a wire," said Oz; "I stood behind the screen and pulled a thread, to make the **4** eyes move and the mouth open."

"But how about the voice?" she enquired.

"Oh, I am a ventriloquist," said the little man, "and I can throw the sound of my voice wherever I wish; so that **you** thought it was coming out of the Head.   Here are

4 *make the eyes move and the mouth open.* The Wizard's interest in mechanical gadgetry and stagecraft was shared by Baum himself. Throughout his life Baum spent considerable time designing ways to create an illusion of magic on the stage and screen. Many of the special effects in his musical plays and silent movies were Baum's work. The cyclone and lion's roar of the 1902 *Wizard of Oz* musical were Baum's ideas. As described in *To Please a Child*, the cyclone was created by revolving a large celluloid disk in front of a spotlight in the balcony and painted on the disk were storm clouds; the rotation of the disk produced the illusion of a hurricane as the clouds were projected on a transparent gauze screen on the stage. According to *The Musical Fantasies of L. Frank Baum*, an effective roar for the Cowardly Lion was produced by rubbing a piece of resin up and down a cord fastened to the center of a drumhead tightly stretched across the mouth of a barrel.

In my introduction I have quoted from an interview with Baum, explaining a number of the effects for the "Radio-Plays," a series of short motion pictures—based upon his fairy tales—manufactured by the Selig Polyscope Co. in 1908. One of the most imaginative of his stage mechanisms was the woodpecker chorus in the unproduced musical "The Pipes O' Pan," included by Alla T. Ford and Dick Martin in their book of unproduced scenarios, *The Musical Fantasies of L. Frank Baum* (Chicago: The Wizard Press, 1958). It is as follows:

The Woodpeckers appear on the various set trees, as cuckoos do from cuckoo clocks, and by mechanically pecking upon xylophone bars concealed just back of the trees, they play the air accompanying the whistle. These mechanical birds are all connected by electrical wires, so that the air may be played by a person in the wings who presses electric buttons on a keyboard.

5 *I was born in Omaha.* In *Dorothy and the Wizard in Oz* (p. 192) the little Wizard continues his history prior to his arrival in Oz. His father, a politician, named him Oscar Zoroaster Phadrig Isaac Norman Henkle Emmanuel Ambroise Diggs. Because this is such a long and difficult name to remember, the young man shortened it to O.Z.; the other initials spelled "pinhead," which he feared might be considered a reflection on his intelligence. He painted the first two initials on all his belongings and, when he joined a circus, on his balloon. Upon his arrival in Oz the natives concluded that he must be their rightful ruler for on the balloon painted in large letters was "O.Z."

the other things I used to deceive you." He showed the Scarecrow the dress and the mask he had worn when he seemed to be the lovely Lady; and the Tin Woodman saw that his Terrible Beast was nothing but a lot of skins, sewn together, with slats to keep their sides out. As for the Ball of Fire, the false Wizard had hung that also from the ceiling. It was really a ball of cotton, but when oil was poured upon it the ball burned fiercely.

"Really," said the Scarecrow, "you ought to be ashamed of yourself for being such a humbug."

"I am—I certainly am," answered the little man, sorrowfully; "but it was the only thing I could do. Sit down, please, there are plenty of chairs; and I will tell you my story."

So they sat down and listened while he told the following tale:

5 "I was born in Omaha—"

"Why, that isn't very far from Kansas!" cried Dorothy.

"No; but it's farther from here," he said, shaking his head at her, sadly. "When I grew up I became a ventriloquist, and at that I was very well trained by a great master. I can imitate any kind of a bird or beast." Here he mewed so like a kitten that Toto pricked up his ears and looked everywhere to see where she was. "After a time," continued Oz, "I tired of that, and became a balloonist."

"What is that?" asked Dorothy.

"A man who goes up in a balloon on circus day, **so** as

o draw a crowd of people together and
get them to pay to see the circus," he **6**
explained.

"Oh," she said; "I know."

"Well, one day I went up in a balloon and the ropes got twisted, so that
I couldn't come down again. It went
way up above the clouds, so far that a
current of air struck it and carried it
many, many miles away. For a day
and a night I travelled through the air, and on the morning
of the second day I awoke and found the balloon floating
over a strange and beautiful country.

"It came down gradually, and I was not hurt a bit.
But I found myself in the midst of a strange people, who,
seeing me come from the clouds, thought I was a great
Wizard. Of course I let them think so, because they were
afraid of me, and promised to do anything I wished **7**
them to.

"Just to amuse myself, and keep the good people busy,
I ordered them to build this City, and my palace; and they
did it all willingly and well. Then I thought, as the country was so green and beautiful, I would call it the Emerald
City, and to make the name fit better I put green spectacles
on all the people, so that everything they saw was green."

"But isn't everything here green?" asked Dorothy.

"No more than in any other city," replied Oz; "but

6 *get them to pay to see the circus.* "Such
skills are as admirably adapted to success
in late nineteenth-century politics as they
are to the humbug wizardry of Baum's
story," writes Littlefield in his article cited
in my introduction. In *Dorothy and the
Wizard in Oz* it is disclosed that the Wizard's father was a verbose politician; evidently Oz learned a few tricks of the trade
from the elder Diggs. Not surprisingly,
American public figures from William Randolph Hearst ("The Wizard of Ooze") to
Lyndon Johnson and Richard Nixon have
been compared to the humbug wizard who
was a good man, but just a bad wizard.
Martin Gardner asks in his introduction to
the 1961 Dover edition: "Are the respected
Wizards of our Emerald Cities really wizards, or just amiable circus humbugs who
keep us supplied with green glasses that
make life greener than it really is?"

Daily balloon ascensions though hazard-
ous were a popular attraction of many
circuses during their heyday in the second
half of the nineteenth century. Barnum's
"Professor" Donaldson made an ascension
near Chicago in 1875 and was never seen
again.

7 *anything I wished.* The Wizard's story
may have been the source for an episode
in Edward Eager's fantasy *Seven-Day Magic*
(New York: Harcourt Brace & World, Inc.,
1962). With the aid of a magic book five
children visit a magic land named Oswaldo-
land; they are accompanied by a stage
magician whose name happens to be Os-
waldo. (In an article on children's literature
in *Horn Book*, March 1948, Mr. Eager explains his admiration for several of the Oz
books.)

8 *looks green to you.* "The Wizard is being overmodest and slightly untruthful," writes Gardner in Note 19 of *The Wizard of Oz and Who He Was.* "When he built the Emerald City he used more emeralds than any other precious stone. The practice of wearing spectacles was never really necessary." After the capture of the city by Jinjur's Army of Revolt in *The Marvelous Land of Oz* the use of green glasses is ended.

9 *I am a very old man now.* This is questionable. It's not likely that the Wizard could be much older than fifty. Although it had been a trading post since the eighteenth century, Omaha did not receive its name until it was incorporated as a city in 1854. The rest of the Wizard's history as well as his dress indicates that he came to Oz in the last half of the nineteenth century. Perhaps his stay in the Emerald City (avoiding all contact with others) has caused him to lose his sense of time and to think of himself as an old man. The average male life expectancy at the turn of the century was fifty years, but the Wizard could not be considered "a very old man" at this age. In fact, the Wizard could not be much older than Baum himself.

The similarity in their ages as well as a few other details suggest that there is a good deal of Baum in the humbug Wizard. The Wizard's stage magic and puns reflect Baum's own personal interests. "After half a lifetime stumbling through the Gilded Age and half the vocations a man could

try," writes MacFall in *To Please a Child,* Baum "had found his fortune within himself, in the humble gift of storytelling. Perhaps he even thought of himself as the Wizard, for as the saga of Oz extended itself through book after book, the Wizard who began as a Prince of Humbug became a genuine Wizard."

10 *green glasses.* An earlier reference to green glasses appears in the "Our Landlady" column, "She Tells How the Agent Deals Out the Corn," the Aberdeen, South Dakota, *Saturday Pioneer,* May 3, 1890. A farmer whose feed crops have been ruined is quoted as saying: "I put green goggles on my hosses an' feed 'em shavings an' they think it's grass, but they ain't gittin' fat on it." (A selection of the "Our Landlady" columns was collected and published by the South Dakota Writers' Project in 1941.)

The wearing of green glasses is also reminiscent of the expression "to wear rose-colored glasses," meaning to see the world as better than it really is. A delightful Oz-like tale is the title story of G. K. Chesterton's *The Coloured Lands* (1938).

11 *shut myself up.* This statement is somewhat inaccurate. The Wizard must have made at least one journey to the land of the Winkies; the Wicked Witch used the second command of the Winged Monkeys to drive the Wizard from the West. But this may have been before he settled in the Emerald City; perhaps his balloon landed in the Winkie Country, and he and his

when you wear green spectacles, why of course everything
8 you see looks green to you. The Emerald City was built
a great many years ago, for I was a young man when the
9 balloon brought me here, and I am a very old man now.
10 But my people have worn green glasses on their eyes so
long that most of them think it really is an Emerald City,
and it certainly is a beautiful place, abounding in jewels
and precious metals, and every good thing that is needed
to make one happy. I have been good to the people, and
they like me; but ever since this Palace was built I have
11 shut myself up and would not see any of them.

"One of my greatest fears was the Witches, for while
I had no magical powers at all I soon found out that the
Witches were really able to do wonderful things. There
were four of them in this country, and they ruled the people
who live in the North and South and East and West.
Fortunately, the Witches of the North and South were
good, and I knew they would do me no harm; but the
Witches of the East and West were terribly wicked, and
had they not thought I was more powerful than they themselves,
they would surely have destroyed me. As it was,
I lived in deadly fear of them for many years; so you can
imagine how pleased I was when I heard your house had
fallen on the Wicked Witch of the East. When you came
to me I was willing to promise anything if you would only
do away with the other Witch; but, now that you have
melted her, I am ashamed to say that I cannot keep my
promises."

"I think you are a very bad man," said Dorothy.

"Oh, no, my dear; I'm really a very good man; but I'm a very bad Wizard, I must admit."

12

"Can't you give me brains?" asked the Scarecrow.

"You don't need them. You are learning something every day. A baby has brains, but it doesn't know much. Experience is the only thing that brings knowledge, and the longer you are on earth the more experience you are sure to get."

"That may all be true," said the Scarecrow, "but I shall be very unhappy unless you give me brains."

The false wizard looked at him carefully.

"Well," he said, with a sigh, "I'm not much of a magician, as I said; but if you will come to me to-morrow morning, I will stuff your head with brains. I cannot tell you how to use them, however; you must find that out for yourself."

13

"Oh, thank you—thank you!" cried the Scarecrow. "I'll find a way to use them, never fear!"

"But how about my courage?" asked the Lion, anxiously.

"You have plenty of courage, I am sure," answered Oz. "All you need is confidence in yourself. There is no living

Winkie followers were forced by the Winged Monkeys to flee to where the Emerald City now stands. In Chapter 20 of *The Marvelous Land of Oz* are reported three visits he made to Mombi the Witch. Glinda suspects that on one of these trips the Wizard gave the girl Ozma, the rightful ruler of Oz, to the Witch. But when the girl ruler and the Wizard meet in *Dorothy and the Wizard in Oz*, there is no recognition on either side of this exchange and no animosity is expressed. But these three visits may also have occurred prior to the building of the Emerald City.

The information concerning the three meetings between Mombi the Witch and the Wizard of Oz is contained in a book (compiled by Glinda's spies) of all that the Wizard did while he was in Oz. Two more details about the Wizard given in the second Oz book but not in the first are that he limped slightly on his left foot (the Scarecrow suspects that he had corns) and that he ate beans with a knife.

12 *I'm a very bad Wizard.* The Wizard is confronted with the psychological conflict between the Role and the Self. The Role is determined by Society, the Self by the Individual. According to the "radical" psychologist R. D. Laing, the split between the Self and the Role may result in schizophrenia—a rift he believes to be societal in origin. The Wizard, however, has not yet made a complete split. Although he is given the role of Wizard, Oz admits that he is only a man albeit a good man. His people think of him only in terms of the part he

is given to play; they cannot even consider the possibility of his being only a man. This presents another conflict. He is feared because he is not understood. He is most dreadful when not seen at all, when his Role is the only thing known of his presence. When the screen falls, his Role falls, and he is seen as his Self, a little old man. Ironically, in Chapter 2, when she is first told to visit the Wizard, Dorothy asks: "Is he a good man?" She only learns that he is a "good Wizard"; but when she discovers Oz, the Terrible, she is disappointed for he cannot live up to his Role. The Wizard's lesson can be seen as the culmination of the experience of the nineteenth century. The old beliefs had been stripped away—Revolution, Darwin, Nietzsche, helped destroy the "old order." Man has had to find a new value, a meaning for his place in the universe; but he must realize that though one may be a wizard, he is also a man.

The Wizard is perhaps a conglomerate of several individuals, including Baum himself (see Note 9). Certainly Baum's Wizard has in him a dash of P. T. Barnum, the "Prince of Humbugs." The charlatan magician is a type character of the nineteenth century; a principal of the cast of Gaetano Donizetti's opera *L' Elisir d'Amore* (1832) is Dr. Dulcamara, the inventor of a patent medicine who makes his arrival in a magnificent balloon. Another contemporary of Baum whose life suggests a comparison to Oz the Wizard is John A. Hamlin, the father of the producer of the 1902 musical. The elder Hamlin won his reputation and fortune with the product "Wizard Oil."

While traveling across country this mid-western circus magician gave demonstrations that promised that anyone who rubbed his hands with Wizard Oil also could do marvelous things. His wide advertising campaign ranged from painting "Wizard Oil" on rocks to the production of musical reviews. When his son Fred Hamlin heard just the name of Baum's proposed play, he agreed to produce it in the hope that the word "wizard" would be as rewarding to him as it had been for his father. During the New York run of the play a rumor was circulated and even printed in the papers that the brothers Hamlin wanted a play based upon their father's famous Wizard Oil and, having decided on the title "The Wonderful Works of the Wonderful Oil of the Wonder Wizard of Oz," they supposedly employed Baum and Tietjens as librettist and composer. There is no truth in this story.

In the 1939 MGM film the Wizard was portrayed by the fine character-actor Frank Morgan.

13 *you must find that out for yourself.* The Scarecrow has already proven that he has the intelligence to use a brain properly. Because he still does not possess one, he as yet has not had the opportunity to abuse a brain. Likewise the Tin Woodman and the Cowardly Lion have shown that the quality of the thing that each desires is already within him. These illustrate, as Gardner has written in *The Wizard of Oz and Who He Was*, "the human tendency to confuse a real virtue with its valueless

outer symbol." The Wizard has already confessed that he knows no magic, yet Dorothy's three friends still ask him to present them with a tangible symbol of what they value most highly. A reversal of this process occurs in *The Patchwork Girl of Oz:* the Glass Cat is given a red stone heart and pink brains for all the world to see, but because she received these before she knew how to use them, she is vain and foolish.

The importance of their journey to the Wizard was not the eventual gifts of a brain, heart, and courage. The journey itself was more important than its conclusion, for through it they learned how to use the gifts they wished from the Wizard and in doing so never needed them in the end. Dorothy did not quite realize what she was saying when in Chapter 3 she tells the Scarecrow: "If Oz will not give you any brains you will be no worse off than you are now." The difference in his present condition is that he now knows how to use a brain. The Wizard suggests that the Scarecrow confused knowledge, the accumulation of facts, with intelligence, the quality to use the knowledge once it is acquired. He has had to gain the knowledge through experience before he can use his intellect.

14 *that kind of courage you have in plenty.* Compare this to the moral of "The King of the Polar Bears" in *American Fairy Tales:* "This story teaches us that true dignity and courage depend not upon outward courage, but come rather from within." As with the Scarecrow and a brain and the Tin

thing that is not afraid when it faces danger. True courage is in facing danger when you are afraid, and that kind of courage you have in plenty."

14

"Perhaps I have, but I'm scared just the same," said the Lion. "I shall really be very unhappy unless you give me the sort of courage that makes one forget he is afraid."

"Very well; I will give you that sort of courage tomorrow," replied Oz.

"How about my heart?" asked the Tin Woodman.

"Why, as for that," answered Oz, "I think you are wrong to want a heart. It makes most people unhappy. If you only knew it, you are in luck not to have a heart."

"That must be a matter of opinion," said the Tin Woodman. "For my part, I will bear all the unhappiness

15 without a murmur, if you will give me the heart."

"Very well," answered Oz, meekly. "Come to me to-morrow and you shall have a heart. I have played Wizard for so many years that I may as well continue the part a little longer."

"And now," said Dorothy, "how am I to get back to Kansas?"

"We shall have to think about that," replied the little man, "Give me two or three days to consider the matter and I'll try to find a way to carry you over the desert. In the meantime you shall all be treated as my guests, and while you live in the Palace my people will wait upon you and obey your slighest wish. There is only one thing I ask in return for my help—such as it is. You must keep my secret and tell no one I am a humbug."

They agreed to say nothing of what they had learned, **16** and went back to their rooms in high spirits. Even Dorothy had hope that "The Great and Terrible Humbug," as she called him, would find a way to send her back to Kansas, and if he did that she was willing to forgive him everything.

Woodman and a heart, the Cowardly Lion has had to find what he values, courage or confidence, within himself and therefore an understanding of himself. Baum realizes, as Sheldon Kopp writes in "The Wizard Behind the Couch" (*Psychology Today*, March 1970), "the possibility of personal growth through coming to accept ourselves, with humor if need be, and of the central role of a loving relationship in solving our problems." Baum wrote "to express his dissatisfaction with Victorian ideas of building character through punishment, grave lectures, and inner struggle for self-control, sacrifice and self-denial." Baum's concern is with a presentation of the reality and worth of the power of the Self. He is not interested in those qualities encouraged by most Victorian literature, "the duties of industry, frugality, manly respect for the weak, and a sober Christian altruism," in the words of Howard Mumford Jones in his essay "The Technique of Happiness" (*The Pursuit of Happiness,* Boston: Harvard University Press, 1954). Since the publication of Baum's book children's literature has followed (as Jones calls it) "the *Wizard of Oz* formula," or the pursuit of happiness. Perhaps this is an unfair generalization, but Baum does support the rejection of social mores and lessons if they do not correspond to the pursuit of the individual's freedom, the origin of which is within the Self.

The Wizard of Oz is a subtle extension of the fairy-tale tradition. Often, the protagonist of a fairy tale searches for a talisman that will cure an illness or a misfortune. M.-L. Franz claims in "The first approach

of the unconscious" (in Carl Jung's book, cited in Chapter 4, Note 4) that the illness is the feeling of emptiness and futility; the desired talisman will return meaning to the individual. And this talisman is merely a reflection of the individual's Self. In *The Wizard of Oz* the Scarecrow, Tin Woodman, and Cowardly Lion each has this feeling of futility; each must find the one thing that will make him whole. The talisman, however, is only a symbol and has no value of its own; only when it reflects the Self is it of value. Now each of the three realizes that what he has longed for has always been within himself.

15 *without a murmur.* This is another pun concerned with heart ailments. By having the Tin Woodman present his request last (the first and only significant time out of sequence), Baum may have been stressing his own desire for a new heart.

16 *agreed to say nothing.* Apparently someone did not keep his promise. Although Dorothy and her friends are supposedly the only ones who know the Wizard's secret, in the second chapter of the second Oz book Tip reports to Jack Pumpkinhead that Oz "wasn't so much of a Wizard as he might have been."

Chapter XVI.
The Magic Art of the Great Humbug.

Next MORNING THE Scarecrow said to his friends:

"Congratulate me. I am going to Oz to get my brains at last. When I return I shall be as other men are."

"I have always liked you as you were," said Dorothy, simply.

"It is kind of you to like a Scarecrow," he replied. "But surely you will think more of me when you hear the splendid thoughts my new brain is going to turn out." Then he said good-bye to them all in a cheerful voice and went to the Throne Room, where he rapped upon the door.

"Come in," said Oz.

The Scarecrow went in and found the little man sitting down by the window, engaged in deep thought.

"I have come for my brains," remarked the Scarecrow a little uneasily.

"Oh, yes; sit down in that chair, please," replied Oz. "You must excuse me for taking your head off, but I shall have to do it in order to put your brains in their proper place."

"That's all right," said the Scarecrow. "You are quite welcome to take my head off, as long as it will be a better one when you put it on again."

So the Wizard unfastened his head and emptied out the straw. Then he entered the back room and took up a measure of bran, which he mixed with a great many pins and needles. Having shaken them together thoroughly, he filled the top of the Scarecrow's head with the mixture and stuffed the rest of the space with straw, to hold it in place. When he had fastened the Scarecrow's head on his body again he said to him,

"Hereafter you will be a great man, for I have given you a lot of bran-new brains."

The Scarecrow was both pleased and proud at the fulfillment of his greatest wish, and having thanked Oz warmly he went back to his friends.

Dorothy looked at him curiously. His head was quite bulging out at the top with brains.

"How do you feel?" she asked.

"I feel wise, indeed," he answered, earnestly. "When I get used to my brains I shall know everything."

"Why are those needles and pins sticking out of your head?" asked the Tin Woodman.

"That is proof that he is sharp," remarked the Lion.

"Well, I must go to Oz and get my heart," said the Woodman. So he walked to the Throne Room and knocked at the door.

"Come in," called Oz, and the Woodman entered and said,

"I have come for my heart."

"Very well," answered the little man. "But I shall have to cut a hole in your breast, so I can put your heart in the right place. I hope it won't hurt you"

"Oh, no;" answered the Woodman. "I shall not feel it at all."

So Oz brought a pair of tinners' shears and cut a small, square hole in the left side of the Tin Woodman's breast. Then, going to a chest of drawers, he took out a pretty heart, made entirely of silk and stuffed with sawdust.

"Isn't it a beauty?" he asked.

"It is, indeed!" replied

the Woodman, who was greatly pleased. "But is it a kind heart?"

"Oh, very!" answered Oz. He put the heart in the Woodman's breast and then replaced the square of tin, soldering it neatly together where it had been cut.

"There," said he; "now you have a heart that any man might be proud of. I'm sorry I had to put a patch on your breast, but it really couldn't be helped."

"Never mind the patch," exclaimed the happy Woodman. "I am very grateful to you, and shall never forget your kindness."

"Don t speak of it," replied Oz.

Then the Tin Woodman went back to his friends, who wished him every joy on account of his good fortune.

The Lion now walked to the Throne Room and knocked at the door.

"Come in," said Oz.

"I have come for my courage," announced the Lion, entering the room.

"Very well," answered the little man; "I will get it for you."

He went to a cupboard and reaching up to a high shelf took down a square green bottle, the contents of which he poured into a green-gold dish, beautifully carved. Placing this before the Cowardly Lion, who sniffed at it as if he did not like it, the Wizard said,

"Drink."

"What is it?" asked the Lion.

"Well," answered Oz, "if it were inside of you, it would be courage. You know, of course, that courage is always inside one; so that this really cannot be called courage until you have swallowed it. Therefore I advise you to drink it as soon as possible."

The Lion hesitated no longer, but drank till the dish was empty.

"How do you feel now?" asked Oz.

"Full of courage," replied the Lion, who went joyfully **1** back to his friends to tell them of his good fortune.

Oz, left to himself, smiled to think of his success in giving the Scarecrow and the Tin Woodman and the Lion exactly what they thought they wanted. "How can I help being a humbug," he said, "when all these people make me do things that everybody knows can't be done? It **2,3** was easy to make the Scarecrow and the Lion and the Woodman happy, because they imagined I could do anything. But it will take more than imagination to carry Dorothy back to Kansas, and I'm sure I don't know how it can be done."

1 *Full of courage.* "Courage" is colloquial for an alcoholic beverage. "The lion gains his courage," observes the reviewer of *The Bookseller and Latest Literature* (July 1900), "though the reader will [be] apt to think it 'Dutch courage' since it comes out of a bottle." C. Warren Hollister reports (in the Spring 1966 *Baum Bugle*) that "courage" is a local brand of beer in Great Britain; he has seen also a beer in Cardiff, Wales, with the name "Brains," but he has yet to find one called "Heart." Also, like that of an alcoholic drink, the effect of the Wizard's "courage" is not long lasting; in Chapter 8 of *Ozma of Oz* when Dorothy asks how her friend has been, the Lion replies: "As cowardly as ever. Every little thing scares me and makes my heart beat fast. . . . To others I may have seemed brave, at times, but I have never been in any danger that I was not afraid."

2 *do things that everybody knows can't be done.* In reference to his own dilemma with patients who expect miracles while under his psychotherapeutic care, Dr. Sheldon Kopp concludes his article "The Wizard Behind the Couch" (cited in Note 14 of the previous chapter) with the Wizard's statement. Dr. Kopp interprets *The Wizard of Oz* in terms of the Rogerian method of treatment. The Wizard acts as the therapist; Dorothy and her companions are patients in search of treatment. He agrees with Baum's suggestion that no authority can magically solve another person's problems; he may give guidance, but the responsibility of the therapy depends upon the patient. A faith in the eventual cure of the individual must be established within himself before any treatment may begin.

3 *It was easy.* How easy indeed! Because his head is stuffed with pins and needles, the Scarecrow thinks he is sharp-witted. Because his heart is silk-lined and filled with sawdust, the Tin Woodman feels he is tender-hearted. Because he has drunk an alcoholic mixture, the Lion boasts he is full of courage. Now the Scarecrow, Tin Woodman, and Cowardly Lion possess concrete symbols of what they have so long desired.

Chapter XVII.
How the Balloon was Launched.

For Three days Dorothy heard nothing from Oz. These were sad days for the little girl, although her friends were all quite happy and contented. The Scarecrow told them there were wonderful thoughts in his head; but he would not say what they were because he knew no one could **1** understand them but himself. When the Tin Woodman walked about he felt his heart rattling around in his breast; and he told Dorothy he had discovered it to be a kinder and more tender heart than the one he had owned when he was made of flesh. The Lion declared he was afraid of nothing on earth, and would gladly face an army of men or a dozen of the fierce Kalidahs.

1 *no one could understand them but himself.* Compare this attitude with the Scarecrow's remarks at the opening of the previous chapter. This illustrates again how the Scarecrow can confuse the meaningless outer symbol with the virtue it represents. Because one has a brain doesn't mean one is intelligent. The Scarecrow thinks as foolishly as he did when he fell in the hole in the road saying that he had no brain to guide him. This is the first of many episodes in the Oz stories concerned with intellectual snobbery. An equally humorous incident occurs in *The Marvelous Land of Oz* when Jack Pumpkinhead has an audience with the Scarecrow who refuses to have a fruitful discussion because theoretically he cannot understand "the language of the pumpkinheads"; they, of course, speak the same language. Also, in the second Oz book is the first appearance of the Woggle-bug, one of Baum's most cleverly conceived characters. The Scarecrow's opening remarks in this chapter are more characteristic of the Woggle-bug's pedantry than of the Scarecrow's generally unprejudiced nature. Once just an ordinary insect the Woggle-bug crawled into a schoolhouse one day, and by listening to the professor's lectures, became "thoroughly educated"; he was caught by the teacher and projected magically on a screen from where, now "highly magnified," he escaped and went out into the world. With all his faults he was one of Baum's personal favorites. He named the dramatization of *The Land of Oz* after Mr. H. M. Woggle-bug, T. E., and wrote a special picture book about him, *The Woggle-Bug Book* (1905). Like Baum, the Woggle-bug's special weakness is the pun. He becomes director of the Royal College of Oz, where students spend all their time at sports and take pills of learning instead of courses (although the Woggle-bug's meal pills can be taken in three courses). The Woggle-bug explains: "You see in this country are a number of youths who do not like to work, and the college is an excellent place for them" (*Ozma of Oz*, p. 258). Such statements, as well as the Woggle-bug's personification in the first chapter of Ruth Plumly Thompson's *The Royal Book of Oz*, may be in part responsible for the poor reception some educators have given the Oz books.

2 *made of silk.* This is an accurate description of the aeronautic balloon of the nineteenth century. Silk was widely used as the material for a balloon, and the glue was generally India rubber dissolved in oil of turpentine. Not until recently have other materials, less expensive than silk, been used.

Thus each of the little party was satisfied except Dorothy, who longed more than ever to get back to Kansas.

On the fourth day, to her great joy, Oz sent for her, and when she entered the Throne Room he said, pleasantly:

"Sit down, my dear; I think I have found the way to get you out of this country."

"And back to Kansas?" she asked, eagerly.

"Well, I'm not sure about Kansas," said Oz; "for I haven't the faintest notion which way it lies. But the first thing to do is to cross the desert, and then it should be easy to find your way home."

"How can I cross the desert?" she enquired.

"Well, I'll tell you what I think," said the little man. "You see, when I came to this country it was in a balloon. You also came through the air, being carried by a cyclone. So I believe the best way to get across the desert will be through the air. Now, it is quite beyond my powers to make a cyclone; but I've been thinking the matter over, and I believe I can make a balloon."

"How?" asked Dorothy.

2   "A balloon," said Oz, "is made of silk, which is coated with glue to keep the gas in it. I have plenty of silk in the Palace, so it will be no trouble for us to make the balloon. But in all this country there is no gas to fill the balloon with, to make it float."

"If it won't float," remarked Dorothy, "it will be of no use to us."

"True," answered Oz. "But there is another way to make it float, which is to fill it with hot air. Hot air isn't **3** as good as gas, for if the air should get cold the balloon would come down in the desert, and we should be lost."

"We!" exclaimed the girl; "are you going with me?"

"Yes, of course," replied Oz." I am tired of being such a humbug. If I should go out of this Palace my people would soon discover I am not a Wizard, and then they would be vexed with me for having deceived them. So I have to stay shut up in these rooms all day, and it gets tiresome. I'd much rather go back to Kansas with you and be in a circus again."

"I shall be glad to have your company," said Dorothy.

"Thank you," he answered. "Now, if you will help me sew the silk together, we will begin to work on our balloon."

So Dorothy took a needle and thread, and as fast as Oz cut the strips of silk into proper shape the girl sewed them neatly together. First there was a strip of light green silk, then a strip of dark green and then a strip of emerald green; for Oz had a fancy to make the balloon in different shades of the

3 *Hot air isn't as good as gas.* Air, often referred to as a "gas," is a mixture of gases. Hot air was used in the first successful balloon flight, that of the French brothers Joseph (1740–1810) and Jacques (1745–1799) Montgolfier in June 1783. The first pure gas to be used was hydrogen, isolated by the British chemist Henry Cavendish (1731–1810) in 1763. In December 1783, the Frenchman J. A. C. Charles (1746–1823) produced the first successful balloon flight by hydrogen, which became the standard gas of balloons in the nineteenth century. The gas referred to by the Wizard is hydrogen (helium was not made practical until after World War I), which though highly inflammable will not cause a balloon to descend when it cools, as does hot air.

color about them. It took three days to sew all the strips together, but when it was finished they had a big bag of green silk more than twenty feet long.

Then Oz painted it on the inside with a coat of thin glue, to make it air-tight, after which he announced that the balloon was ready.

"But we must have a basket to ride in," he said. So he sent the soldier with the green whiskers for a big clothes basket, which he fastened with many ropes to the bottom of the balloon.

When it was all ready, Oz sent word to his people that he was going to make a visit to a great brother Wizard who lived in the clouds. The news spread rapidly throughout the city and everyone came to see the wonderful sight.

Oz ordered the balloon carried out in front of the Palace, and the people gazed upon it with much curiosity. The Tin Woodman had chopped a big pile of wood, and now he made a fire of it, and Oz held the bottom of the balloon over the fire so that the hot air that arose from it would be caught in the silken bag. Gradually the balloon swelled out and rose into the air, until finally the basket just touched the ground.

Then Oz got into the basket and said to all the people in a loud voice:

"I am now going away to make a visit. While I am gone the Scarecrow will rule over you. I command you to obey him as you would me."

The balloon was by this time tugging hard at the rope that held it to the ground, for the air within it was hot, and this made it so much lighter in weight than the air without that it pulled hard to rise into the sky.

"Come, Dorothy!" cried the Wizard; "hurry up, or the balloon will fly away."

"I can't find Toto anywhere," replied Dorothy, who did not wish to leave her little dog behind. Toto had run into the crowd to bark at a kitten, and Dorothy at last found him. She picked him up and ran toward the balloon.

She was within a few steps of it, and Oz was holding out his hands to help her into the basket, when, crack! went the ropes, and the balloon rose into the air without her.

"Come back!" she screamed; "I want to go, too!"

"I can't come **4** back, my dear," called Oz from the basket. "Good-bye!"

"Good-bye!" shouted everyone, and all eyes were turned upward to

4 *I can't come back.* The reason the balloon cannot return is purely practical. The Wizard has failed, in his balloon's construction, to include an apparatus to control his flight. There is no indication in either the text or illustrations to suggest that the Wizard included a valve, or guide rope. By pulling on such a rope for a few seconds, the pilot of a balloon allows the air to escape and the balloon to descend. The only way for the Wizard's balloon to return to Earth is by the unpredictable cooling of hot air. (On the original drawing for the chapter title page in the Henry Goldsmith collection of the New York Public Library is sketched in pencil a guide rope; the finished drawing in pen and ink omits this, perhaps through the suggestion of the author.)

5 *the Wonderful Wizard.* The "humbug" Wizard does return to Oz in *Dorothy and the Wizard in Oz.* He is asked to become the official Wizard of Oz again; he consents and makes his home in his old room behind the Throne Room of the Emerald City, no longer ruler, but soon no longer a humbug.

6 *reached Omaha safely.* The first indication of this, as Ruth Berman suggests in the August 1961 *Baum Bugle,* appears in *The Woggle-Bug Book,* the oversized picture book concerned with the Woggle-bug of Oz in a midwestern American city. In one episode, to escape a "bloodthirsty" laundryman whom he has previously insulted, the Woggle-bug jumps into the basket of a circus balloon, which soars away leaving the enraged laundryman and the real balloonist below. Baum describes this balloonist only as "the Professor," but Ike Morgan's picture shows an elderly, bald little man in circus tights and top hat. Taking the illustration and the locale of the story, one might conclude that the circus balloonist is none other than the little Wizard of Oz. (This is further supported by the Wizard's claim in *Dorothy and the Wizard in Oz* that on his returning to the United States he traveled through the Midwest as a balloonist with Barney and Bailum's Consolidated Shows.)

7. *people remembered him lovingly.* The terms by which his people speak of the Wizard in the second Oz book (after learning that he is a humbug) are anything but loving.

where the Wizard was riding in the basket, rising every moment farther and farther into the sky.

And that was the last any of them ever saw of Oz, the Wonderful Wizard, though he may have reached Omaha safely, and be there now, for all we know. But the people remembered him lovingly, and said to one another,

"Oz was always our friend. When he was here he built for us this beautiful Emerald City, and now he is gone he has left the Wise Scarecrow to rule over us,"

Still, for many days they grieved over the loss of the Wonderful Wizard, and would not be comforted.

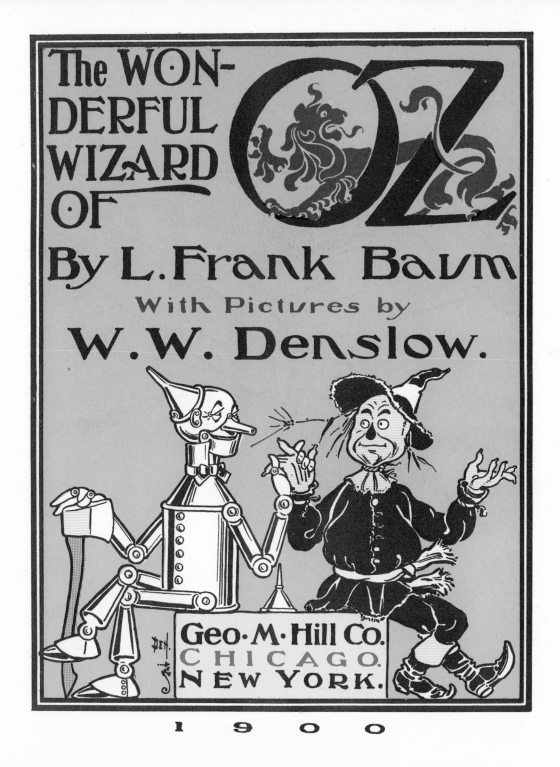

PLATE XX, Title Page

PLATE XXI, Page 93

"She caught Toto by the ear."

PLATE XXII, Page 103

" I am the Witch of the North."

PLATE XXIII, Page 114

" You must be a great sorceress."

" Dorothy gazed thoughtfully at the Scarecrow."

"'I was only made yesterday,' said the Scarecrow."

"'This is a great comfort,' said the Tin Woodman."

" You ought to be ashamed of yourself !"

PLATE XXVII, Page 147

"*The tree fell with a crash into the gulf.*"

PLATE **XXIX**, Page 172

" The Stork carried him up into the air."

PLATE XXX, Page 183

" Permit me to introduce to you her Majesty, the Queen."

"*The Lion ate some of the porridge.*"

PLATE XXXI; Page 195

PLATE XXXII, Page 207

" The Eyes looked at her thoughtfully."

" The Soldier with the green whiskers led them through the streets."

PLATE XXXIV, Page 228

"The Monkeys wound many coils about his body."

"*The Tinsmiths worked for three days and four nights.*"

PLATE XXXVI, Page 251

" The Monkeys caught Dorothy in their arms and flew away with her."

" Exactly so !   I am a humbug."

PLATE XXXVII, Page 264

"'I feel wise, indeed,' said the Scarecrow."

" *The Scarecrow sat on the big throne.* "

PLATE XXXIX, Page 292

" *The branches bent down and twined around him.*"

" These people were all made of china."

PLATE XLI, Page 309

" *The Head shot forward and struck the Scarecrow.*"

" You must give me the Golden Cap."

Chapter XVIII.
Away to the
South.

Dorothy

Wept bitterly at the passing of her hope to get home to Kansas again; but when she thought it all over she was glad she had not gone up in a balloon. And she also felt sorry at losing Oz, and so did her companions.

The Tin Woodman came to her and said, "Truly I should be ungrateful if I failed to mourn for the man who gave me my lovely heart. I should like to cry a little because Oz is gone, if you will kindly wipe away my tears, so that I shall not rust."

"With pleasure," she answered, and

1 *so far as they knew.* "The Royal Historian obviously implies that there may be a good many rulers outside Oz who are stuffed figures," writes Gardner in Note 22 of *The Wizard of Oz and Who He Was.*

brought a towel at once. Then the Tin Woodman wept for several minutes, and she watched the tears carefully and wiped them away with the towel. When he had finished he thanked her kindly and oiled himself thoroughly with his jewelled oil-can, to guard against mishap.

The Scarecrow was now the ruler of the Emerald City, and although he was not a Wizard the people were proud of him. "For," they said, "there is not another city **1** in all the world that is ruled by a stuffed man." And, so far as they knew, they were quite right.

The morning after the balloon had gone up with Oz the four travellers met in the Throne Room and talked matters over. The Scarecrow sat in the big throne and the others stood respectfully before him.

"We are not so unlucky," said the new ruler; "for this Palace and the Emerald City belong to us, and we can do just as we please. When I remember that a short time ago I was up on a pole in a farmer's cornfield, and that I am now the ruler of this beautiful City, I am quite satisfied with my lot."

"I also," said the Tin Woodman, "am well pleased with my new heart; and, really, that was the only thing I wished in all the world."

"For my part, I am content in knowing I am as brave as any beast that ever lived, if not braver," said the Lion, modestly,

"If Dorothy would only be contented to live in the

Emerald City," continued the Scarecrow, "we might all be happy together."

"But I don't want to live here," cried Dorothy. "I want to go to Kansas, and live with Aunt Em and Uncle Henry."

"Well, then, what can be done?" enquired the Woodman.

The Scarecrow decided to think, and he thought so hard that the pins and needles began to stick out of his brains. Finally he said:

"Why not call the Winged Monkeys, and asked them to carry you over the desert?"

"I never thought of that!" said Dorothy, joyfully. "It's just the thing. I'll go at once for the Golden Cap."

When she brought it into the Throne Room she spoke the magic words, and soon the band of Winged Monkeys flew in through an open window and stood beside her.

"This is the second time you have called us," said the Monkey King, bowing before the little girl. "What do you wish?"

"I want you to fly with me to Kansas," said Dorothy.

But the Monkey King shook his head.

"That cannot be done," he said. "We belong to this **2** country alone, and cannot leave it. There has never been a Winged Monkey in Kansas yet, and I suppose there never will be, for they don't belong there. We shall be glad to serve

2 *That cannot be done.* Evidently there are some limitations to Oz magic. This is also seen in the fate of the Silver Shoes at the end of the story. Like our world, the Land of Oz has its own set of natural laws. "Not everything can be done by magic," observes Donald Wollheim in his introduction to the 1965 Airmont edition of *The Wonderful Wizard of Oz*; "only some things are possible and they must be found by experiment and thoughtful ingenuity. That is the basis of the scientific method, too, and perhaps this is one of the things that makes Oz so credible to its young readers of this age of scientific marvels. It isn't too different from the science-oriented world of modern America." A discussion of specific examples of the laws of "Oz Magic" can be found in Robert R. Pattrick's *Unexplored Territory in Oz* (published by the International Wizard of Oz Club in 1963).

In *The Patchwork Girl of Oz* (p. 140) the Shaggy Man speaks in verse: "I'll sing a song of Ozland . . . where magic is a science . . ." Baum clearly realizes the relationship between what has been distinguished as magic and science. Both have the same source: the control and understanding of Nature by Man. Modern sciences, in fact, originated in part from what is now called "magic." Alchemy developed into chemistry, astrology into astronomy. In his introduction to *The Lost Princess of Oz* Baum alludes to the relationship between the sciences and "magic":

Imagination has given us the steam engine, the telephone, the talking-machine and the

automobile, for these things had to be dreamed of before they became realities. So I believe that dreams—day dreams, you know, with your eyes wide open and your brain-machinery whizzing—are likely to lead to the betterment of the world. The imaginative child will become the imaginative man or woman most apt to create, to invent, and therefore to foster civilization. A prominent educator tells me that fairy tales are of untold value in developing imagination in the young. I believe it.

One of the considerations dealt with in Bewley's "Oz Country" is magic and science and their significance in Baum's Oz books.

3 *while Oz was alive.* Is Baum suggesting that the Wizard was killed during his balloon flight back to America? In *Dorothy and the Wizard in Oz* the Wizard returns to Oz alive and well.

you in any way in our power, but we cannot cross the desert.   Good-bye."

And with another bow the Monkey King spread his wings and flew away through the window, followed by all his band.

Dorothy was almost ready to cry with disappointment

"I have wasted the charm of the Golden Cap to no purpose," she said, "for the Winged Monkeys cannot help me."

"It is certainly too bad!" said the tender hearted Woodman.

The Scarecrow was thinking again, and his head bulged out so horribly that Dorothy feared it would burst.

"Let us call in the soldier with the green whiskers," he said, "and ask his advice."

So the soldier was summoned and entered the Throne Room timidly, for **3** while Oz was alive he never was allowed to come further than the door.

"This little girl," said the Scarecrow to the soldier, "wishes to cross the desert. How can she do so?"

"I cannot tell," answered the soldier; "for nobody has ever crossed the desert, unless it is Oz himself."

"Is there no one who can help me?" asked Dorothy, earnestly.

"Glinda might," he suggested.

"Who is Glinda?" enquired the Scarecrow.

"The Witch of the South. She is the most powerful **4** of all the Witches, and rules over the Quadlings. Besides, her castle stands on the edge of the desert, so she may know a way to cross it."

"Glinda is a good Witch, isn't she?" asked the child.

"The Quadlings think she is good,' said the soldier, "and she is kind to everyone. I have heard that Glinda is a beautiful woman, who knows how to keep young in spite of the many years she has lived." **5**

"How can I get to her castle?" asked Dorothy.

"The road is straight to the South," he answered, "but it is said to be full of dangers to travellers. There are wild beasts in the woods, and a race of queer men who do not like strangers to cross their country. For this reason none of the Quadlings ever come to the Emerald City."

The soldier then left them and the Scarecrow said,

"It seems, in spite of dangers, that the best thing Dorothy can do is to travel to the Land of the South and ask Glinda to help her. For, of course, if Dorothy stays here she will never get back to Kansas."

"You must have been thinking again," remarked the Tin Woodman.

4 *The Witch of the South.* As in the 1939 MGM film, Glinda is often incorrectly referred to as the Witch of the North. Baum at least once made this mistake: in *Tik-Tok of Oz* (p. 28) Glinda's Castle is stated as being "far north of the Emerald City where Ozma holds her court."

5 *the many years she has lived.* Not all witches in European folklore were thought to be old crones. Many were said to be beautiful women, a belief that may have originated in the beautiful sorceresses Medea and Circe of the Greco-Roman world. Another beautiful witch-queen in Baum's fairy tales is Queen Zixi of Ix, who like Glinda knows the secret of eternal beauty.

"I have," said the Scarecrow.

"I shall go with Dorothy," declared the Lion, "for I am tired of your city and long for the woods and the country again. I am really a wild beast, you know. Besides, Dorothy will need someone to protect her."

"That is true," agreed the Woodman. "My axe may be of service to her; so I, also, will go with her to the Land of the South."

"When shall we start?" asked the Scarecrow.

"Are you going?" they asked, in surprise.

"Certainly. If it wasn't for Dorothy I should never have had brains. She lifted me from the pole in the cornfield and brought me to the Emerald City. So my good luck is all due to her, and I shall never leave her until she starts back to Kansas for good and all."

"Thank you," said Dorothy, gratefully. "You are all very kind to me. But I should like to start as soon as possible."

"We shall go to-morrow morning," returned the Scarecrow. "So now let us all get ready, for it will be a long journey."

Chapter XIX.
Attacked by the Fighting Trees.

The Next morning Dorothy kissed the pretty green girl good-bye, and they all shook hands with the soldier with the green whiskers, who had walked with them as far as the gate. When the Guardian of the Gate saw them again he wondered greatly that they could leave the beautiful City to get into new trouble. But he at once unlocked their spectacles, which he put back into the green box, and gave them many good wishes to carry with them.

"You are now our ruler," he said to the Scarecrow; "so you must come back to us as soon as possible."

1 *how courageous I have grown.* To look for trouble would seem to me to be just as cowardly as to run from it. As must the Scarecrow and the Tin Woodman, so too must the Lion now learn how to use the Wizard's gift. Each has proven that he has the property derived from the concrete symbol presented to him by the Wizard. In effect, each now is no better than he was before; each virtue is seen only in excess, therefore not seen at all. Each now prizes the symbol above its property. The purpose of the journey to Glinda is to develop their ability to use their qualities (now that they have public symbols for them) through the experience of adventures in unknown territory. The Lion must now face danger to prove to himself that he still has the quality, as well as the symbol, of courage.

"I certainly shall if I am able," the Scarecrow replied; "but I must help Dorothy to get home, first."

As Dorothy bade the good-natured Guardian a last farewell she said,

"I have been very kindly treated in your lovely City, and everyone has been good to me. I cannot tell you how grateful I am."

"Don't try, my dear," he answered. "We should like to keep you with us, but if it is your wish to return to Kansas I hope you will find a way." He then opened the gate of the outer wall and they walked forth and started upon their journey.

The sun shone brightly as our friends turned their faces toward the Land of the South. They were all in the best of spirits, and laughed and chatted together. Dorothy was once more filled with the hope of getting home, and the Scarecrow and the Tin Woodman were glad to be of use to her. As for the Lion, he sniffed the fresh air with delight and whisked his tail from side to side in pure joy at being in the country again, while Toto ran around them and chased the moths and butterflies, barking merrily all the time.

"City life does not agree with me at all," remarked the Lion, as they walked along at a brisk pace. "I have lost much flesh since I lived there, and now I am anxious
1 for a chance to show the other beasts how courageous I have grown."

They now turned and took a last look at the Emerald City. All they could see was a mass of towers and steeples behind the green walls, and high up above everything the spires and dome of the Palace of Oz.

"Oz was not such a bad Wizard, after all," said the Tin Woodman, as he felt his heart rattling around in his breast.

"He knew how to give me brains, and very good brains, too," said the Scarecrow.

"If Oz had taken a dose of the same courage he gave me," added the Lion, "he would have been a brave man."

Dorothy said nothing. Oz had not kept the promise he made her, but he had done his best, so she forgave him. As he said, he was a good man, even if he was a bad Wizard.

The first day's journey was through the green fields and bright flowers that stretched about the Emerald City on every side. They slept that night on the grass, with nothing but the stars over them; and they rested very well indeed.

In the morning they travelled on until they came to a thick wood. There was no way of going around it, for it seemed to extend to the right and left as far as they could see; and, besides, they did not dare change the direction of their journey for fear of getting lost. So they looked for the place where it would be easiest to get into the forest.

The Scarecrow, who was in the lead, finally discovered a big tree with such wide spreading branches that there was room for the party to pass underneath. So he walked forward to the tree, but just as he came under the first branches they bent down and twined around him, and the next minute he was raised from the ground and flung headlong among his fellow travellers.

This did not hurt the Scarecrow, but it surprised him, and he looked rather dizzy when Dorothy picked him up.

"Here is another space between the trees," called the Lion.

"Let me try it first," said the Scarecrow, "for it doesn't hurt me to get thrown about." He walked up to another tree, as he spoke, but its branches immediately seized him and tossed him back again.

"This is strange," exclaimed Dorothy; "what shall we do?"

"The trees seem to have made up their minds to fight us, and stop our journey," remarked the Lion.

"I believe I will try it myself," said the Woodman,

and shouldering his axe he marched up to the first tree that had handled the Scarecrow so roughly. When a big branch bent down to seize him the Woodman chopped at it so fiercely that he cut it in two. At once the tree began shaking all its branches as if in pain, and the Tin Woodman passed safely under it.   **2**

"Come on!" he shouted to the others; "be quick!"

They all ran forward and passed under the tree without injury, except Toto, who was caught by a small branch and shaken until he howled. But the Woodman promptly chopped off the branch and set the little dog free.

The other trees of the forest did nothing to keep them back, so they made up their minds that only the first row of trees could bend down their branches, and that probably these were the policemen of the forest, and given this wonderful power in order to keep strangers out of it.   **3**

The four travellers walked with ease through the trees until they came to the further edge of the wood. Then, to their surprise, they found before them a high wall, which seemed to be made of white china. It was   **4** smooth, like the surface of a dish, and higher than their heads.

"What shall we do now?" asked Dorothy.

"I will make a ladder," said the Tin Woodman, "for we certainly must climb over the wall."

2 *passed safely under it.* Magic forests of trees with humanlike features appear frequently in children's literature. There are two distinctive varieties of such trees in Ruth Plumly Thompson's *Kabumpo in Oz* (1922) and *The Cowardly Lion of Oz* (1923). The forests of Middle Earth of Tolkien's fairy lore contain such trees as Old Man Willow and the Ents. Arthur Rackham's celebrated illustrations for children's classics often picture fantastic elfin trees. (Walt Disney acknowledged his admiration for Rackham's fantastic vegetation in the cartoon film *Flowers and Trees,* the first "Silly Symphony" in Technicolor.) In Canto XIII of Dante's *Inferno* the Suicides are cast into a fruitless wood where they struggle to grow as the trees of the forest; in the shape of gnarled trees, they are eternally tormented by the Harpies who gnaw at their limbs. There are similarities between the description in the Canto and that in this chapter, notably the breaking of a branch that results in great pain to the tree.

3 *keep strangers out of it.* This chapter could easily have ended here; the next lines and subsequent chapter read as an afterthought. Although conclusive proof cannot be found, evidence that this section was written later may be adduced. In the previous chapter the Soldier with the Green Whiskers mentions the forests and the Hammer-Heads of the South, but he neglects to tell them of the China Country. While it has a charm and delicacy that might place it in one of the Valleys of Merryland of *Dot and Tot of Merryland,* the episode in the China Country lacks the robust quality of the other adventures on the journey to the Quadling Country. It is out of place in the action of the story; this

may be a reason why the visitors quickly become uncomfortable in this fragile country. Baum does not state specifically what the Forest of Fighting Trees protects. After overcoming these trees, the travelers are said to be in another forest, which may be a reference to the forest where the Lion becomes the King of Beasts in Chapter 21. Baum perhaps rewrote the opening of that chapter, after he inserted the China Country episode. (This supposition is not so improbable when we consider the deleted chapter "The Garden of Meats," of *The Patchwork Girl of Oz.* Both Baum and his publishers agreed that this chapter was not in accordance with his other work, so Baum eliminated it and rewrote the chapters that had preceded and followed it. See Dick Martin's article in the Christmas 1966 *Baum Bugle.*)

4 *made of white china.* In Note 23 of *The Wizard of Oz and Who He Was,* Gardner suggests the similarity between this wall and the Great Wall of China. Whether this connection has any contemporary social or political implications is not known. Perhaps the growing animosity toward foreigners (which resulted in the Boxer Rebellion in the summer of 1900) inspired the creation of Baum's own country of China. If a theme is to be found in the following chapter, it would be tolerance. Dorothy is told of the sad fate of a China inhabitant who is taken from his native land; she also feels uncomfortable in such a delicate land. A possible political theme would be anti-imperialism. Although she doesn't think that the breaking of a cow's leg and the smashing of a church result in any great loss, Dorothy realizes the possible harm she and her friends might cause if they remain.

Chapter XX.
The Dainty China Country.

W**hile** TheWoodman was making a ladder from wood which he found in the forest Dorothy lay down and slept, for she was tired by the long walk.

The Lion also curled himself up to sleep and Toto lay beside him.

The Scarecrow watched the Woodman while he worked, and said to him:

"I cannot think why this wall is here, nor what it is made of."

"Rest your brains and do not worry about the wall," replied the Woodman; "when we have climbed over it we shall know what is on the other side."

After a time the ladder was finished. It looked clumsy, but the Tin Woodman was sure it was strong and would answer their purpose. The Scarecrow waked Dorothy and the Lion and Toto, and told them that the ladder was ready. The Scarecrow climbed up the ladder first, but he was so awkward that Dorothy had to follow close behind and keep him from falling off. When he got his head over the top of the wall the Scarecrow said,

"Oh, my!"

"Go on," exclaimed Dorothy.

So the Scarecrow climbed further up and sat down on the top of the wall, and Dorothy put her head over and cried,

"Oh, my!" just as the Scarecrow had done.

Then Toto came up, and immediately began to bark, but Dorothy made him be still.

The Lion climbed the ladder next, and the Tin Woodman came last; but both of them cried, "Oh, my!" as soon as they looked over the wall. When they were all sitting in a row on the top of the wall they looked down and saw a strange sight.

Before them was a great stretch of country having a floor as smooth and shining and white as the bottom of a big platter. Scattered around were many houses made entirely of china and painted in the brightest colours. These houses were quite small, the biggest of them reaching only as high as Dorothy's waist. There were also pretty little barns, with china fences around them, and many cows and sheep and horses and pigs and chickens, all made of china, were standing about in groups.

But the strangest of all were the people who lived in this queer country. There were milk-maids and shepherdesses, with bright-colored bodices and golden spots all over their gowns; and princesses with most gorgeous frocks of silver and gold and purple; and shepherds dressed in knee-breeches with pink and yellow and blue stripes down them, and golden buckles on their shoes; and princes with jewelled crowns upon their heads, wearing ermine robes and satin doublets; and funny clowns in ruffled gowns, with round red spots upon their cheeks and tall, pointed caps. And, strangest of all, these people were all made of china, even to their clothes, and were so small that the tallest of them was no higher than Dorothy's knee.

No one did so much as look at the travellers at first, except one little purple china dog with an extra-large head, which came to the wall and barked at them in a tiny voice, afterwards running away again.

"How shall we get down?" asked Dorothy.

They found the ladder so heavy they could not pull it up, so the Scarecrow fell off the wall and the others jumped down upon him so that the hard floor would not hurt their feet. Of course they took pains not to light on his head and get the pins in their feet. When all were safely down they picked up the Scarecrow, whose body was quite flattened out, and patted his straw into shape again.

"We must cross this strange place in order to get to the other side," said Dorothy; "for it would be unwise for us to go any other way except due South."

They began walking through the country of the china people, and the first thing they came to was a china milk-maid milking a china cow. As they drew near the cow suddenly gave a kick and kicked over the stool, the pail, and even the milk-maid herself, all falling on the china ground with a great clatter.

Dorothy was shocked to see that the cow had broken her leg short off, and that the pail was lying in several small pieces, while the poor milk-maid had a nick in her left elbow.

"There!" cried the milk-maid, angrily; "see what you have done! My cow has broken her leg, and I must take her to the mender's shop and have it glued on again. What do you mean by coming here and frightening my cow?"

"I'm very sorry," returned Dorothy; "please forgive us"

But the pretty milk-maid was much too vexed to make any answer. She picked up the leg sulkily and led her cow away, the poor animal limping on three legs. As she left them the milk-maid cast many reproachful glances over her shoulder at the clumsy strangers, holding her nicked elbow close to her side.

Dorothy was quite grieved at this mishap.

"We must be very careful here," said the kind-hearted Woodman, "or we may hurt these pretty little people so they will never get over it."

A little farther on Dorothy met a most beautiful dressed young princess, who stopped **1** short as she saw the strangers and started to run away.

Dorothy wanted to see more of the Princess, so she ran after her; but the china girl cried out,

"Don't chase me! don't chase me!"

She had such a frightened little voice that Dorothy stopped and said,

"Why not?"

"Because," answered the princess, also stopping, a safe distance away, "if I run I may fall down and break myself."

"But couldn't you be mended?" asked the girl.

"Oh, yes; but one is never so pretty after being mended, you know," replied the princess.

"I suppose not," said Dorothy.

1 *beautiful . . . . . . princess.* "The China Princess, fearful that a mended crack might mar her beauty," writes Nye in *The Wizard of Oz and Who He Was,* "lives a lonely and isolated life, avoiding all contact with those who might chip her perfection." Her feelings are not unlike those of Chinese Empress Dowager Tzu Hsi, whose policies against foreign barbarians culminated in the Boxer disaster in the summer of 1900. Baum, however, does not indicate violence on the part of the natives; the only destruction results from the carelessness of the invaders.

2 *You'd eaten up a poker.* Baum is obviously making a pun of the colloquial expression "poker face," or having an expressionless stare. The phrase is said to have originated from the card game, rather than from the metal bar used for stirring fires, but this is debatable. At least one of his contemporaries described Lewis Carroll as having the face of someone who had eaten a poker.

3 *Well, that's respect, I expect.* Baum may have intended this line to be read as a rhymed couplet. This line appears in a revision of this chapter ("In Chinaland," *L. Frank Baum's Juvenile Speaker*) as: "Well, I suspect, they expect no respect." Mr. Joker is the first of several comic Oz characters who speak in rhyme and whose sanity is in doubt. The most famous example is the Patchwork Girl, who, like Mr. Joker, is thought somewhat mad. Mr. Joker is cracked in the head; the Patchwork Girl is made of an old crazy quilt. In the medieval tradition are many examples of court fools who speak in rhyme, the most notable being King Lear's Fool.

"Now there is Mr. Joker, one of our clowns," continued the china lady, "who is always trying to stand upon his head. He has broken himself so often that he is mended in a hundred places, and doesn't look at all pretty. Here he comes now, so you can see for yourself."

Indeed, a jolly little Clown now came walking toward them, and Dorothy could see that in spite of his pretty clothes of red and yellow and green he was completely covered with cracks, running every which way and showing plainly that he had been mended in many places.

The Clown put his hands in his pockets, and after puffing out his cheeks and nodding his head at them saucily he said,

> "My lady fair,
> Why do you stare
> At poor old Mr. Joker?
> You're quite as stiff
> And prim as if
> **2** You'd eaten up a poker!"

"Be quiet, sir!" said the princess; "can't you see these are strangers, and should be treated with respect?"

3 "Well, that's respect, I expect," declared the Clown, and immediately stood upon his head.

"Don t mind Mr. Joker," said the princess to Dorothy; "he is considerably cracked in his head, and that makes him foolish."

"Oh, I don't mind him a bit," said Dorothy. "But you are so beautiful," she continued, "that I am sure I could love you dearly. Won't you let me carry you back to Kansas and stand you on Aunt Em's mantle-shelf? I could carry you in my basket."

"That would make me very unhappy," answered the china princess. "You see, here in our own country we live contentedly, and can talk and move around as we please. But

4 *a china church.* As Gardner observes in Note 25 of *The Wizard of Oz and Who He Was,* this is the only reference in Baum's Royal History to a church in Oz. "The references to religion in the whole Baum authorship are extremely rare," writes March Laumer in the introduction to the Opium Books edition of *Queen Zixi of Ix;* "offhand I recall only the china church which the Cowardly Lion accidentally knocks over in *The Wizard of Oz.* As far as I know it was the only church in Oz; the 'Church' never recovered from this fall!" Laumer suggests that fairies in the Baum books are in place of angels and act almost as deities. I have already considered Baum's religion in my introduction. I suspect the absence of references to religion is due to the decision that these, like those to love and killing, had no place in Baum's books. A notable exception is his *American Fairy Tales,* which has a number of references to religion and religious holidays. As Gardner has noted in *The Wizard of Oz and Who He Was,* two of the few observations of the possibility of an afterlife appear in the "Trot" books. In *The Sea Fairies* is a school of "holy" mackerel who desire to be caught and thus carried off to "glory." In *Sky Island* is the Arc of Phinis where the Blues enter after their allotted time to live on Sky Island. Earlier, in *The Life and Adventures of Santa Claus,* Baum refers to the question of human mortality when one of the fairy Immortals speaks to the evil Agwas: "You are a transient race, passing from life into nothingness. We, who live forever, pity but despise you. On earth you are scorned by all and in Heaven you have no place! Even the mortals, after their earth life, enter another existence for all time, and we are your superiors" (pp. 110–11).

whenever any of us are taken away our joints at once stiffen, and we can only stand straight and look pretty. Of course that is all that is expected of us when we are on mantle-shelves and cabinets and drawing-room tables, but our lives are much pleasanter here in our own country."

"I would not make you unhappy for all the world!" exclaimed Dorothy; "so I'll just say good-bye."

"Good-bye," replied the princess.

They walked carefully through the china country. The little animals and all the people scampered out of their way, fearing the strangers would break them, and after an hour or so the travellers reached the other side of the country and came to another china wall.

It was not as high as the first, however, and by standing upon the Lion's back they all managed to scramble to the top. Then the Lion gathered his legs under him and jumped on the wall; but just as he jumped he **4** upset a china church with his tail and smashed it all to pieces.

"That was too bad," said Dorothy, "but really I think we were lucky in not doing these little people more harm than breaking a cow's leg and a church. They are all so brittle!"

"They are, indeed," said the Scarecrow, "and I am thankful I am made of straw and cannot be easily damaged. There are worse things in the world than being a Scarecrow."

Chapter XXI.
The Lion Becomes the King of Beasts.

After Climbing down from the china wall the travellers found themselves in a disagreeable country, full of bogs and marshes and covered with tall, rank grass. It was difficult to walk far without falling into muddy holes, for the grass was so thick that it hid them from sight. However, by carefully picking their way, they got safely along until they reached solid ground. But here the country seemed wilder than ever, and after a long and tiresome walk through the under-brush they entered another forest, where

1 *a pleasanter home.* A common error in both literature and popular usage is the assumption that the lion is a beast of the forest (e.g., Bert Lahr's song "If I were King of the Forest" in the MGM film). He is a creature of the open countryside.

the trees were bigger and older than any they had ever seen.

"This forest is perfectly delightful," declared the Lion, looking around him with joy; "never have I seen a more beautiful place."

"It seems gloomy," said the Scarecrow.

"Not a bit of it," answered the Lion; "I should like to live here all my life. See how soft the dried leaves are under your feet and how rich and green the moss is that clings to these old trees. Surely no wild beast could wish
1 a pleasanter home."

"Perhaps there are wild beasts in the forest now," said Dorothy

"I suppose there are," returned the Lion; "but I do not see any of them about."

They walked through the forest until it became too dark to go any farther. Dorothy and Toto and the Lion lay down to sleep, while the Woodman and the Scarecrow kept watch over them as usual.

When morning came they started again. Before they had gone far they heard a low rumble, as of the growling of many wild animals. Toto whimpered a little but none of the others was frightened and they kept along the well-trodden path until they came to an opening in the wood, in which were gathered hundreds of beasts of every variety. There were tigers and elephants and bears and wolves and foxes and all the others in the natural history, and for a moment Dorothy was afraid. But the Lion explained that the animals were holding a meeting, and he judged by their snarling and growling that they were in great trouble.

As he spoke several of the beasts caught sight of him, and at once the great assemblage hushed as if by magic. The biggest of the tigers came up to the Lion and bowed, **2** saying,

"Welcome, O King of Beasts! You have come in good time to fight our enemy and bring peace to all the animals of the forest once more."

"What is your trouble?" asked the Lion, quietly.

"We are all threatened," answered the tiger, "by a fierce enemy which has lately come into this forest. It is a most tremendous monster, like a great spider, with a body as big as an elephant and legs as long as a

2 *The biggest of the tigers.* A possible variation of this meeting between the Lion and the Tiger occurs in Baum's short story, "The Story of Jaglon," the first of the "Animal Fairy Tales"; in this story a tiger is the King of Beasts and the lion is the usurper of the throne.

One of the most beloved of the Oz characters is the Hungry Tiger (he is "hungry" because his conscience will not permit himself to satisfy his great appetite) who makes his first recorded journey to the Emerald City in *Ozma of Oz*, but this may not be his first appearance in the Oz books. In *Who's Who in Oz* (p. 99) Jack Snow speculates that the "biggest of the tigers" described in this chapter is in fact the Hungry Tiger of Oz.

3 *The great spider.* Actually this monster, other than its size, resembles other spiders. As with beasts of other mythologies the significance of Baum's creature lies in how it is described; he uses both hyperbole and carefully chosen comparisons. Baum seems to have had a personal aversion to spiders. They appear as monsters in both *The Life and Adventures of Santa Claus* and *Glinda of Oz*. Baum's great spider may be related to other such beasts in literature, like the spider of Edgar Allan Poe's story "The Sphinx," and the spider Shelob of Tolkien's *Lord of the Rings* (1954–1955).

tree trunk. It has eight of these long legs, and as the monster crawls through the forest he seizes an animal with a leg and drags it to his mouth, where he eats it as a spider does a fly. Not one of us is safe while this fierce creature is alive, and we had called a meeting to decide how to take care of ourselves when you came among us."

The Lion thought for a moment.

"Are there any other lions in this forest?" he asked.

"No; there were some, but the monster has eaten them all. And, besides, they were none of them nearly so large and brave as you."

"If I put an end to your enemy will you bow down to me and obey me as King of the Forest?" enquired the Lion.

"We will do that gladly," returned the tiger; and all the other beasts roared with a mighty roar: "We will!"

"Where is this great spider of yours now?" asked the Lion.

"Yonder, among the oak trees," said the tiger, pointing with his fore-foot."

"Take good care of these friends of mine," said the Lion, "and I will go at once to fight the monster."

He bade his comrades good-bye and marched proudly away to do battle with the enemy.

3   The great spider was lying asleep when the Lion found him, and it looked so ugly that its foe turned up his nose in disgust. It's legs were quite as long as the tiger had said, and it's body covered with coarse black hair. It had a great mouth, with a row of sharp teeth a foot long; but its head was joined to the pudgy body by a neck as slender as a wasp's waist. This gave the Lion a hint of the best way to attack the creature, and as he knew it was easier to fight it asleep than awake, he gave a great spring and landed directly upon the monster's back. Then, with one blow of his heavy paw, all armed with sharp claws, he knocked the spider's head from its body. Jumping down, he watched it until the long legs stopped wiggling, when he knew it was quite dead.

The Lion went back to the opening where the beasts of the forest were waiting for him and said, proudly,

"You need fear your enemy no longer."

Then the beasts bowed down to the Lion as their King, and he promised to come back and rule over them as soon as Dorothy was safely on her way to Kansas.

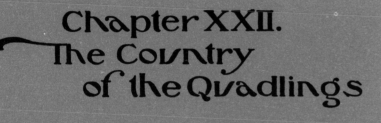

Chapter XXII.
The Country
of the Quadlings

The FOUR TRAVELLERS passed through the rest of the forest in safety, and when they came out from its gloom saw before them a steep hill, covered from top to bottom with great pieces of rock.

"That will be a hard climb," said the Scarecrow, "but we must get over the hill, nevertheless."

So he led the way and the others followed. They had nearly reached the first rock when they heard a rough voice cry out,

"Keep back!"

"Who are you?" asked the Scarecrow. Then a head

1 *Hammer-Heads.* "Hammerhead" is a common name for a stupid person, like the term "blockhead." The creation of these monsters, however, is not limited to this definition. Baum clearly realized a child's understanding of words as "things." He has taken a descriptive compound name and taken each of its parts as a literal description of a fantastic being. In this way he has widened a child's awareness of the possibilities of his world; a child when confronted by an unfamiliar word will frequently speculate on what it describes through his knowledge of its individual parts.

The description of the Hammer-Heads suggests a comparison to toy clowns with pop-up heads. These have round bodies (generally without arms, unless painted on) with heads that shoot up when a spring in the neck is released. The Hammer-Heads are the earliest tribe of comic monsters so characteristic of Baum's fairy tales. One of the most original is the nation of Roly-Rogues of *Queen Zixi of Ix;* these creatures are shaped like enormous basketballs and can withdraw their limbs and head like turtles into their shells. The nearest relations to the Hammer-Heads are probably the Scoodlers of *The Road to Oz;* but instead of shooting their heads, the Scoodlers throw them at any traveler who tries to cross their rocky plain. Far north of the Emerald City on another mountain peak live the Flatheads; their foreheads are so low that they must carry their brains with them in metal containers. Neill's conception of the Flatheads in *Glinda of Oz* shows some resemblance to Denslow's Hammer-Heads.

In *The Emerald City of Oz* (p. 32), the Hammer-Heads are also called "The Wild People."

showed itself over the rock and the same voice said,

"This hill belongs to us, and we don't allow anyone to cross it."

"But we must cross it," said the Scarecrow. "We're going to the country of the Quadlings."

"But you shall not!" replied the voice, and there stepped from behind the rock the strangest man the travellers had ever seen.

He was quite short and stout and had a big head, which was flat at the top and supported by a thick neck full of wrinkles. But he had no arms at all, and, seeing this, the Scarecrow did not fear that so helpless a creature could prevent them from climbing the hill. So he said,

"I'm sorry not to do as you wish, but we must pass over your hill whether you like it or not," and he walked boldly forward.

As quick as lightning the man's head shot forward and his neck stretched out until the top of the head, where it was flat, struck the Scarecrow in the middle and sent him tumbling, over and over, down the hill. Almost as quickly as it came the head went back to the body, and the man laughed harshly as he said,

"It isn't as easy as you think!"

A chorus of boisterous laughter came from the other 1 rocks, and Dorothy saw hundreds of the armless Hammer-Heads upon the hillside, one behind every rock.

The Lion became quite angry at the laughter caused by the Scarecrow's mishap, and giving a loud roar that echoed like thunder he dashed up the hill.

Again a head shot swiftly out, and the great Lion went rolling down the hill as if he had been struck by a cannon ball.

Dorothy ran down and helped the Scarecrow to his feet, and the Lion came up to her, feeling rather bruised and sore, and said,

"It is useless to fight people with shooting heads; no one can withstand them."

"What can we do, then?" she asked.

"Call the Winged Monkeys," suggested the Tin Woodman; "you have still the right to command them once more."

"Very well," she answered, and putting on the Golden Cap she uttered the magic words. The Monkeys were as prompt as ever, and in a few moments the entire band stood before her.

"What are your commands?" enquired the King of the Monkeys, bowing low.

"Carry us over the hill to the country of the Quadlings," answered the girl.

"It shall be done," said the King, and at once the Winged Monkeys caught the four travellers and Toto up in their arms and flew away with them. As they passed over the hill the Hammer-Heads yelled with vexation, and

2 *country of the Quadlings.* Although all maps of the Land of Oz (including James E. Haff's authoritative map) place the traversed area of the last four chapters in the Quadling Country, Baum clearly states here that Dorothy and her companions do not enter the red lands of the South until after they have crossed the Hill of the Hammer-Heads. As indicated by the illustrations and suggested by the text, the countryside between the Forest of Fighting Trees and the farmlands of the Quadlings is a brown land; it is not known if this country is part of Glinda's domain.

3 *green grass and the yellowing grain.* Gardner states in Note 10 of *The Wizard of Oz and Who He Was* that several passages in the first Oz book indicate that Baum was not yet aware of the extent to which animal and vegetable life have the same color as their native land. "Well, the grass is purple, and the trees are purple and the houses and fences are purple," Tip, in Chapter 2 of *The Marvelous Land of Oz*, begins his explanation of this strange phenomenon with the Gillikin Country. "Even the mud in the road is purple. But in the Emerald City everything is green that is purple here. And in the Country of the Munchkins, over at the East, everything is blue; and in the South country of the Quadlings everything is red; and in the West country of the Winkies, where the Tin Woodman rules, everything is yellow." Neill took this to an extreme in his own Oz stories; even the air and skin tint of the natives is the same as the color of the country in which they exist.

shot their heads high in the air; but they could not reach the Winged Monkeys, which carried Dorothy and her comrades safely over the hill and set them down in the **2** beautiful country of the Quadlings.

"This is the last time you can summon us," said the leader to Dorothy; "so good-bye and good luck to you."

"Good-bye, and thank you very much," returned the girl; and the Monkeys rose into the air and were out of sight in a twinkling.

The country of the Quadlings seemed rich and happy. There was field upon field of ripening grain, with well-paved roads running between, and pretty rippling brooks with strong bridges across them. The fences and houses and bridges were all painted bright red, just as they had been painted yellow in the country of the Winkies and blue in the country of the Munchkins. The Quadlings themselves, who were short and fat and looked chubby and good natured, were dressed all in red, which showed **3** bright against the green grass and the yellowing grain.

The Monkeys had set them down near a farm house, and the four travellers walked up to it and knocked at the door. It was opened by the farmer's wife, and when Dorothy asked for something to eat the woman gave them all a good dinner, with three kinds of cake and four kinds of cookies, and a bowl of milk for Toto.

"How far is it to the Castle of Glinda?" asked the child.

"It is not a great way," answered the farmer's wife. "Take the road to the South and you will soon reach it."

Thanking the good woman, they started afresh and walked by the fields and across the pretty bridges until they saw before them a very beautiful Castle. Before the gates were three young girls, dressed in handsome red uniforms trimmed with gold braid; and as Dorothy approached one of them said to her, **4**

"Why have you come to the South Country?"

"To see the Good Witch who rules here," she answered. "Will you take me to her?"

"Let me have your name and I will ask Glinda if she will receive you." They told who they were, and the girl soldier went into the Castle. After a few moments she came back to say that Dorothy and the others were to be admitted at once.

4 *red uniforms trimmed with gold braid.* Miss Matilda J. Gage, Baum's niece, suggests in "The Dakota Days of L. Frank Baum" (*The Baum Bugle*, Spring through Christmas 1966) that the models for the girl soldiers who appear in the Oz stories were the "Aberdeen Guards." These fancifully dressed women carried long wooden spears when marching in parades where they gave demonstrations of their elaborate drills. A highlight of the 1902 musical of *The Wizard of Oz* was the army of marching girls that may have been inspired by Glinda's Guards. Fred M. Meyer, the secretary of the International Wizard of Oz Club, believes that the army of the musical was the prototype of the female Army of Revolt of *The Marvelous Land of Oz*, often viewed as a gentle satire on the woman suffrage movement.

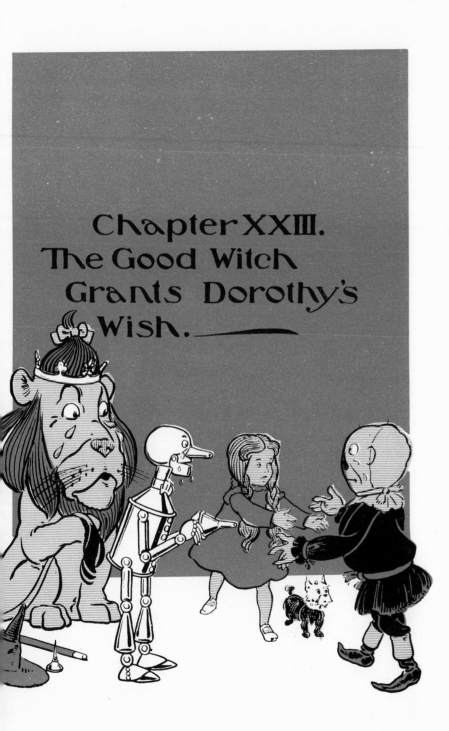

Chapter XXIII.
The Good Witch
Grants Dorothy's
Wish.

Before

they went to see Glinda, however, they were taken to a room of the Castle, where Dorothy washed her **1** face and combed her hair, and the Lion shook the dust out of his mane, and the Scarecrow patted himself into his best shape, and the Woodman polished his tin and oiled his joints.

When they were all quite presentable they followed the soldier girl into a big room where the Witch Glinda sat upon a throne of rubies.

1 *Dorothy.* In this chapter Denslow has pictured Dorothy in the simple dress she wore when she first came to Oz, instead of the one she received when she visited the Emerald City; in Baum's text there is no indication of such a change. Perhaps Glinda by magic has returned to the girl her own dress so that she would not be embarrassed should the one from the Emerald City suffer the same fate as the Silver Shoes.

2 *beautiful and young.* The prototype of Glinda the Good may be Maetta the Sorceress of *A New Wonderland*, 1900 (later *The Magical Monarch of Mo*, 1903). Both dress in white and live in the Southland. In all Baum's Oz books except the first, Glinda the Good Witch is referred to as Glinda the Good Sorceress, identifying her title with that of Maetta. Also, Maetta is described as the most beautiful woman in the world, a claim given to Glinda in the later Oz books. Finally, in *The Woggle-Bug*, the dramatization of *The Marvelous Land of Oz*, Glinda the Good becomes Maetta the Sorceress.

Glinda the Good Witch was portrayed by Billie Burke in the MGM film.

3 *cannot afford it.* Few modern readers are likely to realize the full meaning of this statement. Nineteenth-century customs for mourning were both rigid and expensive, another unwanted burden on the poor. At the turn of the century considerable discussion about a less expensive way for the poor to express their grief was in part responsible for the present flexible customs for mourning.

2 She was both beautiful and young to their eyes. Her hair was a rich red in color and fell in flowing ringlets over her shoulders. Her dress was pure white; but her eyes were blue, and they looked kindly upon the little girl.

"What can I do for you, my child?" she asked.

Dorothy told the Witch all her story; how the cyclone had brought her to the Land of Oz, how she had found her companions, and of the wonderful adventures they had met with.

"My greatest wish now," she added, "is to get back to Kansas, for Aunt Em will surely think something dreadful has happened to me, and that will make her put on mourn-ing; and unless the crops are better this year than they **3** were last I am sure Uncle Henry cannot afford it."

Glinda leaned forward and kissed the sweet, upturned face of the loving little girl.

"Bless your dear heart," she said, "I am sure I can tell you of a way to get back to Kansas." Then she added:

"But, if I do, you must give me the Golden Cap."

"Willingly!" exclaimed Dorothy; "indeed, it is of no use to me now, and when you have it you can command the Winged Monkeys three times."

"And I think I shall need their service just those three times," answered Glinda, smiling.

Dorothy then gave her the Golden Cap, and the Witch said to the Scarecrow,

"What will you do when Dorothy has left us?"

"I will return to the Emerald City," he replied, "for Oz has made me its ruler and the people like me. The only thing that worries me is how to cross the hill of the Hammer-Heads."

"By means of the Golden Cap I shall command the Winged Monkeys to carry you to the gates of the Emerald City," said Glinda, "for it would be a shame to deprive the people of so wonderful a ruler."

"Am I really wonderful?" asked the Scarecrow.

"You are unusual," replied Glinda.

Turning to the Tin Woodman, she asked:

"What will become of you when Dorothy leaves this country?"

He leaned on his axe and thought a moment. Then he said,

"The Winkies were very kind to me, and wanted me to rule over them after the Wicked Witch died. I am fond of the Winkies, and if I could get back again to the country of the West I should like nothing better than to rule over them forever."

"My second command to the Winged Monkeys," said Glinda, "will be that they carry you safely to the land of the Winkies. Your brains may not be so large to look at as those of the Scarecrow, but you are really brighter than he is—when you are well polished—and I am sure you will **4** rule the Winkies wisely and well."

Then the Witch looked at the big, shaggy Lion and asked,

4 *well polished.* Not even the stately Glinda the Good is immune from Baum's weakness for the pun.

"When Dorothy has returned to her own home, what will become of you?"

"Over the hill of the Hammer-Heads," he answered, "lies a grand old forest, and all the beasts that live there have made me their King. If I could only get back to this forest I would pass my life very happily there."

"My third command to the Winged Monkeys," said Glinda, "shall be to carry you to your forest. Then, having used up the powers of the Golden Cap, I shall give it to the King of the Monkeys, that he and his band may thereafter be free for evermore."

The Scarecrow and the Tin Woodman and the Lion now thanked the Good Witch earnestly for her kindness, and Dorothy exclaimed,

"You are certainly as good as you are beautiful! But you have not yet told me how to get back to Kansas."

"Your Silver Shoes will carry you over the desert," **5** replied Glinda. "If you had known their power you could have gone back to your Aunt Em the very first day you **6** came to this country."

"But then I should not have had my wonderful brains!" cried the Scarecrow. "I might have passed my whole life in the farmer's cornfield."

"And I should not have had my lovely heart," said the Tin Woodman. "I might have stood and rusted in the forest till the end of the world."

"And I should have lived a coward forever," declared the Lion, "and no beast in all the forest would have had a good word to say to me."

"This is all true," said Dorothy, " and I am glad I was of use to these good friends. But now that each of them has had what he most desired, and each is happy in having a kingdom to rule beside, I think I should like to go back to Kansas."

"The Silver Shoes," said the Good Witch, "have wonderful powers. And one of the most curious things about them is that they can carry you to any place in the world in three steps, and each step will be made in the wink of an eye. All you have to do is to knock the heels together three times and command the shoes to carry you wherever you wish to go."

5 *Your Silver Shoes will carry you over the desert*. Magic shoes for aerial transportation appear occasionally in legend and literature. An obvious example is the winged sandals of Mercury, the Greek god of trade. Ruth Plumly Thompson writes of a pair of Quick Sandals in *The Hungry Tiger of Oz* (1926).

6 *the very first day you came to this country*. As already seen in the meeting between her friends and Oz, the Terrible, Dorothy, too, has always had the power to solve her own problems; she had to realize for herself the nature of this power. As MacFall observes in *To Please a Child:* "What we want, [Baum] the moralist whispers, is within us; we need only look for it to find it. What we strive for has been ours all the time." The Scarecrow, the Tin Woodman, and the Cowardly Lion always had what they desired, but if not for Dorothy they would not have realized these powers within them.

The significance of the Self develops in Dorothy's case in perhaps a more subtle way. As M.-L. Franz explains in "The Self: symbols of totality," in Jung's book on symbolism (see Chapter 4, Note 4), the Self is often personified as a superior human being. To women this might be in the form of a wise and beautiful goddess (e.g., the Greek goddess Demeter) or a helpful old woman (e.g., the fairy godmother in George Macdonald's *The Princess and the Goblin* and *The Princess and Curdie*, and the Woman-Learned-in-Magic of Andersen's *Snow Queen*). A significant distinction between German and French fairy tales is that the guardian of the protagonist in the first is a "wise woman" (often translated as "witch") and in the second a beautiful fairy godmother. In Baum's story both these common symbols are important. The Good Witch of the North, as the wise old woman, presents Dorothy with the Silver Shoes; Glinda the Good, the wise goddess, tells the girl the secret of the magic slippers. Dorothy must seek out what she needs; then she receives her answer from her Self symbolically in the guise of the witches.

"If that is so," said the child, joyfully, "I will ask them to carry me back to Kansas at once."

She threw her arms around the Lion's neck and kissed him, patting his big head tenderly. Then she kissed the Tin Woodman, who was weeping in a way most dangerous to his joints. But she hugged the soft, stuffed body of the Scarecrow in her arms instead of kissing his painted face, and found she was crying herself at this sorrowful parting from her loving comrades.

Glinda the Good stepped down from her ruby throne to give the little girl a good-bye kiss, and Dorothy thanked her for all the kindness she had shown to her friends and herself.

Dorothy now took Toto up solemnly in her arms, and having said one last good-bye she clapped the heels of her shoes together three times, saying,

"Take me home to Aunt Em!"

*   *   *   *   *

Instantly she was whirling through the air, so swiftly that all she could see or feel was the wind whistling past her ears.

The Silver Shoes took but three steps, and then she stopped so suddenly that she rolled over upon the grass several times before she knew where she was.

At length, however, she sat up and looked about her. "Good gracious!" she cried.

For she was sitting on the broad Kansas prairie, and just before her was the new farm-house Uncle Henry built after the cyclone had carried away the old one. Uncle Henry was milking the cows in the barnyard, and Toto had jumped out of her arms and was running toward the barn, barking joyously.

Dorothy stood up and found she was in her stocking-feet. For the Silver Shoes had fallen off in her flight through the air, and were lost forever in the desert.

Chapter XXIV.
Home Again.

UNT EM HAD JUST COME out of the house to water the cabbages when she looked up and saw Dorothy running toward her.

"My darling child!" she cried, folding the little girl in her arms and covering her face with kisses; "where in the world did you come from?"

"From the Land of Oz," said Dorothy, gravely. "And here is Toto, too. And oh, Aunt Em! I'm so glad to be at home again!"

1 *again.* "It is interesting to note," writes Jack Snow in *Who's Who in Oz* (p. 59), "that the first word ever written in the very first Oz book was 'Dorothy.' The last word of the book is 'again'. And that is what young readers have said ever since those two words were written: 'We want to read about Dorothy again.'"

The illustration on this page originally appeared as the back endpaper of the Hill edition.

342

The Denslow Appendix.

W. W. Denslow and the Scarecrow. A previously un-published self-portrait drawn for Townsend Walsh, pub-licity manager of *The Wizard of Oz* musical. *Courtesy Theatre Collection, New York Public Library, Astor, Lenox, and Tilden Foundations.*

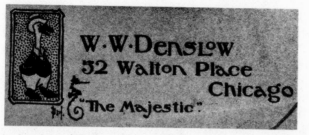

Denslow's drawing of Father Goose which appeared on his personal stationery in 1900. *Courtesy the personal collection of Justin G. Schiller.*

All the books that Baum and Denslow collaborated on were copyrighted jointly in both their names and royalties were divided equally. This joint ownership may have resulted from their having shared the expense of publishing *Father Goose, His Book.* When the two separated, Denslow secured complete control of his illustrations for *The Wonderful Wizard of Oz* and the other Baum titles. To capitalize on the popularity of the musical and claiming to be co-creator of *The Wizard of Oz* Denslow produced a number of "Scarecrow and Tin-Man" works.

He had earlier worked on several projects derived from the success of *Father Goose.* He decorated his personal stationery with a full-color picture of Father Goose. He even drew a "Father Goose" comic page, which appeared in the New York *World* and other newspapers on January 21, and June 22, 1900. (*See* color plate IV.)

With *Denslow's Night Before Christmas* (New York: G. W. Dillingham, 1902), Denslow began to insert characters from *The Wizard of Oz* into his other books. Peering over Santa's bag in this picture book is a toy Tin Woodman based on Denslow's own conception of Baum's creation. (*See* color plate V.) In *Denslow's A B C Book* (New York: Dillingham, 1903), under the letters "S" and "T," are pictures of the Scarecrow and the Tin Woodman (see pages 120 and 161). In the cornfield of one illustration in Denslow's adaptation of *The House That Jack Built* (New York: Dillingham, 1903) is the Scarecrow from *The Wizard of Oz.* (*See* color plate VI.)

For the 1902 musical Denslow drew a series of six lithographed broadsides with illustrations perhaps adapted from his costume de-signs for the musical. Also on the lithographs are verses that may have been written by either Baum or Denslow. The artist Dick Martin suggests that these were intended for nursery wallpaper or perhaps as decorations in the lobbies of theatres where the musical was playing. A number of the drawings from the broadsides were also used as advertising cards for the musical.

Also during the run of the musical, George W. Ogilvie & Co. of Chicago issued a booklet of the original Hill color plates under the title *Pictures from the Wonderful Wizard of Oz* in 1903. (*See* color plate VIII.) These were unused sheets purchased from the Hill company after its failure. Prominently on the cover is a lithographed drawing after a photograph of Fred Stone and Dave Montgomery in costume as the Scarecrow and Tin Woodman. On both the cover and the title page is Denslow's name, but Baum is not mentioned. On the versos of the plates is printed a story, "Adventures of the Scarecrow, the Tin Man and the Little Girl" by Thos. H. Russell (1862–1944). This booklet may well have been designed to be sold in the lobbies of theatres where the musical was playing. This rare piece of Baumiana is reprinted on pages 351-362.

During the successful New York run of the musical the artist wrote and illustrated a picture book, *Denslow's Scarecrow and the Tin-Man* (New York: Dillingham, 1904). It was sold separately and collected with the others in his series of picture books in one volume. To advertise these Dillingham books Denslow designed a full-color book poster with the Scarecrow prominently displayed on the drawing. The story of the picture book may have been based upon an actual dispute between Julian Mitchell, the stage manager, and Montgomery and Stone. (*See* color plates IX, X, XI-XVIII.)

Beginning November 8, 1904, Denslow sold to the McClure syndicate a series of "Scarecrow and Tin-Man" comic pages. The first of these, "Dorothy's Christmas Tree," appeared on December 18, 1904, in the Detroit *Free Press.* In addition to this paper, the Minneapolis *Journal* published eleven pages between December 10, 1904, and February 18, 1905, in its Saturday illustrated supplement. (*See* color plate XIX.) This comic page appeared at the same time as Baum's "Queer Visitors from the Marvelous Land of Oz" and ended only a week before this earlier comic page. Like the "Queer Visitors," Denslow's series concerns the Scarecrow, Tin Woodman, and

The original drawing for a poster advertising *Denslow's Scarecrow and the Tin-Man* and other Denslow picture books of 1904. *Courtesy Columbia University Libraries, Solton and Julia Engel Collection.*

Cowardly Lion on their travels through the United States with a side excursion to South America. Only the first two pages occur in the Land of Oz. Also included as two separate pages are the drawings and story of *Denslow's Scarecrow and the Tin-Man*. These appeared as "Denslow's Scarecrow and Tin-Man About Town" on December 31, 1904, and "Denslow's Scarecrow and Tin-Man Recaptured" on January 7, 1905. The series ends abruptly with the three Baum characters on their way West; and at least three additional pages, two about cowboys and Indians and another called "Denslow's Scarecrow and Tin-Man at the California Flower Festival," were drawn but not published. According to Denslow's account book, McClure purchased no more than those that were published in the Minneapolis *Journal*. There is no mention in the pages of Baum as co-creator.

Denslow apparently attempted to get sole credit for his work with Baum. As early as the "Father Goose" comic pages in the New York *World*, Denslow was publishing under his own name drawings and later stories based upon his illustrations to Baum's books. Baum too perhaps wished to establish his reputation in the newspapers as the creator of "Father Goose"; there is preserved a newspaper story entitled "A Strange Tale of Nursery Folk" about *Father Goose, His Book* and illustrated with drawings based upon Denslow's work, but Denslow's name is not mentioned. This competition between author and illustrator perhaps was the major reason for the breakup of their collaboration. With the success of the 1902 musical *The Wizard of Oz*, Denslow, who was not directly affected by the profits of the play, evidently felt the necessity to establish himself as co-creator of *The Wizard of Oz* as well as to capitalize on the musical's great popularity. In a list of accomplishments, now in the United States Military Academy Library, he made for Arthur Nicholas Hosking's *The Artist's Year Book* (Chicago: Fine Arts Building, 1905), Denslow stated that he "designed costumes and color effects for stage production of *The Wizard of Oz* and originated the characters of Scarecrow and Tin Woodman in that play." Not having been a creditor of Harrison Rountree, Denslow received royalties from *The Wizard of Oz* even after Baum no longer controlled the profits of the Baum-Denslow titles. Perhaps both Baum and Denslow could claim to have created *The Wizard of Oz*, but after the close of their collaboration neither credited the other as being responsible for the success of their greatest work.

Three panels of an unpublished "Scarecrow and Tin-Man" comic page drawn by Denslow, 1904–1905. *Courtesy Columbia University Libraries, two from the George Douglas Hofe Gift, the last from the L. Frank Baum Manuscripts.*

FROM·KANSAS·LITTLE·DOROTHY·TO·OZ·WAS·BLOWN·AWAY;
WHERE·FIRST·SHE·MET·THE·GAY·SCARECROW,·THE·MAN·ALL·STUFFED·WITH·HAY.
IMOGENE;·THE·SPOTTED·CALF,·WAS·GLAD·TO·SEE·HIM;·TOO,
AND·TRIED·AT·ONCE·TO·EAT·HIM·UP·WHICH·SCARED·HIM·THROUGH·AND·THROUGH.

THE·TIN·MAN·IN·A·SHOWER·OF·RAIN·GOT·RUST·IN·EVERY·JOINT,
SO·HE·MUST·CARRY·AN·OIL·CAN·HIS·ELBOWS·TO·ANOINT
NEXT·CAME·A·LION·COWARDLY,·AS·TIMID·AS·A·BIRD;
YET·IF·SOME·DANGER·THREATENED·DOT·HIS·MIGHTY·ROAR·WAS·HEARD.

THE·LION·WISHED·THAT·HE·WERE·BRAVE;·THE·SCARECROW·WANTED·BRAINS,
THE·TIN·MAN·CRAVED·A·LOVING·HEART·WITH·ALL·ITS·JOYS·AND·PAINS
FAIR·DOROTHY·WOULD·FAIN·GO·BACK·TO·KANSAS·AND·HER·FOLKS·
ALTHOUGH·SHE·LIKED·THE·TIN·MAN·AND·THE·SCARECROW'S·JOLLY·JOKES.

Lithographed wallpaper frieze with characters
from the 1902 musical of *The Wizard of Oz*,
drawn by Denslow. *Courtesy Dick Martin.*

SO·TO·THE·CITY·EMERALD·IN·SPITE·OF·WITCH·AND·BLIZZARD,
THIS·FUNNY·CREW·TRAMPED·MILES·AND·MILES·TO·SEE·THE·MIGHTY·WIZARD.
WHEN·THEY·GOT·THERE·THEY·FOUND·IT·FULL·OF·FUNNY·KINDS·OF·FOLK·
CAP·RISKIT·LADY·LUNATIC·THE·ARMY·WAS·A·JOKE.

THE·WICKED·WITCH·THE·MOTOR·MAN·AND·TRIXY·SWEET·AS·HONEY.
GABRIEL·THE·POET·BOY·ALL·THOUGHT·THE·SCARECROW·FUNNY.
FOR·HE·AND·DOT·AND·TIN·MAN·TOO·DANCED·ALL·A·MERRY·MEASURE.
TO·PLEASE·THE·PEOPLE·ONE·AND·ALL·AND·GIVE·THE·WIZARD·PLEASURE.

TWAS·THUS·THE·FOUR·ALL·GOT·THEIR·WISH·HIS·HEART·THE·TIN·MAN·GOT·
THE·SCARECROW·HAD·HIS·BRAINS·AND·HOME·WENT·LITTLE·DOT.
BUT·'TWAS·GOLINDA·GENTLE·QUEEN·THAT·HELPED·HER·SO·I·THINK.
AND·SENT·HER·TO·HER·KANSAS·HOME·AS·QUICK·AS·YOU·COULD·WINK.

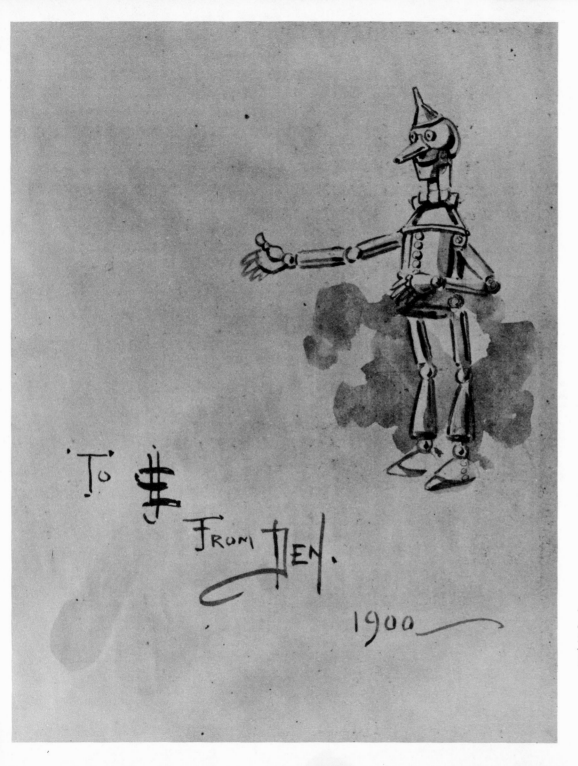

This sketch of the Tin Woodman appears on the flyleaf of the copy of the book presented by Denslow to his friend, the artist J. C. Leyendecker. The original is in watercolor. *Courtesy Bernhard Larsen, Upper Darby, Pennsylvania.*

PICTURES

FROM

The Wonderful Wizard of Oz

BY

W. W. DENSLOW

ILLUSTRATOR OF "FATHER GOOSE," DENSLOW'S "ONE RING CIRCUS," DENSLOW'S
"NIGHT BEFORE CHRISTMAS," ETC., ETC.

WITH A STORY TELLING THE

ADVENTURES OF THE SCARECROW
THE TIN MAN AND THE
LITTLE GIRL

BY

THOS. H. RUSSELL

GEORGE W. OGILVIE & CO., PUBLISHERS
181 MONROE STREET, CHICAGO, ILL.

CHAPTER I

HOW IT ALL BEGAN

The morning was gray and the Little Girl was blue. Of course it was not the kind of blue that some of the people who lived a long time ago used to be when they painted their bodies blue to be in the fashion and keep out the cold. On the contrary, this Little Girl looked pink and rosy, as all little girls should, but she felt blue, as she had often heard her big sister say, when things did not go to suit her. And the morning being dull and gray did not suit the Little Girl at all, for you must know that she had promised a very nice friend of hers, a Boy, that on that very morning she would go with him to hunt gophers in a beautiful park that was The Boy's favorite playground. But here was a cloudy sky, threatening rain, and a dull day indoors, and so the Little Girl was blue.

Now, it is part of the nature of little girls to be like the clouds, which change their appearance often and quickly, and sometimes hide the smiling sun out of pure frolic. So nobody need feel surprised to learn that when a Boy's whistle was heard on the big porch just outside the Little Girl's house, all her blues were blown away, and she ran smilingly to the door. Here stood The Boy in all his vacation comfort of overalls and "barefeets."

"O," said the Little Girl, big-eyed with welcome, "isn't it a shame? We can't go to catch all those gophers, because it is going to rain."

"Aw, rain nothing!" replied The Boy, who attended a big public school, and always tried to talk like the bigger boys. "What's a little rain? That won't hurt us. Besides, if it does rain I know a place where we can hide. I'll take care of you. Come on out and I'll show you how to catch 'em."

Of course that was just like a boy; it is part of his nature to try to lead little girls into danger and then rescue them at the risk of his life, for which they are supposed to love him ever after. So The Boy at once became a hero in the eyes of the Little Girl and away she skipped to find Nurse and kiss a permit from her for the great and risky expedition.

Just then a miracle happened, as miracles often do happen in this good old world to good little girls. The Rain-man, a grumpy old fellow by the name of Jupiter, had had his eye on the Little Girl ever since she tumbled out of her pink-and-white cot that morning, and he had been gloating over the prospect of spoiling her day. But he had been a boy himself once upon a time, and when he saw how glum The Boy looked as he stood in doubt on the Little Girl's porch, he took pity on him and pushed the clouds away, leaving the sky all bright and blue, with no possible excuse for Nurse to keep the Little Girl at home.

So then they started, The Boy and the Little Girl, for the big, wonderful playground that matter-of-fact, grown-up people called the park. Being city children, and knowing the ways of their elders, they did not go hand-in-hand, as children of all ages often do in the country, but better still they went heart-in-heart and were all in all to each other, as boys and girls have been at times since first the world was made.

How wonderful was the prospect that soon opened before

them! Right in the heart of the busy city, and surrounded by its smoke and din, there were the cool, green shades, the splashing fountains, the spreading trees, the winding walks, the many-colored flower-beds, and the delightful little lakes of the famous park; and as the Little Girl and her proud young protector passed from the heated sidewalks into the shade of the big oaks and elm trees, they danced onto the nearest smooth lawn and clean forgot all such commonplace affairs as home and nurses, bath-tubs and books. How could any one remember such things when the roaring of the lions in the park zoo had replaced the rattle of the street-cars, and every step brought nearer new delights?

"I say, Boy," called out the Little Girl, as she ran away from him just for the pure pleasure of being caught again, "isn't this fine? Let's play this is fairyland."

"I'm with you," laughed The Boy, at her side in a moment. "You're a little fairy all right." You see, he was not so young that he didn't know little girls are not altogether displeased at being paid compliments by the proper person.

And then fairyland opened in earnest for the happy pair, though the Little Girl had no idea of the still more wonderful things in store for her before the day was done. The Boy became a giant and pretended to eat her at a single mouthful; then he transformed himself into Jack the Giant-killer and cut off his own head with one stroke of his trusty sword, though how he did it she never has been able to tell. He donned seven-league boots, and made believe to swoop down upon her from a great distance and carry her off to his castle in the air. He became a locomotive, and whistled and puffed under the strain of pulling the private car containing the Little Girl from Chicago to New York in half a minute. He did so many remarkable things, and assumed the shape of so many strange men and animals under the magic wand of the fairy Little Girl, that it was a long, long time before she happened to remember that the main object of the expedition had not been attended to—that they had not yet captured a single gopher. So she mentioned the matter to The Boy.

"O, Boy," said she, "did you forget what we came here for? You know you promised to show me where the gophers live, and to catch some for me."

Then The Boy began to shine with even greater glory in the eyes of the Little Girl, for who but a boy could tell her all about the cunning little creatures that had been peeping timidly at her from their holes in the ground. He showed her how their houses were made with front and back doors, so that they could run into either one when danger threatened; and then, with wonderful patience for a boy, he waited for a chance to dart like lightning upon a gopher that ventured too far from home to pay a friendly visit to a neighbor. Soon the chance came, and like a flash The Boy pounced upon his prey and triumphantly bore the squirming animal to the Little Girl. What did he care for the bites of a gopher, anyway, as long as he had kept his promise, and his playmate had her prize? And how amply was he rewarded when he heard her say:

"I think you are just the nicest boy that ever lived, and when I grow up I am going to ask Nurse to let me marry you."

Then began the greatest gopher hunt of this or any other day. From one end of the great park to another ranged The Boy and his little lady fair. Never were eyes so sharp as his to spy out the little animals as they left their underground houses for a stroll in the bright sunshine; never were feet so swift to beat them in their race for home and safety. Gopher after gopher was cleverly caught and carried to the Little Girl to be admired and petted by her as it lay a prisoner in The Boy's well-bitten hands, and then released at her request to run back home and tell its fretting family of its strange adventures.

But, O, the miles they ran hither and thither, and the time it took to carry on this famous hunt! In quite another part of the big park an anxious Nurse was busily hunting the Little Girl, and the shadows were growing very long as the sun prepared to go to bed in the western sky, when at last she plumped herself down on the grass by the trunk of a big tree, and said, "Boy, I am tired! aren't you?"

Now, when a little girl admits that she is tired, and the evening shadows are falling, she is not far from the Land of Nod, where all good children sleep; and almost before The Boy could say "Jack Robinson," if it had ever occurred to him to make that famous remark, the Little Girl was fast asleep, and he was face to face with the most tremendous responsibility of his short but busy life.

"Now, what shall I do!" he said to himself, as he gazed at the sleeping form. "I can't carry her home, and I guess I'd better run all the way to her house and get Nurse or somebody to come for her before it gets quite dark."

With that, The Boy started off as fast as his tired little legs would carry him, leaving the Little Girl fast asleep in a quiet nook where nobody was likely to pass, except, by chance, a gray park policeman, or maybe a gopher out for a midnight stroll.

CHAPTER II

THE SORCERER AND THE MAGIC LUNCH

"Hello, Little Girl, how do you do this evening?"

At these words, uttered in a thin voice, with a foreign accent quite unlike anything she had ever heard before, the Little Girl looked up to see a little old gentleman with a very bald head and some curly white whiskers, who stood with a broad-brimmed hat in his hand, smiling down upon her. He was very strangely dressed in a green coat with big white buttons, which sparkled in the moonlight and shone like small electric lamps. Of course they were diamonds of the first water, but how was the Little Girl to know that on such short acquaintance? He certainly did not look like any of her father's friends and she was sure she had never seen him before. But then, he had called her by her name, and she was a very polite Little Girl, so in her very best society manner she replied:

"I am quite well, sir, thank you, and I hope you are the same. But, please, who are you?"

At that the strange gentleman laughed outright, and the Little Girl thought that his laugh sounded as if it had come through the funny phonograph her papa had at home.

"Why, Little Girl," he said, "you should be very glad to see me. I happen to be the Sorcerer of this particular park, and as I have just come on duty I shall be glad to show you a few things in my line if you have a little time to spare."

"Thank you very much, sir," said the Little Girl, who was rapidly getting over her first surprise. "But please, sir, will you tell me, sir, what is a park sorcerer? I have heard of park policemen and park phaetons, but I never did hear of a park sorcerer before."

"O my dear," said the little old gentleman, his sides shaking with laughter that made his diamond buttons twinkle like great stars, "I can assure you that every well-regulated park has its sorcerer nowadays. You see there are so many of us here that are hard at work all day long entertaining the public and can only play at night when the ordinary people have left the park. And, of course, there must be somebody official to regulate the doings of the Scarecrow and the rest of the boys. Well, that is the business of the park sorcerer, and here I am!"

"And please, sir, who is the Scarecrow?" asked the Little Girl.

"O I'll introduce him to you presently," replied the Sorcerer; "but first of all let me tell you something about the rest of the park folks. By the way, of course you have noticed the famous statues we have here?"

"O yes, sir," the Little Girl answered quickly. "Why, I know all their names by heart. And I think they are fine, all of them."

"Well, my dear," said the Sorcerer, "how would you like to be a statue, and stand up all day in one position for a crowd to stare at? It's bad enough to be sitting down all day in the same position, as Mr. Shakespeare over yonder does, but when you have to stand up and look pleasant all day long, like most of them, it is very trying to the nerves, and so they have to come down and get a little exercise and amusement after business hours, don't you see, when the public is gone?"

"Why, dear me, sir, that does seem reasonable," said the Little Girl, thoughtfully, "but I really never thought of it before."

"I know you haven't, Little Girl," said the Sorcerer, shaking his head almost sadly. "The public is very careless of its neighbors' comfort. But in this park we try to give our attractions a little amusement after their day's work. Now, how would you like to be an eagle, the bird of freedom, and be caged up inside iron bars all day long? Wouldn't you like to get out and fly high once in awhile? How would you like to be a polar bear and never see a piece of ice all summer? Answer me that!"

"Please, sir, I'd rather be the iceman," said the Little Girl, and then they both had a good laugh and began to feel like old friends.

"Well, my dear," said the Sorcerer, reaching down and taking the Little Girl by the hand to help her to her feet, "if you will come along with me I will show you some of the sights the public never sees. But stay! you must be hungry, my dear, for it is long past your dinner-hour, so we will just whistle for a lunch."

With that the Sorcerer lifted a little black wand which he had been carrying in his hand and gently blew into one end of it. Immediately there rose a sound that seemed to the Little Girl's ears like the faraway whistle of a great steamer. Before the sound had quite died away, a short, sharp bark was heard close at hand, and up ran a funny little black fuzzy dog with a strangely red head and carefully combed whiskers. In his mouth he carried a big lunch-basket, which he dropped at the Sorcerer's feet.

"Abracadabra," said the Sorcerer, and then you should have seen that wonderful dog spread a big white table-cloth on the dewy grass and lay out the daintiest lunch the Little Girl had ever seen. There seemed to be everything she had ever liked or wished for, and though her surprise almost took away her appetite, she soon recovered and ate as heartily as a hungry little girl can. Soon she was ready to accompany the Sorcerer, who stood smilingly waiting for her, and as they started off, hand in hand, the strange dog following close at their heels, she looked around at the remnants of her lunch and started with surprise, for table-cloth, dishes, lunch, and all had disappeared as completely as if they had never been.

"O, we are very careful to keep the park clean, my dear," said the Sorcerer. "We try to set a good example to the public, you see. But come along. Let's go and see the Scarecrow."

CHAPTER III

THE SCARECROW DOES THE HONORS

As the Sorcerer and the Little Girl left the quiet nook in which they had become acquainted so strangely, she could not help expressing a little curiosity about the Scarecrow whom she was so soon to meet. It was only natural, for curiosity has been common in little girls ever since the first little girl made a dolly and dressed it in leaves, long before men learned how to make silks and satins or thought of killing birds for ladies to wear on their hats while petting their pretty little pug dogs. So she said to the Sorcerer as she trotted along by his side:

"Please, Mr. Sorcerer, will you kindly tell me, before we meet Mr. Scarecrow, what kind of gentleman he is?"

"With pleasure, my dear," replied the Sorcerer, not to be outdone in politeness. "You know, of course, that we have a large and growing family of lions here, and also a very fine old family of gophers."

"O yes," said the Little Girl; "I had the pleasure of meeting some of the gophers to-day, and I have seen the lions as I passed along their street."

"Well," said the Sorcerer, "the Scarecrow's business is to keep the lions from eating the gophers when they are out at night, and I am bound to say he earns his salary. He is not a very handsome gentleman, as you will soon see, but handsome is as handsome does, and he does his work well. We try to use him right, as the saying is, and I don't think he has any kick coming."

"O, now, Mr. Sorcerer," said the Little Girl, "you are talking just like a Boy I know, and I am beginning to like you ever so much."

The Sorcerer almost blushed.

"Thanks, my dear," he said, "we strive to please; but look, here is the Scarecrow!"

The Little Girl stopped and looked about her, but all that she could see was a big fence and the trunks of trees.

"Look up, my dear," said the Sorcerer.

So the Little Girl looked up, and there, in the moonlight, she saw a stolid gentleman sitting on the end of a pole, gazing at nothing in particular, and looking as if he had seen better days.

"He doesn't look comfortable," said the Little Girl.

"No, my dear; none of them do at this time of day," replied the Sorcerer. "I haven't called him off watch yet. He'll feel better when he quits work."

And then the Sorcerer once more lifted his magic wand and blew into it. This time the Little Girl felt sure she heard her Nurse singing in the distance a favorite song of hers, called "I've Worked Enough To-day," and looking again towards the Scarecrow, she saw that he had come down from his uncomfortable perch and was smiling broadly at her, like one relieved from arduous duty.

"Little Girl," said the Sorcerer, "permit me to present the Scarecrow."

"I am very glad to meet you, Mr. Scarecrow," said the Little Girl, graciously extending her hand to the new acquaintance. She noticed that his handshake was very cold and formal, not to say flabby, and immediately made up her mind that he must be a person of social importance.

"To what am I indebted for the honor of this visit?" asked the Scarecrow, in a husky voice, which sounded for all the world as if he had been eating straw.

"O, Mr. Scarecrow, I am just dying to know all about you and the rest of the boys Mr. Sorcerer speaks about," broke in the Little Girl, before the Sorcerer could say a word in explanation of her visit. "I want to know just what you do after you get through scaring the lions, and I want to meet all your friends."

"Tell her all you know, Scarecrow" said the Sorcerer; "it's the quickest way out of it."

"Well, madam," said the Scarecrow, who had scarcely seen the Little Girl at all, he was so busy looking straight ahead, but recognizing her as a lady by her voice, "my story is a sad one. The trouble with me is, that too many people take me for a man of straw, whereas I am in reality, a man of importance in this park, as you would understand if you were a gopher. My only pleasure in life is to come down from my perch, once in a while, when the Sorcerer says I may, and have a little fun with my friend the Tin Man, whom you will presently see. But, hold on, that is, don't hold onto me, for I am a little shaky on my pins, but wait a minute! Sometimes my good old friend the Stork does come around and take me out for an airing when I have been badly abused by some of the Rubberneck family that frequent the park. Then, I get a little sympathy at other times from a long-bearded policeman on the nightwatch, who once propped me up on the Diamond Chain, and gave me that beautiful millionaire feeling instead of the stuffy, tired feeling that stays with me all day long. So, perhaps, I shouldn't complain after all."

"I'm sure it's very nice of you to take such a cheerful view of things," said the Little Girl, who believed in scattering seeds of kindness. "But please tell me, didn't you come from a farm? I seem to see a few straws, or wisps of hay, or something, sticking out all over you."

"I don't care a straw what you see," replied the Scarecrow, sharply, "and you ought to know that ladies are not supposed to see everything. Besides, stuffing is very useful in its way, and it's quite the fashion, I'm sure. Ask any dude you know."

"The Boy is not a dude!" retorted the Little Girl, who always knew when her toes were trodden upon. "And if he were here, he'd make you take that back."

"Tut, tut, children!" said the Sorcerer, "no quarreling at this time of night! Leave that to the cats."

"O, Mr. Sorcerer," said the Little Girl, who was greatly interested in a certain Maltese Kitten at home, "what do you know about cats? Have you got any in your park?"

"Have we got any?" echoed the Sorcerer. "What do we keep the poor old Scarecrow here for, except to scare away cats? Aren't the lions big cats, and the tigers, and a lot of the rest of 'em that keep me awake nights? Don't the cats come in here and try to kill our birds? and don't I fix them when I catch them at it? Say, Little Girl, shall I tell you what I did with the last cat I caught with a bird in its mouth?"

"Please, Mr. Sorcerer," said the Little Girl, eagerly.

"Well, my dear, I was bound to stop the killing of birds somehow, so I thought I would make an example of that cat, and I threw it into the lake. Out it jumped, and I cut its head off. Ten minutes later it came trotting after me with its head in its mouth, and by that time I was so provoked that I took its head away from it and threw it square in its face. So, there now, that's what I know about cats!"

The Little Girl looked surprised; then sad.

"Mr. Sorcerer," said she.

"Well, my dear," said the Sorcerer.

"I think you're a wonder," said the Little Girl.

"Not at all, my dear," replied the Sorcerer. "Wait until you meet the Tin Man."

CHAPTER IV

THE TIN MAN AND HIS FRIENDS

The Sorcerer had no sooner mentioned the Tin Man to the Little Girl than a faint tinkling sound was heard near by, and the wonderful dog that had been quietly listening to the conversation with the Scarecrow began to yelp.

"He doesn't like that style of music," said the Sorcerer.

"Why not?" asked the Little Girl. "I'm sure," said she, "it's as good as any music our next-door neighbor's girl can play."

Now, wasn't that a spiteful remark for a nice little girl to make? And wouldn't we be surprised at it if we didn't know that little girls will make spiteful remarks about their neighbors once in a great while?

"O fie, my dear," said the Sorcerer, "you shouldn't make comparisons. But come along and meet the Tin Man. He's in the doctor's hands. Come on, Scarecrow."

Then the Sorcerer placed one hand under the arm of the Scarecrow, who seemed to move with difficulty, and taking hold of the Little Girl with the other, he led them carefully between the trees in the direction of the tinkling noise. Pretty soon a curious scene appeared before them, and it was some minutes before the astonished eyes of the Little Girl could take it all in.

Seated on the stump of a tree, in the center of an open space which seemed almost as light as day, there was a merry gentleman who looked very much like an old-fashioned stove, and all around him were busy little men in leather aprons and spectacles. Each little man had a hammer in his hand, except one, who seemed to be burning out the merry gentleman's eyes with a red-hot iron. At this sight the Little Girl closed her eyes and almost screamed with fright, but the Sorcerer patted her on the head and said:

"Don't mind a little thing like that, my dear. It is only the Tin Man taking a treatment."

"I'll be with you in a minute, Little Girl," said the merry gentleman on the stump, just as if he had been introduced in correct style.

Then the Little Girl looked again, and saw that the busy little men were hammering away at the Tin Man's arms and legs, which they had kindly removed for the purpose, and not knowing what to make of such strange proceedings, she held her peace like a wise little girl and waited until she was spoken to.

"Well, my dear," said the Sorcerer, after awhile, "what do you think of it?"

"I don't know what to think," said the Little Girl. "This is the strangest sight I've ever seen. What does it all mean?"

"Wait until the doctors are through with the Tin Man, and he'll tell you all about it," replied the Sorcerer. So the Little Girl was forced to wait.

Just then she noticed, for the first time, that close behind the busy little men whom the Sorcerer called the doctors there stood an immense yellow lion watching the scene with wide-open eyes. Suddenly, as the Little Girl gazed at him in affright, the lion uttered a shrill cry, like that of a lady in distress, and springing straight up in the air, disappeared among the treetops.

"Whatever does that mean?" asked the Little Girl, staring up to where the lion had vanished like her lunch.

The Sorcerer laughed. "O, that's just like our friend the Lion," he said. "I guess a gopher tickled his toes, and he always goes up in the air when he's tickled."

The Little Girl could not help thinking this was rather strange conduct for a lion, even when the Sorcerer was around, but the Tin Man's arms and legs were replaced by this time, and he was hopping towards her on one leg, holding out a hand that looked like the elbow-joint of a stovepipe.

"How do, Little Girl?" said he. "I'm glad to see you again."

"I think there is some mistake, sir," replied the Little Girl, who was at all times extremely proper. "I do not remember ever having met you before, and I am sure we have not been introduced this evening."

"O, that's all right, all right," said the merry Tin Man.

"You'll know me when I tell you who I am. Why, I'm the statue you stood looking at so long the other day. I was a famous statesman once, and you know all about me. But I get off my pedestal once in awhile, you know, to have a little fun with my old friend, the Scarecrow here, and we're out for a good time tonight all right."

"Excuse me, sir, but I'm sure you do not talk at all like a statesman," said the Little Girl, "and besides, I thought all statues were made of everlasting bronze, while you seem to have come from a tinshop." Even little girls get suspicious of merry gentlemen sometimes, you see.

"O, that's all right, little one," said the Tin Man, with a laugh. "Didn't I tell you this was my night off? You see I get so rheumaticky standing up there on that pedestal in all sorts of weather that I am glad to have a red-hot-iron treatment once in awhile, and of course I have to disguise myself in this outing-suit of tin for the sake of my reputation. You wouldn't have a famous statesman caught out upon a lark at midnight in the bronze clothes he wears before the public in the daytime, would you?"

The Little Girl admitted that there was something in that, and in fact began to sympathize very deeply with the Tin Man. So then he told her that she was welcome to the reserved seat upon the stump which he had just left, and that he would call in a few friends to meet her. "I am tired of being on the stump, anyway," he said, when the Little Girl protested that he was old and famous and ought to take the only seat in sight. Then the Little Girl climbed up on the Tin Man's seat, and the wonderful things that followed she will never forget—no, not if she lives to be as old as Methusaleh.

CHAPTER V

THE SORCERER AND THE ANIMALS

As soon as the Little Girl was fairly seated in the Tin Man's place, the Sorcerer stepped before her, and waving his magic wand, transformed the scene into one of brilliant beauty. Instead of an old oak stump the Little Girl's seat became a throne studded with diamonds, the light from which made even the big brilliants on the Sorcerer's coat look like tallow candles. Little boys and girls, the very images of her own playmates, but oh, so beautifully dressed, danced before her; music that surpassed any she had ever heard played by the big bands in the park filled the air, and it all seemed to come from a single strange instrument played by a young gentleman who looked like The Boy, but was dressed like a fairy prince. Strawberry ice-cream, peaches, and angel cake were served to all within the magic circle by good-looking little colored boys, who seemed to have no feet, but wings, and never waited for a tip. The Scarecrow and the Tin Man did a cake-walk and seemed to have forgotten all their pains and sorrows, until a big oak tree, that had been laughing fit to split its trunk, took the Scarecrow in its arms, and nearly squeezed the straw stuffing out of him. The Lion-Afraid-of-a-Gopher came down out of the clouds and said he had only been up for an airing, and could whip any gopher alive or dead, and all was going as merrily as a marriage-bell when a great whizzing and whirring of wings was heard, and down from the treetops there flew the most wonderful lot of monkeys that ever was seen. There were monkeys with feet like ducks and wings like eagles; monkeys that could talk every language under the sun, and a few more besides; monkeys that thought no more of throwing the Lion on his back and tying him up than they would of eating a peanut; monkeys that finally, at the Sorcerer's command, caught up the Little Girl and her friend the Tin Man and gave them the fastest ride that ever was made in the air, and then brought them back to the scene of this wonderful midnight circus, as gently as if they had never gone at all. And then, when the Little Girl started to climb back into her big, bediamonded throne there was an immense Face without a body staring at her, as if to say, "What a good time you are having, to be sure," and pretty soon there was a big parade of all hands around the arena, with the Little Girl riding in state on the Lion's back and a wonderfully funny park policeman leading the way. The Tin Man followed close behind with an ax, watching for a chance to chop off the policeman's whiskers, while the Scarecrow flirted most outrageously with a spectator who looked strangely like Nurse. Then, at a wave of the Sorcerer's wand, some wonderful creatures, which the Scarecrow called Metazoans, half-tiger and half-bear, bounded into the arena and saluted the Little Girl with mighty roars as queen of the circus, until a big tree fell on them and knocked them into a hole in the ground that opened suddenly and had no bottom.

And the Sorcerer kept waving his magic wand and changing the scenes so rapidly that in less time than it takes to read about it the Little Girl had been to a picnic party on an island with the Scarecrow and the Dog that was so handy at getting up a lunch; she had breakfasted with the Lion and scared him half to death by telling him there was a mouse under the table; she had taken an oil-can and doctored the Tin Man for his rheumatism, and cured him of it entirely; and she had received friendly visits from all the witches and wizards that dwelt in those parts. Then came the Fairy Queen with all her attendant fairies, and the Little Girl received them in state and introduced them to the Lion, who was decorated for the occasion with a golden crown, because the cap of liberty wouldn't fit him. And all the gophers in the park came out and shook hands with her, calling the Little Girl their great and good friend, and asking her to drop in any time she was near their holes. And then she went up in an airship as big as a barn and caught the wonderful waiter-dog winking at another little girl, for which she never forgave him, though she had the satisfaction of pinching his ear and dropping him back to earth. And last, but by no means least, she caught the great Sorcerer himself in the act of telling the Tin Man and the Scarecrow what a very nice Little Girl she was, and that being about as much as she could stand in one short evening she missed all the rest of the wonderful things that certainly must have happened while the park people were at play.

CHAPTER VI

AWAKE AT LAST

"Here she is now! Asleep under that tree!"

The voice was the voice of Nurse, and there were tears in it, for not only Nurse, but the Little Girl's father and mother and sisters and brothers, and all the friends they could find, had been searching for her all over the big park for four hours or more. The Boy, of course, was fast asleep at home.

"Where's the Scarecrow?" demanded the Little Girl, as she was ruthlessly awakened to find herself surrounded by a tearful circle of familiar faces. "And where's the Tin Man? And the Sorcerer, where is he?"

"Why, darling, whatever do you mean? You must have been dreaming!"

"O, I don't know," said the Little Girl, sleepily, "but if I was, it was perfectly lovely, and I'd just like to dream it all over again. Where's The Boy?"

THE END

Bibliography.

A Chronological Checklist of Baum's Writings*

In the preparation of this study I have consulted nearly all of Baum's work, and so I thought it best to include a complete bibliography of Baum's extensive and varying production. I have tried to make this the most complete and accurate listing to date. I am grateful to the directors of the International Wizard of Oz Club, Inc., for permission to reprint material from *The Baum Bugle*. My major source has been the bibliography from the Spring 1966 issue; this listing is an expanded version of that which appeared in the December 1962 *American Book Collector*. *The Musical Fantasies of L. Frank Baum* by Alla T. Ford and Dick Martin has been most helpful in compiling a list of Baum's unpublished plays and motion picture scenarios. Special acknowledgment is due to David L. Greene and Douglas G. Greene for their help in listing major English and foreign language editions of *The Wizard of Oz*. It should be noted that the only short stories and poems listed are those that have never appeared in book form. The lists of books and articles on Baum, his work, and Denslow are highly selective; a checklist of Denslow's work appears in the Autumn 1972 *Baum Bugle*.

Books

The Book of the Hamburgs, a brief treatise upon the mating, rearing, and management of the different varieties of Hamburgs. Hartford, Connecticut: H. H. Stoddard, 1886.

Mother Goose in Prose. Illustrated by Maxfield Parrish. Chicago: Way & Williams, 1897.

By the Candelabra's Glare: Some Verse. Illustrated by W. W. Denslow and others. Chicago: Privately printed, 1898.
> This edition of ninety-nine copies was printed and bound by Baum. Many of the selections in this collection first appeared in newspapers. At least two poems first appeared in the Chicago *Times-Herald:* "La Reine Est Morte—Vive La Reine," June 23, 1895, and "Farmer Benson on the Motocycle," August 4, 1895. A few poems were reprinted in *Father Goose, His Book* and elsewhere.

Father Goose, His Book. Illustrated by W. W. Denslow. Chicago: George M. Hill Co., 1899.
> The pages of verse were hand-lettered by Ralph Fletcher Seymour, aided by Fred W. Goudy.

The Army Alphabet. Illustrated by Harry Kennedy. Chicago and New York: George M. Hill Co., 1900.
> The pages of this and *The Navy Alphabet* were hand-lettered by Charles J. Costello.

The Art of Decorating Dry Goods Windows and Interiors. Chicago: The Show Window Publishing Co., 1900.

The Navy Alphabet. Illustrated by Harry Kennedy. Chicago and New York: George M. Hill Co., 1900.

A New Wonderland, being the first account ever printed of the Beautiful Valley, and the wonderful adventures of its Inhabitants . . . Illustrated by Frank Ver Beck. New York: R. H. Russell, 1900.
> At least one chapter of this book, "The King's Head and The Purple Dragon," appeared in the Philadelphia *Press*, December 9, 1900.

The Songs of Father Goose, for the Home, School and Nursery. Music by Alberta N. Hall (later Burton). Illustrated by W. W. Denslow. Chicago and New York: George M. Hill Co., 1900.
> Denslow drew a new cover design and title page for this selection of *Father Goose* verses set to music. A number of these songs were issued as Sunday supplements of various newspapers during 1900; Hill also published four *Father Goose* song folios in 1900.

The Wonderful Wizard of Oz. Illustrated by W. W. Denslow. Chicago and New York: George M. Hill Co., 1900.
> Baum had expected the first edition of ten thousand copies to be completed by May 1 for presentation copies and the official publication date to be May 15, Baum's birthday. The publication date was postponed until August 1, but copies were not actually distributed until mid-September. Baum prepared an abridgement of his book which appeared in the Phila-

* An alphabetical checklist can be found on p. 379.

delphia *Press*, September 9, 1900. Hill printed ninety thousand copies before January 1901. The next edition did not appear until 1903 under the title *The New Wizard of Oz*, issued by Bobbs-Merrill. A listing of subsequent and foreign language editions appears at the end of the bibliography of Baum's work.

American Fairy Tales. Illustrated by Harry Kennedy, Ike Morgan, and N. P. Hall. Chicago and New York: George M. Hill Co., 1901.
Cover, title page, and decorative borders by Seymour. These stories were serialized in the Chicago *Chronicle* and several other newspapers, March 3 through May 19, 1901. At least one of these stories, "The Magic Bonbons," was republished in *Today's Magazine*, July 15, 1912; here it is copyrighted by Bobbs-Merrill and was probably published without Baum's knowledge.

Dot and Tot of Merryland. Illustrated by W. W. Denslow. Chicago and New York: George M. Hill Co., 1901.

The Master Key; An Electrical Fairy Tale, founded upon the Mysteries of Electricity and the Optimism of its Devotees. . . . Illustrated by Fanny Y. Cory. Indianapolis: Bowen-Merrill Co., 1901.

The Life and Adventures of Santa Claus. Illustrated by Mary Cowles Clark. Indianapolis: Bowen-Merrill Co., 1902.

The Enchanted Island of Yew Whereon Prince Marvel Encountered the High Ki of Twi and Other Surprising People. Illustrated by Fanny Y. Cory. Indianapolis: Bobbs-Merrill Co., 1903.

The Maid of Athens . . . [Chicago]: Privately printed, 1903.
This play prospectus written by Baum and Emerson Hough was probably printed for limited distribution among possible producers for the play that was never produced.

Prince Silverwings. [Chicago]: A. C. McClurg & Co., 1903.
This pamphlet is the prospectus of a play written by Baum and Mrs. Edith Ogden Harrison, based upon her children's book of the same name, published in 1902. This was evidently of limited distribution to possible producers of the musical that was never staged.

The Surprising Adventures of the Magical Monarch of Mo and His People. Illustrated by Frank Ver Beck. Indianapolis: Bobbs-Merrill Co., 1903.
A revised version of *A New Wonderland*. A reissue with new illustrations by Evelyn Copelman appeared in 1947.

The Marvelous Land of Oz being an account of the Further Adventures of the Scarecrow and Tin Woodman. . . . Illustrated by John R. Neill. Chicago: Reilly & Britton Co., 1904.
All subsequent Oz titles are illustrated by Neill.

Queen Zixi of Ix; or the Story of the Magic Cloak. Illustrated by Frederick Richardson. New York: Century Co., 1905.
This first appeared as a serial in *St. Nicholas*, November 1904–October 1905, illustrated by Richardson.

The Woggle-Bug Book. Illustrated by Ike Morgan. Chicago: Reilly & Britton Co., 1905.

John Dough and the Cherub. Illustrated by John R. Neill. Chicago: Reilly & Britton Co., 1906.
This book was serialized in the Washington *Sunday Star* and other newspapers, October 14 through December 30, 1906. A reprint with new illustrations by Laushiu Fan was published by Opium Books of Hong Kong in 1966.

Father Goose's Year Book; Quaint Quacks and Feathered Shafts for Mature Children. Illustrated by Walter J. Enright. Chicago: Reilly & Britton Co., 1907.
Baum planned one more *Father Goose* book, "Father Goose's Party" (perhaps on the same lines as L. Leslie Brooke's *Johnny Crow's Party*), but it was never published.

Ozma of Oz. . . . Chicago: Reilly & Britton Co., 1907.

Baum's American Fairy Tales; Stories of Astonishing Adventures of American Boys and Girls with the Fairies of their Native Land. Illustrated by George Kerr. Indianapolis: Bobbs-Merrill Co., 1908.
A rearranged and enlarged version of the 1901 edition with three additional stories: "The Witchcraft of Mary-Marie," "The Adventures of an Egg" (appeared as "The Adventures of an Easter Egg" in the Chicago *Daily Tribune*, March 30, 1902), and "The Ryl" (appeared as "The Ryl of the Lilies" on April 12, 1903).

Dorothy and the Wizard in Oz. Chicago: Reilly & Britton Co., 1908.
The running title is *Little Dorothy and the Wizard in Oz*.

The Road to Oz. Chicago: Reilly & Britton Co., 1909.

The Emerald City of Oz. Chicago: Reilly & Britton Co., 1910.

L. Frank Baum's Juvenile Speaker; Readings and Recitations in Prose and Verse, Humorous and Otherwise. Illustrated by John R. Neill and

Maginel Wright Enright. Chicago: Reilly & Britton Co., 1910.
This collection of stories, poems, and illustrations from previous books includes the play *Prince Marvel*, which originally appeared as "The Fairy Prince" in *Entertaining*, December 1909; this children's play was adapted from *The Enchanted Island of Yew* and written in the manner of the British toy theatres. (One of the poems, "Mr. Doodle," was republished in the Los Angeles *Times* on July 5, 1918.)

Baum's Own Book for Children; Stories and Verses from the Famous Oz Books, Father Goose, His Book, Etc., Etc. With Many Hitherto Unpublished Selections. Illustrated by John R. Neill and Maginel Wright Enright. Chicago: Reilly & Britton Co., 1911.
A reissue of the *Juvenile Speaker* with a new introduction.

The Daring Twins; A Story for Young Folk. Illustrated by Pauline M. Batchelder. Chicago: Reilly & Britton Co., 1911.

The Sea Fairies. Illustrated by John R. Neill. Chicago: Reilly & Britton Co., 1911.

Phoebe Daring; A Story for Young Folk. Illustrated by Joseph Pierre Nuyttens. Chicago: Reilly & Britton Co., 1912.
Baum had planned to continue the series; at least part of the manuscript, to be called either "Phil Daring's Experiment" or "The Daring Experiment," had been written before Baum and his publishers lost interest.

Sky Island; being the Further Exciting Adventures of Trot and Cap'n Bill after Their Visit to the Sea Fairies. Illustrated by John R. Neill. Chicago: Reilly & Britton Co., 1912.

The Little Wizard Series, six small volumes (*Jack Pumpkinhead and the Sawhorse, Little Dorothy and Toto, Ozma and the Little Wizard, The Cowardly Lion and the Hungry Tiger, The Scarecrow and the Tin Woodman*, and *Tik-Tok and the Nome King*). Illustrated by John R. Neill. Chicago: Reilly & Britton Co., 1913.

The Patchwork Girl of Oz. Chicago: Reilly & Britton Co., 1913.

Little Wizard Stories of Oz. Illustrated by John R. Neill. Chicago: Reilly & Britton Co., 1914.
A reissue of *The Little Wizard Series* in one volume.

Tik-Tok of Oz. Chicago: Reilly & Britton Co., 1914.
Much of this book was based upon Baum's musical of the year before, *The Tik-Tok Man of Oz*.

The Scarecrow of Oz. Chicago: Reilly & Britton Co., 1915.
Some episodes of this book first appeared in the 1914 Oz Film Manufacturing Company's film *His Majesty, the Scarecrow of Oz* (released as *The New Wizard of Oz*). Also published in 1915 by Reilly & Britton was *The Oz-Toy Book*, with cutouts of the Oz characters by John R. Neill but no text.

Rinkitink in Oz. Chicago: Reilly & Britton Co., 1916.
To keep his promise of an Oz book a year for his readers, Baum rewrote this non-Oz fairy tale by adding Oz characters and changing its title from *King Rinkitink* to *Rinkitink in Oz*; the original manuscript was written as early as 1905 but had not been published.

The Snuggle Tales, six small volumes (*Little Bun Rabbit, Once Upon a Time, The Yellow Hen, The Magic Cloak, The Ginger-Bread Man*, and *Jack Pumpkinhead*). Illustrated by John R. Neill and Maginel Wright Enright. Chicago: Reilly & Lee Co., 1916 and 1917.
The first four volumes (from material in *Juvenile Speaker*) were published in 1916, the last two in 1917. Reilly & Lee reissued this series as *Oz-Man Tales* in 1920.

Babes in Birdland. Illustrated by Maginel Wright Enright. Chicago: Reilly & Britton Co., 1917.
A reissue of the 1911 edition by "Laura Bancroft" but with Baum's name on the title page and an introduction signed by him. The "Laura Bancroft" titles were the first books illustrated by Mrs. Enright, who was the sister of the architect Frank Lloyd Wright.

The Lost Princess of Oz. Chicago: Reilly & Britton Co., 1917.

The Tin Woodman of Oz. . . . Chicago: Reilly & Britton Co., 1918.

The Magic of Oz. . . . Chicago: Reilly & Lee Co., 1919.

Glinda of Oz. . . . Chicago: Reilly & Lee Co., 1920.
The next Oz book, *The Royal Book of Oz* . . . (1921), is credited to Baum but is completely the work of Ruth Plumly Thompson.

Our Landlady. Mitchell, South Dakota: Friends of the Middle Border, 1941.
A selection of Baum's columns from the Aberdeen *Saturday Pioneer* (1890–1891).

Jaglon and the Tiger Fairies. Illustrated by Dale Ulrey. Chicago: Reilly & Lee Co., 1953.

An expanded version by Jack Snow of "The Story of Jaglon," the first of the magazine series "Animal Fairy Tales." This book was the first and only published title of a projected series of book reprints.

The Musical Fantasies of L. Frank Baum. Illustrated by Dick Martin. Chicago: The Wizard Press, 1958.
This is a collection of three projected but unproduced plays by Baum: "The Maid of Athens," "The King of Gee-Whiz," and "The Pipes O' Pan." Also included are a monograph on Baum's theatrical ventures and an excellent checklist of his work compiled by Alla T. Ford and Dick Martin.

The Visitors from Oz. . . . Illustrated by Dick Martin. Chicago: Reilly & Lee Co., 1960.
The stories in this collection (heavily revised by Jean Kellogg) are based upon Baum's 1904–1905 newspaper series, "Queer Visitors from the Marvelous Land of Oz."

The Uplift of Lucifer. . . . Los Angeles: Privately printed, 1963.
Compiled and with an introduction by Manuel Weltman. This pamphlet contains "The Uplift of Lucifer, or Raising Hell" (a play written by Baum in 1915 for the Uplifters) and "The Corrugated Giant" (a monologue adapted from *Prince Mud-Turtle*). Illustrated with photographs and contemporary cartoons.

Animal Fairy Tales. Illustrated by Dick Martin. Chicago: The International Wizard of Oz Club, Inc., 1969.
Introduction by Russell P. MacFall. This collection includes all nine of the "Animal Fairy Tales," which had appeared serially in *The Delineator*, January through September 1905, with illustrations by Charles Livingston Bull.

A Kidnapped Santa Claus. Illustrated by Richard Rosenbloom. Indianapolis and New York: Bobbs-Merrill Co., 1969.
Introduction by Martin Williams. This is the only appearance in separate book form of a story originally appearing in *The Delineator*, December 1904, with illustrations by Frederick Richardson.

Johnson, and *Molly Oodle.*
Two unpublished novels, the manuscripts of which are now lost.

Anonymous and Pseudonymous Books

Anonymous

The Last Egyptian; a Romance of the Nile. Illustrated by Francis P. Wightman. Philadelphia: Edward Stern, 1908.

Floyd Akers

The Boy Fortune Hunters in Alaska. Illustrated by Howard Heath. Chicago: Reilly & Britton Co., 1908.
This and the next title are reissues of the two *Sam Steele Adventure* books by "Capt. Hugh Fitzgerald."

The Boy Fortune Hunters in Egypt. Illustrated by Emile A. Nelson. Chicago: Reilly & Britton Co., 1908.

The Boy Fortune Hunters in the Panama. Illustrated by Howard Heath. Chicago: Reilly & Britton Co., 1908.

The Boy Fortune Hunters in China. Frontispiece by Emile A. Nelson. Chicago: Reilly & Britton Co., 1909.

The Boy Fortune Hunters in Yucatan. Frontispiece by George A. Rieman. Chicago: Reilly & Britton Co., 1910.

The Boy Fortune Hunters in the South Seas. Frontispiece by Emile A. Nelson. Chicago: Reilly & Britton Co., 1911.

Laura Bancroft

The Twinkle Tales, six small volumes (*Bandit Jim Crow, Mr. Woodchuck, Prairie-Dog Town, Prince Mud-Turtle, Sugar-Loaf Mountain,* and *Twinkle's Enchantment*). Illustrated by Maginel Wright Enright. Chicago: Reilly & Britton Co., 1906.

Policeman Bluejay. Illustrated by Maginel Wright Enright. Chicago: Reilly & Britton Co., 1907.
This book was reissued as *Babes in Birdland* in 1911 and 1917, the last with a new introduction and Baum's name on the cover and title page.

Twinkle and Chubbins; Their Astonishing Adventures in Nature-Fairyland. Illustrated by Maginel Wright Enright. Chicago: Reilly & Britton Co., 1911.
A reissue of *The Twinkle Tales* in one volume.

John Estes Cooke

Tamawaca Folks, A Summer Comedy. [no city], U.S.A.: Tamawaca Press, 1907.
"Tamawaca" is an anagram of Macatawa, the Baums' summer home in Michigan. This pseudonym is based upon the name of the Virginian novelist and historian John Esten Cooke.

Capt. Hugh Fitzgerald

Sam Steele's Adventures on Land and Sea. Illustrated by Howard Heath. Chicago: Reilly & Britton Co., 1906.

Sam Steele's Adventures in Panama. Illustrated by Howard Heath. Chicago: Reilly & Britton Co., 1907.

Suzanne Metcalf

Annabel, A Novel for Young Folks. Illustrated by H. Putnam Hall. Chicago: Reilly & Britton Co., 1906.
A second edition with a new frontispiece by Joseph Pierre Nuyttens appeared in 1912.

Schuyler Staunton

The Fate of a Crown. Illustrated by Glen C. Sheffer. Chicago: Reilly & Britton Co., 1905.
This book was not released for publication until after half of it had been already serialized in the Philadelphia *North American* in 1905, illustrated by Neill. The Sheffer illustrations were not used and a new frontispiece by Hazel Roberts was included in a reprint about 1912. Baum used as his pseudonym the name of a deceased uncle, Schuyler Stanton.

Daughters of Destiny. Illustrated by Thomas Mitchell Peirce and Harold DeLay. Chicago: Reilly & Britton Co., 1906.
A reprint was issued about 1912 with a frontispiece by Joseph Pierre Nuyttens.

Edith van Dyne

Aunt Jane's Nieces. Illustrated by Emile A. Nelson. Chicago: Reilly & Britton Co., 1906.

Aunt Jane's Nieces Abroad. Illustrated by Emile A. Nelson. Chicago: Reilly & Britton Co., 1906.

Aunt Jane's Nieces at Millville. Frontispiece by Emile A. Nelson. Chicago: Reilly & Britton Co., 1908.

Aunt Jane's Nieces at Work. Frontispiece by Emile A. Nelson. Chicago: Reilly & Britton Co., 1909.

Aunt Jane's Nieces in Society. Frontispiece by Emile A. Nelson. Chicago: Reilly & Britton Co., 1910.

Aunt Jane's Nieces and Uncle John. Frontispiece by Emile A. Nelson. Chicago: Reilly & Britton Co., 1911.

The Flying Girl. Illustrated by Joseph Pierre Nuyttens. Chicago: Reilly & Britton Co., 1911.

Aunt Jane's Nieces on Vacation. Frontispiece by Emile A. Nelson. Chicago: Reilly & Britton Co., 1912.
Russell P. McFall notes in the Christmas 1961 *Baum Bugle* that the "Ode To a Mignonette" supposedly written for the fictitious Millville *Tribune* of this book was written by Baum over forty years earlier for his own amateur newspaper, *The Rose Lawn Home Journal.*

The Flying Girl and Her Chum. Illustrated by Joseph Pierre Nuyttens. Chicago: Reilly & Britton Co., 1912.
Baum planned another addition to this series, "The Flying Girl's Brave Venture," for 1913, but it was never completed.

Aunt Jane's Nieces on the Ranch. Unsigned frontispiece. Chicago: Reilly & Britton Co., 1913.

Aunt Jane's Nieces Out West. Frontispiece by James McCracken. Chicago: Reilly & Britton Co., 1914.

Aunt Jane's Nieces in the Red Cross. Frontispiece by Norman P. Hall. Chicago: Reilly & Britton Co., 1915.

Dick Martin writes in the Christmas 1963 *Baum Bugle* that the 1918 reissue of this book was lengthened by four chapters, due to the development in World War I by that year. So popular was the *Aunt Jane's Nieces* series that another publisher asked to meet Mrs. van Dyne. Instead of revealing Baum's identity, his publishers chose a member of their staff to pose as Mrs. van Dyne at a tea with the other publisher, Mr. and Mrs. Baum being present under assumed names.

Mary Louise. Frontispiece by J. Allen St. John. Chicago: Reilly & Britton Co., 1916.
Mary Louise Brewster was the name of Baum's favorite sister.

Mary Louise in the Country. Frontispiece by Allen St. John. Chicago: Reilly & Britton Co., 1916.

Mary Louise Solves a Mystery. Frontispiece by Anna B. Mueller. Chicago: Reilly & Britton Co., 1917.
This book is said to have been written, at least in part, by Baum's son Harry Neal Baum.

Mary Louise and the Liberty Girls. Frontispiece by Alice Carsey. Chicago: Reilly & Britton Co., 1918.

Mary Louise Adopts a Soldier. Frontispiece by Joseph W. Wyckoff. Chicago: Reilly & Lee Co., 1919.
For three more titles Emma Speed Sampson was employed by the publishers to continue the *Mary Louise* series as Edith van Dyne after Baum's death in 1919. As Mrs. van Dyne she also wrote two titles of the *Josie O'Gorman* series for Reilly & Lee.

Published Songs

Louis F. Baum's Popular Songs as Sung with Immense Success in His Great 5 Act Irish Drama, Maid of Arran. New York: J. G. Hyde, 1882.
A pamphlet containing lyrics and music (both by Baum) of six songs: "Waiting for the Tide to Turn," "Oona's Gift," "When O'Mara Is King Once Again," "A Rollicking Irish Boy," "A Pair of Blue Eyes," and "The Legend of Castle Arran."

The Wizard of Oz, a book of selections and ten pieces of sheet music published separately ("Poppy Song," "When We Get What's A'Comin' to Us," "The Traveler and the Pie," "The Scarecrow,"

"The Guardian of the Gate," "Love Is Love," "Just a Simple Girl from the Prairie," "When You Love, Love, Love," "It Happens Everyday," and "The Different Ways of Making Love"). Lyrics by Baum. Music by Paul Tietjens. New York and Chicago: M. Witmark & Sons, 1902.
The music of the last two songs was composed by Nathaniel D. Mann.

Down Among the Marshes; The Alligator Song. Words and music by Baum. New York: M. Witmark & Sons, 1903.
This song was evidently written for the unproduced musical *Prince Silverwings*, 1903.

What Did the Woggle-Bug Say? Lyric by Baum. Music by Paul Tietjens. Chicago: Reilly & Britton Co., 1904.

The Woggle-Bug, a book of selections and twelve pieces of sheet music published separately ("The Sandman Is Near," "Hobgoblins," "The Doll and the Jumping Jack," "There's A Lady-Bug A'Waitin' for Me," "Patty Cake, Patty Cake, Baker's Man," "Equine Paradox," "Sweet Matilda," "Soldiers," "To the Victor Belongs the Spoils," "The Household Brigade," 'My Little Maid of Oz," and "H. M. Woggle-Bug, T.E."). Lyrics by Baum. Music by Frederic Chapin. New York and Chicago: M. Witmark & Sons, 1905.

The Tik-Tok Man of Oz, a book of selections and fourteen pieces of sheet music published separately ("The Magnet of Love," "When in Trouble Come to Papa," "The Waltz Scream," "Dear Old Hank," "So Do I," "The Clockwork Man," "Oh My Bow," "Ask the Flowers to Tell You," "Rainbow Bride," "Just for Fun," "The Army of Oogaboo," "Work, Lads, Work," "An Apple's the Cause of It All," and "Folly"). Lyrics by Baum. Music by Louis F. Gottschalk. New York and Detroit: Jerome H. Remick & Co., 1913.

Susan Doozan. Lyrics by Baum. Music by Byron Gay. Los Angeles: Cooper's Melody Shop, 1920.
From the 1916 *Uplifters' Minstrels*.

Produced and Projected Plays

The Mackrummins (a comedy drama in three acts) by "Louis F. Baum," never produced and possibly never completed, copyrighted Richburg, New York, 1882.

The Maid of Arran (an Irish idyll in 5 acts), written and produced by "Louis F. Baum," opened at Baum's Opera House, Gilmour, Pennsylvania, in 1882.

Matches (a comedy drama in 3 acts) by "Louis F. Baum," performed at Brown's Opera House, Richburg, New York, on June 3, 1882, and at the Opera House, Syracuse, New York, on May 19, 1883.

Kilmourne, or O'Connor's Dream (an Irish drama), performed by the Young Men's Dramatic Club at the Weiting Opera House, Syracuse, New York, on April 4, 1883.

The Queen of Killarney (an Irish drama), never produced, 1885.

King Midas (a comic opera), book and lyrics by Baum, music by Paul Tietjens, never produced and possibly never completed, 1901.

The Octopus; or the Title Trust (a comic opera), book and lyrics by Baum, music by Paul Tietjens, never produced, 1901.
Two melodies ("Love Is Love" and "The Traveler and the Pie") from this collaboration were later used in *The Wizard of Oz* musical.

The Wonderful Wizard of Oz, book and lyrics by Baum, music by Paul Tietjens, September 18, 1901.

The Wizard of Oz (a musical extravaganza), book and lyrics by Baum, music by Paul Tietjens, staged by Julian Mitchell, opened at the Grand Opera House, Chicago, on June 16, 1902.
Baum wrote two scripts for this production: the first (1901) is faithful to the original text, the second and produced script retains only the slightest resemblance to the children's book.

The Maid of Athens (a college phantasy in 3 acts), a musical scenario by Baum and Emerson Hough, never completed, 1903.

Prince Silverwings (a children's fantasy), scenario by Baum and Mrs. Carter Harrison, music by Paul Tietjens, never produced, 1903.

King Jonah XIII (a comic opera in 2 acts), libretto by Baum, music by Nathaniel D. Mann, never produced, September, 1903.

The Whatnexters, book and lyrics by Baum and Isidore Witmark, never completed, c. 1903.

Father Goose, book and lyrics by Baum, music by Paul Tietjens, never completed, July 1904.
Several *Father Goose* verses were suggested for interpolation in Baum's first script for *The Wizard of Oz* musical.

The Pagan Potentate, book and lyrics by Baum, music by Paul Tietjens, never completed, c. 1904.

The King of Gee-Whiz (a musical extravaganza in 3 acts), a scenario and general synopsis by Baum and Hough, never completed, 1905.
Hough was a popular Western novelist, best known for his *Covered Wagon;* for his children's book published by Bobbs-Merrill in 1906 Hough used the above title of Baum and his unproduced play.

The Woggle-Bug (a musical extravaganza in 3 acts), book and lyrics by Baum, music by Frederic Chapin, staged by Frank Smithson, opened at the Garrick Theater, Chicago, on June 19, 1905.
A dramatization of *The Marvelous Land of Oz.*

Down Missouri Way, never produced and possibly never completed, c. 1907.

Our Mary, never produced and possibly never completed, c. 1907.

The Fairylogue and Radio-Plays (a series of motion pictures and slides based upon Baum's books), written and produced by Baum, filmed by William Nicholas Selig in Chicago, 1908–1909.
Baum supervised the filming and wrote a two-hour lecture for the showing of these slides and movies, which premiered in Grand Rapids, Michigan, September 24, 1908.

The Koran of the Prophet (a musical extravaganza), never produced and possibly never completed, 1909.

The Rainbow's Daughter, or the Magnet of Love (a musical extravaganza in 2 acts), never produced and possibly never completed, February 23, 1909.
Also known as *Ozma, or The Rainbow's Daughter* ("L. Frank Baum and His New Plays" by D. E. Kessler, *Theatre*, August 1909).

Ozma of Oz (a musical extravaganza), book and lyrics by Baum, music by Manuel Klein, scenic effects by Arthur Voegtlin, never produced, 1909.

This is probably the second writing of *The Rainbow's Daughter*. A carbon copy of the typescript is preserved in the Theatre Collection of the New York Public Library at Lincoln Center.

Peter and Paul (an opera), book and lyrics by Baum, music by Arthur Pryor, never produced and possibly never completed, 1909.

The Pipes O' Pan (a musical comedy in 3 acts), book and lyrics by Baum and George Scarborough, music by Paul Tietjens, never produced, 1909.
Perhaps based upon *King Midas* (1901) and/or *The Pagan Potentate* (c. 1904). This and the Baum-Hough scenarios were printed in *The Musical Fantasies of L. Frank Baum*.

"The Fairy Prince," *Entertaining*, December 1909.
Reprinted in the *Juvenile Speaker* of 1910.

The Girl from Oz (a comedy), c. 1909.
This unproduced play was later rewritten as a radio operetta by Frank J. Baum.

The Wonderful Wizard of Oz, a motion picture released by Selig, March 24, 1910.
Baum may have written the scenario for this and the next three films, all made from *Radio-Play* material, plus unused scenes based on *Dorothy and the Wizard of Oz*.

Dorothy and the Scarecrow in Oz, a motion picture released by Selig, April 14, 1910.

The Land of Oz, a motion picture released by Selig, May 19, 1910.

John Dough and the Cherub, a motion picture released by Selig, December 19, 1910.

The Pea-Green Poodle, never produced, c. 1910.
This was evidently based upon one of Baum's "Animal Fairy Tales."

The Clock Shop, never produced, c. 1910.

The Tik-Tok Man of Oz (a fairyland extravaganza in 3 acts), book and lyrics by Baum, music by Gottschalk, staged by Oliver Morosco, opened at the Majestic Theater, Los Angeles, on March 31, 1913.
This is the final and produced version of the play *Ozma of Oz*.

Stagecraft, The Adventures of a Strictly Moral Man, book and lyrics by Baum, music by Gottschalk, produced by the Uplifters of Santa Barbara, California, for their "First Uplifter High Jinks," January 14, 1914.

The Patchwork Girl of Oz, a motion picture scenario by Baum, produced and filmed by the Oz Film Manufacturing Company, released by Paramount Pictures, September 23, 1914.
This scenario was probably based upon the unproduced play of *The Patchwork Girl of Oz*, which had been written to follow *The Tik-Tok Man of Oz*.

The Magic Cloak of Oz, motion picture scenario by Baum, produced and filmed by the Oz Film Manufacturing Company, 1914.
Based upon *Queen Zixi of Ix*. In 1917, Universal combined part of this film with other salvaged film from the Oz company and issued it as *The Babes in the Wood*. A supposedly cut version of the Oz Film Manufacturing Company film was released by the American Pictures Corporation, c. 1920.

The Last Egyptian, motion picture scenario by Baum, produced and filmed by the Oz Film Manufacturing Company, released by Alliance Film Company, December 7, 1914.
Based upon Baum's anonymous novel *The Last Egyptian*.

His Majesty, the Scarecrow of Oz (released as *The New Wizard of Oz*), motion picture scenario by Baum, produced and filmed by the Oz Film Manufacturing Company, released by Alliance Film Company, March 1915.

Violet's Dreams (four one-reel fairy tales), produced and filmed by the Oz Film Manufacturing Company, 1914–1915.
Baum may have written each of the scenarios. One of the films was based on "The Magic Bonbons" from *American Fairy Tales*, released by Victor, Oct. 22, 1915.

The Gray Nun of Belgium, motion picture scenario by Baum, produced and filmed by the Dramatic Features Corporation, never released, 1915.

The Uplift of Lucifer, or Raising Hell (An Allegorical Squazosh), book and lyrics by Baum, music by Gottschalk, staged by Dave Hartford, produced by the Uplifters for their second annual outing, October 23, 1915.

Revived on "L. Frank Baum Night" (January 27, 1920), staged by Max Polluck, with Hal Roach as Demon Rum.

The Uplifters' Minstrels, book and lyrics by Baum, music by Byron Gay, produced by the Uplifters for their third annual outing, Del Mar, California, 1916.

Snow White (a musical comedy), book and lyrics by Baum, never produced and possibly never completed, December 1916.
This was to be based upon an English Christmas "pantomime," with sets designed by Maxfield Parrish.

The Orpheus Road Company, book and lyrics by Baum, music by Gottschalk, produced by the Uplifters at their fourth annual outing, Coronado Beach, California, 1917.

Introductions and Other Contributions

Holton, M. Adelaide, ed. *The Holton Primer*. Chicago: Rand McNally & Co., 1901.
This book, one of the "Lights of Literature Series," edited by the supervisor of the primary school of Minneapolis, reprints the poem, "Where Do the Chickens Go at Night?" from *Father Goose, His Book*. I am grateful to Mrs. Doris Frohnsdorff of Gaitorsburg, Maryland, for discovering and reporting this book to me.

Christmas Stocking Series, The, six small volumes of nursery rhymes and stories (*The Night Before Christmas, Cinderella and Sleeping Beauty, Animal A.B.C.—A Child's Visit to the Zoo, The Story of Little Black Sambo, Fairy Tales from Grimm*, and *Fairy Tales from Andersen*). Illustrated anonymously. Chicago: Reilly & Britton Co., 1905–1906.
Each book contains the same introduction by Baum. In 1911, *The Story of Peter Rabbit*, illustrated by Neill, replaced *Animal A.B.C.—A Child's Visit to the Zoo*.

Baum, Maud Gage. *In Other Lands Than Ours*. Chicago: Privately printed, 1907.
With a preface and photographs by Baum.

Madison, Janet, ed. *Sweethearts Always*. Illustrated by Fred Manning. Chicago: Reilly & Britton Co., 1907.
Box and jacket designed by Neill. Reprints Baum's poem "Her Answer" from *By the Candelabra's Glare*.

Nesbitt, Wilbur D., ed. *The Loving Cup*. Chicago: P. F. Volland Co., 1909.
Contains Baum's poem "Smile."

Lefferts, Sara T., ed. *Land of Play*. Illustrated by M. L. Kirk and Florence England Nosworthy. New York: Cupples & Leon, 1911.
Includes a modified version of Baum's introduction to *The Christmas Stocking Series*. An abridged version of this book was reprinted as *The House of Play*.

Rice, Wallace and Frances, eds. *The Humbler Poets (Second Series); A Collection of Newspaper and Periodical Verse—1885–1910*. Chicago: A. C. McClurg & Co., 1911.
Reprints Baum's poems "Father Goose" and "Captain Bing" from *Father Goose, His Book*.

University Society and the After School Club of America, The, eds. *Famous Tales and Laughter Stories*, vol. 1. New York: The University Society, 1912.
Reprints Baum's story "Juggerjook" (*St. Nicholas*, December 1910). In 1912, the University Society also published the nine-volume *Boy's and Girl's Bookshelf*, which includes Baum's name among the editors on the title page; one volume is a reprint of this anthology.

Skinner, Ada M., ed. *Little Folks' Christmas Stories and Plays*. Chicago: Rand McNally & Co., 1915.
Reprints Baum's short story "Kidnapping Santa Claus" (formerly "A Kidnapped Santa Claus" in *The Delineator*, December 1904).

Uplifters, The. *Songs of Spring*. Los Angeles: Privately printed, c. 1917.
A pamphlet of poems delivered at "The Uplifters' Spring Poets' Dinner" of 1914, 1915, and 1916, containing an introduction and five poems by Baum: "The Massacre," "The Orchestra," "Safety First," "Claudius Raymond," and "An Uplifter's Song of the Shirt." There are several references to Baum in other contributions and "A Toast to L. Frank Baum" by Harry Crouch.

Uplifters, The. *The Uplifter's Hymnal*. Silver Anniversary Edition. Los Angeles: Privately printed, 1938.
Contains several Baum songs from various Uplifters' theatrical productions. (A selection of these songs, "Never Strike Your Father, Boy," "We're Having a Hell of a Time," "Susan Doozan," "Apple Pie," and Baum's "Uplifters' Platform," was reprinted by Alla T. Ford in her pamphlet *The High-Jinks of L. Frank Baum*. . . . Chicago: The Wizard Press, 1959.)

Short Stories and Poems

"The Suicide of Kiaros," *The White Elephant*, September 1897.
Reprinted in *Ellery Queen's Mystery Magazine*, November 1954, with an introduction by Frederic Dannay.

"A Shadow Cast Before," *The Philosopher*, December 1897.

"The Mating Day," *Short Stories*, September 1898.

"Aunt Hulda's Good Time," *The Youth's Companion*, October 26, 1899.

"The Loveridge Burglary," *Short Stories*, January 1900.

"To the Grand Army of the Republic, August 1900" (a poem), Chicago *Times-Herald*, August 26, 1900.

"The Bad Man," *The Home Magazine (of New York)*, February 1901.
Illustrated by Cory. In the January 1900 issue of *The Home Magazine* is Baum's article "The Real 'Mr. Dooley'" (illustrated by Denslow and Morgan) about the Chicago tavern owner who was the basis for Peter Finley Dunn's famous character.

"A Strange Tale of Nursery Folk," Chicago *Times-Herald*, March 3, 1901.

"The King Who Changed His Mind," undated and unknown newspaper, c. 1901.

"The Runaway Shadows," undated and unknown newspaper, c. 1901.
This story also appeared as "A Trick of Jack Frost's" in another undated and unidentified newspaper. This story is believed to have been written for *American Fairy Tales*.

"An Easter Egg," *The Sunny South*, March 29, 1902.
A longer, more detailed version of the story "The Strange Adventures of an Egg" (The Chicago *Daily Tribune*, March 30, 1902), which later appeared in *Baum's American Fairy Tales* (1908).

"My Ruby Wedding Ring," undated and unknown newspaper, c. 1903.

"Queer Visitors from the Marvelous Land of Oz," a series of twenty-seven stories, the Philadelphia *North American* and other newspapers, November 28, 1904, through February 26, 1905.

Illustrated by Walt McDougall. A selection of these stories (heavily revised by Jean Kellogg) appeared in 1960 as *The Visitors from Oz*.

"Coronado, the Queen of Fairyland," (a poem), San Diego *Union*, March 5, 1905.
I am grateful to Oz Club member Scott Olson for discovering this poem.

"Nelebel's Fairyland," *The Russ*, June 1905.

"Jack Burgitt's Honor," *Novelettes*, No. 68, August 1905.

"To Macatawa" (a poem), The Grand Rapids *Sunday Herald*, September 1, 1907.

"The Man Fairy," *The Ladies' World*, December 1910.

"The Tramp and the Baby," *The Ladies' World*, October 1911.

"Bessie's Fairy Tale," *The Ladies' World*, December 1911.

"Aunt Phroney's Boy," *St. Nicholas*, December 1912.
A rewritten version of "Aunt Hulda's Good Time."

"The Yellow Ryl," *A Child's Garden*, August and September 1925.
This two-part story was written in 1906 or earlier. In the July 1925 issue is a short biographical sketch of Baum written by his wife. An eleven-part story, "Invisible Inzi of Oz," begins in the October issue; it was written by two children, Virginia and Robert Wauchope.

"The Tiger's Eye," *The American Book Collector*, December 1962.
A previously unpublished "Animal Fairy Tale."

"An Oz Book," *The Baum Bugle*, December 1965.
A fragment of an unpublished and untitled Oz story. It appeared as one of a series of little-known Baum writings that have been printed in *The Baum Bugle* since Christmas 1961.

"Santa Claus was good to me. . . ." (a poem), *The Baum Bugle*, December 1971.
A previously unpublished poem sent to the Gages, Baum's relatives in Aberdeen, South Dakota, dated December 26, 1911.

"The Man With the Red Shirt," *The Baum Bugle*, Spring 1973.

"Chrome Yellow," "The Diamond Back," "The Littlest Giant," "Mr. Rumple's Chill," and "Bess of the Movies."
The first three of these unpublished short stories are still preserved in manuscript.

Notable Later Editions of *The Wizard of Oz*

The New Wizard of Oz. Illustrated by W. W. Denslow. Indianapolis: Bobbs-Merrill Co., 1903.

After the success of the 1902 musical this edition was issued from the original Hill plates (with a few minor textual differences). Denslow drew a new cover, title page, and endpaper designs. The word "New" was added to the title perhaps to avoid confusion with the play, which was only superficially based upon the original story. This edition was reissued several times in various formats; textual and color plate illustrations were dropped as the color sequences were changed. The plates were leased to M. A. Donohue & Co., a reprint firm, about 1913. Soon after this edition the plates were returned, and Bobbs-Merrill made a final printing from the Hill plates. All editions with Denslow illustrations after 1920 were printed from a reset edition. Later printings include an edition with scenes from the 1925 Chadwick film instead of the color plates, and a "Waddle" book edition issued in 1934 by Blue Ribbon Books with "waddle" toys inserted at the back. The last Bobbs-Merrill edition with the Denslow illustrations has a new cover design and endpapers of scenes from the 1939 MGM movie.

The Wizard of Oz. Illustrated by W. W. Denslow. London: Hutchinson & Co., Ltd., c. 1926.

The Story of the Wizard of Oz. Illustrated by Henry E. Vallely. Racine, Wisconsin: Whitman Publishing Co., 1939.

This and the next two titles are abridgements, issued during the run of the 1939 film through special arrangement with Bobbs-Merrill.

The Wizard of Oz. Illustrated by Oscar Lebeck. New York: Grosset & Dunlap, 1939.

The Wizard of Oz Picture Book. Illustrated by Leason. Racine, Wisconsin: Whitman Publishing Co., 1939.

The Wizard of Oz. Illustrated by W. W. Denslow. London: Hutchinson & Co., Ltd., 1940.

This British edition is illustrated with eight color stills from the MGM film.

The New Wizard of Oz. Illustrated by Evelyn Copelman. Indianapolis: Bobbs-Merrill, 1944.

A "deluxe" edition appeared in 1964.

The Wizard of Oz. Illustrated by Julian Wehr. Akron, Ohio: Saalfield Co., 1944.

This abridgement is illustrated with "animated" movable-part drawings.

The Wizard of Oz. Illustrated by H. M. Brock. London: Hutchinson & Co., Ltd., 1947.

The Wizard of Oz. Adapted by Allen Chaffee. Illustrated by Anton Loeb. New York: Random House, 1950.

The New Wizard of Oz. Illustrated by Leonard Weisgard. Garden City, New York: Junior Deluxe Editions [Nelson Doubleday], 1955.

The New Wizard of Oz. Illustrated by Evelyn Copelman. New York: Grosset & Dunlap, 1956.

This edition includes a number of additional illustrations that do not appear in the 1944 Bobbs-Merrill edition. This Grosset & Dunlap edition appeared in several different formats.

The Wizard of Oz. Illustrated by Dale Ulrey. Chicago: Reilly & Lee Co., 1956.

This edition includes an excellent "Afterword" by Dr. Edward Wagenknecht who also wrote the jacket blurb.

The Wizard of Oz and Who He Was. Illustrated by W. W. Denslow. East Lansing: Michigan State University Press, 1957.

Includes an appreciation, biographical study, bibliography, and notes by Russel B. Nye and Martin Gardner.

The Wizard of Oz. Illustrated by Maraja. New York: Grosset & Dunlap, 1958.

This slightly abridged version was printed in Italy in the format of the Italian edition published by Fratelli Fabbri Editori of Milan in 1957. A slightly different reprint of this Grosset & Dunlap edition was issued later by Duell Sloan & Pearce of New York; an English edition was published by W. H. Allen of London.

The Wizard of Oz. Illustrated by W. W. Denslow. Greenwich, Connecticut: Fawcett Publications, 1960.

This paperback has an introduction by James Thurber, a slightly rewritten version of his article in *The New Republic*.

The Wizard of Oz and the Land of Oz. Illustrated by Rita Fava. New York: The Looking Glass Library, 1960.

The Wonderful Wizard of Oz. Illustrated by W. W. Denslow. New York: Dover Publications, 1960.

This paperback facsimile of the Hill edition includes an excellent introduction and checklist of Baum's fantasies by Martin Gardner. A boxed two-volume set of this and the Dover edition of *The Marvelous Land of Oz* were published in a cloth edition by Dover in arrangement with the Book-of-the-Month Club in 1967. In 1961, Crown issued a reprint of the Dover edition in boards with a new, unsigned introduction.

The Wizard of Oz. Illustrated by Dick Martin. Chicago: Reilly & Lee Co., 1961.

Jean Kellogg abridged this and the first three sequels (issued the same year in the same format) with illustrations by Dick Martin.

The Wizard of Oz. Adapted by Mary Cushing and Dorothea Williams. Illustrated by Claudine Nankivel. New York: Grosset & Dunlap, 1962.

The Wizard of Oz. Illustrated by W. W. Denslow. New York: Macmillan Co., 1962.

Afterword by Clifton Fadiman.

The Wizard of Oz. Illustrated by Ann Mare Magagna. New York: Grosset & Dunlap, 1963.

This edition appeared in several different formats within the next few years.

The Wonderful Wizard of Oz and The Marvelous Land of Oz. Illustrated by W. W. Denslow and John R. Neill. New York: Parents' Magazine Press, 1964.

Preface by Irene Smith.

The Wizard of Oz. Illustrated by W. W. Denslow. Chicago: Reilly & Lee Co., 1964.

This is a reprint of the 1956 edition but with the Denslow illustrations replacing the Ulrey drawings. It retains the Wagenknecht afterword. Besides including several Denslow drawings that have never before appeared in the book, this edition has its cover adapted from a poster issued by Hill in 1900 and its endpapers after those from the 1903 Bobbs-Merrill edition. Copies printed after 1965 have a new cover drawn by Dick Martin after Denslow's work; Rand McNally issued a paperback edition of this edition in 1971.

The Colorful Wizard of Oz. Illustrated by W. W. Denslow. San Francisco: Determined Productions, 1965.

This attractive oversized coloring book reprints the entire text of the book on the versos of blown-up black-and-white drawings by Denslow.

The Wonderful Wizard of Oz. Illustrated by B. Biro. London: J. M. Dent & Sons, 1965.

Unsigned introduction. In 1966, an identical edition was issued by E. P. Dutton & Co. of New York.

The Wonderful Wizard of Oz. Illustrated by Roy Krenkel. New York: Airmont Publishing Co., 1965.

Introduction by Donald A. Wollheim.

The Wizard of Oz. Adapted by Albert G. Miller and designed by Paul Taylor. Illustrated by Dave Chambers and John Spencer. New York: Random House, 1968.

This edition, printed in Japan, is an "animated" toy book of the story.

The Wizard of Oz. Illustrated by Brigette Bryan. Chicago: Children's Press, 1969.

This edition, especially prepared for schoolchildren, is annotated throughout with explanations and pictures of difficult words and terms. At the back is a short biography of Baum and an appendix on precious gems.

The Wonderful Wizard of Oz. Illustrated by W. W. Denslow. New York: Columbia Records Edition, 1969.

This paperback is a facsimile of the Hill edition and accompanies a set of records of the story read by Mildred Dunnock and George Rose.

Translations and Foreign Editions of *The Wizard of Oz*

Le Magicien d'Ohz. Translated into French by Marcel Gauwin. Illustrated by W. W. Denslow. Paris: Denoël & Steele, 1932.

In 1933, Denoël & Steele issued a French translation of *The Marvelous Land of Oz* (with the Neill illustrations) as *Le Petit Roi d'Ohz*.

El Mago de Oz. Translated into Spanish by Jose Mallorqui Fiquerola. Illustrated by Freixas. Barcelona and Buenos Aires: Editorial Molino, 1939.

This edition has been reprinted several times, most recently in 1952.

Volshebnik Izumrudnovo Goroda. Translated into Russian by Alexander Volkov. Illustrated by N. Radlov. Moscow and Leningrad: Ts. K.V.L.S.M. Publishing House of Children's Literature, 1939.
Reprinted in 1941. This adaptation credits Volkov on the cover and title page as author, with a slight reference to Baum. In 1959 an entirely re-written edition was published in Moscow by Soviet Russia Publishers, illustrated by L. Vladimirskov. This edition has gone through several printings, one of which was illustrated by B. Bundin (Tashkent: the Central Committee of Uzbekistan, 1961). This Russian version, in turn, has been translated into various languages, including Armenian, Chinese, Czechoslovakian, Kirghiz, Latvian, Lithuanian, Serbo-Croatian, and Ukrainian.

Volkov's translation of *The Wizard of Oz* has become so popular that he has written two original Oz books. The first sequel, *Urfin Dzhus i evo Dereviannie Soldati* ("Urfin Dzhus and his Wooden Soldiers"), illustrated by Vladimirskov, was issued in 1963 by Soviet Russia Publishers. This book has been translated into several languages, including an English translation by Mary G. Langford, entitled *The Wooden Soldiers of Oz*, illustrated by Vladimirskov, with an introduction by David and Douglas Greene (Hong Kong: Opium Books, 1969). Volkov's second original Oz story, *Sem'Podsemnykh Korolei* ("Seven Underground Kings"), illustrated by Vladimirskov, was issued in 1967 by Soviet Russia Publishers.

De Grote Tovenaar Van Oz. Translated into Dutch by Henrik Scholte. Illustrated by Von Looij. Amsterdam: L. J. Veen, 1940.
Reprinted in 1952 (in cloth) and in 1962 (in paper).

Oz a Csodak Csodaja. Translated into Hungarian by Livia Beothy. Illustrated by Emy Rona. Budapest: Singer & Wolfner, 1940.
A second edition appeared the same year, issued by Uj Idok of Budapest.

Troldmaden fra Oz. Translated into Danish by Kay Nielsen. Illustrated by Harry Hertz. Copenhagen: Tempo, 1940.

Trollkarlen fran Oz. Translated into Swedish by John Wallin. Illustrated by W. W. Denslow. Stockholm: Reuter & Reuter, 1940.

Vrajitorul din Oz. Translated into Rumanian by Camil Baltazar. Bucharest: Editura Socec, 1940.
A new edition of the Baltazar translation appeared in 1965 (reprinted in 1966) with illustrations by Wolny Alexandru (Bucharest: Editura Tineretului).

Der Zauberer von Oz. Translated into German by Ursula von Wiese. Zurich: Morgarten Verlag, 1940.
Illustrated with stills from the 1939 MGM film.

Nel Regno di Oz. Translated into Italian by Maria Luisa Agosti Castellani. Illustrated by Miki Pellizzari. Torino: Societa Apostolato Stampa, 1944.
This translation has been reprinted several times, the most notable being the 1948 edition illustrated with stills from the MGM movie. In 1948, Societa Apostolato Stampa also published Castellani's translations of four other Oz titles: *Oz Paese Incantato* (*The Land of Oz*); *Ozma Regina di Oz* (*Ozma of Oz*); *Il Retorno al Regno di Oz* (*The Road to Oz*); and *Oz in Pericolo* (*The Emerald City of Oz*). The first two titles are illustrated by Pellizzari, the second two by Carla Ruffinelli. In 1948, the same publishers also issued *Il Mago di Oz*, an Italian adaptation by Maria Rosaria Berardi of the MGM film script.

O Feiticeiro de Oz. Translated into Portuguese by Maria Lamas. Illustrated by Hugo Manuel. Porto: Libraria Civilizacao Editora, 1946.

Hukosem Meieretz Ooz. Translated into Hebrew by Chernowitz. Illustrated by Bena Gewirtz. Tel Aviv: Izreel Publishing House, 1947.
This edition has been reprinted several times, most recently in 1963.

Il Mago di Oz. Translated into Italian by Adele Levi. Illustrated by Arturo Bonfanti. Milan: U. Mursia & C., 1949.
Reprinted in 1965.

Il Mago di Oz. Translated into Italian by L. G. Tenconi. Illustrated by F. Bignotti. Milan: Editrice Boschi, 1954.
This edition has been reprinted in several different formats.

Dört Kücük Seyyah. An abridged Turkish translation by Nurcihan E. Kesim. Illustrated by Evelyn Copelman. Istanbul: Derya Tayinlari, 1956.

Il Mago di Oz. Translated into Italian by Emma Sarocchi. Illustrated by Maraja. Milan: Fratelli Fabbri Editori, 1957.
This edition also appeared in English in both Great Britain and the United States, 1958. A French translation, *Le Magicien d'Oz*, was issued by Edition Fabbri of Milan in 1959; reprints have appeared in 1961 and 1966.

Carovnik iz Oza. Translated into Slovenian by Janko Moder. Illustrated by Maksim Sedej. Ljubljin: Mladinska Knjiga, 1959.

Jaduar-e-Shahr-e Zommorod. Translated into Persian by A. Halat. Illustrated by Evelyn Copelman. Tehran: Andisheh, 1959.

Oz Mako Tzukai. Translated into Japanese by Yasunari Kawabata. Illustrated. Tokyo, c. 1959.
Reprinted in 1965. Another Japanese edition, *Oz Mako Tsukai,* appeared in 1939; whether this is the same as the Yasunari Kawabata translation is not known.

Lu Yeh Sien Tsung. A Chinese translation. Illustrated. Taipei, Taiwan: Kuo-ming Ch'u-pan-she, 1960.

Carobnjak iz Oza. Translated into Serbo-Croatian by Alexander Stafanovic. Illustrated by Sasha Mishi. Belgrade: Mlado Pokolenjz, 1961.

O Magico de Oz. Adapted and translated into Portuguese by Selso Luiz Amorim. Illustrated by Gutemburg. Rio de Janeiro: Distribuidora Record, 1961.
A reprint appeared in 1965.

The Magic of Oz. Retold by G. Magidson-Stepanova. Unsigned illustrations. Leningrad: State Text-book Publishing House, 1961.
This edition in English contains abridgements of both *The Wizard of Oz* and *The Magic of Oz.* This textbook is used to teach Soviet children English; the footnotes are in Russian.

Volshebnik Oz. Retold by M. Talinskaya. Unsigned illustrations. Moscow: State Text-book Publishing House, 1961.
On the cover of this English edition is the title *The Wizard of Oz;* this edition is used as a textbook.

The Wizard of Oz. Illustrated by Gopi. Madras: Umadevan & Co., 1961.
An English language edition used as a textbook by Indian students, with a glossary and test questions. The illustrations are adapted from the Denslow drawings. A reprint appeared in 1962.

Carodez Ze Zeme Oz. Translated into Czechoslovakian by Jekub Markovic. Illustrated by Arnost Karasek. Prague: Statni Nikladatelstvi Detske Kniny, 1962.

Czarnoksieznik Ze Szmaragdowego Grodu. Translated into Polish by Stefania Wortman. Illustrated by Adam Kiljan. Warsaw: Nasza Ksiegarnia, 1962.

As Nattu Mayavi. Abridged and translated into Tamil by R. A. Padmanabhan and P. Mohan. Illustrated by Gopi. Madras: Umadevan, 1963.

Acunakara Mantiravati. Translated into Tamil by Gopala Krishnan. Madras: Vairam, 1964.

Der Zauberer Oz. Translated into German by Sybil Grafin Schönfeldt. Illustrated by Peter Krukenberg. Berlin: Cecilie Bressler Verlag, 1964.

Le Magicien d'Oz. Abridged and translated into French by Jean Muray. Illustrated by Romain Simon. Paris: Librairie Hachette, 1964.

Ozu no Maho Tsukai. Translated into Japanese by Fujie Tamamoto. Illustrations after Maraja. Tokyo: Kaiseisha, 1964.

Oz, a Nagy Varazslo. Translated into Hungarian by Klara Szollosy. Illustrated. Budapest: Mora Klado, 1966.

Die Ongelooflike Towenaar van Oz. Translated into Afrikaans by Peter W. Gobbelaar. Illustrated by B. S. Biro. Capetown: Human & Rousseau, 1970.

Books

American Fairy Tales, 1901.
Animal Fairy Tales, 1969.
The Army Alphabet, 1900.
The Art of Decorating Dry Goods Windows and Interiors, 1900.
Babes in Birdland, 1917.
Baum's American Fairy Tales, 1908.
Baum's Own Book for Children, 1911.
The Book of the Hamburgs, 1886.
By the Candelabra's Glare, 1898.
The Cowardly Lion and the Hungry Tiger, 1913.
The Daring Twins, 1911.
Dorothy and the Wizard in Oz, 1908.
Dot and Tot of Merryland, 1901.
The Emerald City of Oz, 1910.
The Enchanted Island of Yew, 1903.
Father Goose, His Book, 1899.
Father Goose's Year Book, 1907.
The Ginger-Bread Man, 1917.
Glinda of Oz, 1920.
Jack Pumpkinhead, 1917.
Jack Pumpkinhead and the Sawhorse, 1913.
Jaglon and the Tiger Fairies, 1953.
John Dough and the Cherub, 1906.
Johnson, n.d., unpublished novel.
A Kidnapped Santa Claus, 1969.
L. Frank Baum's Juvenile Speaker, 1910.
The Life and Adventures of Santa Claus, 1902.
Little Bun Rabbit, 1916.
Little Dorothy and Toto, 1913.
The Little Wizard Series, 1913.
Little Wizard Stories of Oz, 1914.
The Lost Princess of Oz, 1917.
The Magic Cloak, 1916.
The Magic of Oz, 1919.
The Magical Monarch of Mo, 1903.
The Maid of Athens, 1903.
The Marvelous Land of Oz, 1904.
The Master Key, 1901.
Molly Oodle, n.d., unpublished novel.
Mother Goose in Prose, 1897.
The Musical Fantasies of L. Frank Baum, 1958.
The Navy Alphabet, 1900.
A New Wonderland, 1900.
Once Upon a Time, 1916.
Our Landlady, 1941.
Ozma and the Little Wizard, 1913.
Ozma of Oz, 1907.
The Patchwork Girl of Oz, 1913.
Phoebe Daring, 1912.
Prince Silverwings, 1903.
Queen Zixi of Ix, 1905.
Rinkitink in Oz, 1916.
The Road to Oz, 1909.
The Scarecrow and the Tin Woodman, 1913.
The Scarecrow of Oz, 1915.
The Sea Fairies, 1911.
Sky Island, 1912.

The Snuggle Tales, 1916 and 1917.
The Songs of Father Goose, 1900.
Tik-Tok and the Nome King, 1913.
Tik-Tok of Oz, 1914.
The Tin Woodman of Oz, 1918.
The Uplift of Lucifer, 1963.
The Visitors from Oz, 1960.
The Woggle-Bug Book, 1905.
The Wonderful Wizard of Oz, 1900.
The Yellow Hen, 1916.

Anonymous and Pseudonymous Books

Annabel, Suzanne Metcalf, 1906.
Aunt Jane's Nieces, Edith van Dyne, 1906.
Aunt Jane's Nieces Abroad, Edith van Dyne, 1906.
Aunt Jane's Nieces and Uncle John, Edith van Dyne, 1911.
Aunt Jane's Nieces at Millville, Edith van Dyne, 1908.
Aunt Jane's Nieces at Work, Edith van Dyne, 1909.
Aunt Jane's Nieces in Society, Edith van Dyne, 1910.
Aunt Jane's Nieces in the Red Cross, Edith van Dyne, 1915.
Aunt Jane's Nieces on the Ranch, Edith van Dyne, 1913.
Aunt Jane's Nieces on Vacation, Edith van Dyne, 1912.
Aunt Jane's Nieces Out West, Edith van Dyne, 1914.
Bandit Jim Crow, Laura Bancroft, 1906.
The Boy Fortune Hunters in Alaska, Floyd Akers, 1908.
The Boy Fortune Hunters in China, Floyd Akers, 1909.
The Boy Fortune Hunters in Egypt, Floyd Akers, 1908.
The Boy Fortune Hunters in the Panama, Floyd Akers, 1908.
The Boy Fortune Hunters in the South Seas, Floyd Akers, 1911.
The Boy Fortune Hunters in Yucatan, Floyd Akers, 1910.
Daughters of Destiny, Schuyler Staunton, 1906.
The Fate of a Crown, Schuyler Staunton, 1905.
The Flying Girl, Edith van Dyne, 1911.
The Flying Girl and Her Chum, Edith van Dyne, 1912.
The Last Egyptian, Anonymous, 1908.
Mary Louise, Edith van Dyne, 1916.
Mary Louise Adopts a Soldier, Edith van Dyne, 1919.
Mary Louise and the Liberty Girls, Edith van Dyne, 1918.
Mary Louise in the Country, Edith van Dyne, 1916.
Mary Louise Solves a Mystery, Edith van Dyne, 1917.
Mr. Woodchuck, Laura Bancroft, 1906.
Policeman Bluejay, Laura Bancroft, 1907.
Prairie-Dog Town, Laura Bancroft, 1906.
Prince Mud-Turtle, Laura Bancroft, 1906.
Sam Steele's Adventures in Panama, Capt. Hugh Fitzgerald, 1906.
Sam Steele's Adventures on Land and Sea, Capt. Hugh Fitzgerald, 1906.
Sugar-Loaf Mountain, Laura Bancroft, 1906.
Tamawaca Folks, John Estes Cooke, 1906.
Twinkle and Chubbins, Laura Bancroft, 1911.
The Twinkle Tales, Laura Bancroft, 1906.
Twinkle's Enchantment, Laura Bancroft, 1906.

Published Songs

"An Apple's the Cause of It All," *The Tik-Tok Man of Oz*, 1913.
"The Army of Oogaboo," *The Tik-Tok Man of Oz*, 1913.

"Ask the Flowers to Tell You," *The Tik-Tok Man of Oz*, 1913.
"The Clockwork Man," *The Tik-Tok Man of Oz*, 1913.
"Dear Old Hank," *The Tik-Tok Man of Oz*, 1913.
"The Different Ways of Making Love," *The Wizard of Oz*, 1902.
"The Doll and the Jumping Jack," *The Woggle-Bug*, 1905.
Down Among the Marshes, 1903.
"Equine Paradox," *The Woggle-Bug*, 1905.
"Folly," *The Tik-Tok Man of Oz*, 1913.
"The Guardian of the Gate," *The Wizard of Oz*, 1902.
"H. M. Woggle-Bug, T.E.," *The Woggle-Bug*, 1905.
"Hobgoblins," *The Woggle-Bug*, 1905.
"The Household Brigade," *The Woggle-Bug*, 1905.
"It Happens Everyday," *The Wizard of Oz*, 1902.
"Just a Simple Girl from the Prairie," *The Wizard of Oz*, 1902.
"Just for Fun," *The Tik-Tok Man of Oz*, 1913.
"The Legend of Castle Arran," *The Maid of Arran*, 1882.
"Love Is Love," *The Wizard of Oz*, 1902.
"The Magnet of Love," *The Tik-Tok Man of Oz*, 1913.
"My Little Maid of Oz," *The Woggle-Bug*, 1905.
"Oh My Bow," *The Tik-Tok Man of Oz*, 1913.
"Oona's Gift," *The Maid of Arran*, 1882.
"A Pair of Blue Eyes," *The Maid of Arran*, 1882.
"Patty Cake, Patty Cake, Baker's Man," *The Woggle-Bug*, 1905.
"Poppy Song," *The Wizard of Oz*, 1902.
"Rainbow Bride," *The Tik-Tok Man of Oz*, 1913.
"A Rollicking Irish Boy," *The Maid of Arran*, 1882.
"The Sandman Is Near," *The Woggle-Bug*, 1905.
"The Scarecrow," *The Wizard of Oz*, 1902.
"So Do I," *The Tik-Tok Man of Oz*, 1913.
"Soldiers," *The Woggle-Bug*, 1905.
Susan Doozan, 1920.
"Sweet Matilda," *The Woggle-Bug*, 1905.
"There's A Lady-Bug A'Waitin' for Me," *The Woggle-Bug*, 1905.
"To the Victor Belongs the Spoils," *The Woggle-Bug*, 1905.
"The Traveler and the Pie," *The Wizard of Oz*, 1902.
"Waiting for the Tide to Turn," *The Maid of Arran*, 1882.
"The Waltz Scream," *The Tik-Tok Man of Oz*, 1913.
What Did the Woggle-Bug Say? 1904.
"When in Trouble Come to Papa," *The Tik-Tok Man of Oz*, 1913.
"When O'Mara Is King Once Again," *The Maid of Arran*, 1882.
"When We Get What's A'Comin' to Us," *The Wizard of Oz*, 1902.
"When You Love, Love, Love," *The Wizard of Oz*, 1902.
"Work, Lads, Work," *The Tik-Tok Man of Oz*, 1913.

Produced and Projected Plays

The Clock Shop, play, c. 1910.
Dorothy and the Scarecrow in Oz, motion picture, 1910.
Down Missouri Way, play, c. 1907.
"The Fairy Prince," play, 1909.
The Fairylogue and Radio-Plays, motion pictures and slides, 1908–1909.
Father Goose, play, 1904.
The Girl from Oz, play, c. 1909.
The Gray Nun of Belgium, motion picture, 1915.
His Majesty, the Scarecrow of Oz, motion picture, 1914–1915.
John Dough and the Cherub, motion picture, 1910.
Kilmourne, play, 1883.
King Jonah XIII, play, c. 1903.

King Midas, play, 1901.
The King of Gee-Whiz, play, 1905.
The Koran of the Prophet, play, 1909.
The Land of Oz, motion picture, 1910.
The Last Egyptian, motion picture, 1914.
The Mackrummins, play, 1882.
The Magic Cloak of Oz, motion picture, 1914.
The Maid of Arran, play, 1882.
The Maid of Athens, play, 1903.
Matches, play, 1882, 1883.
The Octopus, play, 1901.
The Orpheus Road Company, musical review, 1917.
Our Mary, play, c. 1907.
Ozma of Oz, play, 1909.
The Pagan Potentate, play, c. 1904.
The Patchwork Girl of Oz, motion picture, 1914.
The Pea-Green Poodle, play, c. 1910.
Peter and Paul, play, 1909.
The Pipes O' Pan, play, 1909.
Prince Silverwings, play, 1903.
The Queen of Killarney, play, 1885.
The Rainbow's Daughter, play, 1909.
Snow White, play, 1916.
Stagecraft, play, 1914.
The Tik-Tok Man of Oz, play, 1913.
The Uplift of Lucifer, play, 1915.
The Uplifters' Minstrels, musical review, 1916.
Violet's Dreams, motion pictures, 1914–1915.
The Whatnexters, play, c. 1903.
The Wizard of Oz, play, 1902.
The Woggle-Bug, play, 1905.
The Wonderful Wizard of Oz, motion picture, 1910.

Short Stories and Poems

"Aunt Hulda's Good Time," 1899.
"Aunt Phroney's Boy," 1912.
"The Bad Man," 1901.
"Bess of the Movies," unpublished short story, n.d.
"Bessie's Fairy Tale," 1911.
"Chrome Yellow," unpublished short story, n.d.
"Coronado, the Queen of Fairyland," 1905
"The Diamond Back," unpublished short story, n.d.
"An Easter Egg," 1902.
"Jack Burgitt's Honor," 1905.
"The King Who Changed His Mind," c. 1901.
"The Littlest Giant," unpublished story, n.d.
"The Loveridge Burglary," 1900.
"The Man Fairy," 1910.
"The Man with the Red Shirt," unpublished short story, n.d.
"The Mating Day," 1898.
"Mr. Rumple's Chill," unpublished short story, n.d.
"My Ruby Wedding Ring," c. 1903.
"Nelebel's Fairyland," 1905.
"An Oz Book," 1965.
"Queer Visitors from the Marvelous Land of Oz," 1904–1905.
"The Runaway Shadows," c. 1901.
"Santa Claus was good to me. . . ." 1971.
"A Shadow Cast Before," 1897.

"A Strange Tale of Nursery Folk," c. 1899.
"The Suicide of Kiaros," 1897.
"The Tiger's Eye," 1962.
"To Macatawa," 1907.
"The Tramp and the Baby," 1911.
"The Yellow Ryl," 1925.

Introductions and Other Contributions

"Apple Pie," *The Uplifter's Hymnal*, the Uplifters, 1938.
"Captain Bing" from *Father Goose*, in *The Humbler Poets*, Wallace and Frances Rice, eds., 1911.
"The Christmas Stocking," *Land of Play*, Sara T. Lefferts, ed., 1911.
"Claudius Raymond," *Songs of Spring*, the Uplifters, c. 1917.
"Father Goose" from *Father Goose*, in *The Humbler Poets*, Wallace and Frances Rice, eds., 1911.
"Her Answer," *Sweethearts Always*, Janet Madison, ed., 1907.
Introduction, *The Christmas Stocking Series*, 1905–1906.
Introduction, *Songs of Spring*, the Uplifters, c. 1917.
"Juggerjook," *Famous Tales and Laughter Stories*, the University Society and the After School Club of America, eds., 1912.
"Kidnapping Santa Claus," *Little Folks' Christmas Stories and Plays*, Ada M. Skinner, ed., 1915.
"The Massacre," *Songs of Spring*, the Uplifters, c. 1917.
"Never Strike Your Father, Boy," *The Uplifter's Hymnal*, the Uplifters, 1938.
"The Orchestra," *Songs of Spring*, the Uplifters, c. 1917.
Preface, *In Other Lands than Ours*, Maud Gage Baum, 1907.
"Safety First," *Songs of Spring*, the Uplifters, c. 1917.
"Smile," *The Loving Cup*, Wilbur D. Nesbitt, ed., 1909.
"Susan Doozan," *The Uplifter's Hymnal*, the Uplifters, 1938.
"Uplifters' Platform," *The Uplifter's Hymnal*, the Uplifters, 1938.
"An Uplifter's Song of the Shirt," *Songs of Spring*, the Uplifters, c. 1917.
"We're Having a Hell of a Time," *The Uplifter's Hymnal*, the Uplifters, 1938.
"Where Do the Chickens Go at Night?" from *Father Goose*, in *The Holton Primer*, M. Adelaide Holton, ed., 1901.

Translations and Foreign Editions of *The Wizard of Oz*

Afrikaans. *Die Ongelooflike Towenaar van Oz*, 1970.
Chinese. *Lu Yeh Sien Tsung*, 1960.
Czechoslovakian. *Carodez Ze Zeme Oz*, 1962.
Danish. *Troldmaden fra Oz*, 1940.
Dutch. *De Grote Tovenaar Van Oz*, 1940.
French. *Le Magicien d'Ohz*, 1932.
    Le Magicien d'Oz, 1964.
German. *Der Zauberer Oz*, 1964.
    Der Zauberer von Oz, 1940.
Hebrew. *Hukosem Meieretz Ooz*, 1947.
Hungarian. *Oz a Csodak Csodaja*, 1940.
    Oz, a Nagy Varazslo, 1966.
Indian textbook in English. *The Wizard of Oz*, 1961.
Italian. *Il Mago di Oz*, translated by Adele Levi, 1949.
    Il Mago di Oz, translated by Emma Sarocchi, 1957.
    Il Mago di Oz, translated by L. G. Tenconi, 1954.
    Nel Regno di Oz, 1944.

Japanese. *Oz Mako Tzukai*, c. 1959.
    Ozu no Maho Tsukai, 1964.
Persian. *Jaduar-e-Shahr-e Zonmorod*, 1959.
Polish. *Czarnokieznek Ze Szmaragdowego Grodu*, 1962.
Portuguese. *O Feiticeiro de Oz*, 1946.
    O Magico de Oz, 1961.
Rumanian. *Vrajitorul din Oz*, 1940.
Russian. *Volshebnik Izumrudnovo Goroda*, 1939.
Russian textbooks in English. *The Magic of Oz*, 1961.
    Volshebnik Oz, 1961.
Serbo-Croatian. *Carobjak iz Oza*, 1961.
Slovenian. *Carovnik iz Oza*, 1959.
Spanish. *El Mago de Oz*, 1939.
Swedish. *Trollkarlen fran Oz*, 1940.
Tamil. *Acunakara Mantiravati*, 1964.
    As Nattu Mayavi, 1963.
Turkish. *Dört Kücük Seyyah*, 1956.

About L. Frank Baum

American Book Collector, The. December 1962.
    This special issue devoted to Baum has many fine articles and illustrations on his life and work.
Baughman, Roland. "L. Frank Baum and the 'Oz Books.'" *Columbia Library Columns*, May 1955.
Baum, Frank J. "The Oz Film Co." *Films in Review*. August–September 1956.
Baum, Frank Joslyn, and MacFall, Russell P. *To Please a Child; A Biography of L. Frank Baum, Royal Historian of Oz*. Chicago: Reilly & Lee Co., 1961.
    This is the only extensive biography of Baum and remains the major source for any work on Baum and his Oz books.
Baum Bugle, The. June 1957–1972. Published by the International Wizard of Oz Club.
Ford, Alla T., and Martin, Dick. *The Musical Fantasies of L. Frank Baum*. Chicago: The Wizard Press, 1958.
Gardner, Martin. "The Royal Historian of Oz." *Fantasy and Science Fiction*, January and February 1955.
    In a slightly revised version this article appeared in *The Wizard of Oz and Who He Was*.
"How the Wizard of Oz Spends His Vacation." Grand Rapids *Herald*, August 18, 1907.
Kelly, Fred C. "Royal Historian of Oz." *Michigan Alumnus Quarterly Review*, May 23, 1953.
Kessler, D. E. "L. Frank Baum and His New Plays." *Theatre Magazine*, August 1909.
"L. Frank Baum Is 'Broke,' He Says." New York *Morning Telegraph*, June 5, 1911.
McDougall, Walt. "L. Frank Baum Studied by McDougall." St. Paul *Dispatch*, July 30, 1904.
Mannix, Daniel P. "The Father of the Wizard of Oz." *American Heritage*, December 1964.
Potter, Jeanne O. "The Man Who Invented Oz." Los Angeles *Times Sunday Magazine*, August 13, 1939.
Seymour, Ralph Fletcher. *Some Went This Way*. Chicago: Privately printed, 1945.
    In his autobiography the artist Seymour discusses his association with Baum and several of his books.
Snow, Jack. *Who's Who in Oz*. Chicago: Reilly & Lee Co., 1954.

Tietjens, Eunice. *The World at My Shoulder*. New York: Macmillan Co., 1938.

> In this, her autobiography, the poet Eunice Tietjens and wife of the composer of *The Wizard of Oz* musical describes her acquaintance with Baum.

Torrey, Edwin C. *Early Days in Dakota*. Minneapolis: Parnham Printing & Stationery Co., 1925.

"A Western Author and His Work." An unidentified magazine, c. 1901.

> This early article on the author of *The Wizard of Oz* has been reprinted in *The Baum Bugle*, Spring 1967.

Wing, W. E. "From 'Oz,' the Magic City." *Dramatic Mirror*, October 7, 1914.

> Baum discusses the Oz Film Manufacturing Company.

Worthington, J. E. "Mac-a-ta-wa, the Idyllic." Grand Rapids *Herald*, September 1, 1907.

On Baum's Work

Baum, Frank J. "Why the Wizard of Oz Keeps on Selling." *Writer's Digest*, December 1952.

Baum Bugle, The. June 1957–1972. Published by the International Wizard of Oz Club.

Beckwith, Osmond. "The Oddness of Oz." *Kulchur*, Fall 1961.

Bewley, Marius. "Oz Country." *The New York Review of Books*, December 3, 1964.

> A revision of this study, "The Land of Oz: America's Great Good Place," appears in Bewley's *Masks and Mirrors* (New York: Atheneum, 1970).

Brotman, Jordan. "A Late Wanderer in Oz." *Chicago Review*, December 1965.

> Reprinted in *Only Connect*, a collection of essays on children's literature, edited by Sheila Egoff and others, published by the Oxford University Press in 1969.

Erisman, Fred. "L. Frank Baum and the Progressive Dilemma." *American Quarterly*, Fall 1968.

Gardner, Martin. "A Child's Garden of Bewilderment." *Saturday Review*, July 17, 1965.

> In this article celebrating the centennial of *Alice in Wonderland* is a discussion of Baum's Oz stories and their relationship to the Lewis Carroll classics. Reprinted in *Only Connect*, edited by Sheila Egoff and others (New York: Oxford University Press, 1969).

———. "The Librarians in Oz." *Saturday Review*, April 11, 1959.

———, and Nye, Russel B. *The Wizard of Oz and Who He Was*. East Lansing: Michigan State University Press, 1957.

Hollister, C. Warren. "Baum's Other Villains." *The Baum Bugle*, Spring 1970.

Kopp, Sheldon. "The Wizard Behind the Couch." *Psychology Today*, March 1970.

L. Frank Baum—The Wonderful Wizard of Oz. New York: Columbia University Libraries, 1956.

> A catalog of Columbia University's exhibition of Baum's writing, with an introduction by Roland Baughman and descriptive notes by Baughman and Joan Baum.

Lanes, Selma G. *Down the Rabbit Hole*. New York: Atheneum, 1971.

> A chapter in this analysis of children's literature is devoted to the American fairy tale, including much discussion of several of Baum's books.

Littlefield, Henry M. "The Wizard of Oz: Parable on Populism." *American Quarterly*, Spring 1964.

> A slightly expanded version of this article was included in *The American Culture*, edited by Hennig Cohen (Boston: Houghton Mifflin Co., 1968).

Pattrick, Robert R. *Unexplored Territory in Oz*. Published by the International Wizard of Oz Club, 1963.

Prentice, Ann E. "Have You Been to See the Wizard?" *The Top of the News*. American Library Association, November 1, 1970.

Sackett, S. J. "The Utopia of Oz." *The Georgia Review*, Fall 1960.

Sale, Roger. "L. Frank Baum, and Oz." *Hudson Review*, Winter, 1972.

Starrett, Vincent. "The Wizard of Oz." Chicago *Sunday Tribune Magazine of Books*, May 2, 1954.

> This article was reprinted in Starrett's *Best Loved Books of the Twentieth Century*, a Bantam paperback of 1955.

Thurber, James. "The Wizard of Chittenango." *The New Republic*, December 12, 1934.

Wagenknecht, Edward. *Utopia Americana*. Seattle: University of Washington Book Store, 1929.

> This booklet, the first critical study of the Oz books, was rewritten as the chapter "The Yellow Brick Road" in Dr. Wagenknecht's *As Far As Yesterday* (Norman, Oklahoma: University of Oklahoma Press, 1968).

About W. W. Denslow

American Book Collector, The. December 1964.

> Most of the material (including Dick Martin's checklist of Denslow's work) in this special "Denslow" issue originally appeared in *The Baum Bugle*, Autumn and Christmas 1963 and Spring 1964.

Armstrong, Leroy. "W. W. Denslow, Illustrator." *The Home Magazine*, October 1898.

Baum Bugle, The. Autumn 1972.

Bowes, J. M. "Children's Books for Children." *Brush and Pencil*, September 1903.

"Chronicle and Comment" (column). *The Bookman*, October 1909.

Crissey, Forrest. "William Wallace Denslow." *Carter's Monthly*, March 1898.

Lane, Albert. *Elbert Hubbard and His Work*. Worcester, Massachusetts: The Blanchard Press, 1901.

"A Lover of Children Who Knows How to Make Them Laugh." Detroit *News*, September 13, 1903.

"Our Own Time" (column). *The Reader*, April 1907.

Penn, F. "Newspaper Illustrators: W. W. Denslow." *The Inland Printer*, January 1894.

Snow, Jack. *Who's Who in Oz*. Chicago: Reilly & Lee Co., 1954.

Who Was Who in America, 1897–1942.